I0778878

Bolita

T. Nelson Taylor

A
CineCapture Press
Publication

CineCapture LLC
PO Box 263701
Tampa, FL 33685
Please visit www.tnelsontaylor.com
First Hardcover Edition: August 2011
First Paperback: June 2012
First Electronic Edition: July 2012

Bolita is adapted from a true story. Many character names have been changed to protect privacy and security. Some characters, events, and locations are used fictitiously, or are completely fictitious and similarities to real persons, living or dead, legal entities, incidents, places, and events are coincidental and not intended by the author.

Library of Congress Information in-Publication:

ISBN 13: 978-0-615-52738-3

Printed in the United States of America

Drawings

For my fathers.

bolita: [boh-lee-tuh] Cuban-Spanish literal translation: "little ball".

An illegal form of lottery, popular with working-class ethnic groups during the latter 1800s through the mid-1900s. One hundred numbered small ivory balls are typically placed in a bag for random selection. Brought from Cuba to the United States of America in the 1880s, the games were run by members of organized crime families. Over time, Hispanics developed a name for each number. "La Charada" is based on Chinese origins, creating a superstitious method for interpreting drawings or placing bets according to dreams.

1. Caballo (horse)
2. Mariposa (butterfly)
3. Marinero (sailor)
4. Gato (cat)
5. Monja (nun)
6. Jicotea (tortoise)
7. Caracol (snail)
8. Muerto (death)
9. Elefante (elephant)
10. Pescado Grande (great fish)
11. Gallo (rooster)
12. Mujer Santa (easy woman)
13. Pavo Real (peacock)
14. Gato Tigre (tiger)
15. Perro (dog)
16. Toro (bull)
17. Luna (moon)
18. Pescado Chiquito (tiny fish)
19. Lombriz (brown snake)
20. Gato Fino (fine cat)
21. Majá (Cuban boa snake)
22. Sapo (toad)
23. Vapor (steamship)
24. Paloma (dove)
25. Piedra Fina (jewel)
26. Anguila (eel)
27. Avispa (wasp)
28. Chivo (goat)
29. Ratón (rat)
30. Camerón (shrimp)
31. Venado (deer)
32. Chochino (pig)
33. Tiñosa (turkey vulture)
34. Mono (monkey)
35. Araña (spider)
36. Chachimba (pipe)
37. Gallina Prieta (dark hen)
38. Dinero (money)
39. Conejo (rabbit)
40. Cura (healing)
41. Lagartija (small lizard)
42. Pato(duck)
43. Alacrán (scorpion)
44. Año del Cuero (Year of the Whip)
45. Tiburón (shark)
46. Guagua (bus)
47. Pájaro (bird)
48. Cucaracha (cockroach)
49. Borracho (drunkard)
50. Policía (police)
51. Soldado (soldier)
52. Bicicleta (bicycle)
53. Luz Eléctrica (lights)
54. Flores (flowers)
55. Cangrejo (crab)
56. Reina (queen)
57. Cama (bed)
58. Adulterio (adultery)
59. Loco (crazy)
60. Sol Oscuro (dark sun)
61. Cañonazo (cannon shot)
62. Matrimonia (marriage)
63. Asesino (assassin)
64. Muerto Grande (finality)
65. Cárcel (jail)
66. Divorcio (divorce)
67. Puñalada (stab)
68. Cemeterio Grande (big cemetery)
69. Pozo (well)
70. Teléfono (telephone)
71. Rio (river)
72. Ferrocarril (railroad)
73. Parque (park)
74. Papalote (kite)
75. Cine (cinema)
76. Bailarina (female dancer)
77. Banderas (flags)
78. Obispo (bishop)
79. Coche (car)
80. Médico Viejo (old doctor)
81. Teatro (theater)
82. Madre (mother)
83. Tragedia (tragedy)
84. Ciego (blind man)
85. Reloj (time)
86. Convento (covenant)
87. Nueva York (New York)
88. Espejuelos (glasses)
89. Lotería (lottery)
90. Viejo (old man)
91. Tranvía (tram)
92. Globo muy alto (very high globe)
93. Revolución (Revolution)
94. Machete (machete)
95. Guerra (war)
96. Desafío (challenge)
97. Mosquito Grande (big mosquito)
98. Piano (piano)
99. Serrucho (hand saw)
100. Inodoro (toilet)

Prologue

By autumn of 1975, the city of Tampa, Florida was in a state of near chaos. Fresh from the Vietnam War, Watergate, the Civil Rights Movement, the petroleum crisis, high unemployment, and rapidly rising inflation, Tampa had yet another war to sort out.

Although coexisting for decades, the Cracker Mob was practically on the way out while the Italian families were ever on the annex. Drug smuggling, prostitution, gambling, racketeering, extortion, contract arson, and murder-for-hire were not uncommon for both organizations. Earlier in the 1960s when Castro destroyed their legitimate enterprises in Havana, the exiled Italians returned in full force and continued capitalizing on their existing operations. Through the illegal lottery known as "bolita", mafiosos had entirely taken over Florida's gambling rings. By the '70s, different mob factions mostly learned to work together under the direction of Giuseppe Cantonello, Tampa's local don. The only sticking point remaining was the matter of who controlled the local nightclubs. The "Lounge Wars" raged on with numerous cases of contract arson and contract murder.

Robert F. Kennedy's legacy, the 1970 Racketeer Influenced and Corrupt Organizations Act (RICO, drafted by G. Robert Blakey), gave law enforcement organizations sharp teeth in which to pursue the mobsters. Little did the newly empowered law enforcement organizations know, their war was not only with the criminal families infesting Tampa, but also from every agency level within their own corrupted institutions. This war culminated around the contract assassination of a controversial street detective named William "Bill" Brume.

Bolita

Seminole Heights Serenade

These guys thought they knew what they were doing.

Giuseppe knew better. He wasn't one year past a coronary in Costa Rica before these grave-dancing morons back home went after a cop, actually three, but the FBI never released the names of the other two. Contracting a law enforcement officer was against Giuseppe's omertà, but the others could care less about his old Sicilian ways. Respect had nothing to do with business. They were lucky this morning after missing the first two on their mysterious List of Five, including Benjamin Davidson—the Assistant US Attorney who's been crawling down their necks. So much for sophistication. Cocaine-induced boldness and a crooked cop were going to pay the wage. The morons thought they were doing everyone a favor, including the police department.

Late October, 1975

Wendy barely made a sound on her way out the door with Jeffery and Junior. The boys were getting pretty good at tiptoeing by my bed. Wendy mentioned something about her pills giving her massive headaches, but I didn't give it further thought. I smiled, rolled over, and let the clock march right over my hangover. Oh man, the weather! That third week of October was carrying the first semblance of autumn, and it was enough to make the morning an hour slower than anticipated. 10:03? Last night's meal must have completely drugged me. There was nothing exceptional flickering on TV, except maybe an old Untouchables rerun on Channel 44. That was good enough. I was still too groggy to get up and change the channel, so I sat back at the dining room table, savored my half-drawn Winston, and inhaled a mouthful of coffee. I looked over at the briefcase once again before sticking it back under the bed. I had been staring at it all week in anticipation.

The doorbell rang. *Jehovahs?* I guess they saw the car out front and assumed I was home.

Timing really *is* everything, isn't it? I still felt partly cloudy with a chance of drunk, having not finished my first butt of the day, nor one little cup of coffee. I threw on a bathrobe to cover up my boxers and stupefyingly meandered directly to the door. I noticed my hand twisting the doorknob and that was my last memory before everything slowed down.

I just broke one of my own basic rules! It hit me instantly that I didn't check the window first. It was too late though; the other person likely saw the knob turn, or at the very least, heard the knob moving. I froze for a brief moment in that thought—my hand still on the knob. I was committed.

Things were slow enough already, but when I opened that door, they became much slower. I recalled reading somewhere that cognizant moments happen rapidly. Perhaps, but at this moment, my mind was doing the 100 in under a second. Automatically, I offered my greeting before even catching the person's face.

"Good Morning." I expected an immediate introduction.

The man, dressed in a dark blue windbreaker over a polo shirt, slacks, and loafers, immediately spun around. It's that queer, Graham! State fugitive Herbert Talmond Graham was standing right in front of me, holding a shoebox.

"I got a message for you, cop!" Graham angrily barked before removing his right hand from the box.

A homemade silencer? Where did these fools come up with that? Graham produced one of those practically disposable Mambo .32 automatics with a long, fat cylinder attached to the barrel's tip. I tried to jump back behind the door, but he managed to yank off two rounds first. The first shot hit behind me, impacting the hardwood floor some fifteen feet back. I noticed a spray of blue fibers coming from the end of the silencer as they matted on the other side of the screened outer door. *Air conditioner filter?* The second round grazed my left thigh on its way to the floor too, and it felt no different from the slow, fiery buildup of a wasp's sting.

The gun produced another muted thump, and I felt as though someone threw me down and put a 500 lb barbell on my chest.

"Oh God!" It was the only expression my lungs allowed before collapsing.

Graham stepped through the doorway and took three more shots. He became rather certifiable; staring at me, wild-eyed, as he amateurishly jerked the trigger. Because of that horrible technique, he missed me two times before miraculously managing another round in my general direction. Belly shot. I hardly felt this one. I was too angry.

Graham started to leave, but I jumped up in a rush of adrenalin, grabbed Wendy's heirloom party ashtray, and slung it like a Frisbee at his head. Graham tried dodging the substantial hunk of glass, but was too slow. The ashtray slammed the right side of his noggin, slicing off a chunk of his earlobe. As I fell back down and braced myself up against the kitchen doorway, the weight of that barbell came back. I could hardly breathe. My focus started to go in and out; watching as Graham held his ear and bolted for the front doorway. I momentarily lamented my own aim, not having the satisfaction of watching that queer's gourd paint the walls. Squinting, I barely saw him hightail it with the Mambo down the driveway, and then climb into a green Plymouth sedan that just slammed on the brakes out front. Danny Boy was at the wheel. I should have known.

I choked on the thick air. It felt like trying to breathe through a coffee stirrer in a room that reeked of cordite. I couldn't move, either. My eyes wandered lower, noticing the warmth drain out of me, slowly trickling all the way down to my crotch. I don't know what hurt worse, that pistol or my pride. What stupidity! I'd hit him with that ashtray, but it was no consolation. He got the better of me and it was over.

The only thoughts on my mind now were Wendy and the boys. What a mess I just made. There's stuff strewn all over the floor and the shooting splattered my blood everywhere. She's not going to like this, but there was something worse. I told her I was concrete! She would never believe that now. Our trust was broken.

The pills! That's why she complained. Wendy wanted a little sister for Jeffrey and Junior before they became too old. She kept me amused with her occasional playful hints, not knowing that I *really was* listening to each one. I preferred her thinking I wasn't paying attention for a higher scoring "surprise factor". She must of thought I'd become a classless dingaling.

It began occurring to me that I might die before having the chance to give her a surprise birthday wish. We had our dream home picked out in Land 'O Lakes, but she didn't know I already had it squared away with the bank too. That was supposed to be her birthday present come February; three bedrooms and two separate baths—and on a fresh-water ski lake! Admittedly, I would have enjoyed seeing which room worked best for granting her wishes. With us, new places always meant new everything. It was a paradise, and it only took eleven years from the day I walked out of the academy to save enough for the down payment.

This was going to break her heart. It saddened me to the point of tears. There were so many thoughts going through my mind. I wasn't prepared for this. I should have been prepared. I can't remember the last time I cried. It was probably back when I was a kid after a whipping from my old man. I couldn't help it when I thought about my family.

The next thing I remembered hearing was that Jew lady, Ida, yelling from the front door. Her thick Long Island accent always raked on my nerves, and it momentarily jostled me out of the fog when she screamed back towards the street.

"Someone caul an ambulance! Those bastids went and shawt Bill!"

She came through my door and cautiously over to my side with much timidity. "Dear Gaud, Bill. Hang in there. I saw Sherman go back inside to caul, okay? Bill? Are you there, Bill? Oh my, Gaud!"

I could hear Ida's questions drift through my ears and her tugging at my arm, but I felt no reason to respond. When I closed my eyes, I remembered the sea of red through my lids from the sunlight blazing through the front doorway. I knew I was drifting and the last thing my crowded thoughts explicated was the sound of tires screeching out front.

Boy Blue

"Okay Billy, you next."

I carefully tugged at one of the thin straws my cousin Ricky clutched in his left hand. The stakes were high this time. My cousin, who was actually my best friend, and our best friend Melvin, talked us into avoiding the Army's draft by volunteering with another service. Thing was, we wanted to go through the ordeal together, but couldn't agree on which branch. I wanted the Marines and my crazy cousin Ricky still wanted to jump out of airplanes with the Army's paratroopers. He wasn't just crazy for wanting to jump out of airplanes, he earned the label after getting up several school mornings at 3 a.m. to hunt deer with his father's little .22 revolver. They weren't wealthy enough for superette steak, but venison was freely available on their land. They finally told him to give it up after he wounded several that ran off into the deep woods and became lost. He never found any, but I'm sure the bears were thankful.

Melvin dreamed of the Air Force. In fact, Ricky and I endured the last half of our senior year listening to Melvin ramble on and on about how he was gonna go splash some gooks if he were ever given the chance. It didn't really matter to me. Ricky won the right to pick first from playing odd man out. I was second. The first straw was a long one, so the Army was out, thankfully. I noticed the relief on Melvin's freckly face too.

My uncle's World War II stories of how he survived the Saipan and Iwo Jima assaults sold me on the Marines. He didn't actually see the first or second flag raised on Iwo, but heard about it on the radio. You never visited his house without someone in the family making mention of that event. He didn't mind talking about it so much, but he always paused when mentioning the civilian suicides on Saipan. I couldn't imagine such a scene. The gritty hand-to-hand action the Marines offered completely romanced me, but honestly, it didn't matter what branch it was as long as Ricky and Melvin were there. We were a three-banana bunch.

Slowly the straw revealed its length and apparently, Melvin's chance at the wild blue yonder's shooting gallery was upon us. His jumping up and down brought the furor in Ricky's mother, who didn't like anyone bouncing around on the second floor. She lectured us since birth about the creaky floor joists and the kitchen rattling so violently, dishes were falling out of their cupboards. When she barged upstairs for another finger-waiving blowout, we gave her the news. Suddenly, every plate or bowl we ever broke no longer mattered. Our upstairs thunder rattled her heart from its cupboard, shattering her face in tears.

Neither of us carried a large amount of baggage, so we stuffed a duffel and thumbed it all the way down to Atlanta. The recruiting center for all four services was there, so we enlisted in the Air Force and submitted ourselves for the physical. They had us line up in a huge gymnasium and strip down nude for examination. After which, they took us into another big room with chairs lining the walls. They handed out these big rubber air tubes with a rubber bulb about the size of a baseball attached, and had us wear them on our weak arm's bicep. They handed us a vile for blood collection and then stuck our arms with a needle and tube, which ran down to the vile. Now we had to pump our fists and keep pumping until the vile was full. I think there were about 75 of us in that room and a little more than a half dozen passed out while we were pumping. That gave the rest of us some rare entertainment, but laughing took too much energy. We all grinned wide and kept pumping.

About an hour and a half later, our physicals were complete and they posted the reports outside the gym. Ricky and I were good to go, but Melvin dropped to his knees. Rejected. Jimmy and I both wanted to cuss him out, but the poor boy was already in tears. His dreams were in the trash with his old lady's broken plates. I imagined he answered *her* prayers when he made his phone call back home.

We said our goodbyes and queued for a short bus trip to Georgia Tech's campus for a football game. The next morning, they shipped us out to Lackland Air Force Base just outside San Antonio, Texas. I don't remember much about Lackland other than them constantly yelling at us on the first day. They called us "rainbows" because our clothes were different colors. That stopped when we visited the Green Monster and they issued our uniforms. They buzzed our scalps and sent us to the infirmary next. I remember having four different needles stuck in my right arm, which caused several men to pass out when it was their turn. They taught us how to march too—all the way into the hallways to mop the floors until the wee hours. You were broken on the very first day.

Those first weeks, we marched and cleaned, and went to class, and marched, and ate. It was relentless. We had a conversation piece though.

John Wayne's son, Patrick, shared the same barracks as ours while completing his 90-day wonder duties. He never complained, did all of his tasks, never asked for any favors, and kept his uniforms perfectly maintained. He was a consummate role model just like his dad, which, before boot camp was over, we managed to hear a few of his stories—all of them good. John Wayne was everyone's hero, and I never saw a better western than *The Searchers*, which Pat told us was his favorite.

On Sundays, we'd play football. Ricky and I made quite a few friends on the field, including the tactical sergeant in charge of our squadron. I grew that particular friendship even more after a gag I played on our barracks.

You see, getting any quality sleep at that base became a nightly frustrating endeavor. The base commanders had Taps played every night at 21:00. The lights went out, and we were supposed to go to sleep. Well, the sergeant went off base for the evening and some of the fellas got rather fractious. The barracks guards were switched every two hours and the current one didn't much like the noise, but wasn't a troublemaker, so he let it continue. I rolled around in my upper-bay bunk for an hour before deciding I'd had enough of the whispers from guys under their blankets with flashlights—cutting up, playing cards, or talking about letters to their girlfriends back home. I got fed up, snuck out of my bunk with a pair of boots, and made for the barracks entrance downstairs. The barracks guard was friendly enough; we'd done favors for each other in the past. I whispered to him, "Go along with me," and he said go ahead. I clomped my boots trudging around the front entrance and slammed the door furiously, yelling, "Barracks Guard, open this door!"

The guard giggled and slammed the door behind me while I stormed up the stairs in my loud boots. You could hear all of the fresh airmen running back to their bunks to avoid the heat.

When I made the top of the stairwell, I yelled into the darkness of the upper-bay barracks, "Damnit, I told you people when I left not to make a noise! Hit the floor!"

You could hear a pin drop. I yelled out again, "Damnit, I said hit the floor!"

Everybody jumped out of their bunks and stood at attention at the foot of their bed. They still couldn't see me, so I took my boots off and walked down the aisle between their rows. When I arrived at my bunk, I slipped between the sheets and yelled, "All right now, get back in your bunks and shut the hell up!"

The blanket party that ensued was worth the little pain they doled out that night. They were too duped and laughing to hit me seriously. My little shenanigan was a standing joke for the duration of boot camp. The others even told the TAC sergeant what I had done. He came up to me later and laughed about it hysterically. Evidently, we shared the same sense of humor, and that was necessary to survive this institution.

After a few weeks, our heels were clicking at the same time and our grades were improving. We saw the new groups of rainbows coming off the buses and knew what they were about to go through. They would comment about us ala, "look how sharp those guys are" when we passed by and it made us feel special. Maybe a few didn't, but most of us had a real good time at Lackland.

The TAC sergeant gave both Ricky and me good reviews, so they awarded us our stripes and assigned us to MacDill Air Force Base's 809th Supply & Service Division.

We gave our goodbyes with a weekend of drunken debauchery in San Antonio before hopping on a fresh Monday morning transport bus bound for Tampa. The trip took two long days with a sleepover in Mobile, Alabama. When we arrived late that Tuesday afternoon at MacDill, they assigned our bunks, handed out the base rules, and gave us a short orientation. They handed us the rest of the week off to scout around before next Monday's reveille, so Ricky and I had a few days to explore our surroundings along with some new buddies we met on the bus.

It was a hot and humid week in late July. When we pulled up that Wednesday, the streets were still steaming from a thundershower that passed earlier in the afternoon. There were no air conditioners in the bunks and the evening's swelter brought little relief. We were dying to cool down, so, on the advice of a friendly guard at the gate, we hoofed it a few blocks up Dale Mabry to an air-conditioned tavern. The bartender was used to handling young dumb types, so he poured the cheapest beer, asked where we were from, and if we had seen much of Tampa yet. MacDill had all types coming and going, but the rest of Tampa had only four: Cubans, Italians, Blacks, and Crackers. The locals considered Ricky and me as the latter, but this wasn't anything unfortunate. In fact, we had it better than most around there.

The bartender told us there wasn't much to see or do around town; most of the action for people our age was at the beach. We downed two glasses, and took a cab ride around town anyway. The bartender was right; not much going on and Ybor City's bars didn't look entirely friendly. We ended up back at the same tavern just outside the base and loaded up before the gates closed.

The next morning brought horrendous hangovers, but the boys were determined to see the water, so we caught a ride with some guys exiting the base. My folks once took me to the sea at Kitty Hawk, but I remembered the water being darker, the waves larger, and the sand was course and pepper colored. Clearwater Beach was a veritable paradise. Girls running around half-naked in their bikinis, cheap beer everywhere, clear aqua-green water, and soft sand as white as sugar. Ricky and I thought we'd hit the jackpot and the Air Force suddenly didn't seem like such a bad proposition.

We spent the day flirting with every girl who laughed at our whiteness and I supposed the locals instantaneously recognized folks from out of town as soon as their shirts came off.

"Hey boys, you want us to sign your casts?" They joked.

What they failed to educate us about was how bad of a sunburn you could get, being virtually unexposed and completely numb from the limitless cans of Old Milwaukee. The showers on base provided no relief that evening and that 0530 reveille, like anything at 0530, came much too soon.

The rest of that year was mostly uneventful. We attended our classes and worked in the supply division. Most of us spent just about all of our time on base, buying cases of warm beer, cartons of Winston cigarettes, and losing our paychecks to the squadron's card sharks. We'd watch football on television when we couldn't play it ourselves, and made nickel bets on every play. We also played badminton because the shuttlecocks wouldn't get lost in the snake-infested woods nearby.

We would also go down to the gym and watch the guys boxing or fencing each other. I took an interest in boxing until a welterweight black kid worked me over. I still had an interest, and he taught me a thing or two for which I was grateful. Fencing looked slightly less dangerous, however, so I started learning the different styles including saber, foil, and épée. The fun faded before long; I was only winning half of my matches.

Of course, we hit the beaches at every opportunity too. Picnics with the local girls, more cheap beer (even cheaper from the PX), and volleyball. We had all forms of entertainment available, but the best type, at least for some of us, were the constant practical jokes we played on each other. Probably the two most common were locker hangering and short-sheeting. Of the two, short-sheeting was the longest-running military prank. Almost everybody knew the joke, but occasionally, we pull it on some fresh meat who'd swear up and down both sheets were still on the bed. When they failed an inspection, the obligatory pushups weren't for the faulty bed, but for just plain being stupid after the warning. We had guys coming back from a long night of drinking, throw themselves in bed, and stick both feet right through the sheets. More pushups in the morning.

Locker hangering was a short, sweet affair that all of us lost sleep over every night for months. As the joke went, your locker would have its clasp locked by twisting wire around it from a clothes hanger. We'd have a dawn inspection and trapped clothes meant you couldn't make formation. So, we were all checking our lockers at some point in the middle of the night. Those weren't the only gags.

We did just about anything to get under someone's skin. Anything from wetting toilet paper and sticking it in their boots, to tying knots in belts, to "rearranging" ones footlocker. The only person we never played a prank on was an older, tall, balding fella named Crawford Douglas that transferred out of the Army. "Crawdaddy", as we called him, was demoted several times and never made it past basic Airman, but nobody dared mistreat him, since he was a D-Day Omaha Beach survivor and Korean War vet. He'd come back to the barracks drunk almost every night and tell us stories. Even though we secretly thought he must be a psychotic, Crawford seemed a nice enough guy, but he couldn't remember any of the Ten General Orders if put on the spot. Crawdaddy could recite almost all thirty verses of the "Sanctified Monkey", however. It was some long-winded, drunken poem about a monkey that I've never heard of before, but was hilariously fun entertainment, nonetheless.

Around the seventeenth month in, my cousin Ricky decided he'd had enough of the service and our CO granted him a hardship release due to his mom's health. Still too poor to own a car, he left the way he came in; hitchhiking it back home to Virginia. He met a gal from Chicago, married, and moved up there. I'd get calls from him regularly cursing the weather, so I figured it wouldn't be too long before he came back.

Two years went by before I had a chance to look back. Even though I trained as an in-flight refueler, one of my ears eventually kept me on the ground working the supply and security side of operations. I met a lot of great folks before leaving. Brigadier General Paul Tibbets of Enola Gay fame had become our base commander before he retired and, even though he met us and shook our hands, I regrettably never had my picture taken with him.

The most important person that helped me from the moment I stepped off the bus was Captain Robert Tolliver. He saw me through most of the schooling, kept me out of trouble, and traded favors any time one was needed. His advice was always rock solid and I trusted him implicitly, even when it was time to say goodbye to the Air Force.

We Weren't Cadets

Before my four years were up, I knew that Tampa was the place to settle. I had this apartment already picked out off of Gandy Boulevard, and MacDill was right down the street if I ever needed support. Tampa also had plenty of nightlife and local attractions. Of course, the beaches and their lovely bikinis always beckoned. Our little MacDill clan would hop over to Clearwater on the weekends, keep our bellies full of cheap beer, and play football in the sand in front of the girls. It was perfect!

Captain Tolliver set me right up with an application for the city police department and even had all the blanks already filled. The only line lacking was my signature. One of my service buddies, Mack Poole, had already gone over there two years ago and had been begging me ever since. Why not? The pay wasn't great but the benefits, the low cost of living, and a chance to bust a few heads worked for me. All my friends were still in Tampa as well. Signing that application felt completely natural and before I knew it, I was up at 0500 getting ready for my first day at the academy.

The only thing I remember about that morning was the darkness, my lack of sleep from watching ball with the guys, which meant a heap of black coffee, and fumbling around for my Winstons. Another ten minutes and I hopped in the shower, rinsed off, grabbed a quick comb, and rambled on my old Triumph for the eight minutes it took to get downtown.

I arrived at the department around six, where an officer directed me to a parking spot in the lot behind the building. Another led me over to the cafeteria where they had a fantastic breakfast buffet set up. It wasn't free, but the sixty-five cent price was certainly reason-able. I filled a plate with some eggs and toast, then took a cup full of plain black coffee and sat down.

There were a few dozen of us; mostly younger white and Cuban men, a couple of blacks, and three women. I learned to delineate Cubans from other Latino nationalities over the past few years. They were unquestionably the loudest talkers in the room. A Cuban neighbor in my apartment complex educated me that it was because of their competitive nature in familial conversation. Kids grew up constantly yelling over their siblings, and only the loudest gained attention. This paradox was akin to Middle Eastern revenge. There were no winners, just one ignored blowhard amongst scores of the annoyed.

I never had any problem with the blacks, but apparently, the guy sitting next to me did. He tapped me on the arm twice encouraging me to peer at one of the black guys checking out the young female recruits. I didn't think anything of it until my arm's assailant became visibly angry; enough so that he stood up and started yelling at the man. Everyone stopped what they were doing and looked up at this raging idiot's bigoted tirade.

A supervising sergeant named Thompson ran over and got involved. "What the hell's going on with you, fella?"

I just held on to my coffee and watched the interrogation. The officer got up in the guy's face wondering what the reason was for the disturbance.

"Well?"

It was awful. This fellow must have originated right off a farm in Wimauma, and his exaggerated southern drawl indicated the same.

"Sar, them two naggars over there wuz eye'n them thar wat women…all point'n 'n' stuff. They ain't even supposed ta be in here eatin' with the rest of us, nohow!"

Immediately, disgust showed on the Sgt. Thompson's lean face and you could tell he'd gone through this before when he asked, "Well, do you not like colored people?"

The response was automatic. "No sir, I don't care for them kind and I especially don't care for them trying ta get with our women."

Disappointed, Thompson made the confirmation. "Are you sure?"

The young man skittishly looked around at the others staring back at him. He knew he probably made an egregious mistake, but the slightly walrus-like rookie's pride was too much to backpedal now. "Yassir, I am." As he said it, he took a defensive posture and folded his arms in front.

Sgt. Thompson looked him up and down quickly then looked at each one of us before leaning over to the man. "Come on, fella. Let's take a walk."

Just like that, the sergeant led him out of the cafeteria. Volume in the room instantly exploded with the many conversations pondering what just happened to that guy. It lasted for only a few minutes before the sergeant swung the door back open to address the group.

"Mr. Gooch has been escorted to a post-interview room before being discarded. I'm afraid, he will no longer be joining us. In this regard, I have a message for the rest of you folks. If you are not aware, the city of Tampa happens to be one of the most diverse towns in these here United States. In that regard, we have all kinds: blacks, whites, yellows, Jews, Italians, Cubans, cowboys, Indians, and homosexuals. You name it, we have it. At the end of this academy, *if* you are still here, (he placed a lot of emphasis on the "if') you will be taking an oath to serve and protect. This oath doesn't apply to just 'your kind', it applies to every single living soul out there on the streets. So, I ask every one of you right now; if this is not your belief and you cannot abide by that oath, you should exit the door to my rear immediately."

Of course, you could hear a pin drop. Thompson scanned the eyes of everyone in the room. It seemed as though a full minute passed before he continued.

"All right then. I'll take it we won't be hearing of any more nonsense from you rookies over the next eight weeks." He then turned to the two black men seated towards the corner. "Okay you two, why were you pointing and carrying on about the women over there?"

They both looked at each other for a moment, somewhat afraid to answer before the taller of the two, a muscular linebacker type, had the moxie to face the sergeant. You could tell he had about the same amount of formal education as the person just escorted outside, but this man had a better way about him. He was also a noticeably meticulous dresser.

"Suh, we was only cutting up a little…thinking we had about as much chance at being a po-leese officer as those women over there."

"Hey!" One of the women, a fiery redhead, stood up, taking offense at what that man just said.

He continued, "And that they all looked too good to be doing this kind of work."

The woman sat back down and started teasing her hair. I couldn't tell whether she should take offense to what he said, or to the compliment. To me, it was a brilliant slice of amateur peacekeeping, but the redhead maintained her confused despondency. Sgt. Thompson stopped short of chuckling, knowing he should keep an authoritative composure. His vice happened to be the issuance of sarcastic nicknames. To be sure, we would all have one before the academy graduated. This poor black man just happened to be the first.

Thompson spoke loudly and authoritatively. "Mister, please state your name."

Terrified that he would be escorted out of the room the same as Gooch, the man reluctantly answered, "It's Raymond Coleman, suh, but most folks just call me Ray."

"Well Mr. Coleman, from now on I'm just going to call you Lover Boy." There was a slight flourish of nervous laughter around the room that completely relieved all the tension. "Now, Lover Boy, we aren't going to have any further trouble out of you two and the women, are we?"

"Oh, no suh!" Raymond replied.

"Well that's just dandy, Lover Boy. And, please take it easy on them. Odds are that only one will make it through to the end."

Raymond looked aghast and consoling at the women who were now shocked to hear that kind of hopeless news. If anything, however, it probably served as motivation for the rest of the academy. Women gung ho enough to want to sign up in the first place must have a burr up their ass, I thought. If there was one thing women didn't want to hear lately, it was that they couldn't do something. It didn't matter if they could; they didn't want to hear otherwise.

Ray happened to catch my glance as he sat down. I gave him an expression of approval and he seemed a good man to me. I smiled and raised my coffee cup in his direction before taking another sip. Sgt. Thompson walked back over to his table and sat down. We all turned back around and quietly finished our breakfasts. It was approaching 0700 and time to assemble for morning calisthenics.

They had us line up in the gym and work out for around an hour. Jumping jacks, pushups, jogging around the track, and all sorts of machines simulating different exercises had us working up quite a sweat. The routine was set to some sterilized NASA-style music too. Every time the music stopped, a whistle would blow and we would change exercises or machines. The real entertainment, however, was watching the women attempt pull-ups. After a few days, we started side-betting win, place, or show. After two weeks, it was clear that, although the redhead had a spunky attitude, only this one trim Latin woman could actually keep up with the rest of us. In fact, she was more athletic than a good third of the male rookies. The Tampa Police Department developed its fair share of economic support for the doughnut industry, much like the rest of the country. The third woman gave up and went home after the first week. Our wagers eventually tapered off when it became clear that, no matter how you stacked the odds, there was simply no competition.

At 0800, they gave us thirty minutes to shower, clean up, and back into our civvies; the department didn't issue formal academy uniforms for another decade. Afterwards, we attended specialized classes for the next three hours. Those mostly consisted of criminal psychology, rules of evidence, and how evidence is properly collected, traffic stops, firearms training, explosives, and the history of the police department. The instructors were all heads of their departments, homicide, burglary, auto theft, etc. They all (and I mean every one of them) opened their lectures by informing us how fortunate we were, and how bad they had it during their patrolman days. One patrol captain even went on about how he had to ride in the winter without any floorboards and how he had to beg the grocery stores for flattened cardboard boxes every night. Another, by our count, said he had six extra jobs because the department didn't pay much. Before the day was over, we had another pool going on who was the poorest instructor.

As it turned out, that dubious honor belonged to one of the evidence instructors named Henry Lozello. Not only did he complain about everything, his Spanglish accent was so thick, we strained to understand his lectures. He was also the only one to call us "cadets" even though everyone else called us rookies. I was told later by a major that he liked to pretend the academy was some big outfit like New York's or Los Angeles'—something he must have seen on television. He didn't say it much, but every time he did, I had to restrain myself from laughing.

At 1130, they sent us back down to the cafeteria for lunch. It was an absolutely fantastic country style buffet containing roast beef, fried chicken, Cuban pork, real mashed potatoes, gravy, rice, beans, and all kinds of vegetables. If the city got one thing right, it was sparing no expense on the food, even if they only made a little over a dollar from us in return. They gave us a whopping hour and a half every day for that break. Most of us would finish eating after thirty minutes, so we'd get into groups for studying. Of course, we had some crazy conversations during those sessions. The second day, Ray sauntered over, sat in our group and gave me another reason to wonder about that Lozello character.

"We wuz in Captain Lozello's class this mornin' and all I did was ask a question about a sit-i-ation with me pulling up to a robbury on them Davis Islands. He just went off and said, 'Stop right there joo *Lover Boy*. First of all, joo only be walking the beat while you're working here and second, joo will be in your own neck of the woods and certainly not on them islands. The department don't let no coloreds drive, let alone arrest whites.'"

Mind you, I just came from the Air Force. Blacks not only drove, the Tuskegee Airmen proved they were pretty damn good pilots too. Sadly, what Ray told me was true. Back in the early '60s, Tampa's black cops had to walk their beats, and only arrest other blacks. Only just now were they allowed to eat in the cafeteria with the rest of us. Ray should have known this. I found out later that his dad had been a beat cop for 22 years. I guess he didn't have the heart to tell Ray, or perhaps he didn't want to discourage him before fully committing to the department. In any case, I didn't much care for the outdated policies, but I was just a rookie with no voice.

After the first week, they finally got us to the gun range. They trained us with the standard-issue Smith & Wesson Model 10. It was a .38 caliber revolver with a four-inch barrel shooting standard 110-grain wadcutters. The rangemaster, a sergeant named Harold Hartmann, gave us all the rounds we wanted and expert instruction along the way. He quickly asserted his competence in a demonstration by pumping all six rounds in a three-inch grouping at 25 yards. He was incredible and, with his encouragement, we all thought we could eventually become just as efficient.

Sgt. Hartman knew all the tricks too. At the end of our test rounds, shooting at distances of 8, 12, and 25 yards, he would announce, "All right you rookies, you can put your .38 caliber pencils away." We laughed after he told us about catching two rookies punching holes in their targets with pencils. And yes, they deservedly got the boot for Conduct Unbecoming.

The women, surprisingly, had no trouble handling the pistols, but when it came to training with a shotgun a few weeks later, they ran into serious trouble. That spunky redhead held the butt too far from her shoulder and, instead of leaning into the shot, put her head down. The recoil broke her nose on the first shot, sending the range master running over to grab her before she keeled over crying. The academy was only halfway over and that sergeant from the cafeteria on the first day ended up being correct. Only one of the women made it to the end—Sonja Ramirez. She was as tough as any one of us and, well, much better looking.

After eight weeks, with the exception of a couple of rookies on that last two-mile qualifying run, and one more who couldn't handle one detective's description of a maggot-infested homicide victim, our group was fit to go. On the last day before graduation, they handed out awards in four different categories: Best Shot, Best Academic Score, Best Driver, and Best Physical Condition. As it turned out, they gave me the awards for shooting and driving. It was no surprise when Ray won for best conditioning. Of course, they should have given him another award for Best Dresser. I'd swear the guy was even ironing his gym clothes!

The academic award fooled all of us when they called up Ramirez. Dang! Great looks *and* smart. I know I wasn't the only one disappointed to find out she already had a steady. Naturally, that didn't keep a couple of the guys from hitting on her. She didn't complain though. I got the impression she secretly liked the attention and the power, which is why she may be here in the first place. It didn't matter, really. The end was finally upon us. Academy was over and graduation was the next day.

This was one of my favorite memories from the morning of graduation—signing off on the credit union loan for $105 and heading down to the property room for my first uniform. Blue wool pants and blue cotton shirts, all brand new. And then we drove to a small hardware store just a few miles north of the station for our guns, ammo, and belts. The smell of all the thick, black leather from that shop was unmistakable and unforgettable. I always loved that aroma.

They gave us enough time to get suited up, polished, and on parade by 1000. It was really not that much different from the many military ceremonies in which I had already participated. We stood shoulder to arm's length shoulder, ready for the formal inspection. In our right hand was a brand new Smith & Wesson Model 10. In our left were six rounds of the standard ammunition. The chief made his way down the line inspecting what was left of the 39 original rookies. After our two months passed, only 23 of us remained.

At the end, we all took the oath in front of the city clerk. Everyone of us repeated that we would uphold the local and state laws, the Constitution of the United States, and to protect and serve the public. After it was over and the clapping and hugs dwindled, we were each given our assignments; squad and district. I couldn't wait to get started.

A Tampa Rookie

The department gave the old-timers easier beats, mostly during the daytime, so they could live like normal people. Generally, we had three eight-hour shifts, just like any traditional company—First, Second, Third—but in actuality, we had six distinct shifts because the traditional three shifts had two different starting times staggered by one hour. For example, my first actual time slot was from 11 p.m. to 7 a.m. and the next group came on at 12 a.m. and went to 8 a.m. Even though both groups started at different times, they were both on the Third shift. The other shifts overlapped the same way, meaning Tampa would never have a moment without cops on the street. When they told me which shift I was starting on, they just said "11-7".

I showed up at 10:45 p.m. and grabbed a steaming cup of black coffee at the cafeteria. From there, I went up to assembly, underwent an inspection, and received my first assignment. Back then, the Hillsborough River divided the city into two districts logically titled District 1 and District 2. They also configured the force for two different uniformed divisions: Patrol and Traffic. We had three different platoons that switched shifts each month too. My assignment was to Patrol Division, District 2, Platoon C. Platoon C was on the third shift that month, and our squad had the 11-7 slot.

No sooner did my mind digest the assignment, my Field Training Officer (FTO) tapped me on the shoulder for an introduction. He was a tall man in his late 40s, about 6'1", balding, and about 20 pounds overweight. Cpl. Dick Champney had been with the department for over 22 years and was probably the most relaxed person I ever met. I could tell by his handshake that we'd get along just fine. It was firm enough to ooze confidence without dictating authority, and long enough to convey sincerity without suspicion, or worse, disinterest. He led me down to the garage where the previous shifts were cleaning out their belongings from their cars.

Tampa had two versions of the 1962 Dodge Dart fleet running at the time. They both looked the same, but a few had the gigantic 413 cubic-inch "Max Wedge" V8 engines. Our car had the older 383, but it was no slouch at over 400 horsepower. The cars weren't overly big and heavy, and they, as Dick put it, were "pretty hot". I thought so too. The low rumble of those old big-block monsters was something else!

We climbed in and started to leave. I noticed Dick wasn't wearing his seatbelt, which was newly mandated rule according to driving instructor at the academy, so I had to ask, "Aren't you going to put on your seatbelt?"

Dick Champney did a double take, and smiled. "Tell me, rookie; have you ever seen someone burn alive?"

"No." Of course I hadn't seen anyone burn to death! How many people could have seen such a reprehensible sight? The question immediately made me defensive.

"I helped out on a 10-50 (traffic accident) last year; car flipped over and this man, we thought he must have been 10-55 (drunk), burned up because he couldn't get that belt off. Yeah, sure, go by the regulations and wear the belt if you want. I'm not, and I'd appreciate it if you'd keep that to yourself."

I was puzzled for a moment. *He's supposed to be the shining example as my mentor and already he's breaking a rule?* No matter. I didn't much care for the belt either and he just gave me a good reason.

"I won't tell if you won't," I told him as I took my belt back off.

For radio communications, our identifier was slightly different from our shift designate. Dispatch used the first, second, or third shift number along with a zone number as our identifier. Our district contained six patrol zones, Zones 10-15, and usually only one uniformed patrol per zone. The only exception was Zone 13, which encompassed a small but tough area northwest of downtown and bordered by the Hillsborough River. Zone 13 often needed two patrols due to its high crime rate. My assignment was on the third shift, Zone 12. This zone was a rather large patrol area encompassing most of West Tampa all the way to the bay, and as far north as the city limit. On the radio, dispatchers identified us by our shift and zone, which was "312". Simple enough. There were dispatchers for each district and division (patrol and traffic), making for a total of four. Our particular dispatcher's identifier was "KIB459".

The first couple of nights, Dick rode us all around the zone, showing me its ins and outs. We traded some stories from the service and he gave me crazy tales of rookies that the department quickly fired or disliked because of their antics.

"Did they tell you about Gerald Schwartzman in the academy?" Dick asked.

"I don't recall."

"They gave him the boot after his neighbors started complaining of the way he would mow his grass."

"What's so bad about it?"

"The moron would always wear nothing but these cutoff shorts made from some old dungarees. If that wasn't scary enough, he'd also put on his leathers; firearms and all. Oh, and his duty hat." Champney quizzically glanced in my direction, expecting my slow repulsion.

"No kidding." I started to laugh, but the visualization of some buttery-looking dingaling soon gave Dick his expected results.

"I'm not kidding! The guy was out there cuttin' his grass every weekend like that."

"Any other jewels?" I sarcastically asked.

"Yeah, sure. We had another guy, (he fumbled around trying to remember the name), a Josh Helper…Halper? I can't remember. He went and ruined a good thing we had going with that burger joint, McDonald's. They were giving a free meal to all of us on duty—any day, every day—if we wanted. That wasn't good enough for this guy; he goes and tries to take his entire family in there for a freebie! Off-duty at that! When the manager refused, he created a crybaby scene running everyone out of the place. So, guess what? No more McDonald's. You want to get the department mad at you in a hurry, just take away a free meal! They got sick and tired of his insufferable ass real quick after another month of him skulking around like a playground sissy."

"Let me guess. Conduct Unbecoming?" I confidently surmised.

"No, actually. They assigned him to Zone 13 for two months. He wasn't there more than a week before getting his ass kicked in a brawl. When his partner called it in, everyone took their time.

Took him a month to recover, but he never mouthed off again about anything. I still hate his guts. I still like McDonald's, but I can hardly look at the place without getting my dander up. You've been there before, haven't you?"

"Yeah, sure. Who hasn't?"

On the front half of the third night, we finally received our first call. Around 2 a.m., KIB459 had us respond Code-2 (beacon light on, siren off) to a silent alarm at a bar located on the north end of our zone, near the intersection of Hillsborough and Himes Avenues. Dick took the call, flicked on the car's light and wound up that 383 for all it was worth. We were just a couple of miles off Dale Mabry Highway, so it was only a minute or two before we pulled up to the location.

We learned in the academy to cover opposite corners of the building before going inside. The front door of that bar was wide open, so Dick wanted to cover it himself in case of an assailant's fast exit. He took the front-left corner and sent me around back. It was darker back there, being away from the streetlights. I wasn't afraid though. I remembered that first call being very much like hunting with my old man. I walked quietly back to the corner on the other side of the building from Dick, careful not to step on anything that would make too much noise. Unsnapping the holster to my service revolver, I took up position and waited to hear from Dick. I was on that corner for less than a few seconds before hearing something behind a few clumps of overgrown broom sage on the building's left side. Immediately, I reached for the revolver, and took aim in that direction. Nothing else moved or made a sound, so I looked down, picked up a small rock, and flung it into the weeds. A short Latino man stood up with his hands in the air, and his trouser and shirt pockets appeared stuffed with cash in small denominations.

After cuffing the man and gathering up the loose cash, I walked him back around the front where Dick was coming out of the front door. The look on his face was priceless, especially after what I said.

"Hey Dick, this burglar catchin's easy!"

My FTO just shook his head and walked over to the car to call in a paddy wagon. After finishing with the radio, he looked back over towards me. "You know what this means, don't you?"

I was still guarding the burglar by the rear of the car. Dick's question wasn't clear to me at first, given the distraction. "No. Wait. Right! I won the pool!"

You see, during the beginning of each shift, the entire patrol division would chip in a couple of dollars apiece. The pool was to see who would be the first to catch a burglar that night. Sometimes, a few nights would pass before we caught someone. Sure, we had calls every night, but that didn't mean we always caught the perpetrator. It was only my third night, but Dick told me that the pool was up to its fifth shift without a catch. He started to give his concerns, but I was already on top of what he was going to say.

"Now, Bill, you've only been out here three nights, so it's…"

I interrupted, "I know, I know. Tell them not to worry. Dinner's on me."

The burglar turned around and looked me squarely in the eyes.

"Joo mean, you only been a cop three days?" He had the look of complete surprise and disgust.

"Yeah, that's right. What of it?"

His eyes turned towards my FTO, jokingly. "Oh, man, jefe. Joo gonna have your hands full with thees one here… sneaky son-of-a-bitch!"

Dick took out his baton and pointed it in his direction. "Now, we'll have no more of that, Carmine."

My FTO put his baton back in his leather and started snickering at the frightened look on the burglar's face. "We can't have that kind of language around the youngsters. Besides, I think it's beginner's luck."

He barely got the last words out of his mouth before he and that man were both laughing. I knew it was all in fun at my expense, but that didn't bother me. What took me by surprise was the fact that Dick knew this assailant's name. After the wagon picked up Carmine, I felt compelled to ask.

"Dick, how did you know that guy?"

We were still waiting for the owner to come and take care of his establishment and Dick became quite reflective.

"Rookie, you work an area long enough, observe every detail long enough, look at every face long enough and talk with these people long enough, well…it's not that big of a town, see. These people that live here, most of them wake up, go to work, or stay home. They really don't look around themselves much or try to get to know everyone around them. Complete obliviousness; tunnel vision. You do this job for a while, you'll not only get to know most of your area, but the good and bad people in each neighborhood. And, if you're really good at this, you'll know why these people do what they do. You take Carmine for instance. He used to be a cigar roller just like his daddy. He's had it pretty rough with all the layoffs and whatnot; got mixed up with the wrong crowds and, well, this is the result. The detectives have a big chart on their wall downtown tracing known criminals and their activities. There are three areas on that chart: black, white, and gray. If they do crimes repeatedly, their names show up on the black side. If they haven't done anything in a while, they're on the white. If we're not sure of their status, they're in the gray. Of course, the detectives aren't keeping up with every offender in town, just the higher profile types. It's up to the street cop to maintain his own mental chart. Carmine would be considered a gray since he's back and forth depending on his situation."

Later in the week, I made good on my promise and paid everyone's tab at the Aztec Lounge. It's a little dive about two blocks down from the department and notoriously blue. I think some still held it against me since I still came out ahead twenty bucks after all was said and done, but they quickly got over my beginner's luck. Eventually, I would buy many rounds at the Aztec and became a favorite with Platoon C.

For the next three months, Dick continued my training. On the whole, we had a lot of mundane patrols, but Tampa had its moments. Probably the most memorable during this time was helping out with a plane crash at the airport. A Trans World Airlines Lockheed Constellation belly-flopped on landing and skidded into a ditch. Dick and I ran over and helped the airport police evacuate the plane before she caught on fire, which miraculously never happened. I met the captain from that flight and he personally thanked all of us for the assistance. While he was waiting for the inspectors to arrive, he stood with us and lit up a cigarette before cutting a joke to ease the tension.

"Do you fellas know the nickname for these planes?"

Everyone just stood around shaking their heads.

"They're calling them Flying Whores because they're always on their bellies!"

We got a good laugh out of that one. Sadly, the pilot was right about that model. Apparently, the Constellations were gaining a murderously poor reputation for landing gear failures.

On another occasion, I learned some new lingo. Dick spotted a car weaving in and out of his lane, so we decided to 10-28 (pull over for registration/license check). When the driver ignored us, Dick flicked on the siren and said, "Looks like we got us a rabbit." He meant that we were going to chase down a runner, which this guy was attempting in drunken futility. He ended up taking us to some run-down, old bungalow near the middle of West Tampa, ran the car up into the yard, and started to run inside. I chased him inside the house's screened porch and knocked him down just before he got through the door. While he was on his stomach, I reached back for my cuffs, brought his arms around, and began to clamp him up. That's when the front door swung open and some chubby, middle-aged Cuban woman started wildly swinging her tiny fists into my shoulder and side of my face. I remember getting numb after the first couple of her hits, but I'd had enough. Trying to get the runner on his feet, I had to push her aside. Naturally, she exaggerated the push and fell down. Now, normally this is a source of comedy for me, but what happened next defied explanation.

I must have broken a cardinal rule with the many neighbors who gathered to watch the spectacle. It seemed as soon as I turned around, three or four men started pushing Dick around while he was trying to call a wagon for our rabbit. Since he was wearing cuffs and not going anywhere, I threw him down the porches' three steps and onto the grass so I could help Dick. I didn't have time to get my baton out before they abandoned him and started hitting me from all directions. I couldn't feel any of them. I also didn't feel the many blows my hands were accruing across their facial bones, of which, I evidently broke two; a nose and a jaw on two different brawlers. That didn't stop them though; it was an open melee on the street.

I heard Dick yell into the radio's microphone, "10-24! 10-24! (officer in trouble) Multiple Signal-20's! (mentally disturbed persons)" He gave our location next.

If you wanted to hear something impressive, I can't think of anything much better than the sound of all the responding units' cars roaring towards us. Tires screeched, nightsticks were drawn, and then the *real* violence ensued. They beat those Cubans within an inch of their lives. Officers grabbed the woman off the porch and dragged her by her hair, throwing her into the paddy wagon. There was no mercy for people fighting with cops. This was another rule learned that evening.

On occasion, Traffic Division officers assisted those on Patrol. This was the case in the previously mentioned skirmish. Conversely, our division would help occasionally assist with those in traffic.

My first experience, and probably an excellent break-in by departmental standards, was directing traffic at a large inter-section on the north end of my zone during a typical afternoon thundershower. They didn't issue special clothes for this and, of course, I got soaked to the bones. Drivers would pass by me shaking their heads, and I didn't care much for their pity, but the ones that drove by with the "you must be stupid" look really grinded on me. Even worse, the department didn't allow returning to headquarters for dry clothes. Drainage was poor and during the downpours, water would get over the sides of your shoes. You had to work the rest of your shift dripping. They had me on the "second" second shift, and it ran all the way until midnight. You don't think about this too much when you're standing in the middle of an intersection.

I didn't much care for working the traffic side of things. A buddy named Barry Godfrey validated this while he was work-ing in the motorcycle division.

"Bill, you're not going to believe this... I made a stop earlier this afternoon. Nothing out of the ordinary, right? I just pulled this lady over and she gave me the typical sob story — 'please officer, I can't afford a ticket, not right now...yadda, yadda, yadda.' So I let her off with a warning. You'd think that was the end of it, right? No! One hour later, the captain is calling me back here (headquarters). Would you believe that bitch came straight over here after the stop and smugly bragged about how easy it was talking herself out of a ticket! Oh, they got a pretty good laugh outta that one before confiscating her license as a joke."

Barry was beside himself just after that episode, but he told me later that he'd never give a warning again. That sounded like a smart policy. Why bother with a warning? At best, you'll just become an annoyance for taking up the violator's time. I'd rather give them some value!

The department would sometimes keep things interesting by switching our patrol zones or even sending us to Division 1; "The Dark Side", some called it. After the first month, Dick had me doing the driving, so he insisted showing me some of the "fun" carried on by the Division 1 regulars down in Tampa's estuarial industrial district.

Dick directed us to the most southern end of 20th Street where we met up with a couple of familiar practical jokers; Gerald "Jerry" Immelman and my Air Force buddy, Mack Poole. I met Jerry back at the academy and was well aware of his notoriety as a wisecracking prankster. He was a rather tall and stout blond with a boisterous laugh you couldn't forget—something 18 years of smoking and belly laughing like carnival clown could only produce.

I told him, "You know you missed your true calling as a stunt double for George Kennedy."

"I get that a lot, smart guy." He laughed.

Mack's features didn't stand out in any way compared to Jerry's insisting presence. At the time, my friend was maybe a couple of inches shy of six feet like me, except he had reddish brown hair where mine is sandy brown, and he had green eyes where mine are blue. Mack told me he grew up in the south, but his accent favored more of a western quality. I suppose that if you live around Tampa's cauldron long enough, you slowly lose your identity.

One feature in which Mack excelled was his easy-going gift for conversation. He even knew conversational Spanish, which was rare for his kind, but as I quickly found out, was required knowledge for this town. Mack had a definite advantage and got along with just about everybody he met, including those he pursued.

After we finished with the formal introductions, Dick spoke up with a slight hint of laughter under his breath.

"Hey Jer, why don't you show the rookie here how we like to get around town."

I looked at him, and then over towards Mack, whose eyes had the distinct look of mischief; a look I knew all too well from our days in the service. We climbed back in our cars and drove half a block over to the main railroad tracks that traversed the peninsula. Jerry drove his unit on top of the steel tracks facing north, with the tires straddling the rails; a trade secret of the '62

Dodge Dart. With the engine still purring, he placed the patrol car's transmission in neutral and hopped back out. Both he and Mack started deflating the tires on their sides of the car until the rubber sagged slightly over the rails. They jumped back in, drove down the tracks about 30 feet or so, and stopped. Mack turned around leaned out of his window, motioning us to do the same.

"That's pretty slick, Mack!" I yelled over before driving our car on the tracks just behind them.

Jerry turned around and started laughing maniacally. "Oh, you just wait, buster. This'll be the most fun you've had since watching women at the pistol range."

Dick laughed at that remark since he occasionally served as a backup range master. After he was done, he glanced over towards me and instructed to just let the car idle in first gear after Jerry pulls away.

There we were—two patrol cars taking a trip up the rail system towards Ybor City. Those 383 engines created quite a roar when they floored them. When idling, you could hear a pin drop. We had to keep the cars in first gear or they would accelerate indefinitely, it seemed. I kept my foot on the brake because our car kept creeping up on Jerry's. Dick said I correctly deduced a difference in the two car's idle settings; something the Department's garage would look into later. We made it all the way up to 6th Avenue and they made a left turn onto some other tracks heading west. Mack's voice crackled over the radio.

"All right fellas, turn your lights off and keep about fifty yards off our six."

Dick smiled, but didn't feel the need to say anything other than "10-4". I turned off our lights and let them creep ahead. About a minute later, we were completely off the roadway and cruising quietly between a long valley of darkened warehouses.

Quietly, Mack whispered into his microphone, "Hey boys, keep your eyes down this old rusty building coming up on our left."

I could see a couple of blackish lumps up against that building ahead. As soon as Jerry's car was with a few dozen feet, he and Mack turned on the beacon light, the siren, and the horn; all at the same time. The two lumps immediately jumped straight into the air!

Our lumps turned out to be a couple of sodden skid row rejects half scared out of their drunken wits. Those two panicked their way down the side of the warehouse and around a corner. Jerry and Mack didn't bother giving chase; you could tell from their laughs echoing back and forth on the warehouse's outer walls that they were just playing a cruel trick. I couldn't stop laughing either. A minute or two passed and Mack was back on the radio, hardly controlling his own laughter.

"Bill? You ever see two *transients* move that fast?" Mack was being clever in his use of the word "transient". I came to know his brand of sarcasm in regard to the scholarly titling of bums, crazies, thugs, and other various forms of degenerates. I remembered Lover Boy hardly containing himself when an academy instructor used the term "African-American" in a class. He almost fell over!

Dick handed me the mic. "Mack. Uh...negative. That's probably a record."

Mack laughed, "Ten-four. We're continuing ahead. Stay back the fifty yards again."

I confirmed reception and held the car back until they were again at distance. Both cars idled through the warehouses of Ybor, on and off 6th Avenue's pavement, and then back on the tracks towards downtown. After passing the old Union Station, the tracks led us down Polk Street all the way through downtown to the river. That was the district border, so we stopped, drove off the tracks, and drove two blocks down a parallel street where there was a service station that kept their air compressor running overnight. We crawled over there with our flat tires and filled them up, laughing the entire way. Dick told me that station had a quiet arrangement with our division, but I never knew the full details. Even though headquarters was only a few blocks in the other direction, Dick said the tires wouldn't make it and the mechanics over there would be asking too many questions. Everyone at headquarters knew about the tracks, but officially, they were a big no-no.

Jerry handed the hose over to Mack and then walked over to Dick and me. He was still cracking up from scaring the two deadbeats back in Ybor.

He sauntered over, poked my left shoulder, and laughed, "So Bill, how'd you like that, huh?"

I had to admit, I wasn't expecting to have such an outrageous time riding all over town on the rails. "You guys do that all the time?"

"Sure, but not every night you know. It drives the cockroaches batty because they don't know if we're coming down the street or coming 'round behind. Most times, they just don't expect anything other than a locomotive to be on the tracks. And those hardly ever run at night through Ybor."

Every time they had me assigned to that zone, riding the rails became the shift's highlight. Jerry was right; it drove those people absolutely insane when caught from behind, so-to-speak. The rail run worked well for me, and my shift didn't mind my treating them with their pool money, which was becoming slightly lopsided with my winning half the pots.

Before my three months of training were up, Dick enlightened me on some finery with regard to working with the other patrolmen. There were a few that thought I was making them look bad because I was catching more than my fair share of criminals. They just wanted to put in their time and stay out of trouble until they got back to dayshift. Flat tires were a popular excuse. Some patrolmen would claim flats as an excuse to miss a call, even if it was only a block away. One thing about my FTO, Dick absolutely despised anyone trying to pull that old tire gag. So much so, he would take us out of our zone momentarily to drive by another patrol and make a snide remark in passing from his window.

"Oh, his tires look good today."

He knew they were guilty and put them on the hot seat. With crystal clarity, you could read their lips as we passed by too— "asshole!" The contemptuous jackasses were glaring straight at him when they mouthed it, but knew that Dick was being nice by letting them off the hook with his implied warning. The ones that felt belligerent enough to test Dick's resolve didn't stay in our platoon very long. They likely found themselves assigned to Third Shift, Zone 13 more often if they didn't straighten up.

I wasn't as lenient as Dick. If they hated me for being good at my job, so be it. This was one very important item in which I was always thankful to my FTO—he opened my eyes to corruption.

Hot Lips

By the summer of 1966, I had been with TPD for almost two years. West Tampa became more familiar to me than anywhere I lived previously, even back home in Virginia. I had even picked up enough Spanish to hold a short conversation with appreciative locals. Even better, I got a kick out of spooking some of the Latino shopkeepers by asking them for my Winstons in their language. Some of the bigots, however, would instantly scowl when I spoke to them in Spanish, (*how dare he!*), but most gave me a smile, appreciative that a gringo would give them enough respect to communicate in their language.

Mack and I would sometimes meet way out on the Courtney Campbell Causeway to plunk raccoons, opossums, crabs, or whatever else crawled along the shores. He had been a detective for almost a year and was trying to give me some advice if I wanted to join him. Thing was, he was more of an analyst and I did better working the people on the street. I talked to him about constantly running into people or businesses, and getting the same telltale odor of something that had recently burned.

He laughed, "Bill, that's probably flash paper."

Mack surprised me with his answer, of course. I could see the familiar condescending look in his eyes.

"Flash paper?" I asked.

"Yeah. Didn't you get a briefing on the bolita games a few months ago?"

"I musta been out that day." I lied.

I remembered that boring lecture on local Cuban lotteries, but fell asleep during that part. I never missed a day at work, though!

Mack laughed. I think he knew better. "It's made from nitrocellulose; something like guncotton. It's called flash paper because it burns completely and instantly, leaving no ashes."

Well, that explained the smell. "I think I saw that in a Bond movie once. So, let me guess; I'm probably barging in on some writers or runners, huh?"

"Sounds like it. I don't mess with the old-timers too much unless they get bold. Heck, just about everyone on my wife's side of the family plays, and, well, it's not as if it's hurting anybody. You won't catch me going out of the way for victimless crimes. It's not worth getting hurt, clogging the courts, or wasting precious hours knapping outside the DA's office, which in and of itself is a commission of shear lunacy."

Mack's statement made me considerably ill, especially from a detective who's supposed to be the "shining example".

"They're breaking the law." I sternly retorted.

"Yeah, Bill. They're breaking the law. What am I supposed to do, haul in every granny in West Tampa? Nah. You shouldn't mess too much with them, you know, unless they deserve it. There's this one little market over off Columbus; the owner's name is Miguel. I know he's a writer, but small-time…not worth busting. The way the parking lot is, you can sneak right up on his front door before he has a chance to light his slips. Instead, he always shoves them in his mouth and turns around when I come in, as if I can't see what he's doing. Ha! It cracks me up every time. And, all he does is cuss me out. 'Ay carajo, Mackie! Why joo do this to me!' He'd have to run to the bathroom to spit the wad out and flush. Worse, the flash paper left a bad taste in his mouth for hours. He hated me!"

I laughed at Mack's story, but thought to myself that I'd still bust his ass. I returned to our original discussion about becoming a detective. "I understand. So, what do I need to be doing that I'm not doing already?"

Mack went to his car, came back, and held up a blank Field Interrogation Report (FIR). "Have you filled any of these out?"

"Yeah, quite a few."

"Make a point to fill out as many of these as you can. I found out real quick that the detectives love these already completed because it does a lot of their groundwork for them; understand? Look, you know the only way you're going to be a detective is if other detectives recommended you, right? This isn't some-thing you earn by just doing your time. Look at all these fifteen-year sergeants running around. Doesn't that tell you anything? Pensioner countdowns, the lot. Anyway, you fill out these FIRs any time you get a chance, Bill. If you're on a scene, ask the detective yourself. Initiative — they like that."

I may be somewhat biased in admitting my Air Force friend was, perhaps, one of the brightest people I personally knew. Outside of that, he was something else with a pistol. A hermit crab at 25 yards had no chance! For the next few months, I did exactly as Mack suggested. The detectives knew I was eager to become one of their own, and a few that actually liked me made a point to summon me over for reports. In kind, I didn't keep them waiting very long.

The next six months ended up being some of the most tumultuous in the history of the department, and I was right in the middle of everything. Most of the FIRs I completed were mundane interviews from robbery victims. A few more came from violent crimes, mostly drug or domestic-related. The first report that really got under my skin came from a little boy.

On a late September morning, I responded to an emergency call at a gas station off a busy intersection on the west side of my zone. I was only less than a dozen blocks away, but the column of thick, black smoke let me know what I was in for; or so I thought.

There are moments in your life when everything stops, you become numb, and just execute what you were trained. When I arrived, I didn't remember the first few moments after breaking into a full run towards that fully engulfed sedan. I only remember the flashed sequence: A boy a dozen feet away on the ground, coughing with a smoldering flannel shirt he panicked to remove, and another younger boy trying to climb out of the car's doorway with his clothes and hair completely engulfed in flames.

Foregoing the self-rescued kid on the ground, I leapt for the car and grabbed the youngster by the arm, ran with him several feet away, and started rolling him on the ground to put the flames out. He was maybe nine years old; screaming and crying in excruciating pain. All I could do was hold onto him and yell back towards the station for some water or a wet towel. At that point, my mind allowed me to recall one glimpse of a younger boy in that car. I probably dawdled in contemplation far longer than the few seconds it appeared to take, wondering if I imagined that smaller boy frozen in the flames. I stood up and started to walk over, but the car was much too hot to get anywhere close to the doorway. It didn't matter. God saw fit for me to witness a little seven-year-old kid vanquish in the white-hot broil. His lips curled and receded. Their fat sizzled and splattered the windows like bacon in an oven. There's no soap for a man's eyes afterward; their naivety now and forever tainted.

When the fire department showed up and took over the care for the remaining two boys, the station owner alerted us to a woman locked in his bathroom. She was crying incessantly and not obeying my directives to open the door. The only thing she screamed between sobs was, "Oh God, please forgive me. Oh God, please forgive me." She made me kick down that door and violently yank her away from the sink. I could feel my venomous hate begin raging.

"What did you do?" I yelled.

She would not answer. She just kept crying.

While keeping her in my sight, I pulled out an FIR from my patrol car and walked back over to the oldest boy who was trembling uncontrollably while he sat on the store's sidewalk. The sweat poured off my forehead and onto the paper, smearing some of the basic information I managed to extract. I only managed his name and age before he became a broken record — "It's not her fault. It's not her fault. It's not her fault."

An hour later, a tall and lanky Latin detective named Jose Fernandez walked back over to me after another interview with that woman. He spoke with a slight Spanish accent, but not enough to mispronounce his English.

"You know who that is, Bill?"

How could I possibly know? I'm still in shock from what I just witnessed. "No Jose, I don't."

He held up his ballpoint and tapped it on his clipboard. "That piece of garbage is Samantha Louise Tate from California."

I didn't recall her name but the car's tag was from Nevada. I gave Jose a shoulder shrug and shook my head.

He continued. "They made a report on her a few weeks ago for trying to kill these boys. Tried leaving them in that very same car to suffocate in the Mojave Desert. Can you believe that, Bill? She locked them in a car and walked away in a hundred and twenty-four degree heat. Then, she tried to blame it on the boys, saying they locked themselves in. I remembered reading this last week and just shaking my head. Can you believe that?"

I handed the sweat-soaked FIR to Jose, made for the nearest air-conditioned restaurant with a bottomless glass of iced water, and sat there until the end of my shift wondering what would become of the two boys that survived.

We found out later that Mrs. Tate was a complete mental case after fleeing with the boys from an abusive husband. He wanted their complete custody and, to get back at him, she fled eastward vowing never to give them up...at least, not alive. After her unsuccessful attempt in the desert, she cruelly doused the car with gasoline and threw a pack of matches in the back seat with her curious boys. Some people don't believe in the death penalty. You tell me what value there is in keeping a woman like this around at our expense, afforded the luxury of a natural death. And what about her boys?

Several weeks afterward, the anger slowly subsided and I saw less of the enkindled lips. I was no longer a virgin to my FTO's seatbelt reasoning, but it didn't completely desensitize me or manage my temper. My propensity for street justice reared its ugly head again when I received a 10-16 (domestic disturbance) at a familiar residence in MacFarlane Park. I'd been to this house twice already for drunken husband-wife beatdowns, but when I arrived, I saw that their little boy was bleeding and bruised. A fast scan of the mother and father's knuckles indicated they had both participated in the child's demolition. That was it; the Irish heritage took over when my baton jumped out of its leather and provided a lengthy disagreement with their anatomy. Sure, they went to jail and the boy went to foster care, but I knew the only justice the boy ever received was mine.

Winter had begun to set in our town and in my soul. It seemed those FIRs began to gnaw at me with the efficiency of the local mosquitoes. I was scratching for relief, but receiving little justice on the perpetrators. There were no counterbalances in my life and the professors of its fragility were about to hold another lecture.

A Crickett's Song

In the earliest part of December of 1966, economic and morale conditions in Tampa as well as the rest of the country had become unbearable. Johnson escalated the Vietnam War with over 200,000 on the ground and Christmas was fast approaching. We had our hands full with burglaries and racial clashes. Hate was everywhere and its disease repeatedly consumed my heart.

While on patrol over off Himes Avenue near the middle of my zone, I heard a silent alarm call go out for the zone below mine. It was a break-in at a furrier named Primrose Propers in North Hyde Park and the details came in later of the shootout that ensued.

Evidently, a laced-up young couple from Jersey had made their way down here by robbing fur coat cleaners and decided not to stop upon arrival in Tampa. A motorcycle division buddy of mine was right around the corner and, like many in that division, was a little too gung-ho sometimes. Instead of calling in an observation and waiting for the zone's regular patrol to arrive, he walked around to the building's backside, saw the door crowbarred, and decided to investigate. Thinking the crooks must have already fled the scene, he incautiously entered with a flashlight and a holstered sidearm.

Benny Ray Babbitt and his girlfriend stood up from behind some boxes and gave it to him with a .38 Special and a .357 Magnum. The girl never came close, but Benny Ray hit poor Will Crickett in the chest, stomach, and left thigh before his revolver emptied. Will was still game enough to launch a few in Benny Ray's direction and hit him in the gut. The girl ran screaming out of the building and straight into the arms of the regular patrol, who had just arrived. An ambulance rushed Will to Tampa General, but he didn't make it.

One of the hardest things a patrolman ever has to hear is the fate of a friend broadcast for all to hear. The dispatcher for KIB459, in an uncharacteristically choked-up tenor, announced the condition of Will as DOA. We heard later that, although Benny Ray Babbitt eventually made it to the hospital barely alive, his arrival came 30 minutes after leaving a location not more than five minutes away. This was common during the moratorium on the death penalty, which Babbitt and his girlfriend escaped. His girlfriend later recovered from her baton bruises and received maximum sentences for multiple aggravated robberies, aggravated assaults, and transporting stolen goods across state lines. In the end, Benny Ray Babbitt and his girlfriend received the same sentence: life, no parole. We all thought about how we would handle things if a similar situation arose, and spent hours mooning about the absence of ambulances.

A few days after they cleaned up the scene and released it back to its owners, the detectives had me return to Primrose and get an FIR from the shop's manager. When I arrived, a striking young blond woman introduced herself while going through a pile of invoices stacked up on her otherwise tidy desk. When she glanced up at me the first time, something went off. For a moment, the coldness of the visit went completely away as she stood up to shake my hand. I know she must have noticed my uncontrollable singular glance down her length, but what put me at ease was catching her brilliant blue eyes do the same.

One small consolation, or perk if you will, of being a policeman is the fact we were not completely tied to the clock. As long as you completed your tasks in a reasonable amount of time, nobody complained. I was there for an interview and the questions, as far as the interviewee was concerned, were completely up to me.

Wendy Ness deservedly received the most rigorous examination I've given anyone. Of course, this was to my own benefit. I wanted to know everything about her. It wasn't until she answered a few questions that I noticed she was interrogating *me*. Usually, you couldn't pry anything from my lips, but Wendy became my weakness in fast order.

Before I left, I knew she had only been with the company as a bookkeeper for a year after receiving an associate's degree from Hillsborough Community College. She said she had taken courses in management and had intended to go back when she could afford to do so. She was originally from Houston, Texas and sported a slight drawl; something I found sexy. She liked Elvis as most girls did, but liked Jerry Vale even more. Her favorite food was barbecued pulled pork and she even liked the outdoors. I must have hit the jackpot on a Las Vegas slot machine!

I don't know if she was just looking for any excuse to see me again, but she stated that, according to her invoices, a $400 coat was missing from her company's inventory. The news was particularly distracting since the only way one would go missing would be either internal to her organization, or from someone working the scene on the night of the shooting. Regardless, I had an excuse to call on her again—something I wasted no time in doing.

One thing led to another and I found myself on a double date with Wendy, Mack, and his wife Ann, out for an afternoon at Clearwater Beach. It was starting to warm up again and we found ourselves going over there often. Of course, after a few dates, Wendy and I ditched the chaperones and made off on our own.

I didn't have anything against Mack or his wife, although Ann felt the need to constantly educate us on whatever new legal terms she learned that week while being a court reporter. She was a Cuban-Italian Tampa native with a big sense of adventure; a trait that Mack found irresistibly attractive. Since having a little girl the year before, they've settled down quite a bit, however. I wagered Mack that one day Ann would become a teacher because she wouldn't shut up! That wasn't the reason we wanted to get out of there, though.

I loved Mack's wife, but my eyes were constantly having ideas with Wendy's physique. She was absolutely gorgeous and I couldn't keep my hands off her. The end of her long, blond hair bounced around just above her buxom chest. Her bottom half, in its feminine perfection, bespoke of her athleticism, and her legs were long and firm, but not too firm to lose their curvaceousness. To make matters worse, her posterior was unstoppable when she walked. Her cheeks kept a rhythm in which the finest Swiss clocks could be synchronized, but right now, I couldn't think of better hands for her clock than mine.

It would sound terribly one-sided if I didn't mention that Wendy had a hard time keeping her hands off me either. I'd catch her glances and see her flush lips afterward. When we embraced, she marveled at my rock hard chest and arms by exploring every inch with her hands. On occasion, she would move a hand down my back and pull me in tight so she could examine me entirely. It was at this point that our skillful exits became legendary.

"And…They're off!" Mack jokingly announced.

Fortunately, there was no shortage of motels down the road. We had barely shut the room's door before we had worked through every obstacle between our clothes and our desires. I loved reaching around behind and holding her hair while kissing the length of her body. She would turn around and let me hold her tight up against my body while kissing around the back of her neck. She smelled so good and felt so right. My hands had her piqued. After she got her fill of me, she would turn back around and let me stare into her bright blues.

Of all her features, many of which could have easily been a model's stand-in, her eyes were the most bedazzling to me. They were so expressive, I had no trouble reading her mind and, given our state of intoxicated lust, they never said much other than, "I want to be taken". Of all of her expressions, there was nothing better than looking into her eyes staring up while tugging me towards her lips. Maybe my eyes were saying the same things to her.

Love came fast. Before we let appearances (and disappearances!) ruin our many wonderful weekend rendezvous at the Thunderbird on Treasure Island, we announced our engagement. Finally, it seemed, there was something balancing all that was evil in my life. After a long winter, the warmth of that spring never felt so good.

The Perfect Iceberg

I honestly can't remember a single arrest or interview I made during the season of Wendy. Our whirlwinds took us all over the state almost every weekend and sometimes during the week, depending on my shift. Her boss at the furrier was a nice elderly Italian man that wanted to see her married and settled down. We were nothing close to settled.

Our lovemaking sessions were voracious. It was as though we saved ourselves all these years just for each other. Hours would go by before either of us would towel off or notice a clock, and I don't mean a couple or three; I mean *several*.

Do I remember the waterskiing show at Cypress Gardens or the shootouts at Six Gun Territory? No, I remember the paneled walls at the Starlite Motel in Cocoa Beach, the tiled shower at the Howard Johnson in West Palm Beach and the ice-cold air conditioner at the Golden Host in Sarasota. All of our rooms had air conditioning, but theirs was so cold, the effect on my Wendy was visually stimulating, to say the least. Of all the places we visited, we went back to Sarasota repeatedly. It was just down the road, the prices were affordable and, well, let me just say it was our favorite place for breaking records.

We loved Florida and we loved its beaches. So much so, we went out of our way in locating the most private ones for making out. There was something about that beach scene in *From Here to Eternity* that really turned Wendy on. I was her Burt Lancaster and she was my Deborah Kerr. Eternity. That's how long I would be looking for another woman like Wendy should I let her get away.

"Titie?" (Okay, there's a longer story to this, but she used to call me this as a pet name for the Titanic. As in, she would playfully come up to me from behind when she wanted to make love, reach down into the front side of my boxers, and say, "I want to go sink the Titanic").

"Yes, Ibie." (And, of course, she was my iceberg...but I mean that in the warmest possible context!)

"Can we talk a little bit about what were going to do after we get married?"

Wendy had a playfully easygoing tone. I loved her optimistic plan-making as much as any other making we did, and that cute southern drawl of hers; well, I could go to the grave hearing that sweet tone.

"Well, sure."

The question did catch me a little off-guard. We set a date for late May, but really hadn't thought too much else through since we were constantly exhausting ourselves.

"You know I'm the kind of girl who likes being out and working, right?"

"Yeah."

I was still a little on edge because my father raised me traditionally. I thought of myself as being a bit more progressive, but I wasn't sure where she was going with this so far.

"And, you know I want a family too, so I was thinking..." With Wendy, this was usually not as dangerous as one would fathom. "Actually, I have a couple of questions."

"Okay..." The suspense was beginning to grind.

"How soon can we start having some little ones, and, after they get into school, would you mind my going back to work?"

I thought, *oh, was that all?* "As soon as you want on both, but I beg you for another month after we get hitched. I want as much of you as I can bear until we have to stop. Is that all right?"

I could tell that I immediately turned her on. It didn't take much with us. "But of course!" She whispered.

We were down in Sarasota when she brought up this little conversation, and the reason I remember it so well is because we didn't come out of our room for the next ten hours. When we finally gave it a rest due to utter depletion, she continued elaborating on her master plan.

"Well, how many little ones do you want? I'd like two. One of each."

That sounded fine by me. She could get back to work in as little as seven years if all goes well. "Perfect. And what kind of work do you want to do?"

"I want to continue on with bookkeeping maybe. Or perhaps I can get into management." Her ambitions were exciting and I was in love as much with her attitude as I was the rest of her.

I knew she would have a rough go of any management position, however, and it would take too much time away from the family if she somehow acquired such a promotion.

"Ibie, I don't know your chances of getting into upper management, and it may keep you away from the kids more than you want. Is it the pay or the glory, you're after?"

"Well, kind of both. I mean, I can't tap on an adding machine forever. See?" She pointed to two broken nails on her right hand.

I understood. I was slightly dancing around her reasoning because she might change her mind by the time several years had passed. I rolled over towards her, leaned over, and gave her a long, passionate kiss with a slow release, tugging at her upper lip. "When the time comes, you can do whatever you like."

I got a lot of mileage out of that line and that kiss. Thing is, I meant it.

I knew the planets were aligning for me when Mack called early on a Saturday morning and announced he was the proud father of a baby boy. I never heard him happier than that precise moment. You could hear the pride in his voice because, he candidly admitted over a beer one afternoon, was beginning to wonder if he still had anything left. It had been almost five years since the birth of his little girl and, although he said Ann wanted to space their kids apart a couple of years, this one came a little later than anticipated. I kept this in mind when planning with Wendy, figuring we shouldn't take too big of a break. Sure, we should have some time to ourselves in between, but if we were to have another, they would be closer siblings if their ages weren't so far apart.

Saturday, May 20th, 1967, Wendy's father, Clyde, walked her down the isle of Hyde Park Presbyterian Church. He gave me her hand, winked with a twitch from his faded yellow mustache, and took a seat next to his tearful wife, Bette. Mrs. Ness didn't like being called "Betty" since she married because it sounded too much like Bonnie and Clyde; a joke that never seemed to get old with their Texas friends. The Nesses were proud parents and they adored me for having a respectable job with a promising future. The only problem was her mother constantly worrying about the danger. On this day, her tears were joyous.

All of my closest friends from the department were there, and we all had a great time dancing to some good old big band classics from Glen Miller, Tommy Dorsey, and Sinatra. After the old people left, we got into a little more of the rock and roll stuff. I thought of myself as a decent hoofer, but Mack and Ann stole the show. They were moving around the floor like Gene Kelly and Vera Allen!

By 6 p.m., most of my buddies had gotten to the point where it was a good idea to put Wendy and me on the way to our honeymoon. Our departure was indifferent with most. Our clothes were chock full of rice after ambling down the walkway to my duded-up '66 T-bird convertible. We hugged and kissed everyone, said our thanks and goodbyes, and headed out of town. We made for the east coast down Highway 60, and then down the newer Sunshine State Parkway to Miami. I had to report back on duty June 1st, so we had a full ten days to ourselves. We never spent that much time together, and now we had the rest of our lives!

Our friends and family loaded us up with cash, so I wanted to treat Wendy to something truly special. We spent the first four nights right on the ocean at the famous and luxurious Fontainebleau Hotel. At first, I thought they were going to treat us as second-class dopes, but as soon as I mentioned "honey-moon", the desk manager snapped his fingers, motioned for a bellhop, and had us in a top floor suite. It wasn't one of the ultra-luxury honeymoon suites, but I fathomed it was probably the next best thing. I later found out that they treated cops as well as they did celebrities. They spared no expense in our accommodation and it was a glorious four days of pampering and relaxation. Of course, no evening passed without a voyage from the old White Star line and we made a point to explore every nook and cranny of that pristine suite. I'll never forget that place.

We took two days hopping across the Everglades over US 41. Beyond the Miccosukee Indian Reservation provided some interesting alligator attractions and we found a dinky motel for the night before going to the beach in Naples the next day. The small beachfront town was relaxing and we didn't let that visit go by without another *Eternity* impersonation, but we were really looking forward to our final destination for the next four nights— Sarasota and the Golden Host!

Keep in mind, the only day we didn't devour each other was the one spent in the Everglades because of the paper-thin walls of that particular Tamiami Trail motel.

We managed to save our best for our favorite spot. The first night, we relaxed for a few hours to shake off the beach and the road. We made love only once and fell into the deepest sleep, not waking up until almost 11 a.m. the next day. I remembered Wendy's complacent eyes that morning. I remembered freezing that look in my mind and recalling it for several years afterward because they said "happiness".

We dove in the pool and cooled off before lunch. The end of May's heat was already unbearable and the predictable daily thunderstorms started firing off in the middle of the early afternoon. This worked perfectly for Wendy and me. After swimming, we showered off, threw on some loose clothes, and headed for a nearby steakhouse. We both had worked up quite an appetite, but our hunger was not necessarily for food as it was energy. We both had prime rib, salad, and two glasses of a nice '62 Bordeaux. It wasn't too much and, with the look my bride was giving me, the chances of staying much longer at an empty table grew slim.

You'd think Wendy and I were animals the way we went at it that afternoon. Now, I've heard some folks are all just fine and dandy with a ten-minute run. Heck, they might even feel like they've hit the jackpot if they lasted for 30 minutes. Ibie slid her new silk gown off, threw me backwards in the middle of that king-sized bed, tossed a leg over, and rode to California. To this point, my gal had been somewhat reserved, with a soft moan or a gentle whimper. Not this time. She was quite vocal, almost screaming at the highest pitch. I became frantically worrisome thinking someone might hear through the walls. After a couple of minutes, it dawned on me that any eavesdropping was an impossibility. The Golden Host separated each room with thick cinderblock walls. The windows were thick too, but to make matters easier, the air conditioners were also at the front of the rooms, masking the sound inside. Not only that, Lorrie, the desk manager, remembered us from our previous stays and had one of their two honeymoon suites reserved. They weren't overly luxurious, (After all, we had just come from the fanciest hotel in Florida!) but the astute architects had situations like ours in mind, placing the suites at the far ends of the building with a double wall separating the room next door. For extra measure, the bedrooms were towards the back, so you could close off the hallway between the bedroom, bathroom, and the living room. While I didn't have a problem with occasional "risked extroversion", the privacy of the Golden's suites was most reassuring. Wendy instantly felt my returned attention and gave herself the whip.

Our timing was perfect. An hour after we began, loud claps of thunder started rattling the windows. This couldn't get much more epic, I thought.

"Avast ye, William my Conqueror!" Evidently, Wendy was in a seafaring mood, what with being near the Gulf and hearing the windows pelted by the "waves".

"Yar!" It was my turn and indeed, I pillaged, plundered, and buried more treasure than Captain Kidd. Wendy's insatiable body became my Gardiner's Island and I explored every last acre of her.

The storm only lasted around 40 minutes...I think. I'm not sure, really. Wendy and I did just about everything imaginable over the next several hours. There were breaks, of course. We would cuddle and caress just long enough to let the sweat dry, then find a new trail to the top of another peak. I never could manage more than two. I don't know why; I just felt like that was enough for a day. It didn't stop me from trying to set new records with Wendy though. It almost became a challenge for me to discover her fullest capability. That day and night, we blew right through her previous blistering of six. I have very few regrets, but purposely stopping at nine still bothers me. Nine! It's a number most believe unattainable, even for the most egregious nymphomaniac. I wanted to reserve that mythic ten for another time so we always had something to work for. Although we came close on more than a few occasions, we haven't gotten there yet. Maybe that was the point—the thrill of the pursuit. What if we made the magic number? Would we try topping it? I'd like to think so.

Wendy and I spent the next two days wandering the beaches from Siesta Key up to Anna Maria Island. Each day we returned to our room, my bride carried quite a haul of large conch shells, sand dollars, and starfish. I think she already had some future house decorating in mind. We dined on incredible plates of shrimp, stone crab and lobster, then worked it right back off jiving at a couple of the local clubs. Everyone treated us like royalty. I supposed they saw the new rings and easily figured us out without asking. Bliss. Was this what everyone was talking about?

As much as we hated leaving our Shangri-La, the end of the month was fast upon us. Ibie and I made love a few times on those last days, but after our rampage from the second night at the Golden Host, those sessions took on a different feel. Peaks became more like plateaus; our bodies didn't care so much about how many times as the deepness and longevity of a singular magnanimous culmination. By the time we made it back to my South Tampa apartment, we were completely and utterly exhausted.

It was a good thing we planned a day of relaxation before getting back to work. We cleaned up my place and prepared our clothes. It was our last night of the honeymoon, so I motored Wendy to a quiet little mainstay called The Colonnade. The food was excellent and served an enjoyable honeymoon finale. Wendy and I rode home, took a slow, hot shower, climbed into bed, and lit up a smoke. She came along side me and started borrowing it for her own. I didn't mind — we did that often. Before 9 p.m. we were both falling asleep, cuddling all the way.

The Dark is Shot

A sobering end to our honeymoon occurred when the alarm clock went off at 5:30 a.m. Wendy didn't have to be at work until nine that morning, but got up anyway. I wasn't on the schedule to report until seven, but I liked to get up early and read the paper with some coffee and a couple of smokes before heading downtown. I usually arrived about 15 minutes early on top of that, so 5:30, which was my old MacDill reveille, seemed normal.

That first week back on patrol was more of a victory lap than anything else. They had me assigned to 113, so all the folks along my beat were all approaching me, shaking my hand, and wishing me and my bride a happy life. Back at the headquarters' locker room, it was another story. "Sucker!" they yelled. Not much went on during the 113 slot, so I enjoyed the de facto break-in week as given. The following week, headquarters had other plans for me.

District One, Downtown, Second Shift. For the next two weeks, the new chief, Garrard Smallwood, saw fit to have extra patrols in some of the hot zones close to the projects. 1967 was a year of draft-dodging hippies, acid-freaked fruitcakes, and angry brothers. Ever since Martin Luther King's march on Washington, their neighbor-hoods were on edge. It didn't make much sense, to me anyway, having "whitey" patrol in those areas, but that's what they assigned, and I tried to make the most of the situation.

It was late in the afternoon on a Sunday that I ran into my old academy friend, Ray "Lover Boy" Coleman. I was rolling up Nebraska Avenue towards the train station downtown when I noticed him up against the side of an old brick building across the street, trying to stay out of a downpour. I did a U-turn, pulled up next to the sidewalk, and motioned him over.

"You don't look like you need a shower to me, Lover Boy; hop in."

"Hey! Wild Bill! What's going on, man?" Ray thankfully opened the door and slid into the front seat.

"Ah, well; not too much. Smallwood's got us over here to help you guys out, you know."

"I don' know iffin he's heppin' or hurtin' with that, man. You know the brothers are getting' pretty mean about the Man. You know, your man Mack done asked me about the situation 'round here and I told him what's up. Somethin's got to give, man."

"You're probably right about that, Ray. Bad enough with the war having everyone pissed. Now you got these subversives running around stirring up trouble. If you ask me, your people need to solve their own problems."

Ray laughed, "What the fool you talkin' 'bout, Billy? You know damn well they don't treat us the same. Heck, HQ don't even let us drive, much less have a patrol car. Why even bother havin' us go through that drivin' part in the academy?"

He already knew I disagreed with that policy. The least I could do was ferry him around until he dried off. "Hey Ray, you want to warm up a little? Grab a cup of coffee?"

Ray rubs his arms from being soaked. "Yeah, man. That'd be righteous."

I drove up to a little café around the corner, jumped out and ordered two cups to go. I was growing fond of the local steamed café con leches the local Cubans perfected, but Ray took a standard cup with a cream and two sugars. The rain had dwindled to a drizzle, but I felt bad throwing him out of the car still soggy. That's when I came up with a brilliant idea.

"Hey man, why don't I do your patrol with you and let you take the wheel. What do you think about that?"

"Say what?" Ray must have spilled half his cup spinning around in disbelief.

"Look. You drive the car through those neighborhoods and they'll think you're the boss. Think about that for a moment. A white guy being the passenger instead of the other way around. What do you think?"

"Man, you're gonna get us both in trouble with the sergeant. Uh-uh. No thank you. I appreciate the ride, man, but no."

"Aw come on, Ray. Think about it. If I drive through there, they'll think you're a traitor and stone the car. If *you* drive, it'll make a good impression. Come on! It's brilliant. You know it!"

Ray took a long draw off his cup of coffee, never letting his serious glare leave my eyes. "All right then, but if you get me in trouble over this, you 'n I are gonna have some words."

Ray's seriousness fell away to a wide grin. I was about to give this man a sense of pride he never had in his three years as a beat cop. Sure, I could get into some serious trouble for this, but who's going to know? We loaded up and headed north on Orange Avenue. Ray had the biggest grin on his face; steering wheel in his left hand and a cup of coffee in his right. We made a right down Scott Street and a slow right down Governor Street into Central Park Village, which was the first project develop-ment just north of downtown. It was getting near dark, but you could see some of the neighbors doing a double-take in shock. That alone made it worth the potential reprimand. Ray felt like he was on top of the world too. I wondered what his father would think if he saw his son *driving*. Ray made a point to hit every street in that project and, as slowly as he drove—jawing with everyone that came up to visit—it was about an hour before we finally got out of there.

By then, it was almost completely dark, and the rainwater had just about steamed its way off the sidewalks. I told Ray I should drop him off so I could get back down towards the docks. We were exiting the project's southern end when Ray caught a glimpse in the rearview mirror. Three hoods were running the other direction behind us carrying several boxes that appeared to originate from a photo supply warehouse. They must have hidden behind some bushes and decided to make a run for home just after we passed.

I was impressed that Ray, with no practice in the last few years, knew exactly what to do and handled the car beautifully. He hit the beacon light switch, flipped on the siren, threw the transmission in reverse, hit the gas, got up to about 20 MPH, and slung the car all the way back around. He then threw the car in forward gear and raced back up Governor Street, catching up with the young men and their haul. Ray made it to the corner of Harrison Street at the edge of the project, where we both jumped out with our pistols unholstered and gave chase through the project, heading across Harrison towards Nebraska Avenue towards the eastern side.

It didn't matter to these guys how many warnings or how many threats of firing we yelled, they just kept on hightailing down the street. Of course, Ray, a patrolman on foot, had no trouble running down a straggler, who was too greedy to drop his load and run faster. Criminal stupidity no longer surprised me. The other two wisely dumped their haul back at the intersection and fled. Even though my lungs were punishing me from the years of smoking, my recent exercising allowed me enough stamina to make gains on one of the slower rabbits.

On several occasions in my life, adrenalin rushes slowed the world down around me to a crawl. All it took this time around was the flash of a silver revolver in that kid's right hand. At this point, I could have shot him on site and I'd get very few questions. He had a gun and that was all I needed to fire. I didn't think about firing, however, until he swung that revolver under his left arm to fire in my direction.

"I'm gonna kill you, pig!" He yelled.

I stopped, didn't think about aiming, and sent a round his way. That's when everything sped back up immediately; the point where he dropped motionless to the ground and moved no more. I paused for a few moments and watched his movements. His cohort, a few dozen yards away, turned around, panicked, and ran around the corner of the nearest apartment building. I faintly remember hearing Ray yell at me to get out of there and back to the car. I walked up to the young black assailant and saw that, although he was as tall as I was, he couldn't be much more than 20 years old. He was still breathing, so I had Ray throw his catch in the rear of the car and call an ambulance. When I got a little closer, I rolled the kid over, looking for his gun in case he was pulling something over on me. A cold chill suddenly went down my spine. His revolver was no revolver at all. It was a small silver camera. It didn't register as a camera when he was slinging it around his body like a weapon. That didn't matter.

I can't remember which sounds I heard next, the big V8 engines scorching the pavement in our direction with sirens blaring, or the screams randomly emanating from the 2,000 residents surrounding me in that neighborhood. In no time, a woman, presumably the young man's mother, started getting in my face, throwing punches and screaming at me. Ray managed to haul her away.

"You better get outta here, man."

Ray had a good sense of what was coming next.

In moments, other patrol cars and an ambulance made it to our location. They loaded up that young man and his mother, and then sped off for Tampa General. Even with all the law enforcement piling up on their streets, the malcontents of the neighborhood felt no fear towards us. The powder keg stood all around me and I mistakenly lit the fuse. I knew it wasn't my fault and hopefully the brass would see it my way. I assumed Ray would also give a corroborative interview later.

Half an hour went by. Sergeant Bowers arrived at the scene pissed because of the situation. He told Ray and me to get out of that neighborhood and meet him two blocks away down Cass Street. Before we had a chance to evacuate, our car windows were being shattered with beer bottles and small rocks — anything those people could lift came our direction. As I had hoped, Ray gave the full story to the sergeant exactly the way it happened.

"Well, that doesn't really matter right now, does it Lover Boy?" Bower's sarcasm was unbearably thick as he turned towards me.

"Right before I got to you, it came down on the radio that the boy you shot passed away. Our guy at the hospital said you tagged him right in the lower spinal column. Normally, I'd say that was some piece 'o shootin', but look what we got us now! Holy shit, Brume!"

You could hear some gunfire ringing back towards the scene. Escalation. We assumed it was our guys trying to disperse the crowd. Bowers took another call on the radio and walked back towards us. Thankfully, he never asked who was driving the car at the time, and later, the review panel didn't ask as well. They just assumed I was at the wheel, and Ray and I never told any-one our little secret.

"Jesus Christ, Brume. They're shootin' at *our* guys. Somebody's got a real big pair they must want whacked off. Come on and get in the car, Ray. I'm gonna need you up there. Bill?" Bowers looked towards the rear of the car. "Take that piece 'o shit down to headquarters, get cleaned up, and head back towards your zone."

I made it back to headquarters and took Ray's prisoner over to booking. Before I knew it, a few detectives surrounded me saying I needed to go see Chief Smallwood up at his office immediately. When I got up there, it was a complete beehive. People going in and out, left and right, phones ringing off the hook. Smallwood invited me in and shut the door.

"You wanna tell me what happened out there before the Times and the mayor start crawling down my throat?"

I gave him the full story and he was satisfied that it would easily pass as a justifiable shooting. At the time, it didn't matter if a perpetrator had a weapon. If they ran from a cop giving a direct order to halt, he could cut them in half. Consequently, we had a lot of fatsos in the department during those years.

"All right," said Smallwood. "Forget about going back over to the docks and stick around downstairs. I have a feeling this is going to be a long night if those people want to turn *my* town into another Watts."

Two years before, that part of Los Angeles became a veritable war zone. Smallwood didn't want an Armageddon, so he called everyone up (I mean *everyone*) and started gathering his army. To my surprise, he didn't want my assistance with the several riot squads; he was ordering me to stay put so the rioters would never find me! I desperately wanted to help my fellow officers, but I understood Smallwood's logic. If they spotted me down there, it would just make things worse. In hindsight, it didn't matter. The fed-up, impoverished, unequally-treated masses from those projects started a fireball that lasted several nights and injured scores.

Mack came down from upstairs and shook his head, shrugged his shoulders, and went around back to the assembly area. A short, older-looking detective appeared from the same elevator. Looking exasperated, he took out a handkerchief, wiped his brow, and shuffled towards me.

"Are you Bill Brume?" He asked.

"Yes, sir."

"I am Detective Sgt. Matthews. I was just in a briefing with Chief Smallwood, letting him know what's going on at the hospital. He told me what you did. I would have reacted the same way, just so you know. This was probably going to happen whether we shot someone or not. You know that, right?"

"I suppose. I still should have seen that camera, though."

"Don't be too tough on yourself. It doesn't matter."

I was beginning to get curious why he was talking with me at all. "Thanks. I'll try not to. So, what's going on upstairs?"

He sighed and wiped his brow again. "Ah…the hospital. It's a madhouse down there, you know. People shot, beaten, deep gashes from glass bottles and windows, some burned from fires."

"Did you see that boy's mama?"

"Yeah, but she was hysterical…not letting any shade of white anywhere close without throwing a fit. Kept saying she was going to kill you. Terrible, but if it's any consolation, they'll never put you over there again!"

That didn't make me feel any better. "I didn't think about that. One of these days I'd want to talk to her and let her know it was a huge mistake, but her son didn't give me much of a choice."

Matthews threw up his hands. "Fella, that woman will have to be told by someone else and, even then, she won't be happy unless you're dead. Doesn't matter if her little cockroach was a despicable thief caught in the act. You'll never get anywhere near her without a fight. I tell ya the whole mess is FUBAR."

That was an expression I hadn't heard since the Air Force. "FUBAR, eh?"

"Yeah. You shoulda seen what they were bringing in to the emergency room. I saw a few people that looked like they stepped on a landmine. There was this one young white woman; she came in all beat up wondering around the entrance to the Emergency Room asking if her husband had shown up. Do you wanna hear this? I have a little time before I have to get back over there. You hungry? How's about we get a bite in the cafeteria."

That caught me a little off-guard. How in the world could this guy think about eating at a time like this? How could he possibly want food after seeing so much carnage? If you do this long enough, do you go *completely* numb?

"I'm not hungry, but sure, I'd like to hear the rest of your story."

We walked over to the cafeteria and sat down after he acquired what he needed. Detective Matthews was a man in his late fifties, maybe 5'6" on a good day, wearing a brown jacket, brown slacks, and a fedora like something out of a '40s movie. He removed the hat to eat, revealing his bald and gray head that supported a pair of browlines. I wanted him to go ahead and finish his food before it became cold, but he went ahead with the story, regardless.

"Okay, so this woman is running around the entrance to the ER for thirty minutes or so and finally, they wheeled this guy in on a gurney. He's cut to pieces—head half bashed in. I don't even know how he survived. They're in triage mode over there, so they just bandaged him up real fast, hit him with a small shot of morphine, and let his wife look after him in the corridor just outside the ER's doors. I walked up to them for an interview and this is what they tell me.

"Joann, that was her name, and Kenneth Dettwiler were just cruising down the highway nearby, saw all the smoke and flame of one of the buildings those rioters torched, and thought they'd have a look. They had no idea about the riot because the news hadn't hit the radio or television yet, right? They were just bored and wanted to see what the fire was about, so they come down the offramp and turn right into a frenzied mob that surrounded their car, broke all the windows, and dragged them both out on the street. They tore up her skirt while making her watch several others repeatedly kick her husband on the ground. She said, 'They got all over me with their sweaty body odor, and I felt their hands crawling all over me, grabbing at my places. She told me that, out of nowhere, someone's stronger hands grabbed her by the arms and threw her back in her car, yelling at her to get out of there. She said she panicked and did just that, screeching her tires all the way back onto the highway and over to the hospital.

"By that point, she was crying hysterically, saying she felt guilty for leaving her husband. Mr. Dettwiler reached out his trembling hand and grasped her arm, trying to calm her down. When she finally stopped sniffling, he whispered his story to me. He said, 'I saw her drive away, but there was nothing I could do. She did the right thing. After she got away, they beat me to a...well, you can see for yourself. I must have passed out more than once. After a while, I couldn't feel the kicks anymore. I knew they were still kicking me, but I couldn't feel it. After Joann left, I heard five or so of them making a circle around me. (He started trembling when he got to this part) I heard the hammer of a pistol cock, and then I heard one of them say, 'It's time to kill him!' Then I heard another one say 'Hell no, man! Trouble like that, we don't need.' And then I felt someone get close to my ear and whisper, 'You better play dead', so I did. A few moments went by and someone grabbed the back of my shirt and left arm, getting me to my feet and walking me a block or so towards some firemen. He ditched me and ran back before we got there, but I managed to stumble the rest of the way.'"

"Do you realize how lucky they both were, Brume?" Matthews glanced up at me before taking his last bite of a muffin.

"Yeah, they're both lucky to be alive." All I could do was stare at Matthews' mental blockage ability in eating while describing the absolute worst carnage.

"I saw a little six year old girl down there who wasn't so lucky. Their story started almost the same way; her mom took the wrong street at the wrong time. The mob threw a brick through the girl's window. Some glass hit her in the side of her head, taking an ear off. What kind of sick bastard does that to a little girl?"

He finished his meal, took his paper-handled coffee cup, and stood up. "I have to get back down to the hospital for some more interviews. You take care of yourself and stay away from the zoo."

He shook my hand, donned his fedora, and walked back into battle. I drifted back to the lobby and a secretary met me after searching the department for a while, she said.

"Oh, there you are. The chief told me to inform you to go home and get some rest; you're relieved for the evening. A special FBI task force is on the way from Washington and they'll have a lot of questions for you tomorrow I'm sure. Right now, he just wants you away from here and definitely away from the riot scene."

That sounded fine by me. My mind was cooked and I was seemingly no good for anything but whispered conversation around headquarters. Some of the older bastards were giving me the evil eye for making their fat asses get out of bed. I went down to the locker room, changed into some blue jeans, hopped on my old Triumph, and came home to Wendy. I previously called her to let her know I was okay, but she didn't know much else than what was being reported on the television. When I walked in, she gave me a big hug and a beer. I cooled my bruises off with the can before opening it. Wendy started to cry because her biggest fear was my getting hurt out there and leaving her alone. I told her I was made of concrete and promised her I would always come home. We cuddled and watched the television all night.

The carnage was unreal. The rioters torched several buildings and dozens of victims were in the hospital. Their anger littered the streets with rocks, bottles, and burned-out cars. Florida Governor James Clermont activated the National Guard to keep the riots contained, which they did, but the violence didn't end.

Some of my platoon buddies later told me of their stint on the riot marches through those neighborhoods. They would form a phalanx of cops wearing helmets, batons, and shields to clear the streets. Even though they beat their shields with batons for a harrowing effect, which was ominous and intimidating because of the volume, the rioters still pummeled them with rocks and bottles. When the phalanx made it to the center of the disturbed area, they uncovered a well-protected Mayor who then read a Proclamation of Martial Law. Naturally, protesters responded to the speech with more bottles and rocks, so they released some large German Shepherds that made quick work of the streets and back alleyways. Panic quickly spread amongst the rioters with news of half-devoured limbs fought over by the dogs in the more hidden alleyways. Of course, these rumors were false, but they had the desired effect. When the Schutzhund-trained K-9s arrived, the instant panic that ensued became legend in the department.

Even with the streets cleared, sniper fire would occasionally strike a cop in the legs. The dogs couldn't protect our men from this form of treachery. Ray told me his father got so nervous, he wouldn't even look around a building's corner before reaching around it with his revolver and blasting two rounds. It was amazing that, in those several horrible days of complete chaos, not a single person died by the violence. The only reported death was that of an older patrolman who died of a heart attack upon arrival at the scene. It may have been the Summer of Love in Haight Ashbury, but it was the Summer of Hate in Tampa.

Mack finally caught up with me on the phone. "Did you know I gave the chief a briefing on this very problem just four days ago?"

"No, I didn't." I was in complete astonishment.

"We knew some federal employees and churches were fomenting tactical government subversion in Jackson and Belmont Heights. I gave Smallwood the names. He believed me so we took it to Mayor Knox. Can you believe that buffoon denied everything we said and started ranting that 'no riot was gonna happen in *his* Tampa'? Incredible! So, fella, *we* knew this was about to happen and they just used you as an excuse. I know it's not your fault, Bill. Don't worry if a federal panel or if the press wants to make an issue out of this. Always remember, you were in the right."

I felt a little better after Mack's assurances. After the look he gave me the night before, I left headquarters wondering.

With the rioters contained by our department and the National Guard, Governor Clermont decided to execute a program enlisting around 50 young black men for patrolling the ghettos and keeping the peace. The governor gave them limited powers to work in conjunction with bona-fide police patrols, and issued plain white construction hats. They became known as the White Hats and gained national attention for their successes. It was a huge political triumph for the governor, and to celebrate, he had plaques made for each of the White Hats, commem-orating their achievement. What they didn't know is another story that Mack told me a few years later.

"What I can't figure out is how Governor Clermont signed all those plaques with his right arm in a sling from a flag football accident up in Tallahassee. That must have taken some doing."

I told him the governor probably had some pretty good medication back then. Mack winked. "Perhaps."

Sure enough, when the maelstrom settled, the panels rigorously examined me in every detail. Everyone that offered their opinion to me earlier, with the exception of the boy's mom, was right—justifiable adjudication of force. Wendy and I were relieved and I just wanted to get back to work. They had me on the old 312 shift so I would run into less people that next week. After the riots, everyone was so sick of the violence, the town became rather serene.

That last week of June, Smallwood called me up to his office, plunked a small box down on his desk, and handed me a sheet of paper to read. My wait was finally over.

Detective Brume

"What do you think, Bill?" Chief Smallwood asked.

I recall an unprecedented length of silence following the chief's question. My eyes fixated on the new hardware and what it represented.

"But I thought there wasn't..."

Smallwood interrupted, "Well, that's just the thing, see. We're promoting you under the temporary title of 'Patrolman Detective' until such a time that the budget allows for the actual title. Don't worry, the pay increase is there."

He uttered that last line with a slight hint of sarcasm, since our pay was laughable to begin with.

Smallwood continued, "Major Fielding said you're needed in burglary, so you are going down there to help out."

Of course, he still hadn't answered the main unasked question, so he made me inquire.

"Okay, but..."

"I know, I know. You want to know why we're putting you in after everything that happened. Putting it quite simply, the other detectives requested you, and, well, it was time to get you out of Patrol. Here, take your badge and get down to Property. Sgt. Edward Cantrell in Burglary will meet you there and give you the rest."

Burglary, eh? I knew of the several detective divisions: Burglary, Homicide, Auto Theft, Pawn Shop, Missing Persons, Juvenile, Prevention, and Intelligence. Mack said they put him in Intelligence because he was a great analyst. So why put me in burglary?

"You're pretty good on the street, Brume. Ed had two other detectives specifically request your help. You keep getting more informants like you have already and you'll find this job pretty easy."

I shook his hand, briefly gazed at my new symbol of empowerment, and bounced downstairs as instructed.

Cantrell was waiting, and only gave a few minor instructions. First, he suggested that I purchase a new concealable backup weapon as well as a shoulder holster for my current sidearm. Most were using the Smith & Wesson .38 snub-nosed "Airweight" as a backup, using an ankle holster. That worked for me. Second, he told me it was a three-day sus-pension if they caught any detectives out on the street with either their badge or gun showing intentionally.

"Detectives are supposed to be discreet." He said.

Lastly, he told me I should ditch the Hush Puppies for some nicer shell cordovans.

"Every station in the country has an 'in' with this shoe maker up in Massachusetts. You're gonna bust your ass with those things you got on your feet, and when you do, you'll wish you'd gotten a pair of these."

Cantrell pointed down to his own feet, which were sporting a shiny, brown pair of the shoes he described.

"Take a look at the sole, huh. Do yourself a favor a get a pair. They'd cost $80 to anyone else. For us, they're only $30."

$30 for shoes? I was beside myself, but he had a good point. I didn't want to get in a chase and bust it on a corner. Wendy would understand, so I filled out a credit union order for the cost of two holsters, the revolver, a box of shells, two auto-loaders, and the special order for my new shoes. I was riding pretty high at this point.

Cantrell gave me the rest of the day off with pay, so instead of going to the hardware store, I ran straight back home, changed clothes, and drove over to Primrose Propers, kidnapping Wendy for lunch. After the rollercoaster ride we just took, she may appreciate some good news. As it turned out, she was more than ecstatic, and actually supportive of my purchases. This was but one of her many constant reminders regarding how lucky I am.

When she came home that afternoon, she took a shower and dressed for giving me her warmest affections. Our newly ritualized after-smoke became an excellent platform for deep conversations and, of course, Wendy wasted no time theorizing how we should spend the new money that would be forthcoming. Our plans for raising a family meant buying a house and getting it ready. We decided to start looking around the various neighborhoods when we weren't working. House hunting became our weekend pastime for the next several weeks.

By then, the chief wrangled the necessary budget for titling me as a proper detective. My first hour as such was spent waking up at 7 a.m., getting cleaned up, throwing on some dark gray slacks, a knit shirt, a sports coat, my shiny, expensive shell cordovans, which were well worth the price, and then heading down to the station. Once there, we all filtered into the cafeteria and drank the morning's first cup. This became the ritual every morning for a while.

Those first coffee sit-downs became the war story forum for everyone. Usually, four or five of us would be in each group. Afterward, we all signed in and walked down to that morning's lineup. The lineups consisted of all those criminals busted from the previous day so we could get a good look at them and get more insight. In effect, it was more of a cacophonous zoo.

Detective Sgt. Cantrell usually throttled some of the "more interesting" types during lineup, which was great entertainment. That first session gave me a perfect snapshot of the many mornings to come when he started picking on a queer burglar picked up the night before.

"Okay Goldstein, what do you do for a living?" Cantrell asked the brazenly flamboyant little thug.

"I, uh..."

"I what?" The sergeant demanded.

"I, um, take in ironing." Goldstein effeminately whispered.

"You what?" Cantrell poked, as if he couldn't hear the man.

The man succumbed to his prodding by yelling loudly, "I take in ironing! I iron clothes! Is that a problem?"

The entire room erupted in laughter, including the rest of the lineup that didn't necessarily want to be anywhere near that man. I slowly started looking forward to the daily comedy show because the lineups were different every day and nobody ever became bored.

I never understood how some of those patrolmen were ever satisfied spending 20 years falling asleep in the same neighborhoods week in and week out. Detectives were a different breed. Sure, we were not much different from any other cop, but we didn't suffer career complacency. After all, it wasn't such a giant leap to detective; you only had to show a little initiative because there was no special training for us during that era. The only trait required was keeping excellent notes. That's it! You made detailed notes, and if you had enough for a conviction, you handed them up to the District Attorney for an arrest warrant.

After lineup, I was usually ready for cup #2. That's when you visited your duty sergeant to inform him of your next actions. Of course, this was usually a setup for other matters you may have needed to attend. For example, if you needed a haircut, you'd tell the sarge you needed to meet with an informant and he'd only meet you at the barbershop. This wasn't true of course and Sarge knew better, but he never said no to any of my actions. It didn't matter if I said I was doing interviews at a certain restaurant (meeting Wendy) or at a night-club; he was always onboard. The only thing I had to do was sign for a plain car and be on my way.

I had a lot of fun learning the ways of being a good detective. There were times, however, that the jokes and/or the nature of the business were a little much. The Medical Examiner, Bruce Morgan, had a peculiar habit of eating cookies while performing autopsies in front of us, and worse, liked to make us handle the stainless steel probe when tracing bullet paths through cadavers.

Det. Jerry Immelman, however, was the King of Practical Jokes. One time, however, a prank of his ended up netting a little more than the usual laughter. By now, he had already chalked up several unwitting detectives that fell prey to his microphone key gag. Jerry would stick a toothpick down in the key and break it off with the circuit held open. The other detectives would drive around for several minutes, sometimes hours, before another patrol caught up to them and shut it down. A few weeks ago, this prank ensnared two detectives that were constantly badmouthing the department and their superiors. Dispatch recorded over twenty minutes of their blather before sending a unit. That was the last time that gag ever worked. Everyone became so paranoid, they forever checked their radios before throwing the ignition switch. Jerry didn't stop there, however. He would famously take jabs all the way to the top, driving Chief Smallwood crazy at every opportunity.

The most talked about gag was when he tied some nickel firecrackers on a premeasured string. He tied the string off to an upper floor window and then dangled it down to the window right behind the Chief's office chair. When executing his devious plot, Jerry would hold the elevator on his floor, light the firecrackers and go straight to the ground floor lobby where his partners stood around laughing. The Chief never caught Jerry, even after several times, but he knew.

Smallwood was an old country man from Thonotosassa and had a profound southern drawl. Even though he secretly laughed at Jerry's inventiveness, he would always go through the motions, running down through the detective's offices yelling, "I'm a gonna farr somebody!", and then start a token internal investigation. Jerry *always* had his alibis.

Our star prankster had other gags as well. If you showed a weakness, rest assured, he was all over you. We had a captain named Rodderman that was superstitious and believed in voodoo. Jerry would have all the guys walk by and leave dolls on his desk. Some had pins stuck in various places. Rodderman had a sense of humor, however. After everyone set down their dolls, he would leave the room frantically. The chief would appear moments later saying that the captain had taken the day off due to pains in his back.

I began to catch the prankster bug and, unfortunately, my practical joking coup de grace came at the expense of my old friend, Ray Coleman. I made sure Jerry was with me on a run before attempting my last monkeyshine, and I am proud he witnessed my perfect performance. You see, we didn't have any walkie-talkie systems just yet. Tampa was still somewhere in between the 19th century paradigm of officer's giving verbal status reports ala yelling "Nine O'clock and all's well!" at the top of their lungs, and using personal radio communications. Lover Boy didn't have a car so, when he was on his beat, he would check in using the city's system of call boxes. These were often a simple locked black box on a pole containing a phone patched directly to the captain on duty. On this day, I had taken a live pigeon, locked it inside a callbox I knew Ray was checking soon, and then parked our car just outside of his view. Of course, he opened the box and had a near out-of-body experience. The bird didn't flutter straight up as I had intended. Instead, it flew straight into Ray's chest! His lightning-fast reflexes took over and he mistakenly trapped the bird against his chest. Naturally, he scared everything the pigeon ate that morning all over his shirt. Ray couldn't stop yelling, "Oh God! Oh God!"

Lover Boy, aka "The Egyptian" because of his big nose and green eyes, as you know, kept his apparel meticulously maintained, always starched to perfection. The mess on his perfect threads was devastating. Jerry's belly laughing went on for several minutes and I had to admit, I couldn't help myself either. We had to carefully approach Ray and apologetically give him a ride home, wait until he got cleaned up, and gave him a ride back to his beat before the next scheduled check-in. I learned over time that without levity, an average detective would emotionally implode. It's a good thing Ray had a great sense of humor too, but my capricious hoodwinking was so awful, I swore I'd never do it again.

By Christmas time, Wendy and I saved up enough for a down payment and, after deciding our location should be closer to our jobs, bought a small 1950s home in southern Seminole Heights. That was our gift to each other. Of course, our real gift would come a few months later. Wendy was five months into her pregnancy and everything looked fantastic according to her doctor.

On April 25th, my captain released me from a stakeout so I could be at the hospital when she gave birth to a beautiful 8lb, 4oz baby boy. We named him Jeffrey Alan. I have a son! Throughout the misery of witnessing and interacting with multitudes of the city's worst citizens, coming home to my happy place kept a fragile balance.

I spent the next two years working in the burglary division taking down an assortment of thugs, building up my list of informants, and increasing my worth in the department. There was an old joke that ran around headquarters concerning informants; you arrest all the informants and crime would go down by half. Sadly, that joke isn't far from the truth. For me, creating informants was one of the easiest tasks for a detective. If I saw someone breaking a law — any law — I busted them right on the spot. If it was something small, I'd let them go if they'd work for me. Intimidation was easy. If they didn't want to play, they went to jail. It was that simple. Mack kept telling me I should go easy on some of the nickel-dime gamblers or drug users, but that's what made him a better analyst and me a better street cop.

By 1969, the department was undergoing changes and so were we. Wendy gave birth to our second son, whom she demanded naming Junior. He was another healthy blue-eyed tyke that, admittedly, did share more of my particular features than Jeffrey, so Junior he is. With more happiness came, well, the other side of the coin. The department's forays into drug dealing and prostitution became so often, they created a new detective division. Because of my experience and vast list of informants, I was a natural fit for the city's new Vice Squad.

Ray's Sunshine

I loved doing interrogative interviews. Those became a quintessential art form in determining truth, cause, and effect. My hope for humankind increased on a daily basis when, after amassing thousands of interviews, I discovered that most people, even those committing crimes, were typically honest. I mean "honest" in its native sense, of course. Interviews were sometimes hit or miss. Sometimes, you ran across someone that in no way was telling the truth because a fact or event couldn't possibly have happened the way they described. If you weren't sure, all you had to do was ask if they'd take a polygraph examination. The liars always declined.

Once the interviewing process was complete, if I felt I had enough evidence to nail the culprit, I sent them down to booking and referred the case to the District Attorney. The only aspect of this job I despised was sitting around the DA's office. The solicitor's attorneys moved like molasses, leaving us out in the hall waiting up to two or three days in the hopes one would break loose just to take a deposition. My caseload had grown to over 60, so the waits were becoming unbearable. I wanted to get back on the street and *work*. With the current system, however, we were overloaded most of the time.

In the early part of 1970, Chief Smallwood called a few of us up to his office for a conference. Drugs, burglaries, and violent crimes were getting out of control in the black neighborhoods, and the patrolmen in those areas didn't have the resources to combat the internal networking that slowly developed over the preceding years. There were a dozen of us in that office. Most were curmudgeons from bygone eras just waiting on their 20-year pensions. I waited to see if anyone would offer a solution. Nothing. For me, the answer was clear as a bell, so I spoke up.

"Hire more black detectives."

The chief didn't say a word. He just sat and smiled at me. None of the others said a word either. They only gave acknowledging expressions or scowls depending on their prejudices.

"Thank you, Brume. That's what I had in mind. I just wanted to hear it from someone else's lips. Does anyone have any objections to my promotion of a black detective? Anyone?"

Of course, no one uttered a word because that meant their job, or at least, a mountain of scrutiny.

The chief continued, "Bill, do you have anyone in mind?"

"Yes sir. I think Ray Coleman would make an excellent detective."

"Lover Boy?" The chief cackled.

Immediately, the room erupted in laughter. Evidently, my prank from a couple of years earlier had enshrined Ray as a legend. After it died down, Chief Smallwood dismissed the rest of the detectives and spoke to me alone.

"Bill, I know you're a friend of his, and I know this will be a pretty big day for the department and the city. You go pick up Coleman from his beat and bring him back up here. There will be reporters from the Times and the Tribune outside by the time you get back. Thanks again for speaking up."

I couldn't believe it. After I messed up a good part of that community, the chief saw fit to have me personally deliver Ray's promotion. What a politician!

I wasted no time signing off on a plain car and headed over towards Ray's beat. Ray was on his lunch break inside a little joint on a corner north of Ybor City. Given the ethnicity of the neighborhood, I thought it best not to honk the horn and bring unwanted attention. Instead, I just got out and went inside to get him. Fortunately, the diner was mostly empty. Ray had turned around to see who was coming in after getting a warning from the proprietor. I could read the proprietor's lips through the window too. "Who in the hell is this dumb cracker?"

The place was so tiny, he tripled as the cashier, the cook, and the waiter. Nonetheless, he immediately recognized me and began complaining to Ray that I should leave.

"I don't wanna be known for no kid killa comin' in *my* place."

Since the riots, I ran into a few blacks that simply closed their eyes to the truth, or were just as prejudiced as some of the old-timers working in the department. I felt it necessary to defend myself and perhaps plant a seed of reconciliation in the neighborhood. Ray beat me to the punch.

"Now come on, Simon! You know that boy was bad—stealin' everyone's TVs for smack. Take it easy."

Ray's words didn't comfort the proprietor, so I pulled up a chair and continued what I was going to say.

"Fella, I understand how you feel, and believe me, I wish things didn't happen the way they did. Truth is, that boy pretended to pull a gun; not just on me but Ray too. What are we supposed to do? I don't have anything against anyone, but I know there're a few around here that would like my head. Maybe I can get you to see differently. I'm not a bad guy, and I didn't want to hurt anyone."

"Yeah, well tell it to the boy's mama." The old cook was having none of it. He set his mind in stone before I ever walked in the door.

"Damnit Simon! Why you gotta be that way?" Ray became frustrated.

"Well, at least I tried, sir. Since Ray was there, maybe he can give it to you straight when he gets back."

Ray turned around to me with lightning speed. "Back from where?"

I paused a moment and, even though I knew he hated me, gave a friendly wink to the cook before nudging Ray's arm. "Back from headquarters. The chief wants to see ya."

Ray's big green eyes became as big as eggs. "Say what?"

"Hop in; I have some news for you. Come on!"

Ray's curiosity got the better of him. He couldn't wait to ask before getting in the car. "So what's this all about, Bill?"

I lit up a Winston, climbed in the car, and spoke through the opposite window. "How'd you like to be a detective, Ray?"

Ray was slow to get up in contemplation. I could tell his gears were sapping all the energy from his limbs. All he did was give me a sarcastic smile and threw up his hands. "Aw, come on, Bill. You know damn well they ain't never gonna make me no damn detective!"

"Ray, I'm not kidding. Get in the car. The chief's waiting for you right now if you want the job."

Ray didn't speak another word before jumping down Alice's rabbit hole. He was still tense from the joke I pulled last. "You betta not be pullin' my leg or nothing, Bill."

"Relax, Lover Boy. This is on the up and up. We had a meeting this morning about your little problem over here and the chief asked for a solution. I told him to hire another black detective and when he asked who, I told him *you*. Voila!"

"Oh, so I have you to blame then. Okay, okay, I'm game. I don't believe it, but I'm game."

I put the car in gear and took off back down the station. Ray didn't say much; he was still skeptical. By the time we parked inside the garage, the news had already spread throughout the building. A few of the older detectives couldn't help but get a few last minute jabs with statements like 'we gotta lotta expectations of you now, boy.' Most just stared as I brought him up. A few went so far as clapping. They knew what this day meant.

Normally, it was a pretty big day around the department when someone made detective. It was almost like someone getting made in the mob, except the champagne was cheaper and you had to wait until after your shift to drink it. A black man making detective was still a big deal, however. I rode the elevator up with Ray to the chief's floor and reporters were already spending bulbs before the doors were all the way open. He wasn't used to the attention, but it was starting to sink in. Ray Coleman became Tampa's third black detective.

The newspapers paraded Ray's name for several days with positive reactions throughout the poorer parts of the city. Every little victory made by a person of ethnicity gave multitudes hope for true equality. The move by the chief not only paid off politically, Ray's eventual reporting became a bonanza for several divisions needing crucial cross-discipline intelligence.

At first, they assigned Ray to train under Tampa's second black detective in the Robbery Division. Together, they helped reduce the area's crime rate by double digits. Smallwood made good use of those figures when arguing with the mayor for budgetary increases. When the chief hired yet another black detective to take over Ray's spot, Ray came to my little world.

The Match

Through Ray's informants, our West Tampa narcotics raids became more often and with greater yields. We started putting a real hurt on their operations, hauling in duffle bags full of marijuana and heroin. That's when things started taking a turn. We'd go on club raids and, by the time we arrived, the places were empty. Or, we'd go hit a house, and the evidence was nowhere in sight. We didn't know how the dealers were tipped off, and I had an idea, but it wasn't something I could float just yet.

I went on a bolita raid once with Mack. By the time we arrived at the front door of that market, the old man just sat there laughing behind the candle on his counter. Talk about humiliation! There were other miscues.

We were coming down the street of a bolita peddler's house that we knew hadn't been tipped off. When the lead car dropped off our point man before parking, the driver didn't tell anyone he was going to back his car in the driveway across the street first. When he did, the point man hopped out and the rest of the raid flew in, hitting the wrong house. Of course, the peddler across the street had ample time to disintegrate his slips.

Tip-offs went on for several months until the department hit a big break with the arrest of Martin "The Match" Sanchez. During the past several years, the Criminal Intelligence Division had been tracking a multistate arson ring under the McClellan Committee's direction. For a modest fee, the mob would take care of your overburdened mortgage or your failed business through means of "accidental" incineration. It was usual practice having the suspect interrogated several times by each detective division. I was third on the list after Mack and a homicide detective had their fill. Before I entered the room, Mack met me out in the hallway.

"You be careful with this one, Bill. He's one sick son of a bitch."

Mack was usually playful in character. I knew it would take a lot to rattle his cage. When he met me out in that hallway, his eyes were filled with complete reprehension and disgust.

"What the hell, Mack?"

I tried to get some insight before heading inside, but Mack was too out of spirits for further conversation. He just threw up his arms and continued walking down the hall. I pursed my lips, shrugged, and went on inside.

Handcuffed to a chair at the opposite end of the table sat a man perhaps in his late forties. He had long, black hair combed back over his lengthy sideburns and down his back to just beyond his shoulders. His ethnicity appeared somewhat of a mix between Latino, American Indian, and a dash of Cracker. His denim dungarees, cotton button-down shirt, and denim vest reeked of cigarettes. Out in the hallway, the smell was the usual pine cleaner, institutional paint, and the peculiarly reminiscent smell of an elementary school — freshly shaven pencil. Considering the company and his repulsive odor, I truly felt as though I just climbed into a garbage dumpster. Martin Sanchez never noticed me when I sat down. His eyes faced my direction, but he appeared as though he were in some sort of a trance. I quickly surmised that I would be conversing with a Signal 20, so I quickly cut to the chase.

"Mr. Sanchez, from what I understand, you're going to prison for a very long time. Detective Poole tells me you may be the type of person that would do a little negotiating. What do you say that your help may be, let's say, of some benefit to yourself with regard to a reduced sentence or perhaps a little leniency behind the bars...special assignments and so forth. Could we count on some cooperation?"

The Match never blinked. He just sat there, completely ignoring my offer. I knew I had to reach him through other means. He didn't care about the punishment. I'm beginning to believe he didn't care about his compensatory reward for the fires. Ah yes, the fires.

"Is it the heat? The dance of the flames? The destruction? Or is it that you're making us run around after you that turns you on? Which is it, Sanchez?"

That was it! Sanchez blinked leisurely and refocused his bloodshot eyes on mine. Slowly, a grin developed revealing several misaligned and brown front teeth. His voice had a distinct local flavor; Cuban Cracker. This was a mix of a very slight drawl, Latin tone, and sprinkled with occasional Cuban inflections.

"I read of men that lived in the wild with the bears, and with the coyote, and the snakes. Men who learned to live with the monsters," said Sanchez.

"And fire is your monster, right?" I asked. Sanchez looked apathetic and continued his grin.

"Some can't live with the monsters, jefe."

I rolled my eyes, curious of his hatred, but knowing of what atrocity in which he alluded. "You mean the two boys they found in that restaurant last week."

He grinned wider. "When I researched my affliction, I came across a term describing what happens to some people when they burn."

"What's that, Martin?"

"It's a boxing term called the 'Pugilistic Attitude'. I've dreamt of seeing it for myself, and those two hosses from the east side, well…" Sanchez tilted his head back and drew a big breath between his teeth before continuing. "…made my year."

Mack briefed me on Sanchez's capture. He was right; this guy was one sick bastard. The Match stopped lighting fires himself after growing bored with simple destruction. He wanted death too. He autographed his "projects" by pouring gasoline on the floors and splashing it on the walls. This is where The Match got his nickname: He'd next take out a box of thick wooden matches, place one's tip between his thumb and the sandpaper on the side of the box, and flick it far inside the structure, causing an instant fireball. He practiced this so often, the tips of every one of his fingers were callused and scarred with sulfur stains. He didn't have to burn his fingers anymore, he would just go dangle a bag of smack off 22nd Street north of Ybor and the world came to him. Of course, the two young men he picked up for a job that night were too strung out to bother paying attention to anything else than dumping ten gallons of leaded gas all over Cuba Linda's terrazzo. It didn't occur to them that the stove, oven, and hot water heater's pilot lights were still burning. By the time their canisters hit their last gallons, they were incinerated. The responding firemen had the blaze out quickly and ran inside, only to discover both men fried extra crispy. One was nothing more than a charred, black lump on the ground. The other was completely petrified in his stance, clearly displaying the pugilistic attitude — as if one was taking an athletic posture when boxing. By the way Mack described it, the similarities between this incident and the boy I witnessed burning, were striking. The sickness of those memories flooded my mind. I could feel hate's nausea welling again.

"So, you admit walking in to see how those boys burned, Marty?" I asked.

"Look cop, I admit to nothing. You got that? Nothing!"

"Okay if you say so, Marty. But I gotta tell you that those firemen that walked in there after putting out your handiwork — they found a shoeprint near the kitchen's side window. What you want to bet when forensics gets through, it matches one of your boots. What do you think?"

"Hey man, I…"

"Come on, Marty. Help us out here." I interrupted. There was a hint of capitulation in his voice.

"Look man, I ain't admitting to nothing. Besides, if I tell you anything, they gonna start comin' after me, no? You gonna protect me?"

"You work with us and I assure you, no one will get within a half mile of you."

Sanchez became sarcastic. "Heh. I know a couple of skinnies from back in Korea that did better than a half mile."

"Well, we're not in Korea, now are we."

"I'd probly be better off there after talkin'."

"Hey Sanchez, you gonna give us anything or do I need to send you back downstairs?"

I grew impatient, but thought he was about to pop anyway. I let several moments pass, observing his fidgetiness increase as the clock ticked.

"If you gonna start lookin' somewhere, maybe you should look across your street first." On his third interview, The Match finally started giving us something to work with — a direction.

"Across the street? What, the bail bondsmen?" I tried coaxing more out of Sanchez's dark abysmal, but he just lowered his head in complete withdrawal.

I heard a knock on the one-way glass at the front of the room. Someone wanted me outside, so I got up, opened the door, and walked around to the other side of the glass. Mack and Captain Rodderman had returned, caught the last part of the interview, and wanted to coach me a little further. Mack had a few more details.

"Bill, you know we've been running surveillance for a couple of weeks across the street, right?"

I nodded.

"We caught the first two tip-offs with a line tap, but someone put the brakes on it."

Mack gave me a look I'll never forget. My mind instantly fogged up. I could hear the distant horns emanating across its harbor, but the warnings went beyond the horizon. His glance, however—the glare of qualmish sarcasm—penetrated the obscuration. Internal corruption; the nastiest insinuation any cop could make, and Mack just lowered the boom. Someone tipped off the bail bondsmen, which means someone, at least on the detective access level, was on the take. What about the bondsmen? There were three offices across the street. Which one?

"Bill, I'm returning to the interrogation with you. There are a few more items we need to know."

What was I going to say to my friend? *No*?

"After you!"

I led Mack back into the interrogation room. He sat at the end of the table and I took up a stool just off his right so I could see his notepad. Sanchez immediately perked up and offered some jocular sarcasm in an attempt to break his own stoic tension.

"So now we're havin' us a Poole party. Ha ha."

Mack was all business. "That's good Martin. Your originality astounds us."

Sanchez was unfazed. "Well, what can I do for you gents?"

Mack came straight to the point. "You can start by telling us who's tipping off the bail bondsmen."

"What's in it for me?"

"You know I don't have the power of the pardon, but what I *can* do is try and get your sentence reduced for cooperation."

"Try?" Sanchez sneered.

Mack was sharp in his interrogations. This was probably the fifth time I've participated on a high-profile purging. His fluid and vast tactical repertoire usually paid high dividends, and with typical alacrity. He favored a mix somewhere between "the easy way out" and "dire consequences". I didn't have to guess too hard that he was about to pull the old Mutt and Jeff routine when we both sat down.

"Yeah, try. You know I can't pardon you, Sanchez. Right now, you're looking at an Old Sparky concert in less than five if you can't cough up more information. Is that what you want? Ride the lightning? It won't be the cakewalk they gave you ten years ago, but maybe I can at least keep you off the chair." Mack later told me of Sanchez's prior conviction and whopping five-day clinical sentence.

The Match erupted in maniacal laughter, rolling his eyes to the ceiling. Moments later, realism set in and his complexion reflected a wisp of fear. His expressive hazel eyes dove from the ceiling to bouncing randomly around the floor. I ceased the opportunity.

"Come on, Marty. We can't keep you out of prison. You know that. You do a little hound-doggin' for us and we can find you a comfortable room at a hospital for a while. Understand? No Death Row. It's the best we can do."

Somewhere in the midst of Martin Sanchez's diseased mind, a synapse squeezed the trigger of clarity. He gave Mack and me a sober look and started giving us some details.

"Look, man. I don't know who they got on the inside. I don't know which bail joint across the street is ratting ya'll out either. I just overheard that bit while scoping a job at a bar."

Mack's face excitedly lit up. "Which bar?"

"No way, man. I'm not givin' no names, entiendes? If they knew I talked, they'd plug me no matter where you have me put up. Shit, for all I know, it's one of *you* assholes and I'm already dead."

Mack and I both knew we were dealing with something bigger than just some contract arson. This man was the key to connecting the main suppliers of cocaine and marijuana for the entire bay area. Mack attempted another coaxing.

"Sanchez, you don't have to give me the guy's name. How about the name of the bar. Can you do that? Just the name of the bar and we're good for today."

"Aw shit, man. You gonna get me killed." Sanchez became most uncomfortable.

Mack turned towards me and said, "You see that? The maggot points his fingers but gives us nothing. Come on, Bill.

Let's get the hell outta here. Scumbag's gonna fry. I knew Mack was just going with the game plan, so I played along again.

"Now hold on just a second. I'm going to let Mr. Sanchez have one last opportunity. What about it, Marty? You can't even give us one little clue where this place is? Something?"

Sanchez looked disgusted for a moment. It was the kind of look you get when you're utterly disappointed in yourself for not letting the dog out when he begged you for over twenty minutes, and you discover the reason for his begging the hard way.

Sanchez peered angrily into my eyes, and with a scornful tone, winked, "Take a *dive*, cop!"

Those were Martin Sanchez's final words for the day. Neither Mack nor I could get another syllable from his lips. He would only sit and stare blankly at the floor. Mack and I looked at each other and shrugged, and then left the room for some fresh coffee.

"Take a dive? What in the Sam Hill do you think he meant by that, Bill?"

I was at a loss. Sanchez's eyes kept flashing in my mind, leaving a silhouetted impression much like the sun or a light bulb does after you gaze in its direction. "I dunno, Mack. Dive? This town is full of dives. Heck, the Aztec down the street is the very definition of a dive."

Mack pursed his lips and stared down the hallway for a moment. His super-human analytical gears were smoking from the speed and friction.

My friend's face was about the easiest on the planet to read, meaning Mack was a terrible bluffer at the card table. Any time he was telling a fib, his cheeks would become red with some sort of a rash. They did the same thing when he was drinking too. He finally snapped out of it and started walking down the hallway at a fast pace.

"Come on. Let's take a little ride."

Curiosity never ceased at the department; if you had a hot lead, there was no point in mulling it over. We simply signed off and hopped in a plain car, zipped through downtown and then onto Kennedy Boulevard, heading west. We arrived at the corner with Tampania Avenue about two miles from downtown and Mack took a fast right into the parking lot of Randy's Lounge. It was about 10:45 in the morning and there was only one other parked car on the property. Mack backed into a space towards the rear of the lot and stared at an eight foot cinder block wall on the opposite side of the lot, about 50 yards away. He left the engine idling for a moment, so I had to ask.

"Randy's? It's a drag queen bar isn't it? What brought you over here?"

"Bill, do you know what's on the other side of that wall?"

"What are you, crazy? I've never had to set foot in that godforsaken place. Don't want to either...unless I have to. I suppose you already know, right? Been here before, have you?" I started joking around with Mack with a nudge on his right shoulder.

He started laughing. "No, but some patrolmen that were regularly called over here for clearing some hateful infiltrators have been in there. That bar has one feature none of the others have; a swimming pool."

"A drag queen bar with a swimming pool. Oh, that's rich...and disgusting at the same time. Who runs it?"

"Like most of the bars, the *real* owners are the mafia—probably one of Tresedici's places, but most of the queer clubs around this area are operated by Angel Vargas. You ever heard of him?"

Salvatore Tresedici. Why does his name always come up? I've heard Sal's name in rumors and innuendo behind a myriad of capers in this town, usually involving bolita raids on joints housing that coincidentally happened to have his cigarette and pinball machines. I never met him personally, but I ran into the lawyer for his boss once, a fella by the name of Paul Gravina.

He was speeding up South Tampa street one afternoon when he was late for a trial. I made a stop on him, but since he was nice and honest with me, I didn't write the citation. Gravina was the lead attorney for the Trucker's National Union boss, Jack Mollar, and also Giuseppe Cantonello, the famous Sicilian who controlled every bolita racket in the state. I met him only once at a grand jury hearing. Snazzy dresser. I honestly didn't see what all the mystery was surrounding this guy. He looked like the typical old man watering his lawn down the street.

All of us loosely followed the Italian families and their escapades. Giuseppe's main love was running casinos. Although he maintained a low-profile family-driven life—splitting homes in Tampa and Miami—he had been a major-league casino operator in Havana.

The Italians liked growth.   After Cantonello's father succeeded taking over bolita operations from Cracker Mob leader, Chucky Banks, Giuseppe spread the game to every corner in the state. Everyone was playing, but the real action was in Havana. He had two or three big casinos in operation down there, all seemingly legitimate too, in the late 1950s. Of course, they also served as laundering and debarkation points for the burgeoning drug trade.

When Castro's revolution ceased power, they closed down the casinos, scooped up the owners, and threw them in prison. I read where Paul Gravina risked his own freedom, flew down there, and eventually won Cantonello's release. Gutsy. The only thing left for Giuseppe to do was continue running bolita and drugs back in Florida...at least, as far as we thought. Proving it was another matter.

Salvatore Tresedici had been Giuseppe's underboss for over 30 years, and, if you ask me, he was probably getting a little impatient to become the boss. Regardless of their reputations, they were very respectful to me. I grew to appreciate their sincerity, but kept the whole mob thing at a distance. That was for the feds. From what I suspected around the office, it was getting too easy to get sucked into the mafia's world, and someone that evidently did was now whom Mack and I were after.

"Vargas? No. Well, just the name, maybe. What of him?"

"This guy's a real character. Wait 'til you meet him..."

I got to thinking; *meet him*?

"I've had to interview him on several occasions already because surprisingly, only one of his clubs ever burned, and it was a real pile of dung. I suspected it was only for the insurance money since the other places were making bank. Yeah, meet him! I don't want to look him up at his house though. He's probably sleeping anyway and it'll be funnier if we show up here later. You game?"

"I suppose." I said reluctantly.

Mack always enjoyed ruffling the feathers of the other side. Admittedly, I did too. Rousing a drag queen bar during primetime, however, didn't float my boat as much. The last time I walked into a gay bar, I felt like I had to run home and take a quick shower, washing away all the unwanted desirous looks. It was easier for me to walk into some greaseball restaurant and mess with the old-timers. The bolita merchants were buying extra candles these days too. Mack felt like we were on to something much bigger this time, and I believed him. He fired up our big brown Dodge and had us back at headquarters in just a few minutes. We were set for taking an afternoon break, but the FBI that met us in the lobby had other plans.

Nosey

"Hi Mack. Is this Detective Brume?"

Even though I've only spoken to him briefly on the phone, I quickly recognized Special Agent Leonard Karman's voice.

"Yeah, Lenny." Mack replied.

We shook hands and briefly exchanged pleasantries. Behind Agent Karman stood another suit escorting none other than Major George Dulles—the head of Vice!

"Hey Mack," said Karman, "I'll give you a call later this afternoon. Right now, you might oughta go up and see Smallwood. I think he's expecting you two."

Mack and I were dumbfounded. Dulles? What did he do? We traded theories during the short ride up the elevator, but our heads shook upon opening the chief's door. In the back of our minds we suspected the worst, but were praying it wasn't him.

"I suppose you ran into Lenny downstairs." Smallwood had a knack for the obvious. "Come on in and have a seat."

I felt like we were in trouble, but Smallwood had the feel of disgust and change rather than anger. I had always admired that in leaders; not dwelling on trivial matters, and moving forward decisively. After a long sigh, he gave us the bombshell.

"You know, usually when a crime happens, we (he pointed towards us) go after the perpetrators. It appears that crime has come to us. You saw Dulles downstairs. Lenny picked him up today after a year's worth of federal wiretaps on this place. Can you believe it? He's the son-of-a-bitch that's been yakking across the street all this time. And worse, Lenny tells me that they've had an abnormal amount of mob conversations emanating and terminating at this department. Folks, we're not going to the mob, the mob is coming to us!"

Mack's squinted eyes echoed my own anger. I had a partner shot and several raids quashed by that bastard and, now that the evil had a face, I wanted payback in spades. Before the chief continued, we heard a small bump at the door. I got up quickly and swung it open, revealing Major Henry Lozello evidently recovering from a crouched position in front of the door's keyhole.

"What the hell's the matter with you Henry?" Mack asked in a sarcastic tone.

Timidly, and with a rapid stutter, he made a lame excuse. "N-nothing. I...I n-needed to see the Chief."

Smallwood was right on top of him. "Well why didn't you just call me?"

"U-uh, u-mm, I...uh, heard you were still in the building, so I just came up."

I couldn't help myself and burst with laughter. Lozello, in his embarrassment, focused a disgruntled gaze in my direction before the chief resumed his query.

"Well? Is it *that* important? As you can see, we're in a meeting."

"N-no, I don't s-suppose so." Lozello cowered.

"Okay then, I'll see you first thing in the morning." Smallwood didn't wait for his response; he just sternly closed the door in his face. It wasn't quite a full slamming of the door, but a little stronger than normal. We returned to our seats and Smallwood continued.

"Mack, I'm putting you in charge of Criminal Intelligence. Congratulations. Bill, I want you to take over Dulles' spot in Vice, and I want you to work closely with Mack and Lenny. I'm promoting you to Sergeant. What? Don't look so surprised, you two. The FBI just saved the city a captain's salary and pension. We can afford it this time."

Even though Smallwood was congratulatory about our promotions, the tone of his voice continued with stern determination.

"I want you two to keep an eagle's eye out around here. Mack, you report directly to me. Bill, make your regular reports to your lieutenants, but if you get something internal, you bring it straight to me and nowhere else, understand? "

Mack and I left Smallwood's office and headed downstairs for a fresh cup of coffee. This day was turning out to be a whirlwind for the both of us, and we still had a long way to go before it was over. We also had some downtime waiting for Lenny's call, so we ran to our offices and dropped the news on our wives.

Wendy, ever supportive, was ecstatically cheering over the phone. Junior was only two years away from going to school, which meant she could return to work soon. It also meant our income would increase enough to afford our dream house. Although we liked the convenience of our home in Seminole Heights, our family had rapidly outgrown two bedrooms and one bath, which, it seemed, we were all waiting on at some time or another.

The only problem with the promotion was that it meant my working even kookier hours; a fact that I had to convey in staying out on the job later with Mack. That piece of news met with mixed reviews. Sure, Junior was old enough now and causing less hassle, but there were *two boys* at home with little or no backline support since Wendy's folks moved back to Texas last year. When Mack hung up with his wife a few minutes after I did, you could read his face. He just rode the same seesaw. We looked at each other for a moment, knowing our playground had become considerably larger.

The secretary buzzed in about fifteen minutes earlier than expected with Lenny's call. We scrambled over to Mack's private office since it had more than one phone, closed the door, picked up the handsets, and listened. What no one else knew (not even Chief Smallwood), was that Mack possessed a line scrambler. I had him set me up with one the next week.

"Hey fellas, did Smallwood fill you in on the situation?"

We gave Lenny our briefing on the infiltration concerns, but that was all we had.

"Okay. Well, if he didn't already tell you, Bill, your old duty sergeant was the one tipping off the bail bondsman."

Mack spoke up. "He did tell us that, Len."

"Okay then. I suppose he told you about the high number of contacts going to and coming from known RICO interests?"

"Yeah, those too." I added.

"Excellent. I wanted to let you know that we originally intended letting Dulles carry out a few more tips so we could trace his outside contact's hub and hopefully discover where everything's going. Whoever they were calling has a network large enough for contacting every bolita writer, club owner, and dope house in town within five minutes. If you think about that for a second, it's rather impressive."

Mack sat back in his chair with a look of apprehension. Whatever he was about to say, it bothered him.

"Len, can you tell us which bondsmen across the street were taking the calls from Dulles?"

Lenny paused and laughed for an uncomfortable moment. "It's not your brother-in-law, Mack. You can relax. The fella we're after doesn't sound anything like him."

Brother-in-law? I thought. I didn't notice my jaw on his desk, but Mack did. He squinted and just waved a hand at me in such a way that made his relationship trivial to the conversation going forward, and that he'd explain later. The revelation caught me completely off guard. For a moment, I felt that Mack should have given me that little piece of information a long time ago. It wasn't quite betrayal, but for a slight instant, it sure felt like dirt. He never mentioned he had a brother-in-law working bonds across the street.

"Okay, then who?" Mack asked.

"Let's see. Sam is on the far right, correct?"

"Yeah." Mack patiently replied.

"Big Sam is your brother-in-law?" I blurted towards Mack while palming my phone's mouthpiece. Again, he waved me off, allowing Len's reply.

"Then it's the place on the north end, in front of your headquarters' parking exit. They've got a perfect view of any-one coming or going. The proprietor's name..."

"Red Markete." Mack interrupted.

"You know him?" Lenny asked.

"Only professionally. He seemed nice enough by me. Flew under the radar, I guess. Now that you mention it, not all, but most of the bolita runners usually wound up in his bail office. What are you going to do with him?"

"The IRS is working on a tax case while we continue running taps. We probably won't get much else out of him now, and the tax case will award more time than the RICO offense alone. The tap's already there, so if we get anything in the next few months, it will just be a bonus."

I had one burning question. "So Lenny, *who* do you want us to keep an eye on?"

"Bill, right now, everyone. Just keep your eyes open and if you have anything to report, make sure you run it through Smallwood first."

Mack had a final postulate. "Hey Len, Bill and I are headin' over to Randy's in a little while. You want to bring your swim trunks and join us?"

"Randy's?" Lenny paused. "Isn't that one of Vargas' places? Oh Jesus, you mean that freak show place with the pool?"

"Yeah." Mack laughed.

"Err. No thanks. Why are you going over there?"

"Bill and I got a hot tip that may be your other end of Red's calls. Not sure, but it's worth paying Angel a visit. You sure you don't want to come?" Mack snidely laughed, fully aware of Lenny's professed homophobia.

"Hell no! I'm not going in there unless I'm wearing a rubber suit and sporting a hundred pairs of cuffs. Forget it!"

Both of us laughed before hanging up with Lenny. It was starting to get late in the afternoon. We began concentrating on the task at hand; a meeting with Angel Vargas.

Racing Down the Drag Strip

Mack and I decided on 6 p.m. as our best time for arrival. Vargas would probably be available just before dinner, and the creepy types probably wouldn't show up until later that evening. We had plenty to contemplate on the way back over to the lounge. Specifically, Mack's omission of his brother-in-law's establishment.

"*Mack?*" I asked in a facetious tone.

"Yes dear." He already knew what I was going to ask, so he played along with the tone.

"You mind telling me why you never mentioned something pertinent like your brother-in-law running a bond joint?"

He glanced over towards me in a way that was befitting consternation, but also acknowledgement.

"To tell you the truth, when Lenny said it was a bondsman across the street, I nearly had a heart attack. I don't know what all Sam's into, and for the sake of my wife, I tend to not look his direction too often, so you know. We go over to his place for special occasions and the kids play like normal. He has two boys that are a hoot and my sister-in-law makes some of the tastiest panisado you've ever had. Sure, he and I chat about some of the cases that come through, and some of the characters he puts up with, but that's about it. Half the time we swing by, he's asleep because he's out most of the night running his business."

"I appreciate the dossier, but that didn't answer my question."

Mack took a playful yet cynical posture. "Well, smarty, because I didn't think it was important."

"Fair enough." I told him I'd get over it, and besides, our ride down old Lafayette Street had brought us back to the corner with Randy's Lounge. I took a deep breath when Mack pulled the car into our same spot from that morning. Now, the lot was over halfway full.

The evening was still too fresh for necessitating a bouncer at the front entrance and, when Mack and I ambled in, a tubby-looking strongman was just waking up to our presence down at the end of a short, but dark hallway. Immediately, he put his newspaper down and stood up to run interference. Mack paid him little attention, scanning the spaces behind him while I flashed my shield. Of course, reaching into my jacket meant flashing the hardware beneath that any astute adversary quickly comprehended. Anytime I reached into that location, I made a habit of checking the opposition's eyes. He knew.

The interior of the lounge consisted of two bars; the smaller one towards the building's right side serviced a vast gaming area full of pool and foosball tables, pinball machines, and a jukebox. All of the machines, unsurprisingly, displayed distinctive Southland Amusement stickers on their coin doors. The flooring on that side of the lounge was terrazzo in bad need of a polishing, and the walls had portraits of exotically costumed pageant winners from previous years. The only lighting on that side came from those over the pool and foosball tables. Although the tables were nicely lit, our eyes had to adjust momentarily until we could see that most of the clientele currently occupying this room were either playing games or seated along the walls, and all were likely making conversation about the two obvious detectives that just walked in.

"Mack, you see what they're playing, don't you?" The closest tables probably overheard my laughing.

"Yeah, Eight Ball. What of it?" Mack responded while gauging reactions from nearby onlookers.

"Lady's game. Kinda figures, doesn't it?"

A loud miscue simultaneously occurred with the end of my sentence, causing a grumble two tables away. A gargantuanly tall, but well-attired queen (if there is such a thing) rose from his crouched bridge with the look of disgust. I walked around to his side of the table, plunked down two pieces of chalk and said, "These are free, you know."

He actually laughed and took the advice. I supposed people of this nature were victimized by daily ribbing, so it rolled off.

The left side of the building was much more ornate. The far left wall displayed a stage protruding about 12 feet from that wall and was about 20 feet wide. Behind crushed red velour shrouds that hung from the ceiling were several small light banks. There were large loudspeakers on each side of the stage, probably for a band or the second jukebox near the large rectangular bar that filled the entire back wall. In the middle of the room was a square, wooden dance floor with a mirrored ceiling overhead. Many small lights surrounded a crystal chandelier in the middle of that ceiling. A few were lit, giving luminous reflections on the walls and floor below. The lounge's front wall was lined with semi-private booths slightly raised off the floor and had benches made from a most uncommon brown corduroy.

Randy's most unique feature was the sliding wall on the main bar's backside. When open, it revealed the only swimming pool at a "public" lounge—at least in Tampa. We scanned the dance area and saw only one couple keeping to themselves. *Not Vargas,* I thought. The doorman, butted in.

"Hey you guys; is there anything I can help you with because, frankly, having you two stand around the front entrance is probably bad for business. You know what I mean?"

That didn't set well with me, and before Mack had a chance to say anything, I was already barking.

"Look here, ya little greaseball, if we wanna sit here for a while, we certainly can, but why don't you do us a favor and scare up your boss."

He threw up his arms, not wanting a scene caused on his behalf. "Okay, man. I don't want no trouble. He's with Tuesday out back."

Mack interrupted, "Tuesday?"

"Yeah, isn't that what day it is?" The doorman replied.

The comment struck Mack for a moment before the doorman explained.

"You know; Tuesday. The boss has a girl for every day of the week."

"That's not terribly original." Mack quipped.

The doorman paid the remark no attention. "They're still out by the pool. Go past the changing rooms behind the bar and they're probably seated towards the back left. That's where they usually sit"

As we left, I noticed him pressing a small button similar to a doorbell. I supposed he was alerting someone towards the rear of our impending arrival. Sure enough, a much larger Italian-looking fellow stepped out from a small nook on the other side of the changing rooms, making his presence known. He didn't impede our progress towards the pool; he was simply there for Vargas' reassurance.

The pool was probably not much bigger than a standard South Tampa backyard swimming pool, and only four people were actually in the water. Another half-dozen were soaking up rays while relaxing on padded lounge chairs sipping cocktails. Seated behind a table under a large umbrella was a mixed couple.

Angel Vargas had long, straight, black hair, bobbed at the middle of his neck, wore mirror-finish Aviator sunglasses, a thick, white terry bathrobe with a big red monogrammed "V" on his right breast, and a damp pair of swim trunks. On his left relaxed a dark brown-skinned woman with short hair, who wore a tight brown string bikini. I caught myself looking a little longer in her direction than I should have—probably long enough for Vargas to notice, and declare it a weakness. Admittedly, even though I didn't go for black women, she was beautiful. I was married and loved my wife, but in my opinion, there's nothing wrong with beauty's admiration. It's no different from staring at a Bouguereau or Renoir. Besides, nobody's *that* married.

Vargas removed his sunglasses and stood up, shaking our hands. "Gentlemen, allow me to introduce myself. I am Angel Vargas, and this is Miss Tuesday."

I felt Vargas' icebreaker and decided to play along before Mack could get anything out. I quickly shook the woman's hand. "And what a lovely day we're having."

Vargas couldn't help but laugh. I was sure he had heard most all of the witticisms concerning days of the week by now, but timing conquered all. Mack attempted to say something again, but Vargas had already offered a seat at his table in the shade. He snapped his fingers towards the bar and its tender appeared in a flash. Vargas turned back towards us as we finished introducing ourselves. His lips tightened and his eyes grew vaguely distant.

"Can I offer you both something to drink? Anything?"

Mack ordered a club soda with lemon. I asked for plain water. Vargas continued.

"I had a feeling you might be paying me a visit soon."

"Why do you say that?" Mack replied.

"These fires. Nasty business what someone's doing."

"Yes it is."

"And you caught the man responsible for these, no?"

"We don't know yet."

"Come on, Detective Poole. I know they spare my clubs for some reason, and I know that when faced with death, people will say *anything* to cheat it."

A moment later, the bartender appeared with our drinks. The glasses weren't cheap and the water didn't taste like the normal Tampa City tap water, either.

Vargas spared nothing with his bars. Mack later informed me that when Vargas first started operating, Tampa was awash in mom-n-pop taverns with few distinguishing features. Even though Vargas is himself a heterosexual, he was the first in town capitalizing off of the newfound sexual openness that the country's metro centers were experiencing. We soon discovered, however, that his bars were also breeding grounds for narcotics distribution, male prostitution, and a strange new disease nobody could quite put a finger on.

Mack became impatient. "Angel, you seem okay to me, but let me tell you what you're up against. (Here comes Mack's famed used of the 'Already Know' tactic) You're getting heat from the feds and they've got your bartender on tape with Red Markete. He's one of the bondsman across from headquarters."

Vargas put his sunglasses back on and turned his head away. Classic emotional concealment for liars.

"I don't know anything about that."

That was it; the meeting was over. Vargas would not talk any further and we didn't want a scene. The man standing behind us at the opposite end of the pool was a wildcard and we had no other business being there. Besides, the scenery was slowly becoming more of a carnival's freak show than I cared. I think it was the tall mulatto with the bulging two-piece that finally made me gag. Upon getting up to leave, Vargas evidently couldn't resist a laugh-infused parting shot.

"Give my regards to Major Dulles, okay?"

Mack didn't say anything else at that point. We just walked back up front, cordially thanked the doorman, and left empty-handed. When we made it back to the car, Mack got in and sat for a moment before hitting the ignition.

"Did you get anything out of that, Bill?"

I thought for a moment. "Well, that last remark confirms Dulles was probably working with them. And, he recognized that his clubs were being spared by the fires."

"That's close, Bill, but what I heard from him disturbs me far worse than I would have thought."

"What?"

"We didn't bring in Sanchez until earlier today. They already pulled Dulles away by the time we brought Sanchez into interrogation. Even if he had time and made the call, Lenny would have gotten the tap and told us."

"So it doesn't stop at Dulles." I surmised.

"Apparently not."

"Then who?"

Mack cranked the car and we headed back towards the station. "That is the $64 question now, isn't it?"

Wexler's Rock

For the next year and a half, Criminal Intelligence and the rest of the department's divisions initiated a full effort in the attempt to uncover and gather a rock-solid case against our internal monsters. It wasn't easy. Penny-ante narcotics and a few rarely-unprepared bolita writers were the only raids we successfully executed. My informants were begging to produce larger potential suspects; many of the usual primetime players. None of those raids were successful, however. Either they were gone, or they were present, but their places were clean. I couldn't even catch them with a token amount for harassment! Nonetheless, we continued our assaults in hopes that they would make a mistake, which they were making without realizing it on *every* raid.

Secretly, we announced select raids in a certain way to certain participating individuals so we could observe their reactions and other behaviors. Most everyone else believed we were simply on a raid, but we were also on another safari. It became clear to me that our token raids were never against any of the known operations of the larger traffickers. Our department was actually working *for* those traffickers by arresting any perceived competition! After lengthy analyses, my heart sank. I felt utterly duped and dirty. While we had been keeping some drugs off the streets, we were only making the *real* problem much worse.

Still, we managed to determine a point of commonality with a few of those raids. His name was Lieutenant Dennis Wexler, and you can easily imagine the cartoon nickname Mack enjoyed taunting him with thereafter.

My light bulb went off after he had an exposé in the newspaper about an investigation I knew nothing about. I should have easily been angry, being the Head of Vice (or is it *in* a vice?). Instead, my mind rummaged through possible motives.

Wexler and a couple of his cronies sent a paid informant to infiltrate a Land 'O Lakes nudist camp with drug connections. It sounded normal until the bust literally uncovered a city patrolman named Howard Johns and his wife. Normally, Internal Affairs would have undertaken an investigation involving a dirty patrolman, however, Wexler never claimed prior know-ledge of John's involvement. Curiously, Johns had already provided one of my detectives with tips pointing in the direction of the larger syndicate. I wondered if this was Wexler's retaliatory nuisance. Yes, Johns was evidently a kooky user, and he certainly deserved the bust, but in the back of my mind, Wexler probably executed a minor housecleaning contract.

Mack had his hands full as well. He didn't make any friends at the sheriff's office when he tossed a grenade in their latrine. You see, many of the state's upper-echelon intelligence units formed a semi-secretive group back in 1963 specifically for sharing information on organized crime. They originally denied the Hillsborough County Sheriff's Department's entry because of some stoolie, the group suspected, worked for the mafia. Of course, as soon as the new sheriff was elected a year later, they investigated that deputy and fired him shortly afterward.

Years later, Criminal Intelligence again denied membership for the Sheriff's Office. Mack was the head of the Criminal Intelligence's state governing body this time, and his reasoning was because their sheriff department's structure had reporting filtered through department heads and not directly to the sheriff. Mack wouldn't tell the papers he didn't like their department leader, opting to blame their systemic differentiation instead. Of course, that didn't play well with the sheriff, who had a particular talent for coddling the press. Because of this, our beloved young mayor Richard Gregorri felt it was time to get out and make a king's ransom in the private sector. I have no trouble saying that was a loathsome decision. With him gone, I knew we were in for some changes.

Lenny called me for meetings on a regular basis throughout 1974. By then, we had been up to our ears with his office and the military in working counterinsurgency cases concerning the local colleges. The distractions with Vietnam gave the commies plenty of momentum, and we helped weed out some of their plants. When we made it back to the main internal corruption investigations, Lenny said there were taps coming in from

Giuseppe Cantonello's top soldiers indicating a connection with Wexler and Lozello. In light of this, I initiated a few tails on Wexler and immediately gathered more entertainment than I had bargained.

On one hand, the surveillance uncovered Wexler's alcoholic routine involving a stop by his favorite joint—the Collegiate Restaurant off Fowler Avenue. Paul Moretti, who was a known lieutenant for Cantonello, owned the place. There was nothing illegal about this, but it easily raised every red flag in my mind. On the other hand, I couldn't help but laugh at this spoon-fed misfit. He'd get so completely drunk at the Collegiate, our tails were not only following him for intelligence, but also for public safety since he couldn't keep his car between the lines. If that wasn't enough, when he arrived at his house, he would stumble from his car over to this large rock in his front lawn, lay across it, and then pray to its magic powers, wishing for a well-deserved promotion to become the chief. That story was second-hand, though. I personally tailed him one evening and found it was only *mostly* accurate. While it was true Wexler ritually copped a few potions and weaved his way home, he didn't actually grope his lawn ornament. He did slap it on his way inside the house while mumbling something unintelligible, however. That was close enough for me. I told Lenny, he'd end up helping us more than whomever he was reporting to before this was all over. That's when Lenny called a meeting with Mack over by Mack's house in Town 'n' Country at a breakfast joint called the Ranch House.

Mack was off that day, but came over after dropping off his wife and kids at a swim club just around the corner. He wore a Hawaiian-style cotton shirt with shorts and a pair of sandals, which was an awkward contrast to my sports coat and Len's three-piece.

"I don't know how to tell you boys this, but we have every indication that you need to start a full folder on Henry Lozello."

Just like that, Mack and I were working by proxy almost full time for the FBI.

"I also want to put you two in touch with a relatively new Assistant US Attorney named Benjamin Davidson. He's about your age and just as aggressive as you are, Bill." Leonard added.

I remembered the name at the time, but the logic escaped me. "Davidson? Wait a minute. I seem to recall his name associated with Angel Vargas'."

"That's right. The man defended him in numerous criminal cases; mostly misdemeanors. Some of them after raids you executed."

Davidson's motives became suspect, I thought. "And now, he's a mafia turncoat?"

Lenny laughed, "No, no, Bill. Lawyers will defend just about anybody for a buck. That's their job, you know. We regard Davidson with the highest integrity. It just so happens that Vargas is into him for almost $40,000 in fees and he isn't paying."

"Revenge?" I asked.

"No.   Well, it's more akin to Davidson's not being contractually bound to save him, so-to-speak. And, his new job is just about as powerful as they come...almost untouchable. You could say revenge, but I prefer to think of Benjamin's particular focus as his job description by choice."

Well, that was that. Mack and I were now fully in the thick of an FBI mafia and police corruption investigation. I left the meeting in a complete fog, realizing the consequences of any mistakes. It could easily mean my career, but I had this sinking feeling that it could be much worse if I really screwed up.

The next week, I received a message to meet Benjamin Davidson at his office downtown. Upon arrival, his secretary showed me into his office where he and Mack were already chatting about some of the incidents we observed. As Lenny mentioned, Davidson was about my age, but quite taller with a resounding and confident voice. He instantly reminded me of Broderick Crawford, the actor. Behind him were the typical laudatory awards; a bachelor's diploma cum laude from a Massachusetts college (which explained his accent), various academic honors, a juris doctorate from a DC university, his various bar memberships, and most prominently, the John Marshall Award for Outstanding Legal Achievement.

"Hi, Bill. Good Afternoon. Mack said a lot of nice things directed your way." Davidson said.

"Why, thank you..." I was at a loss on his preferred name use so I gave him the standard pause.

"You may call me Ben." He quickly helped my predicament.

"Ben, thanks. Leonard Karman was quite complimentary of you as well."

"Please have a seat, Bill. You a ball fan?"

I knew he was starting with the small talk to get a feel for me. I liked this tactic as well. You can tell a lot about a man by his sports.

"Baseball or Football?" I asked.

"Both."

"Yeah, I like both. Me and the boys have been keeping an eye on Hank Aaron's run, and how about the Big Red Machine, eh?"

Of course, Ben was a frustrated Sox fan, so it was good to have a couple of strong teams milling about.

"You're right, Cincinnati is something else. We went down to Al Lopez Field back in the spring and caught a couple of their training games."

"Nice. I took my two little boys there and they got a poster signed by the whole team. I think Mack did too."

Mack chimed in. "Yeah, all but Pete Rose. Good thing my boy is a Johnny Bench fan or I would have been up the creek. You know I get my hair cut by Lou Piniella's brother, right Bill?"

"No, I didn't know that. I suppose the conversation is on Lou most of the time?"

"Not as much as you'd think. They're just regular guys like anyone else. Good folks."

"What about football?" Ben asked.

Mack spoke up first. "Now we're talking my language."

"You gotta like Miami." I offered.

Ben jumped in. "Yeah, but I think their time has come and gone. You keeping up with the Steelers? Mean Joe Greene and Terry Bradshaw? Watch those guys."

Mack deferred. "You know I had a class a couple of years ago at UT with big John Matuszak and Freddie Solomon. Nice guys. They called me their secret weapon after I ran off a photographer making films of their practices at Phillips Field."

"Is there anybody you *don't* know, Mack?" Ben asked.

"Evidently a few in our department." He quipped.

Just like that, our friendly conversation abruptly turned towards the business at hand. Ben's Steeler smile dropped and his eyes refocused on mine.

"Mack and I were discussing Lozello and his cronies a few minutes ago when you walked in, Bill. Right now, both you and

Mack are probably feeling like your situation is rather precarious, to say the least. For me, it's quite simple. You bring me enough evidence for a water-tight RICO case and I'll have a grand jury crawling down their necks in a New York minute."

"What is it, exactly, that you need, Ben? What I mean is, what type of evidence will work best?" Mack asked.

"Catching him with known associates isn't enough. At the very least, it would only cause some embarrassment or at the most, a demotion, in which case, our interested parties will likely shuffle the deck, per normal. That's not what we want. What you need to do is catch him committing an egregious felony with a known mobster and I can stick him for 20 years per count. Judges aren't granting leniency or early paroles lately. You get me two counts each on the bastards and we're golden."

Even though I've heard the reference to RICO in several landmark cases since 1970, those were mostly federal, and I didn't know all the attributes.

"Ben, would you cite some specifics. What exactly would we try to nail them on?" I asked.

"It's likely you won't catch them doing some of the dirtier soldier/enforcer work. Those jobs are for the expendable types, you know. Usually, ex-cons, hooked addicts or family members that were too dumb to climb the ladder and became generally disliked by other members. Tough love. You'll want to look into the extortion, embezzlement, obstruction of justice, murder-for-hire, narcotics, gambling, money laundering, and bribery ilk. Work the taps, nail them in conspiracy."

My mind started clicking with all of the possible scenarios. I had a feeling I could eventually link them with Vargas, or even Cantonello and Tresedici, but it was going to take some undertaking. Worse, the subjects had their own intelligence network and were right on top of me. Mack felt the same pressure. We weren't pushing on the expendables any longer. I knew if we started pushing, they were ready to push back as hard as they needed to get the heat off. Mack still believed the CIA rumors floating around that Cantonello had something to do with the Kennedy assassination a decade earlier. If that was the case, they wouldn't have any qualms in dispatching a couple of lowly detectives. Ben was a reassuring team leader and made most of my concerns disappear.

"And, don't worry about taps. You need a tap, you call Leonard."

We left Davidson's office raring to get busy, but slightly overwhelmed. It's not exactly as if Mack and I were experienced investigating high-ranking internal figures. Who is?

Mack evidently had his strategy worked out. "Bill, I'm going to keep tabs on Lozello and Wexler. What do you think about working it from the other end?"

"What, you mean Tresedici and Cantonello?"

"No. You probably won't get much surveillance on the old pros. I mean Vargas, Moretti, and Sanchez. We'll have to work on The Match. He knows more than he leads on. Moretti's probably a tight-lipped traditionalist, but Vargas... If you ask me, he's the weakest link."

"Why?" I asked.

"Because he's not Italian!" Mack laughed.

When I woke up the next morning, Wendy handed me the Tribune. Mayor Gregorri had formally announced his retirement effective at the end of the month. That was only three weeks away, and we knew we had to work fast because the buzz around the department was—whomever the council selected as the new mayor—Smallwood was definitely out. He knew it and so did we. Damn it, Gregorri! His timing, usually impeccable, couldn't have been much worse.

Mack offered his usual wisdom. "Look them right in their eyes and smile. Just be nice in person. They'll suspect less."

His advice just wasn't in my nature.

Mayored Out of Our Minds

A chance encounter at the downtown Maas Brothers had me in touch with my academy favorite, Sonja Ramirez. She dropped out of the department during her first pregnancy not more than two years after she started. Sonja told me of her three children attending school, and of her lucky husband, which was something she might have thought necessary for any number of reasons, but most likely from the obligatory visual compliments that, after her three kids, were the definition of obligatory. Back in the day, I surmised she got an ego boost if anyone came close to hitting on her. In a way, I felt somewhat sorry for her decline. Nonetheless, we had a fruitful conversation.

I told her about my wife's desire for returning to work, and Sonja provided me an excellent reference. She was leaving soon for a security management position at her company's newer location on Tampa's west side, and she carried strong referral power with her general manager who was desperately looking for a replacement. The timing couldn't have been more perfect. Junior was already in the second grade and Wendy hit the ceiling at her old furrier's job. The only problem I had with the whole thing was that she would be making more money than I would. Bragging rights. I'd never been in this situation, but if it meant getting a nicer house, I was okay.

A week later, Wendy successfully interviewed for the security management position and they hired her on the spot. We were just starting our celebration when Mack phoned me in a panic.

"Man, you're never gonna believe what Lenny just laid on me."

"Well, spill it quick, fella. Wendy just got a new job and we're over here doing a little celebrating."

I knew Mack wouldn't be calling me unless he had something heavy. I wanted to hammer my position home, so in case he had something that was going to ruin our evening, he'd hopefully steer clear. Of course, that didn't happen.

"Oh, well, tell her I said congratulations. Is she making more than you now or something?"

Mack's insight killed me sometimes. I don't know if it was something in my voice, or the fact he just liked tweaking me and everyone else sometimes. His reputation as a troublemaker had been steadily growing. It was a necessary evil, in my opinion. I had learned how to deflect or throw the sarcasm right back.

"Yes. As a matter of fact, I was thinking of retiring unless you've got something *really* important."

Wendy almost threw her glass of wine at me while Mack thought of something clever to say. "Yeah, well, you might think I'm joking when I tell you this. Len's got a tap of a call between that numbskull drunkard council chair, Bobby Henderson, cooking up a vote placing Lozello as the new chief."

"No kidding." I said.

Yup, that ruined the evening. My synapses hit overload pondering the ramifications of a dirty chief. It made me angry, but I was trying to stay somewhat festive for Wendy's sake.

Mack apologized and hung up. As the wine sunk in, I became slightly on the bitter side. Wendy stuck around and I gave her a massage, with probably stronger hands than normal since she was constantly giving warnings. *Lozello.* Here was the guy that could hardly speak English properly, getting sentences backwards because he was thinking in Spanish. Here was the guy that gave little insight during investigations, and annoyed everyone by sticking his nose in all the wrong places. Here was the guy that wasn't even fit as a patrolman when he began and they assigned him to gather parking meter proceeds on the city's three-wheeler. Many of the old-timers joked about that saying, "He collected a little for the city, and he collected a little for himself." Here's the guy we nicknamed "Linus" because he couldn't go anywhere without his security blanket named Wexler, and previously Dulles.

"Ow!" Wendy yelled just before dropping her cigarette on the carpet. "Look, if you're going to take Mack's call out on me, I can just sit with the boys and watch television."

"Sorry." That's all I could say in my defense. I refocused my attention on my bride. If I let them get to me, they've already won.

Two days later, Mack had me rendezvous with him and one of his patrol buddies out at our old opossum plunking spot on the Causeway. A gruff voice greeted me with a handshake stronger than a pro linebacker's. Like just about every cop I knew, the requisite medium foam coffee cup occupied his left hand. We all traded jabs at our increasingly inept superiors, save for a few, then Patrolman Terry Perkins dropped his Little Boy.

"Yeah, you ever heard of a man named Jimmy Furtelli?"

"Isn't that one of Cantonello's lieutenants?" I replied.

"Exactly. Well, get this… I arrested him on a DUI charge last night. The guy was completely wasted and kept going on and on about how he'd be out before the night was over, and no charges were going to stick because '*we*' just put in your new chief."

"Is that so." I took a stern sip of coffee while Perkins continued his account.

"So I asked him, 'We who?', and he says, 'Go fuck yourself'. So, I'm thinking this guy's only got a pair because he's three sheets to the wind, right? I ask again, 'who you think's so big around here, you can rig the top spot', and he says, 'Oh, just Big Sal and Bobby, that's who.' He said Linus was sittin' at the table when the decision was made."

"So it's true then." I concluded.

Careful to leave Perkins in a plausibly deniable situation, I cautiously asked Mack if anyone else knew.

"Have you dropped this on our Washington friends, Mack?"

"No, not yet. First thing in the morning."

"What about downtown? I added.

Perkins felt minutely insulted at my dancing around.

"Look, Bill. I don't know if Mack told ya; we go back a ways…do a good bit of huntin' and such. You don't have to two-step the obvious. I know you mean Davidson. It's not like the man's a spook, you know."

Busted. All I could do was joke with Mack. "So why isn't this guy a detective already?"

He laughed and then pointed towards the sand in front of us. "So, is this where you guys used to throw out a squirrel or something?"

"'Possum, yes, until our fireworks excuses stopped working with dispatch. I think Smallwood got tired of covering for us with the whole 'sound travels further over water' bit. Crying shame." I answered.

We sat around for a while, sipping on coffee and Winstons. Perkins seemed like a decent fellow and I put in a word for him with Major Fernandez.

Mack told me two days later Smallwood called him up and had him run all the way over to his house in Zephyrhills to collect the chief's office key. The man was so upset, he couldn't personally hand the keys over to such an imbecile, as he put it not-so-delicately. I felt for Mack's substitution in replacing the chief for the disdainful task handing those keys to Lozello personally, but I think he was simply following his own advice. *"Be nice and don't let them see it coming."* I didn't forget.

Lozello must have thought there was a change of heart with us and tried to reciprocate. The second week he was there, he started showing up wearing these expensive suits from Hong Kong. That's when it started—the slow, but sure encapsulation the mafia attempts by offering small gifts. Little by little, they suck you in until you're bought. Vargas gave Lozello two $300 suits and he thought it was a good idea to pawn one of them off on me. I followed Mack's advice...well, kind of. When Linus handed me the suit, I accepted it graciously. When he left for the day—always before the rest of us, mind you—I took out my Swiss Army knife, shredded the thing to pieces and hung it on one of the parking garage's rafter's in plain view. I don't know if he ever figured out it was the one he gave me, but the thing stayed there for nearly a month.

Lozello's case file was expanding exponentially. Lenny was calling me on a weekly basis for updates and pretty soon, I didn't know if I was working for Tampa or for the feds. It seemed like, over the next few months, Linus and his comrades tried everything in the book to get us off their case. When they weren't hitting on me, they were hitting Mack, Major Fernandez, Lover Boy, or any of the other good cops.

They had one of their expendables, Det. Sgt. Raymond Hilliard, write some bogus article in a local periodical so they'd boot us from the Florida Intelligence Unit. Mack was their leader! Well, the evil plot didn't work and we knew Hilliard was dirty.

The moron flaunted his little 18-year-old piece 'o tail from Tennessee around town, so we got ahold of her, miked her up, and made a pleasant little recording.

Ben Davidson called us and started laughing. "You should have seen the look on his face when I told him he was looking at 20 years on a Mann Act felony.

It was a seldom-used law, but if you needed to bust a horny old gobbler for pseudo-prostitution, the Mann Act was a convenient outlet.

Davidson told us it was sometimes a lucrative idea to let the smaller fish return to the pond. Hilliard would likely yield more gold since his violation allowed Lenny probable cause for another tap. Our investigation was running along smoothly until we hit another snag.

We thought interim Mayor Bobby Henderson's appointment was pretty much a joke. I had to wonder if Gregorri intentionally clued everyone in by having him sworn on April 1st. In no coincidence, bar tabs at the Aztec approached record levels. The new inside joke on campus was saluting anyone giving you headaches with three fingers, meaning you preferred a three-fingered drink to their nonsense.

Two and a half months downstream, department suspicions of Henderson's alcoholism heightened after he appeared at an award function honoring the Tampa Fire/Rescue Department for response times on heart attack calls. Of course, he dies right there at the podium after having one himself. Word was, The Match implicated his involvement with his arson ring, and someone whispered the impending indictment in his ear just before his opening speech.

I wasn't remorseful of the bastard, mind you, but it pays to know where all your enemies reside. I read Sun Tzu's philosophies in the service and they applied just as relevantly to a police department. Now we were going to have *another* interim mayor and only heaven knew how things would go until October's election.

Mack and I shared diligence on every aspect of the case. He started with immediate family ties (the usual motive) and discovered Lozello's sister was a manager for New York company named Central Stevedores; a long-suspected bolita and narcotics laundering front owned by the Letto family. The Letto's were under constant surveillance by Lenny's folks. Our cases began merging towards an inevitable conclusion. We were all pursuing the mob and the mob was pursuing the City of Tampa.

Internalized Fears

Levity. It's a state of consciousness that I find hard to maintain sometimes, but Mack saw humor in almost everything. If he caught a bolita writer choking on slips because their candle wasn't ready, he laughed. Their embarrassment was worth more than endless (and often pointless) paperwork ending in their eventual expedient return to criminality. There were many examples.

The summer of 1974 found Tampa under the leader-ship of its second interim mayor, Milton Grant. Since he was only in for a short term, Grant's strategy included no major policy or personnel changes until the public elected a new mayor that October. If there were any positive attributes for our Polk County farm-raised mayor, it was that he didn't allow the mafia any major advances either. They already had their chief, a friendly state attorney, a handful of judges, and some other local officials. The only thing missing was a longevity guarantee. Naturally, political muckraking became an everyday occurrence.

Chief Lozello, much to my amusement, caught his first sharp criticism after an unsuspecting deputy caught him in an illegal poker game while he was vacationing at a Pinellas beach with some of his buddies and their wives. While the women were unwittingly contributing to their melanoma cases out on the sand, the men enjoyed air-conditioned Georgia skins. Because of their thick cigar smoke, they left the room's sliding balcony door wide open. Unfortunately, the condos shared a common balcony and, as fate would have it, a local county deputy happened by Lozello's two-alarm poker shindig, looking for information regarding a stolen car parked next door. He didn't know he stumbled into Tampa's Chief of Police, and Lozello wasn't inclined to laud his true identity either. Embracing his departmental nickname, he gave the deputy "Linus" as his name, and an address at 1710 N. Tampa Street—Tampa's police headquarters. In hindsight, the group made a huge mistake allowing outsiders anywhere near their party, but it was a harmless low-stakes game, right?

The stakes were low until that deputy reported the information back at his office a few blocks down the strip. His sergeant recognized the address immediately and made a visit to the condo the next day, instantly recognizing Lozello. The sergeant didn't say much, and let the men continue their vacations. Professional reciprocity, or so Lozello thought. Of course, the sergeant conveniently failed to inform him he was sending a memo to his sheriff—a man revered for unwavering scruples. A week after the memo circulated around Pinellas County Sheriff's Office's hierarchy, the news leaked to a local paper. The telephone rang in Lozello's room and he received an unwelcome surprise.

"Chief, this is Everett Caseman with the Times. I don't mean to disturb you on your vacation, but..."

"Well, you are." Lozello interrupted.

"What can you tell me about the poker game?"

"I don't know anything about no card game, Caseman. Even if I did, I wouldn't talk to *you* about it."

Eventually, the frustrated reporter ran with an article, and the embarrassment forced Mayor Grant to make a small example of his chief. He docked Lozello a day's pay and issued him a formal written reprimand for Conduct Unbecoming.

You see, Mack found this hilarious. Lozello got his hands slapped and the embarrassment was worth far more than any adjudication. While I admittedly found Lozello's predicament humorous, the underlying principles in departmental ethics were practically down the tubes. The shining example was losing its luster and his poor example meant the entire petty criminal world felt vindicated. In fact, they now had a role model.

The department's next predicament came in the form of an alcoholic detective named John Robert Skitter. John loved two things in life: the martial art of karate and, antithetically, single malt scotch. We used to joke with him about his "blows to the head". Not surprisingly, he never understood our double entendres.

Over the previous three years, we were hearing rumors of Skitter's questionable activities. He stayed mostly to himself over in Robbery and didn't ruffle any of the other detectives' feathers unless a sporadically rare wisenheimer comment floated around the floor about his drinking. I equated Skitter with any other gray-liner. I thought he mostly stayed out of trouble like most, but when times got tough, he ventured towards his old pals. Mack and I decided to start keeping track of him and, after only a month of taps through Lenny, we acquired a line on massive theft Skitter had set up for Vargas. We put together a small greeting party with three detectives and two uniforms in backup. Mack and I were going out with Ray Coleman at the time when Skitter and a well-known button man for Angel Vargas were supposedly hitting the Saturday night ticket proceeds at the Florida State Fair.

The main office for the fair was a well-protected brick building located on the other side of a tall wooden wall near the sprint car track. We discovered that weekend tickets to the races and the fair itself totaled over $120,000 on a weekend night, so this was no small-stakes arrest. We wanted Skitter, but we also wanted his coconspirators. If all went well, we could possibly take down a dirty cop, a middle-ranking mobster, and best of all, Vargas. It was just after 8:30 p.m. when our two unmarked cars arrived at the rear of the main parking lot close to the racetrack.

"What do you think, Mack?" I asked, pondering the noise from the race raging just on the other side of the lot.

"Lenny told me they planned on parking close to that track wall around ten or so tonight. After they hit the office, they said they'd throw everything over the wall by the second light pole just over there."

Mack pointed towards the track and we assumed the races would be over by the time anyone would dare step on its surface. We walked through a few hundred yards of parked cars and took a position some four rows back from a makeshift gravel road running the length of the racetrack's wall.

"Well then. Since we's got to wait an hour, I hopes y'all don't mind me having a look at that there race." Ray said.

I started to speak up with a concern regarding the possibility of Skitter making one of us if he happened to scout the location beforehand, but Mack threw his hand in front of me before I could say a word.

"Go right ahead, Lover Boy. Don't stay too long though. If you see anyone get within 50 yards, you make for a dark corner of the parking lot. All right?"

"You got it, man."

Ray shimmied across the gravel road, across a small ditch, and over towards the racetrack's wall. The crowds watching the races were located on a grandstand at the other side of the oval, so his chances of detection were minute. Mack started giggling uncontrollably, slapping my right arm with the backside of his left hand. The imported and damp red Georgia clay lovingly let the drivers countersteer all the way around the track so long as their tires spun freely, and poor Raymond didn't notice any spray from the spinning tires flying over his head from the pack's last lap. Mack didn't let his own unfortunate childhood experience get in the way of Raymond's education either. My arm started smarting after several more slaps from Mack when Ray found a half dollar-sized knothole in the fence and tried to take a peek. Not only did the first car send a perfect clod into Ray's peephole, when Ray backed up in pain, the rest of the pack showered him in cold, wet mud.

"Oh my God, I can't take it!" Mack yelped in mad laughter.

I don't know where Mack suddenly discovered his mean streak, but it was almost as good as the callbox gag. Again, there was Ray with his perfect threads perfectly sabotaged. I felt for him, but this wasn't my fault. I was in tears, too. If he wasn't such a good sport about his informal education, I'm sure my laughter wouldn't go unchecked. Ray had a pretty good sense of humor after several years on the job. All he could do was wipe it off and join in his spectacle.

"All right, all right. Laugh it up, you two. Y'all's is coming sooner or later." Ray said.

We kept laughing.

Thirty minutes passed and the noise from the track died down. While Ray cooled, we strategized how to handle the bust.

"Ray, just before your shiner, did you get a chance to look around." Mack asked.

Ray rubbed his eye, still finding grit behind his swollen lid. "Yeah, but only for a moment. Couldn't see too much. They had stacks of tires all up against that wall, but I saw all them racecars comin' 'round, and I saw the seats over yonder, too. I couldn't see that building you was talkin' about though, Mack."

"You probably wouldn't. That's another hundred yards beyond the tracks southern wall. Well, they won't have any problems getting anything over that fence if they've got tires to climb up."

We were approaching the window Lenny gave for the hit, so we summoned the uniforms to our position. They were a couple of younger guys we trusted after working a few years and reading their FIRs. Jimmy Diaz was a tall and lanky patrolman that seemed cool when under pressure. Mack mentioned him frequently when talk of hiring new detectives went around. Herman Smith was another patrolman we liked, but probably couldn't survive a foot chase if he had to run more than twenty-five yards. He wasn't obese or anything that drastic, but he was certainly overweight. When Mack gave us the game plan, the logic seemed slightly backwards, but I caught on to his sense of humor.

"Okay, here's how we're going to run this. Bill, Jimmy, and I will take the car, but only *after* they have the evidence. When the car first pulls up, I want Ray and Herman taking the office runner."

"Say what?" Ray raised his voice in immediate disbelief. "You wants me to go chasin' the delivery boy halfway across this park with Herman? You gots to be crazy!"

"I ain't gotta take no abuse from the department's poster boy, sarge." Smith grumbled immediately. "He's probably right, though. Isn't Jimmy a better choice?"

Mack laughed sarcastically. "Yeah, but you need the exercise and besides, if he takes off, we still have the fastest hundred in the department standing right next to you."

"Mack, don't you think we should be on the other side of that fence somewhere before they show up?" Ray asked.

"I thought about that Ray. Too risky. If the runner makes you before making the drop, we've got nothing. How about the two palm trees just beyond that gate down the far left corner of the track wall?" Mack pointed towards the extreme southeastern corner of the track.

"I suppose that'll do. You sure them trees is thick enough to hide behind?" Ray joked.

"Oh, ha-ha, detective. What the hell have you got all over your jacket anyway?" Herman whispered.

We all laughed. Patrolman Smith held his own.

Mack finished his instructions. "Anyway, you two — you see a bag go over that wall, you take the guy down. We'll handle the car. Remember; wait until he throws it first, all right?"

Ray and Herman took off for their position and the rest of us steamed in the humidity. We watched for any activity around the racetrack's second light pole and grew anxious after another forty minutes slipped by. Suddenly, an unmarked car from our own lot gingerly stopped on the road next to the wall precisely at the second light pole. Our first reaction was to draw our .38s and jog over there, but Mack held us back.

"Wait for the bag!" He whispered at the top of his whis-pering voice.

The car sat for a moment. I noticed the orange glow of a cigarette drawn by the driver. A passenger opened his door, which was on our side of the car, and walked around to the back of the car. He opened the trunk and went around to the driver's side where he leaned up against it, conversing with the driver. From our position, we noticed Ray holding his arms open as if to ask what's going on. I motioned him to be patient. A moment later, three huge black garbage bags sailed over the fence and into the ditch by the car. The first bag startled the car's passenger since it landed only a few feet away. Throwing his unintentionally crushed cigarette to the ground, he gathered up the bags and loaded them in the trunk. I glanced back over towards the trees where Ray and Herman were hiding. They had already split. We crouched down and duckwalked to the last row of cars before springing our trap.

"Bill, take the driver. I'll take the pickup guy. Jimmy, cover yourself with this last car here and keep us blanketed, okay?"

"Yes, sir." He said, nervously.

Detective John Skitter didn't quite know what to do. From behind his steering wheel, his headlights faintly showed a man in a suit waving a badge, but that's not what eventually gained his undivided attention. Staring down the end of my gun barrel made him momentarily forget he had a lit cigarette in his mouth. It wasn't until after it burned a hole through the fabric surrounding his crotch that he received an excruciating reminder. I demanded his hands on the wheel, but Skitter wasn't through having kids either. Coolly, he handled the pain and repositioned his posterior over the smoldering ash, slowly extinguishing it by suffocation. I could tell something wasn't quite right with him, but wrote it off in consideration of his well-gossiped addictions.

The passenger didn't much like the end of Mack's gun barrel either. Before he realized he was staring down Mack's .38, his right hand was halfway under his jacket.

"Hold it!" Mack yelled and pointed his pistol towards the man's hand.

The man withdrew and slowly held up both hands.

"Mack Poole? Is that you?" Skitter's voice nervously emanated from the car's interior.

While keeping a keen eye on the man in front of him, Mack cautiously replied, "Who's asking?"

"Jesus Christ, Mack. This is John Skitter. What the hell's going on?"

"I'm not talking to you right now, Skitter. And you better inform your friend here not to move a muscle while I disarm him."

"Do what he says, Furt."

"Furt?" Mack asked while reaching into the man's jacket and removing a .25 automatic from his shoulder holster. The man's expression faded to a dull frown. After Mack finished frisking him, he continued. "As in Furtelli? Nick Furtelli?"

The man's frown grew to a scowl. "Yeah, what of it?"

"Keeping good company lately, eh Skit?" I jabbed.

Skitter kept his cool, opting for conversation.

"Mack, do you mind if I climb outta here?" He asked.

"Bill, you know the drill." Mack said.

"I suppose you do too, John. Stick your hands out of the window and open the door from the outside."

Detective Skitter did so, and then slowly swung the door open.

"All right, now keep your hands on the wheel." I reached into his jacket and removed his Airweight.

"Bill, don't forget the other—and get the keys from the ignition."

I had Skitter climb out of the driver's seat and I frisked him completely. Like many of us, he had an extra piece strapped to the inside of his left ankle.

After Mack was satisfied we were no longer in danger, he ordered everyone to the rear of the car. By this time, Ray and Herman showed back up with a short, scruffy-looking, middle-aged sap wearing a soiled baseball cap, an old windbreaker, and a pair of greasy dungarees.

"How'd it go, Ray?" I asked.

"About as Mack figgerd. He saw Herm and me trotting after him and the son-of-a-bitch took off. I caught up and stepped on his heel."

"He looks like he's in a little pain, Ray"

"You assholes ain't got nothin' on me. I ain't done nothing wrong. Ow!" Ray side-kicked the same twisted ankle.

"Okay, Skitter. Let's have a look at the contents of your trunk." Mack pointed towards the keys in my hand. "Let's open her up, Bill."

"Is that what this is about? Oh man, are you guys in for it." Skitter laughed.

"And you're in a lot of trouble Skit. I don't see much funniness about going to jail and losing your family." I countered.

"Well be my guest, gents." He said.

As the trunk lid flew up, exposing the three garbage bags, Mack began opening the topmost bag and started reading Skitter his rights.

"You three are under arres…" That's when Mack's eyes grew wide and his speech surrendered. "What the hell are these, John?"

"That's what I tried to tell ya, Mack."

Mack frantically searched around the bags emptying their contents into the trunk. Miniature teddy bears. Probably over 200 of them about the size of an average man's fist. Mack took out a small pocketknife and spit two random bears to make sure it wasn't a concealment job, but he found nothing but stuffing. He spun around and gave me his patented goddamnit look.

"You were saying, Mack?" John Skitter snidely remarked while leaning over the trunk.

"What the hell are you doing with all these bears, John?"

"I should be asking you why the hell the depart-ment's got five cops chasing after a bunch of teddy bears!"

"Well, why is you sneaking 'round throwing them over a damn wall in the fust place, Skit?" Ray jumped in.

"You shut your negro mouth, Lover Boy." Skitter growled.

"Well?" Mack asked.

"Well, what?" Skitter snorted.

"Answer Ray's question."

All of us could tell Skitter was searching his mind for the best excuse. He had to know how shady it looked palling around with a known RICO interest, let alone covertly collecting plush toys thrown over the wall of a state fair's racetrack.

"It's really none of your business, but a friend of ours bought these to give to his girlfriends."

"He has 200 girlfriends?" Mack asked.

"Probably more. He's a well-known flirter—likes to charm the girls. He bought these at a discount from Gustav over there and said he'd throw them over the wall if we met him at a certain time. The whole deal was under the table since his boss doesn't like him making extra book.

"You see! I ain't done nothing wrong!" Yelped Gustav.

"Don't be getting' on my nerves again." Ray lifted his foot, silencing the wiry carnival operator.

"Who?" Mack asked.

"What?" Skitter replied.

"Who were you talking about just before, John."

"Rather not say."

"Rather not, or can't? Because, if you don't tell me, I'm sure the chief might have a problem with your running errands with a mobster in a company car."

"Lozello? Please. I think you know where your complaint will end up."

Mack became physically agitated. You could tell he lost half the enamel on his teeth in the few minutes after our fouled bust.

"Let him go, Ray." Mack said.

"Do what?"

"Let him go, I said."

"Can't I get an evadin' charge or something?"

"Won't stick. You know that." Mack contended.

Ray let his prisoner loose and almost got another kick in before doing so. The shifty worker was slightly faster.

"Yeah, and you'll be lucky if I don't sue your asses for brutality!"

Herman withdrew his baton and stepped towards the man's direction. He immediately ran away in a painful limp.

"Bill, give John his firearms back. We're letting them go."

"I won't mention the two bears you tore up, Mack." Skitter laughed.

"John, I think you know by now what you're doing. You want to hang around with these types, you know where that ends up. You want to keep risking the gavel, that's your prerogative."

"And you keep up harassing us and you know where that'll end up." Furtelli blurted.

I got angry with his threat. "Where's that, Nick?"

"Nicky, shut the hell up and get in the car." Skitter demanded.

"What about my hardware?" Furtelli asked.

Mack removed the gun out of his jacket pocket, released the clip, unchambered a hollow-point round, and racked the slide off, temporarily dismantling the .25's firing capability before handing the parts back to Furtelli.

"We used to practice putting these back together in the army, you know," Furtelli said, "Got it down to around five seconds."

I was unimpressed. "Have you ever timed it with a .38 in your chest?"

Furtelli grumbled and climbed in the passenger's seat, careful not to drop any of his pistol's parts. Skitter gave us a cold grin, hit the big Monaco's ignition switch and respectfully refrained from spitting gravel.

"Jesus Christ, Mack! What'd you let 'em go for?" I asked.

"Come on, Bill. We've got virtually nothing on them. What am I gonna do—take them in for a misdemeanor with a RICO association charge? Davidson said that wasn't enough."

"We could have gotten Skitter fired, and Furtelli off the street for a while. What about that?" I asked.

"No. We don't want any petty vengeance, Bill. I know you, Ray, Jimmy, and Herm want a little payback. Give it some time. Right now I just wanna know what happened with our intel."

"Sarge, you mind if we head back?" Herman asked, still slightly out of breath.

"No. You and Jimmy can go. I'll debrief you tomorrow after we get some answers."

After the uniforms vacated, Ray said, "Hey Mack, the way I sees it, we just got made. I mean, your Karman fella shoulda know about them teddy bears unless it was a setup."

"I think he's right, Mack. Lenny's people play at the highest levels, you know? Had to be a setup." I added.

"I'm not so sure, but we'll find out first thing Monday. I'm calling it a night."

Mack's puzzlement dragged our spirits lower. I didn't sleep well that night. I kept hearing the distant crackle of the fairgrounds' public address system advertising one of the sideshows wherein a woman magically turns into an ape.

"Go-rilla! Go-rilla! Go-rilla!" They repeated that over and over. I couldn't get it out of my head!

I never slept well after losing a battle, but after researching every detail, I concluded we did nothing wrong, procedurally. The problem rested solely with Lenny.

I arrived at headquarters earlier than normal that Monday morning. Unsurprisingly, Mack was also in his office and on the phone. I assumed he was speaking with Lenny, and before I turned towards my own door, Mack's arms were motioning me to come over. Indeed, Lenny was on the other end of the line, and from what I could tell, Ray's theory proved unfortunately correct. All of the words they used in Lenny's tap were uncharacteristically direct. In other words, they were using "money" and "cash", when they would have normally said "merchandise", "goods", "objects", or some other generalization. If it was any consolation, Lenny commended Mack for practicing restraint and letting them go. The FBI wanted a bigger case and they didn't want the deck shuffled.

The following two weeks were relatively quiet with the exception of Ray's informants coughing up several smalltime dealers all peddling identically composited heroin. One talked openly of the amount that recently hit town—highest quality and professionally packaged. In the back of my mind, I knew it meant there was a large shipment that washed in, and a newer player likely marketed it.

A boisterous fracas echoed throughout the department's open stairwell later that month. Our entire floor witnessed two Internal Affairs detectives escorting a major named S. O. Lidwicki to the detention block. After the noise disappeared, word quickly circulated he was arrested for embezzlement. While Lozello did a fair job of keeping his cronies in order, he wisely rejected those that were greedy bond made mistakes. Department rumors told of a secret partnership with the chief and Lidwicki likely sharing profits from the embezzled parking fines, but when an anonymous tip rang into Internal Affairs, Lozello threw him to the wolves. We were talking and laughing at Lidwicki's demise, especially since nobody liked him. We wondered if IA would turn any attention towards Lozello, but he was also just intelligent enough to keep his hands clean.

The buzz hadn't quite left the room before it suddenly fell quiet. I was previously jawing with Ray, seated on a desk right behind me, when his expression displayed contempt. He motioned me to turn around. All I remember about that particular moment was that my eyes slowly started at the bottom; recognizing the lavishly designed white Italian shoes, white slacks with a bleached gator-skin belt, a maroon-striped double knit polyester shirt with a wide collar, and a matching white jacket. When my eyes made it up to the long, straight black hair and sideburns, it became apparent Angel Vargas was paying *me* a visit.

Of all awkwardness, why me? Why in front of all these detectives would the man pay me a visit—at headquarters, nonetheless? I had to admit, this was far superior in gutsiness than when Mack and I visited his drag bar. Whatever the reason, he was here, and he had been holding his hand out in anticipation of a handshake for over three seconds.

It was a rare day when many of the detectives were actually in their offices. Most times, we're out in the field, so I wondered if Vargas knew this and carefully calculated this visit to somehow embarrass me with the unavoidable question-filled fallout from such a visit, especially if I took his hand. I made a completely conscious decision and gave him the warmest welcome. After a moment of obligatory, unintelligible mumbling in the background, Vargas and I sat down.

"I can't say I'm not flabbergasted by your lack of intimidation in visiting the lion's den, so-to-speak, Mr. Vargas."

"And why should I? You should feel no intimidation coming into one of my fine establishments, no differently than a public citizen visiting any of our government's fine institutions. Am I wrong?"

"Of course not, but I have to admit having a higher anxiety visiting one of *your* clubs as opposed to the library downtown."

I paused and fired up a Winston to break the tension, offering one to Vargas, who declined.

"Well then, you may be able to help me then."

"What do you mean?" I asked.

"Detective Brume. My lounges do well because I am a fan of the business. I love what I do."

"And what's that exactly?"

"I find a niche and market it extensively."

"Queer bars."

"Alas, it was my brother Randy who inspired the idea."

"So the place is named after him?"

"Yes. And before you ask, he *is* of the other persuasion, but this idea alone is not why my operations are successful.

"When I first started working as a bartender, I quickly discovered why people visited certain clubs. They desired being surrounded by like minds — people that were like themselves with the same interests. Tampa has an endless supply of mom-n-pop shacks serving the same cheap booze. What makes any one of them stand out? The cleanliness? What game is on television? The bathrooms? The girls working the tables?"

"I see your point."

"Everyone wants a good time and anyone can learn to keep a decent bar, but not everyone can select a proper theme. So, that's why I came by today, Detective Brume."

"You want me to help you with a bar. I don't think..."

"Señor, you must not think of a place as just a bar, but more as a place of entertainment. This is what I love. Ideas!"

I didn't know what Vargas was up to, but I played along. If he divulged anything useful, the dialog couldn't hurt.

"What about a sock hop?"

"A what?"

"You know. A fifties joint. A dance place with checkered floors, chrome and red everywhere, red vinyl seating, Jive, Twist, Jitterbug, and the Lindy, east-west swing stuff — the fifties. I think it's making a comeback."

"I love it!" Vargas said while he stared into my eyes before continuing.

"By the way, Miss Thursday wanted me to send her regards."

I knew it. Vargas saw me eyeball his woman on our visit and he's testing me. I thought I'd better play it cool.

"Today's Monday. Where is your Monday girl?"

"I wasn't aware you've seen her. Do you think she looks better?"

"Oh, no. I hadn't seen any of the others besides Thursday. I just..."

"They are all exceptional. Miss Monday is waiting for me downstairs. We are going to the Tropicana for some deviled crabs. Would you like to join us?"

He knew there was absolutely no way I could be seen out in public associating with a known federal interest, unless, of course, I was undercover. I would have to decline his offer but maintain the friendly discussion. Admittedly, I found Vargas rather pleasant—certainly not the stereotype you see on television.

"I'm afraid I can't. Can I take a rain check?"

Vargas' face lit up. The way I said "rain check" inferred sincerity and he picked up on the tone.

"Absolutely."

With that, Vargas stood up in preparation for departure. Before shaking my hand, he reached into his jacket pocket, withdrew something, and placed it on my desk. It was one of the teddy bears identical to the lot from our busted raid.

"The man with two hundred girlfriends." I mumbled in muffled irritation.

Vargas knew he had us that night and was rubbing it in. "The ladies do wonders for these. You can't find them just anywhere, you know. I wanted you to have one for your wife."

"I appreciate it, but I can't accept..."

"No, no! I insist. Please regard it as compensation for helping me with a new club theme. Fifties...I could make a small fortune, you know."

"I don't doubt it." I let him leave the bear on the desk.

"I am going to hold you to your word on that rain check, detective."

"I'll be in touch."

"When?" Vargas said playfully.

"Please give my regards to Miss Thursday." I looked him in the eye as I shook his hand. He turned around and eased out of our floor, disregarding all of the bewildered looks and spilled coffee as he passed the other's desks.

"Say, Billy. Are you crazy, man? And what the...Aw, no! That ain't one of them bears is it?" Ray was all over me as soon as Vargas' elevator door closed and he could no longer see us.

"Shhhh! I don't want everyone to know." I whispered.

Ray turned around to see if anyone else was actually paying attention. I knew someone couldn't pass by my desk without a "Hey Bill, keeping good company, I see."

Ray lowered his voice and continued with his concerns. "You ain't gonna actually meet with this cat, are ya Bill?"

"Already have once. I dunno, Ray. I gotta go see Mack. I don't want to get in over my head."

"Yeah, you do that."

My friend gave me the look of a parent when they knew their child was making a mistake. I knew this because I've had plenty of practice with my own boys lately. This felt like opportunity to me and I didn't want to throw it away.

I was fumbling the bear around in my hands as I contemplated Vargas' abyss. My fingers unconsciously explored every nook of the toy until it disturbed my concentration by finding a loose seam. My head dropped and my eyes refocused on the toy because my right index finger disappeared well inside its plush interior. I felt something sharp, but pliable, like the edge of some paper. With both hands, I held the seam open and extracted a small roll of money. Five crisp Franklins. I stared at the money for a few moments. *Compensation,* I thought. I just accepted a payoff without realizing it. Why? I was going to take the bear up to Mack, but now I had to think about this legally. No, I wasn't culpable. I didn't know there was anything inside the bear before its acceptance, so I am not liable. This is evidence as far as I was concerned.

Mack was delighted to see me at his door while he finished up a phone call. As soon as the handset hit the base, the teddy bear showed up on his desk's calendar. His playful demeanor became a stoic glare.

"Where the hell did that come from?"

"Didn't anyone tell you Vargas just came and paid me a visit?"

"Are you kidding me?"

"Of course not. You and I need to talk."

I plunked down the fresh hundred dollar bills and briefed him on the visit. Mack was amazed at Vargas' bravery and tenacity.

"It sounds like we've got until Thursday to come up with a plan for your visit." Mack concluded.

We were definitely on the same page and I felt completely relieved.

"What do you think we should do next?" I asked.

"Get Lenny onboard. He'll need to know about the bear and the money."

Mack turned on the scrambler, dialed his direct line and Len picked up immediately. After a brief explanation, we decided it was best to meet that afternoon, so we bounced over to a small café in Hyde Park and sat in front of three freshly poured mugs and a clean ashtray.

"You don't have to go through with this if you don't want to, Bill. If things get out of hand on this one, we can't always be waiting right around the corner, you know." Lenny relayed his concerns.

"I know. That doesn't bother me. What I need to know is what you want me to do, exactly. I mean, the guy just gave me five hundred for nothing. He was even bold enough to bring one of those damned bears and give it to me personally."

"It's a personal business these guys are in, Bill." Lenny retorted.

"I understand."

"Do you know where you're meeting him yet?"

"No. I said I'd be in contact."

"Great, so you get to pick the place."

"I suppose."

"Mack filled me in about Vargas thinking you may be...um...unfaithful, given the right situation with one of his girls. Is that the impression you're getting?"

"I think so. But I *am* a faithful man, sir, just so you know. I have no intentions of..."

"Oh! I know you can deal with that. We're not asking you to adulter the girl. Just use her as an in with their organization."

"Understood. So what's the gig?" I asked.

"Let's have some ground rules first. They gave you a $500 payout. You have it?"

I put it on the table. "Yeah, it's right here."

Lenny put it back in my hand. "Hang on to that. It's evidence, but it'll just get logged and sit around doing nothing. I'll sign off for your expenses, so keep it in case they ask you to buy something."

"Like what?"

"Anything. As long as you have the cash they gave you, they'll know you didn't hand it over or give it to your wife. You need to appear slightly aloof and liquid."

"Okay."

"Next. If they want you to take future payoffs, take them unless they are ridiculously high. In other words, don't appear too greedy. You're a dirty cop, not a pig. Understand?"

"What's too much?"

"Probably anything over five large."

"Got it."

"Third, don't stop busting the little guys. You have to keep appearances with your department. Just don't mess with Vargas' people. We'll take care of that."

I was beginning to feel like I'd signed on to an Apollo mission.

"Fourth, this is just you and Mack on this one. Everyone else has to think you're on the take."

"What about Ray Coleman?"

"Don't think so, Bill. He's not a bad cop, but this has to stay small."

"I understand."

"Lastly, don't get shot. I don't want to read about you in the paper. I don't care how serious anyone thinks this business is, it's not worth dying."

It's not as if I would disagree with him. "Okay, so what am I doing?"

"Having fun!" Lenny laughed. "Seriously, all you're doing is gathering information about their operation. I want to know everyone involved, who the official contacts are, and how they're running their operations. We won't stop until you've inked everyone to a grand jury hearing."

"I kind of envy you, Bill." Mack lamented.

"Oh yeah?"

"Sure! You're gonna get some fine grub and get to stay away from home at night. You've got a free pass."

"I'm gonna have to hire a maid for Wendy."

"I know a girl who'll clean your whole house, do laundry, and even windows for $15 a week."

"Give me her number." I said.

When Mack and I returned to the department, we received a message asking to return a call from Benjamin Davidson. We rolled to Mack's office so I could listen too. Ben picked up and gave us some news.

"Did you hear about our little breakthrough today?"

"No, Ben. What happened?" Mack asked.

"The Match just said he's gonna roll on that supermarket job he botched last year. Mentioned Letto."

"Yeah?" Mack was exuberant. I knew who they were talking about but I didn't know Emilio Letto personally. All I knew was that he was a top Cantonello family member.

"Yep. We don't have the interview down yet. That's going to happen in the morning. Do you think you can drive by Letto's place tomorrow and make sure he's in town?"

"No problem." Mack replied.

We hung up with Davidson, excited about the prospects of bringing down a top man. I wondered how that would affect my situation, but concluded it was out of everyone's control except Cantonello's. Mack and I made plans to record a phone call that I would be making tomorrow afternoon, setting up my meeting with Vargas. He made plans to call on Letto in the morning.

The Ballad of Emilio Letto

No match for a scorching summer sun, the dense fog finally cleared by 10:30 that Tuesday morning. Mack told me later he was on his second café con leche, slowly sipping the steamed milk while his car idled down Warren Avenue's bricks.

"All I intended to do was just drive past the place and see if they were home. Before I made it to the corner, I hear this older man's voice coming from his huge bungalow's porch yelling, 'Hey Mackie! Hey Mackie! Don't embarrass me by not stopping. Come on up for a talk.' What am I supposed to do, ignore the fella?"

"I would have."

I had no taste for being social with the enemy. The whole Sam and Ralph routine was so unnecessarily pretentious.

"One of these days you're gonna learn you have to talk to these people, Bill. They end up giving you more information."

"Well go on with your story. It's not like I am going to talk to *them* on Thursday or anything."

Mack gave me that look again and continued. "All right, so I pull the car over and go up a few steps to Emilio's front porch, which was quite nice by the way."

"I'm sure it was." Mack was completely disregarding my sarcasm.

"And there he was — some supposedly tyrannical mobster that was maybe five-nine and around two hundred pounds, in a light pair of trousers and an undershirt that had a fresh coffee stain or two — inviting me for a sit-down."

"Which, of course, you did."

"He asked me how things were at the department, but it was just the generalized light stuff. When I got to him, I understood why he called me up on the porch. He said, 'Mackie, joo know ees not goin' too well for me, don'tchoo?' And I tell him I didn't know anything in particular. He went on, 'Joo know I wish things coulda been a little different with me. None of thees woulda happened.' So, again I tell him I'm not aware of exactly what…and he interrupts me. 'Joo know that business in Lakeland, no? Got messed up pretty good. They're sayin' I'm a, what did he call me… a liability.'"

"So did you ask him?"

"Ask him what?"

"Ask the guy if he'll turn state's evidence. What did you think?"

"Of course, silly. I said, 'You know we can protect you; keep you from being hit.' He turned towards me, looked me straight in the eye and said 'Joo know I cannot do this, Mackie.' I didn't quite know what to do next except console the guy."

"Oh brother. You really *are* a case. You know that, Mack?" I laughed.

"Sure, laugh. So get this…I continued by asking, 'Is it that bad?' And he replied, 'I think so, Mackie. They gave me the kiss, so that's it for me.' Bill, this guy's about to get hit and he knows it. He's accepting it!"

"Isn't that their way. What do they call it?"

"Omertà."

"Yeah, that. Once they're made they can't squeal or something. Family business and all that?" I asked.

"That's the deal. All right, I guess he's gonna get it, so I started fishing. I asked him if he knew anything about the murder of Chucky Banks. He's supposedly rumored to be involved with that, you know."

"And?"

"He laughed, 'This will go to my grave Mackie, but I can tell joo I wasn't the one that cut his throat or bashed in his face.'"

"So he knows who did it, but won't say."

"Yeah. Man, I'd love to be the one that broke *that* case." Mack happily admitted. I'm sitting on the porch with a convicted felon and known big-time family member and he's talkin' to me like father and son."

"Well, at least you got some info on the Lakeland fire. Can we get a subpoena before they get to him?" My gears began spinning.

"He really didn't admit to the act, Bill. Just knowledge, but I don't know that it's enough for a judge unless we get something corroborative from Sanchez."

"Did you get anything else from Letto?"

"Nah. I didn't stay that long…had to give Ben the information he wanted."

"What did he say?"

"Said we can't do anything until Sanchez rolls."

"That's cutting it close." I surmised.

Of course, that was an understatement. The department received a call late Wednesday evening from Tampa General Hospital's security detail. Letto's panicked wife contacted them several hours after Emilio was supposed to return from an in-town lunch. They reported her sobbing statement wherein she said Emilio uncharacteristically hugged her on the way out the door, kissed her on the lips, looked her straight in the eyes, and said he loved her. She said he hadn't done that in over thirty years, which is why she knew something was wrong. She waited until 9:30 that night just in case he wasn't off on another one of his afternoon escapades with a mistress, but he never came home. Mack called me that night with the report. It wasn't what I needed to hear just before going on the inside with Vargas.

The Flying Grasshopper

"Hey Bill, my people said you made the call, but I haven't heard the tape yet. Are you meeting him?" Lenny asked.

I knew he was as anxious as a new daddy. Penetrating any level of a mafia family was fantasyland for the FBI.

"Yeah, just a little while ago as a matter of fact."

"Well?" You could hear Lenny's excessive enthusiasm oozing.

I laughed, "Calm down Len! I'm meeting him at Lilliput's Lounge around three. Geez, can't wait on the tape can ya?"

"Is there anything else I need to hear on it?"

"Nah. All he did was give me the address, even though I already knew where the place was, and we agreed on the time. No other small talk other than his saying he and Miss Thursday were looking forward to my company."

"Miss Thursday, huh? Not pushy or anything is he? Heh! Excellent, Bill. Lilliput's? Isn't that down near the west end of LaFaye...uh...Kennedy."

"Yeah, that's the one. Just before the plaza."

We hung up and before long, it was zero hour. I threw on a decent pair of blue slacks and a short-sleeved shirt. My Smith & Wessons were whining for the adventure, but I could only take one and that would be the Airweight on the left ankle. Lenny also gave me a radio bug and a cassette tape recorder/receiver. I wondered what would happen if they found that on me. Surely, this Thursday wag would put her hands on me. *Oh man, what am I getting myself into?* Wendy would never approve of that, even if it was for official business. Curiosity. *Did I still know how to relax and keep the interest of a woman?* I guessed that tonight I would find out. *What about the bug?* I left it behind. Maybe I could get away with it when they trusted me, or perhaps when I knew for sure I wouldn't have a pair of hands exploring too many places.

It was blistering hot that day, but nothing the breezes from my topless T-bird couldn't handle. I donned my Aviators and whisked westward towards the bay, down to Kennedy and west five blocks to the lounge. I parked, stamped out a smoke, and headed through the front door that was propped wide open. I took my glasses off and allowed my eyes time to adjust to the half-lit interior.

Even though I just finished smoking, the odor inside was stronger—something in between cigars, a pipe, countless cigarettes in beer-soaked ashtrays, and fryer grease used to make grouper sandwiches. The ceiling was rather low, maybe just over seven or eight feet; just high enough for ceiling fans that helped the paltry two air conditioners that filled what used to be windows on the left wall. I'm sure they ran constantly, humming away while their condensation dripped onto the hot asphalt outside.

There were only two customers sitting at the end of a long bar towards the back watching a rare weekday afternoon baseball game. I could see down the hallway back to the kitchen. One of the doors in that hallway was open, allowing its light to cast a shadow of a person swaying back and forth as they worked a phone. The back door at the end of the hallway was also propped open for increased circulation. I walked in a little further and behind a large, square post was an older, well-dressed man showing a teenaged-looking boy how to make a drink.

"Come Che, watch me make this drink." The man said to me.

I recognized the voice and I could clearly see him now. It was Giuseppe Cantonello. I felt the tingle of uncertainty, but Cantonello eased my nervousness with his easygoing nature and, well, my own curiosity. Wendy and I weren't cocktail connoisseurs, but we knew how to make the few that pleased us. When it came to something exotic, we left that to the experts.

"Che?" I asked.

"Just a minute while I show this young man how to make a proper drink." He said.

Giuseppe was pouring something green and frothy into a cocktail shaker and, after several moments of loving agitation, poured the concoction into a martini glass.

"There, you see? Perfect." Cantonello said in a slight Sicilian accent.

"You want to try it, Che?"

"What is it?"

"It is called the Flying Grasshopper."

"I think I've heard of it."

"You may have heard of the older plain Grasshopper, but not the Flying version."

"What's the difference?"

"The original is made with equal parts Crème de menthe, Crème de cacao, and fresh cream. A nice drink for the ladies if you want to keep the breath fresh, but if you want a more romantic evening, replace the cream with a decent vodka."

"Flying. I get it. So, what's with the Che you called me?"

He smiled and handed the shaker to the young man who let no time waste in his own battle against sobriety. Cantonello laughed, "That is what I call these Chattanooga FBI agents with their poor taste in fashion."

I didn't know if I should have been offended, but I was more amused and curious. "But I am not an..."

"Oh, I know you're not one of them, detective. Yes, Angel left me alone for a moment while he and his girl ran an errand. And, this boy needed a hand learning how to properly entertain a woman."

"Fashion?"

"Yes, anyone who wears blue pants and brown shoes is either a queer or with the Bureau. Since you've got that ring, the decision is simple, no? Besides, I know where those shoes come from. Nice, but every agent in the country wears them. Easily recognizable. If you want something better, you let Angel know. He's a nice guy, you know. I don't like some of his businesses, but he is not like that. He's a nice guy."

Before the afternoon was over, I wouldn't be able to count how many times Cantonello repeated Vargas was a "nice guy". It seemed rather odd to me that the reputed King of Florida was just a regular man like anyone else. He was still on top, but his aging and the Cuban debacle took their toll. I didn't know if I had another chance, so, like a boy asking some old WWII veteran about his battle experiences, I asked Giuseppe about his trouble in Cuba.

"You're lucky I don't mind talking about that now. Ten years ago, I woulda had your knuckles bent backwards; I was so angry at that two-timing bastard Castro. I'm kidding of course, but I *was* that angry.   The government has everyone cozy after that vagabond brought over the Russians. If they only knew the whole story."

"The buzz downtown is that the CIA enlisted you for an assassination attempt."

Cantonello slowly wiped the excess green froth from the bar top and grinned. He didn't make eye contact however when he said, "You know, I had the top places down in Havana. We knew Batista might lose, so the safest thing to do was keep both sides entertained.   We gave so much money to these people...for Castro's guns. I thought it wouldn't matter who ended up in charge, we would be okay, you know."

A convertible Cadillac El Dorado motored to a stop at the front entrance. Angel Vargas climbs out of the driver's seat and walked around to the passenger side, removing Miss Thursday and a striking blond. I heard the phone conversation terminate in the back and witnessed the grand appearance of Anthony Rizzo; Cantonello's primary driver and a department legend. He gained popular infamy downtown in the late Fifties after a high-speed chase ended with him in cuffs, but only after he outran several patrolmen *in reverse*. He's not as young, but his 6'4", 240 lb physique still loomed.

"You ready, Pino?" Rizzo asked as he trudged past us at the bar.

Cantonello quietly leaned over towards Rizzo's ear and grumbled, "How many times do I have to tell you, huh? Don't call me that in front of guests."

I guess he had to keep appearances.

"Sorry Mr. Cantonello." He then helped Cantonello with his jacket and handed him his signature beige pork pie.

"Maybe we get a chance to talk some more, Che." Cantonello suggested.

Rizzo smirked when Cantonello used that name. Vargas, who was halfway groping one of the girls while entangled up against the side of the Cadillac, caught a glimpse of Rizzo's colossal frame and decided he should make haste.

"Hey, who's the blond with Angel?" Rizzo asked.

"I'm sure you will be introduced in a moment, Tony." Cantonello advised.

The old-timers didn't like it when a fella took interest in someone else's woman. It didn't matter if Vargas had one or a hundred, unless he offered otherwise, they were his.

I waited by the bar while they exchanged salutations just outside the front entrance. Vargas handed the car keys to Rizzo while Rizzo held the passenger door open for Cantonello. Rizzo then climbed into the driver's seat, cranked the car, turned on the air conditioning, and closed the powered roof. Vargas, Miss Thursday and a mysterious young woman, not much older than 22, entered the bar. Vargas noticed me, but once he removed his sunglasses, his eyes darted about the room, showing concern that there wasn't anybody watching the bar. The young man that learned how to make a grasshopper must have been a trainee, I surmised. At that moment, the men's room door opened and the young man reappeared. Vargas momentarily left his lovely company and tactfully scolded the young barkeep for leaving the register unattended.

Vargas didn't have a temper. His management etiquette dictated nurturing and guilt over fear of punishment, which was probably why he was liked by almost everyone in the industry.

"I am very sorry about this, Detective Brume." Vargas said, apologetically shaking my hand. They have me run the place, but it is not what I'd call a signature Angel Vargas establish-ment, if you know what I mean."

"For sure." I replied, with my eyes purposely fixated on his company.

"This is my friend Trudy." Vargas said as I briefly took her hand. "She is just down from Burlington, Vermont. Ever been there?"

"Can't say that I have, but they have lovely people there, it seems." I replied, catching a wisp of her freshly-shampooed locks. She giggled while I continued. "And what do you do in Burlington, Trudy?"

She giggled again, sexily pivoting from side to side. "I am in the nursing program at the university."

"A nurse! Great choice."

Impatient, Vargas made sure I wasn't being rude to his other guest. Of course, I knew she was there, and building up a little tension may have kept her unfocused. I knew why I was there.

They wanted information and weren't sure if I was corruptible. That was Thursday's job and she was ready to work.

"And, you remember Miss Thursday, of course." Vargas interrupted.

My eyes locked with hers. She seemed immediately vulnerable. A moment ago, her body language oozed confidence. Now, she was mine for the taking and I knew it. We embraced and I didn't quite give her the customary peck on the cheek, but more of an intentional partaking of her bouquet with a wetter than normal kiss. She would either wipe me off afterward or let it dry depending on her intentions. Without seeming too terribly obvious, she blushed slightly and never let her arm retract from my side. We stayed somewhat embraced all the way to a back room where Vargas had a private lounge. It was a small, but comfortable alcove replete with its own living room suit, television, card table, and several chairs. Vargas flicked on the television and found a game show for background entertainment. Even though it was an *I've Got a Secret* rerun, it covered the light drone of the air conditioner on the back wall. I led Thursday towards the couch while Vargas and Trudy made themselves comfortable on a love seat. A moment later, the young bartender appeared at the front corner taking drink orders.

"Thursday, Bill?" Vargas asked.

"Go ahead." I told Miss Thursday.

"Um. Nothing too strong."

"I just learned how to make a grasshopper. Would you like to try it?" The young man asked.

Thursday looked quizzically at me, then over towards Vargas and Trudy.

"Don't ask *me*," said Trudy. "I've never heard of those."

"Did the old man show you how to make it?" Vargas asked.
"Yes."

"Then you learned from the best." He turned back towards Thursday. "You should try it. That's a good starter."

Starter? I had the feeling this might be a long afternoon. How was I going to avoid getting drunk and making a bad decision? My tolerance was okay, having the usual game day benders with my friends, but my confidence in keeping up with barflies was shakable.

"I'll have one if Trudy has one," said Thursday.

Trudy nodded and the girls' curiosity would be satisfied. Vargas looked over towards me in anticipation of a drink order. I had to think quickly. Beer? That filled me up and made me lethargic. So did the sweet drinks. Martinis were too strong to start. I needed something athletic.

"Gin and tonic with a twist of lime."

"Excellent choice. I'll have the same." Vargas ordered.

I wasn't going to start any conversation concerning business. Whatever business Vargas had in mind for me, he would have to initiate that dialogue. I imagined that having the girls close by, the immediate strategy was to get me loosened up.

I took out a smoke and fired it up. After two drags, Thursday took it from me and sucked half the thing down her lungs. Provocatively impressive, but I wasn't that easy. When the drinks arrived after several minutes of light chat, we started paying a little more attention to each other. Trudy was exceptionally vivacious, quaffing half her drink in two gulps, but paying for it when the rush of mint hit her nose. Vargas slowly sipped his tonic, as did I. We were both sizing each other up when Thursday caught my attention by leaning into me and placing her free hand on my chest. I wasn't as hard as I was eight or so years ago, but I wasn't out of shape, either. I didn't think my father would approve of a black girl hanging on to me, but she was cute, warm, young, voluptuous, and her thin, green mustache drew me to her pillowing lips. Right there, I could have. It was a definite invitation. Something held me back. She read my hesitation and slowly licked the frothy grasshopper circularly round her those luscious lips. Oh, it was murder! I had to think quickly. I grew tired of referring to her as Miss Thursday and I felt the time was right since she was apparently there for my pleasure.

"Do I have to keep calling you Thursday, or can I get some genuineness from those marvelous lips of yours." Compliments work every time, I thought.

Thursday glanced over towards Vargas, who wasn't paying her any attention since Trudy was no longer interested in mere verbal intercourse.

"Delena, but my friends just call me Dee."

"So what do I call you?" I playfully asked.

"I'd rather you make that choice, but whisper it in my ear."

I leaned over, put my lips against her left earlobe, and whispered slowly, "Hello...Dee."

I still had it. The heat immediately began to well from within her. When a woman has her body in such close contact, hitting her broiler's button is unmistakable. I probably shouldn't have been so forward, and luckily, Trudy was excusing herself for the restroom, motioning Delena to join her. A temporary reprieve!

I was beginning to doubt my fidelity's strength. Men can say what they want to, but given the right circumstances, chivalrous claims of abstinence are nature's indulgent masquerade. Just after they were around the corner, which Vargas double-checked, he got down to business.

"You seem to be enjoying yourselves, no?"

I laughed. "More than I should, you know."

"I could never be married. Why make a vow you know you can't keep."

"Honesty is the most noble of virtues." I don't know where that piece of philosophy came from, but it slipped out. Must have been the gin. Unfortunately, the fact that I was in the room with a known mobster (flirting with one of his girlfriends no less!) made me a hypocrite. I managed a twisted smile denoting my sarcasm. It worked.

"I suppose you are here because you are curious. Curious of how you can make a decent addition to your unfortunate detective's pay, no?" Vargas inquired.

I took a long sip from my tonic and nodded.

"You must know that you won't start with anything much too important."

"I gathered as much."

"Good. These things take time. Years, in fact."

Slowly the alcohol worked its magic, but I was still in complete command. "So, what do you need?"

"Like I said, nothing much. Maybe you make sure your people look a little harder at my competition. Maybe I give you some small fish and let them be thrown back in the sea." Vargas savored his lime twist. "Maybe you let me know if I make a mistake before I make it."

"You sure you're not making one now?" I don't know why I asked the question. Perhaps I wanted to keep a jocular feel. He took it as I intended—in stride.

"I don't think so. What about you?"

"I don't think so either, but I gotta be honest with you Angel. I'm a married man, I *did* take the vows, and I actually *do* love my wife. Delena's a nice girl and all, and I don't mind playing around a little, but I can't go any further with her, understand."

Vargas smiled widely. "But of course! And, I am glad you were honest with me. You see, I don't want any more human cesspools like some of your colleagues. While they may do some favors here or there, they are completely corrupt and greedy. They make mistakes. I need people with a little more integrity. I need sharp people who think on their feet. I need someone who can maintain control of himself, like you. I am happy you told me about your wife. She has a good man."

"Ah, flattery."

Okay, so Thursday was another test I passed — well, kind of. Sure, I was married with kids, and I did love Wendy, but that moment was my weakest. If the situation were slightly different, I might have failed.

"Are you okay, Brume?" Vargas asked, apparently wondering if my mind drifted away from the subject.

"Yeah, sure. Just had a thought, that's all. Probably thinking I should not be seen around here for a while. I don't want rumors flying around the department, that is. You should've been there to see the gossip flying after you left the other day. Cops probably think I'm on the take already."

"As a matter of fact, after we finish here today, we shall probably not meet for a very, very long time." Vargas added. "And when we do, it will not take place at such a public venue."

I heard the clamor of female giggling and prattle down the hall. The girls were returning just as Vargas and I concluded business.

"Well, how about it, Bill? Can we have a harmless little affair?"

I winked and nodded as the girls entered the room. Vargas smiled and finished his cocktail. We ordered another round and talked about the Miami club scene, which Vargas had many stories about comingling with Hollywood stars and New York's finest. He winked at Delena and she turned her seductive powers down a notch. While she maintained an appearance of interest, and continued her close proximity, there was certainly less heat between us. That atmosphere was generally and genuinely friendly.

That second round was it for us. The afternoon shift was arriving and he intended taking full advantage of the two girls as soon as he could. They didn't have to say so much, but it was in their body language. We exited Lilliput's, hugging and kissing goodbye all the way. I shook Vargas' hand and told him I would be in touch next week. He nodded in agreement. I hopped into my T-bird and went directly home.

The timing couldn't have been better. The boys were down the street, playing at a friend's house. Wendy was just finishing up cleaning a sink full of dishes. I crept up behind her seductively and proceeded to make love to her with a veracity not quite seen for several years. She didn't say anything about the gin on my breath because she already knew I was undercover. She knew that if I was coming home to her and getting into her skirt I was not getting into someone else's skirt. She was indelibly practical in our marriage and I promised I wouldn't place myself in a position of danger like that ever again. After today, however, I often wondered if I really was the concrete I claimed.

Trick or Trick

"Well, I was right about one thing, Lenny. I wouldn't have gotten away with wearing a wire."

"We were wondering if you'd survive." He laughed.

"Do you have any special instructions?"

"No, not really. These things take time, you know. We're going to have to play by their rules for a while—keep them interested, and keep you out of trouble."

"So I have to lay off them?" I asked.

"Not exactly. Do as he says—lean on his competition and throw a few of his lackeys in the slammer—but keep diligence up on his operations."

The first cooler wisps of mid-October magnified my morning coffee enjoyment. It was a brief reminder of many cool summer mornings in Virginia; waking up to the aroma of frying bacon, eggs, and my parent's percolating magic. Before my mind had taken the first bite, however, I almost choked on the newspaper's front page.

Milton Grant says, "No more Halloween Trick-or-Treat"

Interim Mayor said on Monday, "We don't live in times that allow it anymore. It is too dangerous", hoping parents would store their children at home on the night of the 31st, and end the tradition of trick-or-treating. "They should have costume parties and get-togethers instead."

When asked about the suggestion, Tampa Police Chief Henry Lozello said, "This idea is great. Problems would be eliminated in traffic accidents, night crimes and less children on the streets."

"Wendy, get a load of this. Lozello and the Mayor want to end Halloween!"

"What?"

"Come here and read this, you're not going to believe it."

Wendy had finished with folding some of the boy's clothes and drifted over for a look.

"That's insane! Talk about political suicide." She said in complete amazement.

"They're making it easy for the competition, aren't they?" I laughed.

"I suppose so!" Wendy replied, giving me a light nuzzle on the back of my neck.

Of course, a week later, voters elected a new mayor and it wasn't Milton Grant. I still missed Gregorri and didn't see any candidate I thought worthy except a long shot named Dickerson. The city's voters decided on an insurance salesman named Richard K. Pike. We didn't have anything against the man, but some of his connections made us wonder. The fact that he let Lozello remain chief was a pretty big clue.

During the holidays, the department was primarily concerned with thefts. People were trying to save money, but gasoline was creeping upward and that meant higher prices all the way around. Naturally, folks gravitated towards the lesser expensive items or gave up entirely. The new mayor saw fit in having Lozello skim detectives specifically for shutting down pimpless whores, massage parlors, and vacating the homeless, since our skid rows were overflowing. Most of those operations were competing with the mob or wouldn't submit to their protection schemes, so they targeted those first. When the families saw the progress, they rewarded the mayor with enough budget for a brand new fleet of patrol cars. Lenny called me and delivered some disquieting news.

"Bill, the latest is, your chief has taken residency at a home owned by Cantonello. His name's not registered with the property, but we know he's been using the place as a second residence."

"Where?"

"Off Boulevard."

"Everyone's over there. Heck, that's just down the street from me."

"You mind driving by?"

"Yes. If I'm spotted, it'll get back to Vargas. They won't like it. I'm only supposed to watch his comps. What about Mack?"

"You're right. I'll see if he will."

Mack took Lenny's offer and confirmed Lozello's existence in the neighborhood. The problem was, Mack was spotted by half the residents on that block who were either friendly to the Cantonellos, or were actual relatives. Word evidently leaked back to the chief because the very next Monday, the second week of 1975, Lozello shuffled the entire department and disbanded the Criminal Intelligence Unit permanently. We were all headed for reassignment and had little choice in the decision-making. Mack and I wasted no time contacting Lenny and Davidson about the shakedown. Ears were everywhere it seemed, so we decided to meet at a small roadside ice cream parlor in Clearwater. Mack and I rode together, but when we arrived, only Lenny was visible.

"Davidson dropped me a line just before I hit the door. Said he's tied up in a deposition. Are you both okay?"

Mack went first. "I've been through these before; it's not that big of a problem for me really."

"Where are you being assigned?"

"I had a choice, but I thought the radio room would be best right now."

"That's perfect actually." Lenny thought for a moment. "Yes, you could monitor just about everything from there, couldn't you?"

"That was my thinking." Mack replied.

"And what about you, Bill?"

"I've not decided yet. They want me in Burglary but I'm sticking with Vice. I Figure I can still keep up with the boss' shenanigans that way."

"What about Lozello?"

"That's who I meant."

I watched Lenny become distracted with Mack's feverish attack on his ice cream. "Ah. Okay. Mack, what is that?" Lenny asked.

Mack broke concentration and licked off the mustache he recently grew out of infatuation with Dennis Weaver's character from *McCloud*. Mack's hunting buddy, Terry Perkins, even told me he had the matching coat and cowboy hat!

"Butter Pecan. My wife got me hooked on it. Rather tasty."

"Evidently." Lenny replied drolly.

By February, most of the arson investigations were wrapping up due to The Match's redacted testimonies. When I received a call to help with a homicide investigation that tied in with another competing lounge to Vargas', I thought someone was sending me a message. I thought they were sending everyone a message.

On a chilly afternoon, with a brilliant blue sky and breezy conditions, someone decided that the owner of Patriot's Pub on Columbus' west side made a mistake. Broken glass appeared scattered in a 30 ft radius all around the front step. Blood and matter covered most of the shards, and the body of a man laid upon them, practically decapitated by a large caliber weapon. Nothing much remained above his shoulder except the remains of his shattered neck, half of his jaw, and half an ear. The rest had been scattered up against the entryway, including a mostly-intact scalp and skullcap. The bartender told me he and a squatty Italian owner named Arnold Botticelli were loading in a new glass top for the bar when two men drove up with skidding tires just a few feet away. From the car's rear window protruded the barrel of a 12-guage shotgun and, as soon as his boss turned around while holding the heavy glass, they exploded his melon.

Judging by the carnage, I concluded the hitmen used a deer slug. Birdshot would have only peppered his face and might not even have killed the poor bastard. Buckshot would have destroyed his face completely, but only a deer slug could make a man's skull completely explode. Forensics was busy surveying the scene, so I decided to locate the missing bullet, venturing inside for a look.

Logically, if the bullet managed to make it through the man's skull and into the front entrance, its trajectory inside the building would be limited. The back wall opposite the front entrance was only twenty-five or so feet back, and in its middle stood a jukebox. Its glass window was broken, and the needle was stuck at the scratchy end of a warped-sounding 45 record. I walked up, looked inside, and there it was; a bloody lead slug, slightly flattened on one side, spinning around the middle of Bachman-Turner Overdrive's "You Ain't Seen Nothin' Yet" single.

After a lengthy pause staring at the record, my eyes drifted upwards toward the back corner of the jukebox. The vendor's sticker was from "Tampa Entertainment Partners, Inc." That was Carlos Salazar's company—Sal Tresedici's one and only competitor. That night I tried to locate Vargas and see if this was something I needed to clarify. After work, and after the boys ended their evening, I made a call to Randy's trying to locate him. I knew Lenny had my line tapped, so if there was anything said, his crew would catch it. Unfortunately, his bartender told me he wasn't there and that I might be able to catch him at another bar. He gave me the number for The Trade's Restaurant located on the other side of East Bay, down by the phosphate docks. When I called and asked for Vargas, the man on the other end of the line paused for a few moments, then relayed that Vargas would not speak to me over the phone, but I was welcome to join him over there. We hung up; I took a finishing drag off a Winston and threw on a decent shirt before heading back out. Wendy looked concerned, but she was too tired to give me any grief, so we just kissed briefly and gazed into each other's eyes before she patted my butt and pushed me out the door.

Cruising past the shipyards and crossing over a chilled East Bay, which forced me to turn on my aging T-Bird's heater, the dim lights of a solitary establishment slowly came into view across the water. Wendy and I ventured here once before when a friend suggested they had the best deviled crabs in town. He was right, but the place was a little out of our way, so we didn't make the trip often. The parking lot was still made of crushed seashells, and the owners recently refurbished the old wooden building's façade. They kept the original wood floor, however, and it creaked slightly at the front entrance. At the far corner of the dining room sat Angel Vargas and Anthony Rizzo, finishing the last of a smoked mullet dinner while enjoying a beer and smokes. They motioned me over and I sat down after a round of handshaking.

"I hope you didn't mind driving out here. You see, I suspect the phone lines, especially yours, are tapped." Vargas wasted no time in his opinion.

"Completely understandable."

"What can I do for you today, Detective Brume?" Vargas asked.

His demeanor seemed relaxed, but his body language seemed twitchy. I believed he knew exactly why I was there, but in his heart, he would rather avoid the question I had to ask.

"Did I miss something?"

"What do you mean?" Vargas asked.

"I mean, did I miss someone you wanted me to look after?"

"You'll have to forgive me, Bill. I still don't follow you." Vargas maintained his evasiveness.

"You don't know anything about what happened earlier at the Patriot?"

Vargas wiped his mouth from the beer he quaffed. I could tell he knew by the way he rolled his eyes. I was looking straight at them when I asked about the Patriot. I didn't know why he kept up the charade.

"What happened at the Patriot?"

I glanced at Rizzo in disbelief. He maintained his distant glare. It was the kind of look someone gave when they were actually paying attention to you, but didn't necessarily like what you were saying.

"Botticelli got his head blown off. Wasn't anything left but his neck and an ear."

Vargas didn't like the graphic description. His complexion grew slightly pale. Evidently, violence was not something he enjoyed—especially the hands-on part. He tried to hide his disgust with a display of remorse, but I think he knew why I was asking.

"That's terrible. Arnold was a nice guy."

I laughed. "Evidently someone had a different opinion."

"To be sure." Vargas agreed. "So why are you asking me about poor Arnold?"

"Thought you might take a notion that I wasn't paying attention to the right people or something."

Vargas looked around the dining room, making sure someone new hadn't taken a seat too near. "Bill, relax. Have I not said how much I appreciated your help downtown?"

Vargas was, of course, speaking about the massage parlors and pimpless whores we effectively recruited under his umbrella.

"Yes, and we thank you very much." I referred to his gracious payments. "This matter caught me by surprise, see. Gut reaction. Instead of their having an accidental fire or a friendly visit, there's been a change of method. Gone Chicago. I got it."

"You're ahead of yourself, Detective."

"Well, am I wrong?"

Vargas shrugged. "What am I supposed to say? These things are not up to me."

"Well, what do you want me to do, Angel—look the other way? I got the feeling someone wanted me there for some reason, that's why I'm here."

"Bill, if someone was trying to tell you something, I would be the one to do it, and you'd hear directly from me." Vargas swiftly countered. "And I don't want you doing anything you aren't already doing. At least, for now."

I finished half of a glass of water, tamped out a butt, said goodbye and walked outside to my car. I paused for a moment and lit another Winston while staring at the dilapidated signs across the street marking the entrance to the old Auto Park drive-in theater. I was feeling somewhat lost, so I climbed in my car and motored home. Wendy met me at the door with a message to call "the office". The number she handed me was Lenny's, who was waiting patiently for my call.

"Bill? I understand you worked the Patriot shooting earlier. That true?"

"Yeah."

"Thoughts?"

"Vargas is dirty but he's not giving anything up. Said basically it was over my head and that he didn't make those decisions."

"That's consistent with conspiracy. Murder, at that. Good work!"

"Thanks Len, but I'm a little worried."

"How so?"

"That scene I worked this afternoon. Something's fishy about it. They didn't need me there. Homicide and forensics had it covered. I get the feeling someone wanted me there to send a message."

"I see." Lenny pondered.

"You don't want a grand jury indictment yet, do you?" I asked, since Lenny seemed gratified.

"Oh, no. Not yet. As far as I'm concerned, we still want two more levels and your boss. You're very close, so you have to practice extra caution, Bill."

"Do you have anything useful on Lozello lately?"

"No, but one of my guys mentioned something about his going regularly to the University of Tampa's campus at night. Nothing else."

"Okay, Lenny. I'll see if that produces anything. Good Night."

"'Night."

We hung up and that was the last contact I had with Lenny for a few weeks. As far as I was concerned, the mission objective just changed from Vargas to Lozello. I immediately started a new surveillance plan involving the chief's college activities and his wife's employer, Central Stevedores.

I received a package in the mail from Washington a few days later. Inside was a brand new Nikon F2 35mm camera, a standard 50mm lens, a Nikkor 300mm telephoto lens, four rolls of high speed film, and instructions for proper exposure. I thought, *My God this is over $1000 in camera equipment!* There was a letter from Lenny stating that the gear would be especially useful if I could use it effectively.

"You know the old adage, 'It's not what you know; it's what you can prove in court!'" He wrote.

I bought a case for the outfit and kept it in my car, but not before taking some test shots of the family. By the end of the roll, I had most of the exposure scenarios that Lenny instructed might become necessary. I also had some great new shots of the boys and Wendy. That camera came into heavy use over the next few months, but when I needed it most, the blasted contraption was nowhere around.

Set Up

The evening turned rather gusty while Mack and I waited. The sabal palms' leaves clattered and folded, while others found their way to the University of Tampa's grounds. The temperature was only a mild fifty-eight degrees, but blowing in straight off the gulf proved chilling.

"Here." Mack said, holding a dark blue jacket.

"What's this?" I asked.

"See if it'll fit. I keep an extra in the car for times like these. Ann or someone's always underprepared."

Mack handed me a fleece-lined windbreaker and relief was immediate. "Thanks!"

"My mother-in-law works at Speedline. She gives us all a new one every year."

I usually wore a sports jacket, but that wasn't cutting it tonight. The temperature was also making my camera's metal body and lens finder frigid propositions. Around 9:45 that evening, through the heat distortions of our car's hood, I snapped Lozello holding a briefcase while conversing with several others at the building's front steps. A younger female, carrying a purse, textbook, and notebook, walked by our car. Mack, thinking quickly, hopped out and asked her a few questions. I hid the camera temporarily in the front floorboard and then glanced over my shoulder catching Mack flirtatiously chat with the young woman before climbing back into the driver's seat, reaching for our coffee thermos. I've not seen Mack's bubbling overconfidence in quite some time, so the fact that he was taking his sweet time pouring a fresh cup meant the revelation from the woman would be most entertaining.

"He's lecturing." Mack spoke after a long draw across his cup's steam.

"Lecturing? I asked. "On what?"

"She didn't tell me."

"Isn't that a..." I pondered while Mack continued.

"Conflict of interest? Possibly. If he's drawing a paycheck, the local PBA might take an interest. I have several friends in there; some of which could probably tell me if he's double dipping.

He was. When Mack confirmed this with his old sociology instructor, who also happened to be married to the school's disbursement officer. Mack didn't waste any time bringing this to Lenny or Davidson before going straight to the Policeman's Benevolent Association. He was still rightfully sore about the department shuffling and his Florida Intelligence Unit's disbandment. There were several high-ranking members inside the PBA sympathetic to the reshuffle, and they didn't much care for Lozello, either. A claim was filed, the city council met, and it was determined that the chief and two other senior officers were violating their charter. In record fashion, the chief lost his part-time gravy before the news leaked to the media.

I don't know how, but word got back to Lozello that Mack and I were the ones responsible for his embarrassment. I figured it came from some gossip at the PBA. Granted, he should have notified the PBA more anonymously, but Mack usually took the direct route. One thing police work teaches you is the removal of intimidation. Packing a little heat never hurt, but just about every detective paid for his badge in casualties of the flesh.

Lenny and Davidson didn't mind, either. As far as they were concerned, Lozello's side-job wasn't a RICO offense and bared little weight, other than bolstering their eventual character assassination in court. In fact, both Lenny and Davidson were grateful for Lozello's distraction while they formulated strategy after the department's shakeup.

Mack and I walked around with renewed confidence. These people weren't invincible, even though they constantly portrayed themselves as such. And so it went, back and forth for the next two weeks. Our punishment came in the form of working late calls. Just after the beginning of March, I had worked several long nights straight, dealing with a growing stream of drugged-up whiners crying about their arrests. At my weakest moment at the end of a long shift, my integrity was again tested.

No one heard the screams of a plain-clothed detective from the concrete parking lot behind headquarters. At least, no one that I noticed. I saw four legs dancing wildly around the other side of a plain car. When I rounded the last fender, a handcuffed Hispanic man was on top of someone, beating them frantically with a fist composed from both hands. I didn't think. I reacted, jumping him from behind and throwing him up against the chain-linked fence behind the car. The man attempted to bite my shoulder, and I was without a nightstick. Short of pulling out my revolver, my adrenaline-rushed anger sent several blows to the man's midsection. I never noticed his defense with the cuffs. If my hand made contact with any part of those, it meant breaking something. I don't know if I would have felt it, either. He gasped for air and fell to his knees in complete pain. I uncuffed one of his hands, threw him to the ground on his stomach, and then recuffed both hands so he couldn't use them again. I then wiped the sweat off my face and went back around to the other side of the car where a policeman was recovering. I stopped cold for a moment when I caught his severely scuffed face.

Detective John Robert Skitter wiped some blood from his lower lip and laughed. "Bet you didn't think your night would end like this, huh?"

I didn't know what to say. *Skitter? The karate expert?* All I knew was, if I knew it was Skitter before I arrived, the prisoner would have been given more time.

"Jesus H. Christ, Skitter! What the hell's going on?"

He didn't say anything; he was still catching his breath. His prisoner, on the other hand, managed more than a moan.

"The son-of-a-bitch ripped me off!"

"You shut your mouth!" Skitter yelled frantically.

"Well, did you?" I asked.

Skitter turned towards me with the glare of hatred. "Did I what?"

"Did you rip the guy off, like he said?"

"Yeah, check him. I had $300 on me and that son-of-a-(cough)-bitch took it from me, man!"

"Skitter, you know I can't do anything about this, but if I see you showing up with a new watch tomorrow, I just might. You got enough trouble as it is, don't you?"

"Good luck with that, ace. You just wait, this ain't over."

"What's that supposed to mean?" I got in his face, but he backed down, not saying another word.

"Look, I'll try and make you a deal. You get the FBI off my back and I'll get Lozello off of yours." Skitter snidely referred to the department's internal feuding.

"I'm sorry. What?" I wanted Skitter's clarification.

"You get the FBI looking the other way from me and I'll tell the chief that this was in self defense."

I became enraged at his questioning my professional integrity. I calmly uttered through my clenched teeth, "You know damn well that I was rescuing a fellow officer, Skitter."

His sarcasm continued. "I'm not so sure about that, Brume. But I'll guess we'll find out."

I should have known they'd put the fix on the Hispanic. The following Monday, I'm called directly up to the Chief's office. When the door flew open, I saw Skitter seated in front of Lozello's desk next to an empty chair. I took my seat and Lozello commenced his fallacy-ridden Spanglish tirade.

"Seems we got ourselves a poco problema, cabelleros. I've got a real piece-o-dirt in holding downstairs with two cracked ribs claiming—how did he call it?—'Brutalidad'."

"You must be joking." I laughed.

"No, no. He does have himself two broken ribs and they treated him for that at the infirmary before bringing him back to holding. Did joo do it, Brume?"

"No!" I shouted.

"You didn't hit the guy?" Lozello asked again, glancing towards Skitter. "This detective here says he saw you do it."

I glared angrily at Skitter. "Yeah, I hit the guy in the stomach and knocked the wind out of him, but I never hit the man's ribs."

"I find that hard to believe, Brume. How else could this have happened?"

"Well, why don't you ask Skitter!"

I could tell it was a set up and now I had to see it through because there wasn't much else to do at this point. Half the department rumored Lozello was getting rid of the good cops systematically. I shrugged it off as paranoid hearsay. Now I knew.

"I asked Detective Skitter and he told me a pretty funny little story, Brume. Joo wanna hear it?"

"I don't know what nonsense this dirtbag told you, but I know it's a lie." I growled.

"Oh, wait. You're gonna love this." I looked at Skitter right in the eye while Lozello outlaid the most outrageous claim. "Seems our dear Detective Skitter has interests within the federal level. Enough so, it landed him a grand jury subpoena this morning, so he tells me. And then when I asks him about it, he tells me you'd get the FBI off his back if I would get off yours."

"Ha! I never told him that, chief. In fact, he told *me* that very thing last time I saw him. He's lying."

"Am not, Brume. Don't come after me because you broke that man's ribs!" Skitter yelled.

"I didn't break that man's ribs and you know it. I'm guessing you cracked a couple and told him you'd break more if he didn't roll on me. Heck, chief, the prisoner even told me Skitter ripped him off for $300." I turned back towards Skitter. "I saved your sniveling little ass and this is how you play it?"

"Knock it off, Brume." Lozello sternly scrapped. "I think *you're* lying!" He yelled.

I sat back down and for once, my clarity in an intense situation played well.

"He's the one lying, Chief and I can prove it easily with one phone call."

"Oh yeah? To whom?" Lozello barked.

"I'm not the one making the call, Chief. You are. You call any polygraph technician you want and we'll settle this matter right now."

Skitter jumped straight out of his chair. "I want my lawyer!"

Chief Lozello contained what should have been his typical leery nature and asked, "And who is that, Skitter?"

"Barry Lunsford."

"Then go get him." Lozello ordered.

Skitter, picked himself up and scrambled hurriedly through the chief's door. I turned back around and Lozello had a scowl on his face.

"You're both lying." He snarled.

"I'm not lying, Chief. Your liar just left this office, and when I hit him with the polygraph test, you should have known."

"I'm not going to hit Skitter with a lie detector test, Brume. I'm going to hit *you* with the test."

"What?" The demand surprised me.

"You can't do that, Chief. It's illegal."

"If it's illegal, why did joo just ask me to test Skitter, huh?"

"Ah, this is incredible..." I mumbled. "For his reaction!"

"Yeah, Brume; I knew that. 'Liars always refuse' is the saying, no? Well, what about you, eh? You will submit to the test by this Thursday or I'll have your badge."

I got up and left the room. The others told me later that every glass window in every door on the three floors adjacent Lozello's rattled when I slammed his door. I would have felt better if his window crashed violently to the floor in my anger, but alas, it didn't. I had to take comfort that others were, at least, aware of a problem.

Of course, everyone in my circle was aware of my dilemma. Davidson was sympathetic to my situation and had agreed to represent me if they actually carried through with the firing. He warned me that the process would take some time, however. When the city was a litigant in a losing case, the courts naturally dragged their feet, figuring any funds they kept in the bank for any length of time would draw interest.

Mack was visibly angry when I gave him the news that afternoon. He promised that we would nail the bastard and all this would be over before too long. All we had to do was finish making our case and get to the grand jury.

Lenny was actually delighted. I didn't know what to make of his reception at first, but he started laughing hysterically when I gave him the news.

"You don't worry about a thing, Bill. Let them fire you. You'll just have more time to spend working for me," he said.

The pats on the back were encouraging, but the logistics of it all hit home when I spoke to Wendy later that night. She was starting to grow weary of the whole situation and feared mostly for my health. She had a great job with Maas Brothers and made more money than I. It was enough to get by, and I was sure the case would break with a reinstatement and, as my daydreaming allowed, a tidy promotion. Still, she cried on my shoulder in worry. We had both gotten used to our situation, but she was feeling the tremors of an impending earthquake.

Regardless of Davidson's legal specter, I was brought up to recently-promoted *Captain* Wexler's office where he demanded my badge for not obeying a direct order to take the polygraph. I had no problem handing it over. That was it. The City of Tampa Police Department fired me.

Flying Solo

There was a certain relief in my freedom from the department. All the protocols were gone and I answered to nobody's schedule but my own. All of my personal connections were still there if needed, and I was also mostly free from obligations I made with Vargas' pact. My only valid concern was money, or lack thereof. Lenny kept me supplied with petty cash for use in operations, but there was technically no salary paid. I was not on the federal payroll and carried no GS grade. I was an extraordinary informant in qualification, but an ordinary informant nonetheless.

I started thinking about scoring and skimming dealers that I knew carried large amounts of cash. It was dangerous, but a good skim or two and I'd have a year's salary. Catch 'em off guard, call the uniforms and show them *most* of the money. The problem was, it could get back to the department if the dealers complained about the amount. They never actually claimed any amounts because the higher it was, the dirtier they looked. It was perfect. There was another problem, however. Sooner or later, it would get back to Vargas, which could prematurely ruin Davidson's case. Ben wanted Cantonello, Tresedici, and Lozello. The way everything was set up, however, none of those guys would ever share any legal exposure. They must make a mistake. Making mistakes were rare. They usually only happened when someone got greedy or made a provocative gesture. I began theorizing how someone in their position could make such a mistake. How could I provoke the organization into making a strategic error? My gears ground for several days and I finally decided that the mob classically made their own mistakes. If Mack and I continued diligence on the organization, sooner or later, they would come to us. I didn't have a long wait.

Tampa's lounge wars began well over a decade ago and the small battles were sporadic at best. There were small-time murders reminiscent of Botticelli's along the way, but most of the time the owners kept it less personal. Arson was the preferred method because the owners received the message and their insurance companies picked up the tab. On some occasions, the owners allegedly called up the people they thought were culpable and thanked them. As it turned out, Botticelli's execution, as I feared, was just the beginning of their more direct methodology.

Lenny phoned me late on an April afternoon with the news. His team recorded a session involving Vargas and a suspected professional assassin named Guillermo Mendez from Fort Lauderdale.

"Never heard of him." I said.

"One of our agents heard Vargas refer to him as Santa Claus. That ring a bell?"

I thought about it for a moment. "No. But I suppose you're going to tell me why Vargas calls him Santa Claus."

"Sorry no, I was hoping *you* could." Lenny replied. "Regardless, Santa's coming to town and I don't really care if the bastard knows who's naughty or nice."

"Funny." I said.

"Seriously. The point is, who's on his list."

"You think he had something to do with Botticelli?" I asked.

"We're not sure. The guy likes shotguns, but so does half the underworld since they're untraceable."

"Shotguns, huh." Of course, the sight of Botticelli's decapitated corpse flashed in my mind. "Brutally effective."

"Right. I am letting Mack know about this too, of course. You guys acquire any knowledge, don't hesitate calling me."

I signed off with Lenny and it wasn't even a full week before Mack was calling for a meeting. He swung by my house with a tape recorder and played a copy of a frantic emergency call from a vending company proprietor named Carlos Louis Salazar — the same company who owned the jukebox at Patriot's Pub.

"*This* is an interesting specimen, Bill. Have a listen." Mack excitedly presented the recording.

I noticed him annoyingly survey my reactions, even anticipating them before something dreadful occurred. This was the same reason I made a rule with Wendy; never watch a movie the other has already seen. We loved experiencing new things together. The tape, however, was something I never wanted Wendy's ears partaking.

Mack depressed the Play button and the tape's hissing drama began.

> [click]
> "P-p-please.   Someone…please send a car over here."
> "What is your emergency, sir?"
> "Just, please, can joo just send a car over here?"
> "Sir, please state your name and address."
> "Oh, God! There he goes again. Get down! Ayos mio! W-what?"
> "Sir, you need to give me your name and address."
> "T-t-thees is Carlos Salazar at my c-c-company T-Tampa Entertainment. Oh God! He gonna…"
> (loud explosion and glass breaking)
> "Sir? Sir?"
> "Y-y-yeah?"
> "Okay Mr. Salazar, I am sending a unit over to you, but I need to know what's going on so our people aren't in any danger, okay?"
> "Oh dear God, l-l-lady, can't joo hear the fuckin' gun?"
> "You're being shot at, Mr. Salazar?"
> "Jes!"
> "Who is shooting at you, Mr. Salazar?"
> "I don't know dees, woman. All I know is eets some white car with a one a dem double shotguns p-poking out from the back window."
> "Mr. Salazar, there is a patrol on the way to your location. Can you stay on the line with me?"
> "Jes!"
> "You said it was a white sedan?"
> "Jes. Four doors, white."
> "Do you know the make, or maybe a tag number?"
> "Hey lady, joo think I'm sitting here with a fuckin' binoculars?"
> "No, Mr. Salazar, I'm just trying to help. So, no make or tag?"

"No...wait. Chevy maybe. I don't know. Joo know
I'm behind a wall here. The last time I looked, dey
almost tooken my head off! Wait...I think dey gone.
I hear the siren. Aye Dios!"
[click]

Mack turns off the recorder and asks, "What do you think?"

"I think shotgun."

"Anything else?"

"Yeah. A couple of things, actually. First, it means the
shooter's likely Lenny's Santa Claus. Second, it means he's not as
professional as they said; he's rather sloppy, in fact. My guess is,
he's rather timid and lacks confidence. Third, and this is my
personal favorite, it means the likely conspirative kingpin is none
other than Salvatore Tresedici."

"Excellent! I deduced the same, with the exception of the
insight on the shooter's lacking confidence. Nice touch, and I fully
agree."

"I guess the Radio Room's not so bad after all, eh?"

"Nope. Just about everything's going through me, but I still
miss the interviews."

"Think you'd get much more out of Salazar?"

"Not really, but he may have some other stories tying John's
motive."

"John?" Mack's sudden use of that name caught me off guard.

"Tresedici. Wait. You don't know that old joke? As long as
you worked at the department?" Mack was stunned in surprise.

"Joke? I guess that one slipped by."

Mack shook his head and laughed. "Tresedici. That's Italian
for three sixteen. Some of the immigrants changed their names to
numbers back in the early 1900s, and they hate it when you call
them by their number. His is three sixteen but instead of the
numbers, we just call him John."

"From the bible verse."

"Exactly."

"And it drives him crazy." I guessed.

"Nothing funnier than witnessing a Sicilian temper."

"I'll remember that."

Mack and I relayed a copy of the tape to Lenny, who was
morbidly pleased with Tresedici's inclusion. I say morbidly
because it comes at Salazar's expense. Apparently, he was a

marked man, and if we played this bait correctly, the second man on the mob's totem pole was ours.

"What about Cantonello?" I asked.

"Word is, he's down in Costa Rica, sunning his Sicilian beak. Our people in Miami are working on a tax case, but you know how accountants work. The forensics will take several years before we have an airtight case."

"What's going on in Costa Rica?"

"Don't you know? Lenny looked surprised. I was getting used to this, however.

"Gee, um, no, Len."

Lenny laughed boisterously. "Why, it's the new Havana!"

"Really."

"Well, not quite. They are setting up some casinos and hotels but not on the same scale. Most of the mob's money moved to Vegas, but if you want the climate, Costa Rica. It's not so much for the gambling though. It's another staging area for the cocaine coming up from Colombia."

"And Cantonello's been down there how long?" I asked.

"Off and on about two years now." Lenny replied.

"But I just saw him a few months ago."

"Like I said, off and on. He visits Tampa and Miami regularly, but most of the time, he's down there. He's either paranoid about our investigation or helping with the narcotics. Either way, it's a matter of time."

"Okay, so what do I need to be concentrating on right now?"

"Same as you were doing. Stay on top of Lozello and Vargas."

Lenny handed me an old mug shot of Santa Claus. It wasn't what I expected from his Hispanic surname, and I immediately decided he was a straight European descendant. His hair was light brown in color and longish, covering three-quarters of his ears and highlighting his long sideburns. His eyes were as blue as mine and he had fair skin. One feature that stuck out, literally, was his nose. It was slightly wider than normal and bulbous. From the shot, I thought he may have been an alcoholic, but the photograph could have been taken while he was drunk. He also appeared in the casual attire that became synonymous with the '70s. His denim jacket over a striped T-shirt echoed so much. *Sloppy*.

Mack told me the department ran extra patrols by Salazar's company and house for nearly a month. After nothing else happened, the patrols ceased. That wasn't the end however. Almost two months later, Mack called me in the middle of a family dinner, telling me Salazar was in the hospital with third degree burns and shrapnel from his car exploding. If at first...

The next day Lenny called, and his voice carried one of the most succinct and terse tones I haven't heard since working with my old FTO.

"Bill, I need you to meet me at my field office ASAP."

"Something wrong?"

"No. But you need to hear a new tape from a recent interrogation with The Match.

Of course, I wasted no time hopping on my old Triumph and scooting downtown.

Lenny flicked on the tape player and the middle of a conversation crackled in a speaker.

> [click]
> "So, you think you can get me the good stuff?"
> "I got you the gun you wanted, didn't I?"
> "Yeah, but I can check a damn gun. I can't check your merchandise without gaining too much attention. You know what I mean?"
> "My guy's good. Take it or fuckin' leave it."
> [click]

"Who was that?" I asked.

"That was The Match talking with, we think, Guillermo Mendez."

"Santa Claus?"

"We think so."

"Sounds like they were talking about explosives to me. And, let me guess — these were used yesterday on Salazar?"

"Likely. That's not the worst of it, though." Lenny reached for the tape player.

> [click]
> "No, that's fine, man. You know what'll happen if it turns out no good." (the voice laughs maniacally)
> "Yeah. You gonna make me number six on that list. So fuckin' what. I know it's good."

"You just watch that smart mouth of yours or I'm gonna move you to number two ahead of that lawyer Davidson."
[click]

"Holy Jesus. You've got to be kidding me!" My mouth was completely agape.

I peered deeply into Lenny's eyes. They were as cold and emotionless as some of the veteran pilots' at MacDill during Vietnam. He said nothing.

"Well, Jesus, Lenny. It sounds like they've gone and made a… Well, why do they want Ben out of the way?

"Did you forget Vargas is into him for forty large?"

"Guess so. But that ain't enough, if you ask me."

"He represented Vargas on numerous occasions. Several of his underlings, too. Ben never reached the level of Paul Gravina's fame and (coughs) fortune, mind you, but he professionally defended several of Gravina's underlings."

"Gravina? Cantonello and Mollar's lawyer? You're making me sick."

"I know. It's a tough concept, Bill, but remember—they consider themselves consummate legal professionals following their oaths implicitly. They're not bad people."

"Come on, Lenny. Not bad people? Gravina represents a known mafia kingpin and a union thug. Just because it was their legal right to represent their sorry asses doesn't make it okay in my opinion, oath or not. What if an innocent man rots in prison because one of these *professionals* successfully defends a guilty murderer? You're telling me they can walk around with a clear conscience because of some oath?"

"Believe me, Bill, I completely understand. I think it's academic in Ben's case, however. You know he's going after these guys and their panicking to the point of assassination, supposedly."

"Why now?"

"Convenience. The report mentions Vargas still owes Ben some legal fees. Loss of narcotics traffic, having his nightclubs under constant surveillance, his bosses giving him heat. The motive's there."

"If you ask me, Ben knows he danced with the devil and wants his hands washed." I said.

"I don't want to speculate on Ben's motives."

Lenny wanted my concentration focused on Vargas, so we spent the next several minutes discussing Santa Claus. I stared at his picture and fixated on his bulbous nose.

"What's the dope on this one, anyway?" I asked.

"Mendez is originally from Medellín, Colombia. He immigrated to Miami with his family in 1962, but his parents are deceased. The father was into gambling and prostitutes. His mother was a bolita writer. One day in 1966, the father came home drunk and found the old lady sexually gratifying a young runner, who escaped through their kitchen door before the old man blasted him with his pistola. Mendez comes by for a visit two days later and discovers his mother in the middle of the living room floor covered with blowflies and their maggots. The father shot her no less than five times; twice in the heart, once in the head, once in the mouth, and once in her vaginal area. The old man saved the last round for his left temple."

Lenny placed his finger on the photograph and continued. "So, young Mendez there placed the report, had them buried, and has been in and out of the Miami-Dade system ever since."

"What offenses?"

"Mostly violence related. Bar fights and accusations of extortion. He did a year for robbery back in '68."

"Only a year?"

"Report said he robbed a lounge down in Hialeah, and they were gonna give him five, but he flipped on the joint's smalltime marijuana dealings and they reduced the sentence."

"Then he should have been dead or at the very least hurt badly as soon as he was released." This was usually the case for rats.

"Not if he was doing a favor for someone else. I fathom he was only attacking the competition."

"And got caught! How did that happen, anyway?"

Lenny handed me the report and pointed towards the pertinent paragraph.

"Says right there. 'Apprehended 3:42 a.m. Located in female restroom.'"

"The guy's an idiot!" I laughed.

"Yeah." Lenny agreed, rolling his eyes and sighing. "But he's been off the radar for the last five years, until a few months ago when the pictures were taken. Polk County picked him up off the side of Interstate 4—passed out drunk with serial-less .25 auto on the front seat."

I threw up a finger, interrupting Lenny. "The .25 was made before 1968, right?"

Lenny acknowledged affirmatively. "Of course. If it wasn't, they'd have him on a five-year felony possession. He wasn't on probation at the time, so they had to let him go."

"Everything you've told me about this guy so far says "sloppy", Len. He missed Salazar..."

"Barely." Lenny included pointedly.

"...Okay. Barely. He blew his robbery, he was caught drunk on the side of a major interstate, and his appearance... He's an amateur!"

"That should make him easy to find, which is what my guys are working on. In the meantime, I want you to flush him out in the open. Lean on Vargas' operations a little, but also keep up surveillance on your old boss."

"What about Ben?" I asked. After all, they were after *him*.

"We're running protection for Ben, don't worry. Mendez won't have a chance." Lenny assured me not to concern myself so much with Ben Davidson, whom I now regarded with slight animosity.

Two more arsons and another shotgun volley ended April's tumultuous infighting amongst the nightclub owners. Although no owners died in the skirmishes, their anxieties became heightened. Vargas hired two extra bodyguards and had office cots installed at every location. He paid managers a little extra if they slept on premises and made sure a girl or two made their jobs a little more interesting during the wee hours. Some of his competition wasn't so brilliant, however.

The first arson was rather simple. The place closed at 1 a.m. on weekday evenings, and by 2:30, it was on the ground smoldering. The second incident was another matter. The owner enjoyed much of the same business savvy as Angel Vargas and shared the same epiphany, implementing an overnight watchman at his establishment. Unfortunately, the man lacked common sense. He had iron bars installed on every door and every window to keep undesirables out at night. When he locked their deadbolts from outside, however, he doomed his poor manager to a premature cremation.

Last week Mack shared some photos gleaned from a friendly violent crimes detective involving a shooting at a tavern on Nebraska Avenue's north end—a tough neighborhood. Two black men cruised up in a flat brown Pontiac LeMans station wagon and lobbed two barrels worth at the front door. The bouncer picked himself up, brushed the broken glass off his jacket, whipped out a .38 Special, and hit the car twice, blowing out the rearmost driver's side window. Mack read the bouncer's interview and said the bouncer was angry at himself for missing the driver from less than fifteen yards. It was a classic error, yanking on the trigger always pulled the shot towards your shooting hand. I guessed someone either chopped or repainted the car the next day. To my knowledge, it never reappeared even after making a public description and reward offer.

I ran surveillance on Central Stevedores off and on for the next month and spent two rolls of film on Lozello's sister coming and going. I became familiar with most of her outfits. Wendy helped identify most of the manufacturers and they were indeed very expensive, even for a manager. I fathomed they were likely the standard gifts similar to the Hong Kong suit I left in the police garage. I also took several rolls of deliveries offloaded at the docks. Lenny's analysts determined they were nothing out of the ordinary.

My informants were coming up dry no matter how hard I leaned on them. Since I no longer carried a badge, they felt less threatened. Two told me to go to hell before I gave them my retirement gift; a stop by the local payphone to call my old partner. Lover Boy would have them picked up when it was most inconvenient.

I spent several mornings standing on several West Tampa corners across from the bolita merchants. It would usually take half my cup of coffee before they noticed me. The typical responses were: milling around for a few moments in panic, making the frantic phone call, and flashing their breakfast wagers upon their ever-vigilant candles.

Most of May was rather quiet. Wendy spent her first three workweeks unabated while I took extra chores around the house, including ferrying the boys back and forth to school. We caught a few ballgames watching the minor league Tarpons at Al Lopez Field. Tickets were cheap and most of my old buddies from the department sat nearby, catching me up on the latest complaints about Lozello.

The last week of the month, the boys' school term finished. Wendy and I saved up some extra cash and were curious about Disney's new Space Mountain, so we took off to Orlando for the weekend. It was our second trip to the place since its opening, but we had a better time now that the boys were old enough to enjoy most of the rides. The classics were still delightfully entertaining; the Haunted Mansion, the Hall of Presidents, The Pirates of the Caribbean, the Eastern Airlines ride, 20,000 Leagues Under the Sea, and It's a Small World were irresistible. The only problem was getting the repetitive theme songs out of our heads. I remember telling Wendy during one of those rides, "If I had wings, darling, we'd leave the boys with a sitter and hit Sarasota next Saturday." Blissful lines like those always brought a hug and kiss. We didn't get to Sarasota that next weekend, however.

I had been secretly squirreling away extra funds for two years, saving for a down payment on a property Wendy and I looked at in Land 'O Lakes. Money was tight as it was, but I still managed the little extra. We were on schedule for a nice Christmas if I played my cards right. If that meant missing a weekend jaunt or two out of town, I had no problems. The following week was academic.

The Freezer

Wendy mastered Spanish breaded steaks and rice as an inexpensive dinner, but I had been missing her patented Sunday roasts for a couple of months now. If we didn't have family over, it was usually one of my lonelier old friends from either the department or Wendy's store. We had Ray and his family visit for dinner once. His folks were incredibly appreciative and well mannered, which is more than I can say for a select few neighbors gawking unapprovingly upon Ray's departure that day. Two even made jocular comments afterwards like, "Hey Brume, you trying to get our property taxes lowered?" or, "How was the fried chicken?"

One of the few neighbors that always respected our privacy, but appreciated having a policeman in the neighborhood was Ida Heinemann. Her accent made my skin crawl, much the same way as Jean Stapleton's, except Ida's was even worse. Her husband, an insurance salesman, had passed two years previously, leaving Ida alone and infrequently visited by her grown kids who resided back up north. Sometimes she would cook a traditional Jewish feast and have us over so she could feel some sense of belonging. Retired and without anyone to care for, Ida became the neighborhood mother—always nosey, but in the caring sense. She didn't hold anything back when it came to conversation either. After the riots, she harassed Wendy for weeks thinking *they* were coming to our neighborhood and *they* would burn the houses down if *they* ever found out where I lived. Women were so naturally panicky but I regard this as a generalization having personally known a few that weren't, thankfully.

Mack had phoned saying he needed to see me right away. Wendy was listening to our conversation from the other side of the bed that morning, but she was used to uncontrollable interruptions by now. Her eyes were so expressive and readable; she gave me an entire paragraph with one blink.

"Honestly Bill, if Mack's calling you so early in the morning, must you insist on rhetorically asking if it's important, knowing darn well it is?"

After I briefly muted the phone's mouthpiece and gave a lovingly playful finger shushing, I apologized to Mack, who continued.

"She's right you know."

"Yeah, yeah. Always kissing up to the ladies, Mack. You do the same thing with the 'is that right?' after someone tells you something too! What can I do for you, hillbilly?"

Mack always took my ribbing in stride. His tone was rather alarmed, however. "You can meet me right way, that's what."

"You can't..." I attempted hijacking the meeting to our present phone conversation, but Mack insisted.

"Not this time, Bill. Meet me at the huntin' camp."

That's what we eventually started codifying as Ben T. Davis Beach when we knew the lines were tapped. You could hear the clicks every two minutes and, since my liaisons with Vargas, Lenny felt it necessary. We didn't meet exactly at that beach, but just a little further down the causeway, where all of us relaxed and sometimes used rodents for target practice.

"Give me thirty minutes." I said before hanging up and then sliding behind my old gal while she brushed her teeth. Wendy's worry had taken over, and her posterior's deflection nullified any chances of an extended shower.

The morning's haze had already blown away with a stiff sea breeze, but my T-bird's vinyl was scorching. I ran back inside for the towel that Wendy stood clutching in anticipation of my return. Suffice to say, she'd become accustomed to dealing with skirts on the lowest rack of my Ford oven. While she normally kept her buffer stored in the cars themselves, she had removed the towels for washing. So went our rhythmic Sundays.

Mack, as usual, was already waiting for me on the causeway. I didn't recognize the car he was driving, however; it was a newer and larger Thunderbird painted a hideous shade of beige. I felt much better about my good old '66. Mack didn't care that much about cars, so it must have been for his wife, I thought.

When I pulled up, he shook his head while rolling his eyes, as if we were in some sort of a competition. He hated lack of punctuality, but only if it was his own. His wife was partly Cuban, so she must have driven him absolutely batty on a regular basis. Nonetheless, he always laughed instead of scolding.

"'Bout time you got here." Mack chortled.

"I'm five minutes early, ya rookie." I shook my friend's hand and asked about the car.

"What the hell is that butt-ugly thing?"

"It's a newer T-bird we picked up from the bond lot. Only 7,800 miles." Mack stated.

"What's with the big scratch behind your door?"

Mack's pride eased slowly down his throat with a sigh. "My dad-burned son ran into it with his bicycle. I'm gonna have to get it painted before it goes back."

"Back?"

"Yeah. Wife hates it. She can hardly see over the hood anyway, but it doesn't matter—it's a lemon. Been in the shop three times already for some vapor lock problem. I didn't much care for it either, but she thought she wanted one of these boats, so I let her have it. Guess she misses her old Falcon."

"What happened to the station wagon?"

"That trip we took to California last year did a number on the suspension. Besides, that thing sucked the gas. After I ran out in Homosassa, miles from anywhere, and had to hike, that was the end for me."

"Well, why'd you let it get so low?" I laughed.

"I didn't!" Mack yelled. "My boy emptied the darn thing playing around up there."

"Jesus, Mack, he's only eight!"

"Yeah. Hindsight." Mack frowned.

I kept laughing. "You don't need a car, Mack. You need a less hyper kid."

"Already took care of that." Mack grinned.

"How."

"Took him to see *Jaws* last week. Little guy's afraid to take a bath now. Thinks it's gonna come up out of the drain!" Mack's grin exchanged itself for a slightly devilish cackle.

"You're a twisted bastard sometimes; you know that, Mack?"

"Absolutely! You just wait, buster. Your two are getting close to that age. Gonna cost you plenty."

"I don't doubt it." My eyesight refocused on his newer car. "Anyway, whatever's under that hood can't be much better than the wagon."

"Yeah." Mack admitted solemnly.

We leaned up against the fronts of our cars for a moment before Mack began the real reason for our visit.

"Things just got a little more dangerous for you and me, Bill."

"We were never that sheltered, Mack, but what's the deal."

"Ran across a communiqué yesterday. There's an internal investigation going on as we speak."

"About?"

"You remember Terry Perkins, right?"

"Yeah, the patrolman that busted Jimmy Furtelli. My kind of guy."

"He's a detective now…"

"No surprise." I added.

"Anyway, he and another fella you know, Gary Weaver…"

"Gary?"

"Yeah, Gary. Will you let me…never mind." Mack grew frustrated at my interruptions. "They were heading up a take-down in Ybor at some restaurant yesterday. Before you ask, they're okay, and the raid went well—busted two writers, found a half-pound of heroin, and about nine grand."

"Nice."

"Yeah, except that when they got back into the kitchen, Weaver said he did a double take on one of the freezers that had some pictures taped on the door."

"Doesn't sound too out of the ordinary. We keep some pictures, too."

"They were of us."

Mack didn't have to repeat it, but the discovery took a few moments to digest before I uttered the first syllable.

"Oh. Damn."

"Exactly."

"Just us?" I asked.

"Gary found twelve more. Eleven were detectives, eight from our department and three from Hillsborough. The other was on your federal taskforce."

"Who?" I asked pointedly.

"From your taskforce?"

"No, I mean, who as in do we know all of them?"

"I've met a few, yes. I don't know everyone you know, especially this 'Jim' working from your side. Lover Boy was one; Jose Fernandez was another. That's not the worst of it, though. The photos were our official department photos, not shots taken in public."

Instantly, my focus went beyond Mack's face and out into the bay. I remembered that moment well, for it was a blatant reminder that we were fighting a covert war from both sides.

"The investigation is internal? Hell, Mack, the problem is internal!" My temper soared.

"Don't worry, it's already been sent to the newspapers. They'll be all over this before Tuesday. Watch." Mack said.

"I wish I could be so confident. They don't report everything, you know."

"Sure, but you know there's a couple of them that know half the department's corrupt."

Mack often seemed like his exaggerations stabbed at the dark sometimes, although historically, most proved correct. After all, the department originally chose him as an ace analyst with Criminal Intelligence and he served for many years developing a reputation as the James Bond of the department. One newspaper columnist even went so far as actually printing "he's Tampa's 007" after a single-handed bust back in the late '60s. But everyone back then thought of Bond as the ultimate comparative policeman, except Fleming's policeman was, and still is, an international playboy.

As a detective, the people you most trusted were hardly ever wrong when they gave their opinions. I used the exact same approximation with informants. If they lied once or gave me some whackjob theory, I quickly discounted and discarded them in a jail cell somewhere. Mack remained one of my most guarded friends, and he proved himself worthy of that relationship yet again.

By Tuesday, June 3rd, the Times slung an unglamorous shot on the front page of the local beat hinting at government corruption and a bust in Ybor that contained some interesting evidence, but fell short of revealing the outright government scandal. I was disheveled, but not completely dissatisfied.

While investigating a tip involving the recent bombings, Lenny sent one of his units by with a message asking me to call him as soon as possible. When he picked up the other end of the line, his voice seemed the most focused I had heard in months.

"You know about the photos already. We're petitioning a grand jury that's supposed to convene around the beginning of November. I'm already receiving interference from the usual culprits on the state and local levels. Evidently, they aren't revealing much, which, as you know, indicates contrition."

"Tell me something I don't know."

Lenny laughed. "Okay. You don't know that I want you, specifically, to find out who gave the owner's of that Ybor lounge the photographs, and you don't know which holding room we're using at the department for your interrogation."

"Knowledge is king." I replied coldly.

Lenny wasted no time relaying the whats and wheres. Before the afternoon was over, I waltzed inside the police department as a deputized federal officer and, after addressing a dozen or so wisecracks of congratulations for escaping the menial local level, rested my fresh con leche on a table opposite the surviving owner of Pepe's Tavern off 7th Avenue in Ybor. I say surviving because during the raid, his partner, an older Italian man that had a life of rich foods and endless cigars, collapsed into full cardiac arrest while our guys were cuffing him. He was gone before the ambulance arrived.

The survivor, a man named Paco Jimenez, was a squat middle-aged Cuban with a standard '60s do, parted left, and he had a rather unkempt mustache with tobacco stains. His breathing was somewhat labored, perhaps from his oversized belly pushing against his lungs. His short gulps were also a byproduct of nicotine deprivation, so I offered him a smoke and lit it myself.

"I know joo, jefe. Joo ees one of them from the photographs, no?" He stole a long draw from his cigarette during my reply.

"It would seem so, Paco. What can you tell me about those?"

"Ay, nothing much, jefe. Those belonged to my partner, joo know."

Right away, Paco starts with the dishonesty. It didn't matter so much if you were a lawbreaker, I despised dishonesty more. My expression didn't allow Paco any comfort either. He recognized my generosity in offering the cigarette, but the inbred Latino guilt trip hadn't kicked in yet.

"Look, Paco, while I'm positive the investigators that came before me filled you in on your situation, your actions make me feel like you need a review."

Paco scratched his balding head, fending off the bravado he would normally portray.

"You were found in possession of banned narcotics in such volumes that warrants the maximum sentences for distribution. The authorities found you with cash in sufficient amounts to verify that distribution. Your partner is deceased because of this lifestyle and from the looks of it, you may not be far behind."

Paco took that as a personal insult, which it was, but I intended the statement from the viewpoint of concern, not disrespect.

"But the worst of your offenses, Paco, is the possession of the photographs."

This fact didn't seem to bother Paco at all; rather, he became fidgety in the sense that he wanted to state something that disposed of the seriousness. "These photos, I tell you, belonged to my partner."

"They were in *your* possession."

"Okay, so these were in my bar, so what? What's the penalty for possession of these photos?" Pepe mockingly asked, as if to taunt the legal ramifications.

"Those photographs are not a joint or two some patron laid on you, Paco. They aren't a lid, or an ounce, or even an entire bale, señor. They aren't a five-year racketeering slap for gambling, either. What they *are* is a RICO conspiracy charge with a sentence not less than thirty years, and if you don't tell me where they came from, I'm going to personally see that it's without parole. Tú sabes?"

Paco's eyes were like an owl's from behind the smoke of my complimentary Winston. Coming into the station, and surviving the local's interrogations gave him a false sense of security that now crumbled.

"You see, Paco, the locals here may not have informed you of the federal ramifications. Those tend to be more severe and the prisons far more harsh."

The stream of smoke, once steady as a rock while it climbed towards the ceiling, was now considerably shaky. I continued pounding away at his machismo.

"A person such as you probably wouldn't last long in a federal facility, Pepe…"

"Okay, okay!" He yelled. "I understand," as he paused to contemplate his demise. "A girl showed up with them the other night."

"A girl. Out of the blue." I never resisted sarcasm. "What was her name."

"Aw gee, I dunno, jefe. Debbie, I think."

"What does she look like?"

"Well, she has the blond hair, a ring in her nose, long legs and, black."

I was taking notes of the girl's description, and the pen stopped as soon as he softly mentioned the last part. My eyes refocused from the paper to him. "Excuse me, did you say she was black or wearing black pants."

"No, she had on the dungarees."

"Were they black?"

"No." Paco fidgeted. "She is."

"Wait a minute. You're saying she's black, but had blond hair? Are you sure?

"Si, I mean jes, jefe. It was a wig or something."

"And she was tall?"

"Maybe, but she had on these really high heels. What do you call them — platform choos?"

"I guess."

I was holding back the visual of this older dumpy man with a young bubblegum-chewing black girl, but my curiosity took over. "So…you like playing in the jungle, Paco?"

"What's that suppose to mean, jefe?"

"You know. I mean do you prefer black women?"

"What?"

"Hey, you know what they say; 'to each their own', you know. It doesn't matter one way or the other to me, Paco."

"They okay, jefe, like anything else that is free, joo know? I just don't go around the street with them in my arms."

Racist pig, I thought. "Yeah, I know what you mean. What did you mean by 'free'?"

Jimenez slumped in his chair, searching for a way out of this line of questioning.

"I got nothing more to say about that, jefe."

"Okay, Paco. I just need to know why you needed the pictures."

Jimenez grew annoyed since he had already answered the question without realizing it. I often snuck a repeat to test attentiveness. About half of the time, the technique worked wonderfully, and often the interviewee unwittingly answered a question they successfully deflected earlier. It wasn't working on Pepe.

"I told joo before, those belong to my partner."

"Well he's dead now, isn't he?"

Jimenez didn't appreciate the reminder and, in retrospect, I probably shouldn't have said so much.

"He's dead because of joo people, jefe."

"No, Paco. He's dead because he had a weak ticker from the booze and drugs. He's dead because his conscience caught up with him when we walked through the door. There's no reason to be angry at us, Pepe. We're doing our jobs and you guys all know what you're doing. You play the game like everyone else. Now, do you want to tell me why your partner had those pictures or do I need to show you some mug shots of your potential roommates?"

Again, I easily circumvented Paco Jimenez's motivational lacking. I may not have been able to gain the prostitute's handlers, but that business would be a piece of cake. Lover Boy knew them all, their pimps, and all their parents. Tampa's black community was a small town nestled within a medium city. If Ray didn't know, his dad was the fallback. Between the two, and a handful of others, including the former White Hats that stayed in town, everyone was covered.

"Okay, jefe. As God is my witness and I hope Carlos don't come back to haunt me, he wanted them to study if one of joo came walking by the door. The numbers, joo know—poof." He made a hand gesture imitating flash paper detonation, blowing the last puff of his cigarette's vapor from his lungs.

Paco Jimenez and his partner were bolita writers, drug dealers, and associated with the underworld's fringe benefits. They weren't bosses or even high on the family food chain. With all of the activity going on, the likelihood of one or both of the thugs from an Ybor tavern requesting, and worse, actually gaining access at the top levels of the police department for smalltime needs seemed feasible, yet highly unlikely. I left that book open just in case the department had become so incredibly bold as to egregiously flaunt corruption, the simplest reason might actually contain the truth. My efforts would lead me back in contact with an old friend whom I trusted implicitly since the first day of academy.

Ray Coleman had just returned from his annual family vacation in South Carolina. He told me of his dreams of retiring to a simpler life in the piedmont just west of Columbia. I reminisced with him about my own country upbringing long ago in Virginia, and how one could leave your wallet on the front seat of your car and the keys in the ignition without a care in the world.

Ray and his father loved the locally caught mullet, so it became a tradition whenever I saw him to show up with about ten pounds worth fresh from the causeway docks. I tried his wife's cooking once, and constantly cursed myself for not inviting myself over more often. For now, my only hunger was information.

Ray put the word out for the whereabouts of a young "social worker" named Debbie, but that was only to confirm what he already knew—the only pimp handling anything outside of the neighborhood was a political high roller named Gerome Franks, Sr. He and his son ran a funeral home to launder profits from a pool hall he also ran. His son, Junior, was serving his third year of a federal racketeering charge after being busted in an international prostitution ring.

Ray informed me situations like these required delicate treatment. If his query reached the wrong sort, young Debbie's whereabouts could drastically change, since they've also been rumored to purposefully dissolve assets when no longer equitable.

"Ray, you don't think they'll kill her, do you?"

"Probably not, but if'n it somehow gets out she's being sought by the feds, then Gerome won't play. You know what I mean?"

"I'll keep my fingers crossed."

Mrs. Coleman poked her head out from around the corner of her kitchen, wondering why I was standing up with my car keys on hand.

"Oh, no you don't!" She jacked; waiving her finger from side to side. "Just where do you think *you're* going?" Ray's wife wasn't a creature to befoul—and her high school social studies students would agree—but I had to get by Lenny's field office before he left for the day.

"Mama, don't you lip Bill like that, he's got to go do important business now!" Ray intervened.

"Have to go, Bev. Sorry."

"Always going somewhere, aren't you Bill? And just who's gonna eat all this fish you brought over?"

"I wish it were me, Bev!"

"Well don't go blaming me if you don't get enough of my cooking, okay?"

"Not in a million years, Bev."

I smiled, shook Ray's hand, and hit the door. His neighbors were always giving me strange looks as I walked back to the car—wondering why in the hell some white guy has to go and mess up the neighborhood. They knew Ray was a cop, otherwise, any honkey visiting around there was probably up to no good.

"Ben, under what circumstances would official police portraits be given to anyone outside the department?"

Davidson examined the question only briefly before his bellowing laugh ricocheted off all four of his offices walls. I told him he'd give us all tinnitus before our retirements, but he never changed his volumes, or his booming nature.

"Heck Bill, you'll have to ask someone higher up like your old major. I bet he'd know.

"Can you take a guess?"

"Off the top of my head, I'd say it would only be for publication with a newspaper story; you know—like you see anytime you make a major bust or if you get an award.

"Sounds plausible. Who would authorize those?"

"Can't say for sure, but probably the highest level, if not the chief. You need to ask Fernandez. Do you have his number?"

"Mack does. I'll call him."

Ben pushed his phone across to my side of his desk. "Here. I'd like to hear what he has to say."

Surprised by Ben's atypical impatience, I reached across and dialed Mack's number. Three rings later, he picked up and started blabbing about a home run his boy hit at a baseball game yesterday.

"I didn't think he'd hit it!" Ben could hear Mack's voice squawking rapidly on the earpiece. He went on for a minute more before giving me Jose Fernandez's number and we hung up.

"What was all that about?" Ben asked in amazement.

"Funny. He told his eight year old son that he'd buy him a puppy if he homered."

I didn't get my ears covered in time. "Ha! Well, he asked for it."

"Kid slammed it so hard, the ball has a huge blemish."

I dialed Jose's extension directly and he immediately picked up the receiver.

"Hey Roadrunner, how are ya? Remember me?" I asked.

Jose earned the nickname after winning every single department marathon since the late fifties.

"Bill! Hey, man. Doing fantastic!" Jose's greetings were always upbeat.

"Major Fernandez, I have to ask you a question about the photos problem. That okay? You know what I'm talking about?"

"Yeah, sure. I don't know what I can do, but you can ask."

"Do you know who authorizes their release?"

"Yeah, Bill. I do. That has to come from the top. From the chief."

"Do you know why someone would want those pictures, Jose?"

"They send them for the reporters, or departmental publications. Sometimes for exhibits in court."

"Anyone else?"

"Not that I can think of."

"Jose?"

"Yeah?"

"I know it would throw up too many red flags if you go around asking who made the request for the photos, but if you happen to catch any talk, would you mind giving me a call?"

"Sure thing, Billy. I got no problem with that."

"Thanks, Jose."

I sat with a blank expression, but the gears were turning upstairs again.

"Bill, the way I see this, there are only three questions that need answers: Who requested the pictures from the chief, who did the chief release the pictures to, and to whom does our little Debbie belong?"

"One of my old partners has a line on the hooker; says she's probably one of Gerome Franks' girls."

"As soon as he's able to confirm that, we'll have him deposed."

Ben's face seemed lost for a moment, and I guessed correctly that he was pausing on my account.

"What's the matter?" He asked.

"Jose said it was either reporters, interdepartmental publications or reports, and then he mentioned courts."

"We don't know if those are the only circumstances," said Ben.

"I understand, however, if those are the main circumstances, then the only requests from the outside would come from reporters or the courts."

"Why would the newspapers need fourteen different plain-clothed detectives photos in the first place, Bill? That doesn't seem plausible to me unless they were putting together a large expose or some awards presentation for the department. Furthermore, your photograph was included, right?"

"Yes."

"Then a newspaper report seems less likely. In fact, I can't think of a single reason why photos of previous employees would be released."

I thought about the other alternatives; internal theft after an approved request and so forth, but the court system was more of an unknown. Who could make the request unless it was for a case. If that was the scenario, I knew of no cases involving all fourteen of the detectives pictured.

ReMatch

"Martin Philipe Sanchez, raise your right hand. Do you solemnly swear to tell the truth, the whole truth, and nothing but the truth, so help you God?"

"Ours is not to do or die..." Sanchez's uncontrollable laughter echoed throughout the small chamber, which prompted the deposing prosecutor's cries for civility.

"Just take the oath Sanchez, or I'll have your certifiable rear back up to Marianna for good."

"Aw. And I was hoping for a heppin' or two of them mashed taters at Four North later." Sanchez cracked, referring to Tampa General's psych ward.

The prosecutor ignored him and continued. "So help you God?"

Sanchez waved his hand disrespectfully and dismissingly. "Yeah, yeah. Whatever. I do."

I glanced over at the stenographer as she stamped "FPLT", ending Sanchez's last sentence. She hardly made an expression, but the Match's preceding antics managed raising her painted brow more than once.

"Mr. Sanchez, the Friday before last, on June 13, did you not converse with a man by the name of Guillermo Mendez for the purpose of his acquiring illegal explosives?"

"You have it recorded, don't you?" Sanchez quipped.

"Does that mean your answer is a yes?"

"I guess."

"And, Mr. Sanchez, in that conversation you referred him to a known associate of yours in Miami named "Nano". Is that correct?"

"Nope." Sanchez flatly replied.

"No? I don't understand, Mr. Sanchez. 'No', as in you didn't have the conversation, or 'no', that you believe it was someone else?"

Sanchez beamed insolently around the room. "Neither."

"Then what do you mean by your reply?" The prosecutor furiously asked.

"I really don't know him that well, so that 'known associate' thing you're laying on me just ain't true. I just know him as a source. Never did any business with the man."

"Nano?"

"That's what everyone called him."

I knew what it meant but the prosecutor didn't, evidently. He must have been the only one in the room that didn't understand. I flashed towards the stenographer and her raised brow. The prosecuting attorney paused to review the meaning with his colleague, who also struggled with his own composure. After a few moments, the prosecutor returned.

"Is this a joke nickname? Kind of like calling a big man 'Tiny'?"

Martin Sanchez couldn't contain himself. "They didn't call him that because of his height, man."

The raspy laughing from gargled lungs returned, but Sanchez wasn't alone. A few others snickered without hesitation, which prompted another disdainful scolding.

"Mr. Sanchez, you'll keep the childish commentaries to yourself."

Of course, the prosecutor's warnings careened off Martin Sanchez's unrepentant gaudiness as easily as skipping a rock across a frozen pond.

"Did you or did you not refer Guillermo Mendez to this man called Nano?"

"Sure did."

"Thank you," said the prosecutor, exhausted with the lengthy extraction. "And what can you tell us about him?"

"Who?"

"Nano!" The prosecutor yelled.

"Nothin', 'cept for if you wanted something to go boom, you went through him."

"Why not you? Didn't you use explosives too?"

"Once, but I didn't dig it."

"Why not?"

"Not my style." The Match stared at the attractive stenographer who sat a dozen feet away to his right. "Over too fast, you know. Some people like it that way. Not me. I want to savor the moment, man. Slow and easy."

The stenographer raised her brow until she caught Sanchez's wolfish stare. She gulped and put her head back into the machine. FPLT. I never caught her raising her brow again during the rest of the deposition.

"Mr. Sanchez, you are heard on the tape referring to a friend — I assume a mutual friend, and the party you attended previous to the phone call." Sanchez rolled his eyes frequently at the foregone statements. The prosecutor continued. "Can you tell us about the party and what was discussed?"

"Oh man, that was some night. Can't remember much after about two."

"Where was it?"

"Lilliput's"

"Tresedici's place? Was he there?"

"He's always there. It's his place, ain't it?"

"Did he talk to you about the job and the explosives?"

"He just pulled me to one side and said he had a tree stump he wanted removed."

"What do you think he meant by that?"

"What do I think he meant by that?" Sanchez's laugh reappeared as he repeated the prosecutor's question. "Hey man, I don't ask too many questions, you know what I mean? They say they want to blow up a freakin' tree; I don't give a rat's ass. Wasn't that on the tape?"

I remembered Mendez mentioning so much, but nothing more. If Sanchez actually wanted us to believe the mob dabbled in random forestry, he was nuts. Then again, he really *was* nuts.

"Mr. Sanchez, can you tell us a little more about the party?"

"Not after two." He laughed.

"Before."

"You had guys there. They know."

"For the record, personnel from the Federal Bureau of Investigation were indeed monitoring the location on that particular evening. They did not, however, monitor your conversations, Mr. Sanchez. You were wearing a listening device, were you not?"

"Yeah, but..."

"And would you care to inform us why the device stopped working only ten minutes after you arrived?"

"It did?" Sanchez played dumb until he remembered the verbal lashing he received by an agent that picked him up off the street around 3:45 the next morning.

"I mean, hey, it's not my fault some chick threw a glass of wine on me!"

We all knew better, including the deposing prosecutor.

"Of course, Mr. Sanchez, which is why we would like to hear your account of what happened during your three sober hours following the demise of our equipment."

"Nothing, man. We just drank and had some fun with the ladies."

"Fun with the ladies? Aren't you a married man, Mr. Sanchez?" Suddenly, the prosecutor realized he was finally pushing the right buttons.

Just as when Mack and I first interrogated The Match, his egocentric bravado began to collapse. "This ain't getting' back to my old lady is it?"

"That depends on you, Martin."

"I don't want to talk any more about the party, ya hear?"

"I'm afraid you need to fill in a few gaps for us Mr. Sanchez, or we take you out of the program, understand?"

Like before, Sanchez was cornered. "Look, man, there wasn't much going on. Sal put this guy on me and he asked about the dynamite, so I gave him Nano's number."

"You didn't discuss anything else? Because, we have two phone records within thirty minutes of your arrival going long distance to Boston."

I remembered one of Ida Heinemann's kitten's pupils expanding to size of nickels while playing with a feathered toy she made. Sanchez' abysmal wells were just as large after the prosecutor's Boston remark. It was Body Language 101. Since two years before, Suffolk County Massachusetts suffered over 60 for-profit arsons. There were an additional 120 hate-related arsons that I read about, putting the city in a near state of emergency.

"Turn off your machine and tell that lady to stop typin'." Sanchez nervously demanded.

"I have no intention of doing so, Mr. Sanchez."

"You will turn it off or I'm not saying another goddamn thing."

The prosecutor looked around the room for a moment, gathering the puzzled reactions from all of those involved. I watched his Adam's apple bob as he cleared his dry throat. With a shrug, he pointed his finger, motioning the stenographer and the tape recorder operator to cease activity. He then turned around to Martin Sanchez, who laughed while dealing with his involuntary buildup of nasal mucus.

"I'll talk to you about up north, but you gotta sweeten my deal." He said.

The prosecutor grinned, but offered little comfort. "Mr. Sanchez, I'm in no position to offer you anything except avoiding a permanent residence up in the panhandle. Besides, you're not offering anything yet, now are you?"

I witnessed Sanchez's confidence abruptly return. The grin. The chalky laugh. The raspy cough that almost always followed.

"You morons haven't got a clue."

"Oh really?" The prosecutor's temper quickly flared. "We've got you on fourteen arsons and second-degree homicide. The only reason you're not rotting upstate is because you've bargained your way out temporarily."

"Temporarily?" Sanchez laughed.

"What? You think you can waltz around after a confession without completing your cooperation requirement? Hey pal, that's revocable at any time we deem you aren't in compliance. Maybe you want to think about that for a moment."

Sanchez didn't think about it for more than six seconds. "What do you want?"

"Talk to me about Boston. You did some work up there? For whom?"

"I'm not spilling anything without a deal."

"What are you offering?"

"Ain't no what…it's who."

"Okay then, who?"

"No names until I got a deal."

Sanchez folded his arms. Defensive posture. He wasn't budging. I motioned the prosecutor over. The lanky, balding man in his early 40s leaned over. I quickly realized his deodorant wasn't cutting it, so I backed up slightly.

"He's not going to give you anything right now," I told him. "Maybe he can give you a description or something."

"Look Mr. Brume, this is just supposed to be a deposition, not an interrogation." The prosecutor quipped.

"I don't see his council advising against it." I said. "He wants a deal.

The prosecutor agreed and turned back around to Sanchez who stared at me, remembering his failure upstairs at the police department.

"Mr. Sanchez, can you tell me anything about Boston? You don't have to name names right now, but if you could give me the gist, that may work."

"You said you couldn't make a deal."

"I'll be in touch with those that can."

Sanchez looked at his attorney, who nodded. Sanchez then sat back in his chair and pinched the bridge of his nose before continuing.

"Suppose I tell you I may have lit more than a few places. And maybe there's more than a couple dozen working the game up there."

"Couple dozen what, Sanchez?" The prosecutor asked.

With another raspy laugh, he continued. "Like I said, you ain't got a clue. People you think would never touch this stuff. This whole little blue rubber ball you call a planet is nothing but a world of lies. You know how it goes," he laughed, "people you think are suppose to be on your side are stabbing you in the back. Ain't so much the property owners as it is the sales agents, you pigs, and even the assholes you pay to stop the fires I start."

The room's wind vacated suddenly. I don't remember how long the silence lasted after Sanchez's bomb. I only remember how the silence ended.

"Brume, please get Agent Karman over to my office immediately. I'll meet you both up there in ten minutes," squinted the prosecutor. The deposition was over.

Stumped

By the time I arrived at Tampa General, doctors already had Carlos Salazar too sedated for interrogation. His family, enraged from the many investigators' houndings, became understandably protective of their beloved's rest. Their frigid stares cocked the inevitable if I were to insist, so I didn't.

"No such thing as a second warning around here, Bill."

I'm not one for flinching, but Lenny's cruel observation and subsequent pat on my right shoulder managed spilling a few drops of my treasured coffee.

"Jesus, Lenny!" I switched hands with the coffee cup and shook off the blistering-hot liquid.

"Oops! Sorry about that." He said with a slanted grin.

We took a few steps away from Salazar's doorway and the ice-cold reflections from within. Lenny and I understood we weren't welcome when Room 424's door authoritatively closed moments later.

"Let's go downstairs; I'll get you a refill." Lenny said, still grinning from his menacing surprise attack.

My handler's rare public appearance gave me concern for the conversation that followed. I joked about his spooking the joint, but the underlying tone in his voice never broke away long enough to entertain a momentary escape from the fact that *I* was now in danger.

"Bill, I know you've been paying attention to this, but you remember the tape I played you?"

"Which one?" I asked.

"The last one between Martin Sanchez and Guillermo Mendez."

"Mendez?"

"The one that calls himself Santa Claus."

I paused momentarily to recall the scenario. "Yeah. I do. Are you telling me *this* is what they were talking about? Thought so."

"So you read Salazar's dossier?"

"It's been a while, but the peg leg's not hard to miss."

"Old stump."

"Poor bastard's life was saved by that leg you know...well, kind of. His family told me he lost it in Korea. Land mine." Lenny said.

"Now, twenty and some odd years later, he has it blown off again. Nice."

"Why the sour look, Len?"

Over the previous few years, I've come to interpret Lenny's expressive face rather easily. He wasn't much different than anyone else in this regard, and I could tell there was something else that bothered him.

"Oh. I don't know how to tell you this Bill, so I'm just going to come right out with it. I've just learned this hit on Salazar probably isn't the end."

"To what extent?"

"Not precisely sure, but a couple of our guys seem to think an enforcer was brought up from Miami for housekeeping on a package deal involving Salazar, Davidson..."

"Ben?"

"Yeah...and three others."

"And you think I'm one of them."

"After today and the Botticelli hit? Come on, Bill. They warned Salazar and, in making sure you were at the scene, likewise for you. You see what happened to Salazar."

"Lenny, there hasn't been a waking moment I've not contemplated the Botticelli hit. What am I supposed to do? Nothing?"

"Settle down. Nobody's asking you to just sit back and let things happen. We just don't want our best assets in more danger than necessary."

"I can take care of myself."

"I know. I just don't want you exacerbating the situation. Let the locals deal with the small fish. You stay focused on Linus."

"What about Ben?"

"He's been briefed on his situation and we've already taken protective measures. Our Orlando office is taking care of it. They're moving him around hoping that someone slips on a tap.

It worked a few times in New York, so they're implementing the same tactic everywhere else. Between Las Vegas and Chicago, we're stretched thin. I have another case we're surveilling in Oklahoma City that ties in with your boy Vargas that could pan out in the next couple of weeks. Now would be a great time to take a short break if you're thinking about it."

Although my right hand was probably stinging and swollen from the coffee burn, I never recalled feeling anything else after listening to Lenny's concerns. The Fourth of July was next weekend and my family was not doing much more than sitting around our crowded Seminole Heights sweatbox. Before that Friday came, I emptied every last bit of cash from my secret house fund and spent the next two days negotiating the dream home Wendy selected a few months earlier. I thought it was a bunch of bologna, but the Arabs didn't much like our friendship with Israel and decided to play games with the oil supply, aggravating an already sour economy. That was good news for me, however, the builders were almost running over themselves trying to get a deal—*any* deal—closed before interest rates went too high. At the end of two days, I not only had our new home secured, the builders conceded a thousand dollars in extras, and a bonus screened porch. *Wendy's going to crown me king for this one*, I thought.

As if the house deal wasn't sweet enough, the down payment came in at a few hundred dollars less than I originally planned. The timing was impeccable. That Thursday before Wendy returned from work, I loaded up the car and prepped the boys for a weekend trip to Cocoa Beach.

If there's a list of life's most enjoyable moments, mine must include the moment of surprise. I can't limit this to moments of happiness when little Jeffrey or Junior open a Christmas present, or when I sent a dozen roses to Wendy while sitting half a block away with a pair of binoculars. I received the same sort of pleasure when busting down a dealer's door, or informing a suspect that their assumption of a light sentence was grossly mistaken. I lived for Wendy's astonishment and wasn't disappointed. When she came home and saw us in the car with all bags packed, all she had to do was hop in, which she did eagerly and without questions until we were well down the road.

"Cocoa Beach? Whatever in the devil made you want to go there?" She asked.

"Just wanted to get away for the weekend...treat the boys to something neat. I haven't told them where else we're going."

At that precise moment, the boys halted their terribly one-sided game of slaps and took up a curios position standing just behind our seats.

"Oh, Bill don't tease them so. What did you have in mind?"

"Not much—'cept maybe a tour of Cape Canaveral!"

Wendy drew a deep breath in excitement, but the boys didn't understand me, I supposed. Well, they heard of the place, maybe, but not the context.

"It's where the astronauts blast off." I said.

That was all it took. For the next thirty minutes, my boys may just as well have been super balls trapped in a cube with no gravity. NASA previously announced their launch intentions for the last Apollo mission a couple of weeks later, but that didn't matter. They were going to see rockets and the men who operated them. By the time we arrived at the beach, Wendy and I were both ready for a shower and a drink.

We had a temporary setback when a reservationist informed me that their hotel was booked solid over the next two weeks. Being that I was flush with cash, I didn't have a problem with a more expensive venue. Another spot was just up the street and they had a vacancy; a nicer room on a fifth floor overlooking the ocean. I never told Wendy that the room was $35 a night, which was the most I've ever paid, and she didn't ask. In the back of my mind, I knew she *had* to have some idea, given my cheery demeanor. Even if Wendy did, she quickly forgot about it after her first cocktail.

After we unpacked, she led the boys down to the water while I grabbed a shower and had a look around. Money well spent. The room was fabulous and the view incredible. I relaxed with a beer on the balcony while the family played below. Wendy didn't last long, however, and came back after only thirty minutes. After the boys rinsed the beach off, she hopped in for her own lengthy shower; something she'd grown famous for over the years. The boys hated sitting around and waiting, so I quickly devised some flash entertainment.

Part of that exorbitant room rate included accoutrements not normally found in our regular bookings. One nice touch was the inclusion of standard stationary alongside the room's telephone. I supposed they never fathomed one of their guests using this for kid's entertainment, other than perhaps some infrequent drawing contests or general scribbling. The boys and I were in the mood for flight! I divvied each a sheet of paper and we began our contest to see whose paper airplane would fly furthest.

We only knew the two basic paper airplane patterns: short and long. Both Jeffrey and I chose the short designs and Junior opted for the long. Both of the short planes floundered in the unsteady breezes, while Junior's headed straight for the water, taking a nosedive into the sand just several yards shy. Much to the boy's delight, I handed out three more sheets of paper. This time, all of us fabricated the basic long design. Jeffrey took off running for the balcony as soon as his was complete. Unfortunately, he hastily forgot to fold his wings upward, so his made a quick nosedive and wobbled its way down to the scrub bushes directly below. I walked over to the balcony and let mine go; watching it sail about twenty yards out before a breeze turned it down the beach where it landed another thirty or so yards away. Junior carefully folded each crease on his design and then positioned the wings for maximum balance. He could hardly reach over the balcony, so I held him up a few feet for a clear launch. The glider poetically danced between the air currents, waltzing and occasionally stalling, but never deviating from its magical flight out to sea. It was a mesmerizing sensation witnessing God's whim. I caught myself staring at the sea before the boys tugged at my pants for more paper. That's when a brilliant idea hit me.

I heard Wendy's shower turn off, so there probably wasn't enough time for another full contest. Instead, I quickly folded another long plane and had the boys follow me out to the balcony.

"Watch this."

I took out the Zippo lighter from my shirt pocket and lit the plane's tail. As soon as the tail became fully ablaze, I sent the plane towards the sea. Of course, the design reduced itself to ashes before reaching the water, but it worked as an interesting improvisational firework. Even better, *I* was the coolest! Both boys let out a chorus of awesomes and neatos for over a minute before Wendy interrupted to inform us she'd be ready to go out in five minutes. That was just enough time for one more flaming paper airplane, which the boys demanded. We didn't get any complaints and the first one harmlessly extinguished itself in the sand, so I didn't mind.

The second flight of the Phoenix didn't go so well. The design was okay, but I threw it hastily without straightening the wings. I watched in horror as the plane glided, or rather, plummeted its way down to the scrub bushes with plenty of fuel to burn. That sent me in a panic out of the room and down five flights of stairs — much to the amazement of several other gawking guests. I made it down there just in time to stamp the fire out before the bushes ignited. And, I could hear the laughter emanating from several other balconies just above me. Brilliant idea.

When I returned, Wendy's puff of smoke and sarcastic grin said everything, but that didn't stop her.

"Here less than an hour and you're already trying to burn the place down. Typical."

I had to laugh. "Come on. Let's go eat, I'm starved."

List of Five

The middle of the next week saw me back at work for Lenny. I sat in his office, smoke drifting upward from my left hand while grazing his department's reports from Oklahoma City. His pacing was what bothered me the most—endlessly back and forth. The anxiety was all too apparent.

"A sheriff." Lenny pounded. "Those idiots tried to take out a sheriff."

"Well it looked like the old man had it under control to me." I replied, looking over the report.

It told of a questionable private eye, who was a former Florida State beverage controller, and how he brazenly attempted the assassination of an older Oklahoma City town marshal named Phillip Jackson. According to the report, Andrew "Drew" Geraldson stalked Jackson by sitting at the end of his street with a shotgun barrel sticking out of his white Cadillac Eldorado's window. As if the car wasn't flamboyant enough, Geraldson's description stated he was a portly 6'3" tall, had white hair, and wore a gaudy white Italian suit with cowboy boots. I laughed when reading Jackson's newspaper statement. "He was as conspicuous as a hippo in a bathtub."

"Bathtub, right?" Lenny asked.

"Yup!"

"Keep reading."

Geraldson revved up his car and spun towards the marshal, who was about 150 yards away. The old man was sharper than he anticipated, lobbing two rounds from his service revolver through the Cadillac's windshield at an impressive 40 yards out. Even though he missed Geraldson, he scared him so badly, Geraldson slammed on the brakes hard enough to bloody his own nose on the steering wheel.

"I talked to Marshal Jackson earlier this morning, Bill. The guy's 63 years old, been with the department for over forty years, and never fired his pistol until that moment."

"And he never blinked before doing so. My kind of guy!" I said.

Lenny nodded and motioned me to keep reading. The report continued with circumstances surrounding the attempted murder, and when it came down to Geraldson's known associates, Angel Vargas' and Santa Claus' names appeared.

"Oh, *those* idiots."

Lenny scratched at his chin. "Yeah. Unfortunately, while you were on vacation, Vargas slipped out of town. I have two field observations placing them in Oklahoma at the time of the attempt."

"Okay. So why was Geraldson the point man?" I asked.

"I don't get it. He worked numerous cases for Ben Davidson; the press loves him! And yet he flipped like a switch."

"Then I suppose you've already talked with Ben."

"Yeah. He became rather ill. We didn't bother with too many details. He has enough anxiety as it is. He said it probably had something to do with revenge. You know how these types are. They bought Geraldson off somehow. You don't go to seed overnight unless..."

"I've got a good idea."

"Bill, I know what you're thinking and I need to remind you to let our guys handle surveillance on Vargas. At the rate he's exposing himself, it's only a matter of time. Keep the tail going on Lozello."

"Aw come on, Len!" Nothing worse than having one's hands tied. I could keep my thumb on the old man and I was only thinking of making a phone call to Vargas. Just one phone call, that's all I ask."

"And what are you going to say? 'Hi Angel. Why did you go after Jackson?' I don't want him tipped off; understand?"

I knew when Lenny wasn't going to budge. "No, but don't worry about it. It's your operation."

"Bill, you don't have to patronize me. I'm not doing this because I think you'll bungle it or something. I'm doing it for your own security. The last thing I need is the person most familiar with this case taken out."

"I'm flattered." Capitulation came with the flick of my Zippo.

Lenny's demand became even more stressful when I received an early morning call from none other than Vargas himself two weeks later. I knew he was simply using my tap to grandstand for the agents listening, but the *way* he said it brought back the pity.

"Bill, you remember what I told you about this madness with the bars, no? And now they try to burn my brother's place to the ground. The roof is still smoking! You should go have a look for yourself. Can't you do something about this?"

"Randy's? What do you mean? Do you know for sure who did it?"

"Don't you?"

There was a brief pause before I answered. Vargas was up to his old tricks; using the open line to somehow implicate me or taunt the eavesdroppers.

"Of course not."

"Well, you know. People talk. People listen. I think maybe you can scratch my back a little, no?"

"Look, Angel; first of all, I really don't know who burned the place. Second, it doesn't do me any good to speculate. I mean, come on; the place practically begs for it by any half-lit redneck passing by. And lastly, I just want you to know that, on a personal note, I appreciate the time we had. On the professional end however, you know I cannot speculate or otherwise divulge any information to people in your position."

"…in my position."

"'Fraid so."

"And what exactly *is* my position, Bill?"

Another uncomfortable pause. I let that speak for itself.

"Please, Angel. The one thing I can tell you has already been said, and that is the truth; I don't know anything about your brother's arson case. Your call is the first I've heard of it."

He hung up on me.

It was the last time I remember speaking with Vargas directly. I always thought that he, or someone in his family, was sending me messages, however.

From the moment he hung up, I began preparing. I took extra caution and made my moves with more deliberation. I approached doors with greater caution, my ears listened more intently, I spent more time at the range, and I kept my firearms meticulously maintained. Lenny was right, though; Vargas was nothing more than a distraction, and he underscored this at a sit-down with me and another one of his operatives at a small café in Hyde Park. He introduced me to an older fella named Harold Savage before taking our seats.

After a cute waitress wearing a uniform more befitting an airline stewardess took our orders, Lenny opened up.

"I read the transcript of your conversation with Vargas. You did the right thing."

"Well, it was true, Len." I said.

"I know. And, I think we all know who had a part in it. Nonetheless, it's not that important right now."

He looked around to make sure nobody was in listening range. There were only about a dozen tables in the place, it was late on a Tuesday afternoon, and there were only three other tables occupied. Two of those also had conversations echoing through the room, so we had little chance of an eavesdropper.

"Go ahead, Harry," said Lenny.

Agent Savage cleared his throat as he glanced in my direction begrudgingly. I could tell what he had to say wasn't going to go down well.

"You remember that detective we busted named Hilliard?" He asked.

"Ray Hilliard?" I replied. "That piece of trash we threw back after a Mann Act warning? Yeah. What about him?"

"He was my assignment."

"Okay." I nodded without thinking much else.

"Outside of the old man constantly running around after the jailbait in Temple Terrace, the run's been mostly fruitless. This morning, the guy decides to take a trip down to Ybor. I tail him all the way inside the Tropicana's doors and take a position two tables away. A few minutes later, your boy Vargas strolls in with some blond chick and an older Italian-looking man. The place was kind of busy, and even though I was close enough to make out bits of their conversation, I couldn't hear everything. They started mumbling something about Colombia and then *he* walked in."

"Who?"

Agent Savage's kept his eyes focused on the tabletop while he spoke until he slowly rolled them up at mine.

"*Your* assignment."

I immediately felt the guilt. Lenny knew I should have been spending more time tailing Lozello. Especially if he was having a meeting with RICO implications. It was almost what we wanted. Almost.

"I guess I should have been there, then?"

Lenny interrupted. "On any given day, I would say so, but not today, Bill."

"I couldn't hear much. Just bits and pieces, but what I heard was enough. They were putting together a hit list. Five people, I think."

"Names?" I asked.

"Couldn't make them all out...just partials. Maybe heard Salazar's name. Maybe Davidson too. Not sure. What I heard clear as crystal was Vargas bringing up *your* name, Brume."

"Yeah?" I laughed. "And what was the response?"

"I thought he was joking when he said it, but my back was turned." Agent Savage's words became dicey—clearly overrun with emotion.

"Who?" I asked impatiently.

"He said, 'someone ought to put a goddamn bullet in your head.'"

"Who?" I demanded.

"Lozello!"

"Perfect." I sat back against my chair's backrest, arms folded.

Savage continued, "After he said it, both Vargas and the older guy laughed. I thought they were joking, but a moment later, Hilliard gets up, throws his napkin on the table, says he's had enough, and hits the door. I didn't follow him."

I sat for a moment before asking the obvious. "Did the others say anything else?"

"Nope. They just laughed and finished their coffees. Wait; they *did* mention something about October, but all I caught was the month. No particulars."

Lenny cut in. "Bill, you're probably thinking that meeting was enough to nail Lozello, but you'd be wrong. The..."

"I know. The conversation's too spotty to hold up in court. Don't worry; I'll keep an eye out."

"Thanks." Lenny sighed. "And stay on top of Lozello. Doesn't take much intelligence to figure out something's going down in a few months time. We also need to figure out who is on Vargas' list."

It never fails. Our bosses give us a directive and it sounds easy enough to follow. Tail Lozello. That's it. Simple, right? Never. Only the most successful managers fully understood the difficulties experienced by their underlings. I likened this phenomenon to other examples of nature's simplicity: Lenny can tell me to stay away from the other planets orbiting this case, but neither he nor I have any control on their individual behavior. Worse, they have a fragile duplicity that has them circling around something warm and delightful until it eventually destroys them. Whenever they feel threatened by it, where do they gravitate? Me.

Not two days after my meeting with Lenny and Savage, events provided clear proof of my theorem. A bar owner by the name of Pappy Hernandez got on the phone with me in a state of Spanglish panic, complaining about some orange and black van circling his block with a shotgun barrel sticking out of the passenger's side something or another.

"Why are you calling me?" I asked.

"I call the police. They do nothing. I call a friend of mine, he gives me jour number."

"Who?"

"Angel." He said calmly.

"Oh yeah? What did he say I could do for you?"

"Nothing. He just gave me jour number."

"Did he tell you who I was?"

"Er…no. He didn't."

"Interesting."

"Okay. Who are you?" He said.

"I'm, um, with the FBI. Name's Brume."

A moment passed. "Jou're crazy."

"Not even a little bit, but my wife may argue differently."

Hernandez calmed down and even laughed. "I should probably not be talking with joo, but Angel did give me jour number. What am I supposed to do?"

"I dunno, Mr. Hernandez. Get different friends?"

"Hey Brume, Angel's a good friend of mine, joo understand?"

And, there they went with the "good friend" bit again. "Of course. It was a joke."

"Ah. So. Can joo help me?"

"Not much I can do, Hernandez."

"Please call me Pappy." He insisted. "Not much? As in nothing?"

"Not much anyone can do without more information. I assume you gave the police department a description of the van. Did you get the tag number?"

"No. All I saw was the barrel and I ducked down below the window."

"So all we have is a general description of an orange and black van. There's got to be a few dozen of those running around here. Too little to go on, you know."

"I got a good idea."

"Who?"

"When I know for sure, joo know. I call joo first. That okay?"

"If that's what you want, Pappy. I can direct the information through the proper channels."

"That is fair enough. This business, well, I hope it ends before somebody gets it."

"I know what you mean."

As we hung up, I really didn't know what to think. I know that Lenny's boys recorded the conversation, and I'd probably get another reminder from him, but what am I supposed to do? Brush him off? Let him get killed?

From the time I graduated from the academy to when I became a detective, I always thought the world of crime was black and white. The good guys never broke the rules and those who did were the bad guys. You do this long enough, you find out that not all the good are all good, and the bad guys aren't all bad. The common denominator with both sides is that it's human nature to eschew disappointment. We want our friends happy and sometimes we'll do whatever it takes to make them so. Who likes saying no? I was no different from anybody else. I knew these guys weren't 100 percent bad like Mack said, and lately, I tried to cater to their better nature. That didn't work every day, however. Some mornings, I found myself still intimidating the punks on the corner or stalking the bolita writer's storefronts. I had friends all over. I had no enemies, except maybe one, and that was probably Lozello.

Later that afternoon, Mack called me with an angry warning.

"Hey Bill, you'll never believe what just happened to me at home."

"Mack! Long time..."

"You'll never believe it, Bill."

"Okay. I'm gonna go out on a limb here and say someone just tried to hit you from a van."

He paused momentarily. "I'd ask how you knew that, but I'm assuming I'm not the first."

"Was it an orange and black with a gun port?"

"Orange and black, all right. Probably a Dodge, but I couldn't tell you for sure. And I didn't notice any gun port. He...the driver, I mean, had the barrel sticking out of his window. Son-of-a-bitch drove by my house twice."

"Jesus, Mack. What happened?"

"Nothing. I grabbed two of my huntin' rifles and had them scoped at 50 yards on the second pass...think they saw my boy through the window. Kinda spooked him a little, though. I had him hide behind the couch with his own rifle, just in case."

"For the love of... Did you call anybody yet?"

"Oh yeah. I called our buddies at the sheriff's department since it's their jurisdiction, then I called Jose Fernandez."

"I'll send it on to Lenny too, if you don't mind. That's the second one I've heard about today. They tried to hit Pappy Hernandez too, so you know."

"Well, if I see the bastards come by here again, I'm just gonna touch 'em off and ask questions later. And you better watch your ass too, fella."

"Huh." I laughed. "Every day, Mack."

Agent Savage arrived on time that next Wednesday afternoon, handing me a fresh cup of coffee as I climbed in the passenger's side of his car. Lenny called earlier that day explaining that he was temporarily yanking me from Lozello to cover a suspected hit on Ben.

It was later that morning when we pulled up in a parking lot across the street from Lilliput's. Harold had some fun stories working for Lenny over the years. I could tell he was somewhat bitter about working some of the suspected subversion cases during the 'Nam era, however.

We sat while cars came and went from the beauty salon's lot where we parked. A plain sedan drove up to Lilliput's entrance and out popped Angel Vargas—alone. He stepped inside and, a few moments later, he and two other men walked back out. I immediately recognized one.

"What do you think?"

"Looks like a couple of deviants to *me*." Savage said.

"That's Guillermo Mendez—Santa Claus. Who's the other?" I asked.

Savage quickly set the focus on his 35mm and snapped a few pictures. "Dunno, but did you catch the barrel under his jacket? Ah. Never mind."

Before I had a chance to confirm Harold's observation, Vargas had already handed the car's keys to them and they jumped in. Savage handed the camera to me and hastily hit our car's ignition, forgetting it was already running. That set off a loud screech that made Vargas' head turn. I just sat there, thinking Vargas just made us, but the glare coming over our backs and across the windshield obscured his view. Vargas evidently didn't think much of it, or just assumed we were probably stupid women since we were in front of a salon. Whatever the explanation, he walked back inside, leaving us safe.

I looked over at Harold who looked back at me with the driest swallow. "Oops."

He placed the car in reverse and backed out, leaving the salon's lot and taking up a 200-yard tail on Vargas' car, heading east on Kennedy. I remembered them taking a left on Dale Mabry, and then hopping on the interstate heading north.

When we were close to the on-ramp for I-4 Eastbound, Savage sighed, "Uh-oh."

"What?"

"They're heading towards Orlando. See?"

He pointed out their turn signal and lane change. "Better call it in, Bill."

I hopped on the radio for the update. As a precaution, the bureau had already moved our friend Ben from his suddenly-not-so-safe house. When word had arrived that the hit was on the way, they had a couple of well-armed types waiting quietly inside with a full tactical team hidden around the corner.

We followed that car for over an hour and a half all the way to Winter Park, just on the northeast side of Orlando. I didn't know the exact location of Ben's house and neither did Savage. I'm not sure if Vargas' men knew either. They drove around for over thirty minutes, going through several neighborhoods without stopping. Finally, they hopped back on the interstate and headed back towards Tampa. Savage and I broke off the tail and met up with some other agents at the Orlando field office. We handed over the film for analysis, discussed the run, and then headed back to Tampa after a short lunch.

"Made?" I asked.

"Len Karman thinks so." Savage replied.

"I don't."

"Why's that?"

"Vargas didn't make us and he had no way of warning them after they left."

"Then why did they just drive around Winter Park all that time without stopping. If they knew there wasn't a tail, they would have gone through with it, right?"

"Hard to say, Bill. I've heard of runs like this. Maybe someone tipped them about the general location; maybe even the neighborhood, but not the exact address. Maybe they want to shake us out. Maybe they had other business going down in Tampa and knew this would divert some eyes. Who knows. What I *do* know is that Davidson is not lying face down on some hokey shag."

Lenny's technician's developed the negatives from Savage's camera later that afternoon and confirmed their intelligence. The person traveling with Santa Claus was a "watched" escape artist named Peter Danforth Lewis. According to his prison guards, cellmates affectionately called him "Danny Boy", but it wasn't because of any Irish heritage; he was actually Jewish. They called him Danny Boy because he was a favorite with the bulls — building up their confidence and companionship by trading his services. That was his modus operandi. After a few days, he would have one of them give his face a good once over so he'd got a free ride to the infirmary where it was easier to escape. The ploy worked the first few times until they wised up and let him bleed the night away. So, what does he do? Hire some fresh ambulance chaser wanting to make a name for himself by filing a suit against the state for denial of his medical rights. They immediately threw the case out.

Lenny's brief went on to say they released Lewis back in May as part of an exchange deal for testimony. He supposedly snitched on another prisoner bragging about a prior murder he had committed. Thing is, the DA suspects he and the prosecutor were lying, so they're keeping an eye on 'ole Danny Boy here.

Lizards of Lounge

On an early Saturday morning, with my shirt already soaked with sweat from mowing the lawn, Lenny whisked his government-issued Dodge into my driveway, asking if I minded a short visit.

"Not a problem at all Lenny, if you don't mind giving me a moment to get cleaned up. Is it an emergency?"

"Not yet." He calmly replied.

Lenny had that cold look again, and I knew it was probably serious enough if he was bouncing to my driveway on a Saturday morning. His frigidity spoke volumes.

The cold shower felt good, but it only lasted long enough to get the soap on and off. The military two-minute drill paid off sometimes. I threw on a pair of slacks and an undershirt then strode back over to the kitchen where Wendy kept him occupied with a fresh cup of coffee.

"Sorry to trouble you guys, Bill. Take a look at today's front page. Do you recognize the car?" Lenny sipped at his coffee.

I studied the picture for several moments before noticing the caption, "Lounge Wars Continue". The scene involved a half-burnt Cadillac with a destroyed engine compartment and a huge hole in the windshield in front of the steering wheel.

"Whose is this?" I was fixated on the photograph and didn't bother reading the article.

"That's Pappy Hernandez's car."

"He dead?"

"No. It's in the article; there was only one person in the car, but it wasn't him."

I scanned the article quickly before Lenny grew frustrated.

"Who is Christopher Garcia?" I asked.

"That's his daughter's boyfriend."

"Holy Jesus! He lived through that?" I looked again at the hole in the windshield.

"The dynamite was either weak or they miswired the device. Either way, the bomb detonated under the driver's seat and ejected him through the windshield. He's lucky he doesn't have a broken neck."

"Oh that's awful!" Wendy said, glancing at the newspaper as she passed.

"Sorry, Mrs. Brume. I didn't mean for you to see that."

"It was for Hernandez, of course." I said.

"That's why I'm here, Bill."

"Yeah?"

"I want you to interview Hernandez and see why he thinks someone wanted him dead."

I looked at Lenny and wiped my still-sweating forehead with the towel I brought from the bathroom. "You mean Vargas, don't you?"

He shrugged, "Probably, but I want to know why."

"Wouldn't Hernandez's interview already have been taken by TPD?"

Lenny laughed and put his hand on my shoulder before exiting. "Geez, Bill. You know I can't trust anything officially printed from that inept institution. At least, not right now."

I laughed.

When Lenny drove away, Wendy came up from behind and threw her arms around me. My mind wandered inside the photograph in the newspaper. She put her head next to mine and wept ever so slightly. "When will this be over?"

I almost blurted, "When the right people are either dead or behind bars", but opted for a less inflammatory approach.

"Soon, I hope."

Craving the wind, I saddled up on my aging Triumph and rambled over to one of Hernandez's taverns on South Tampa's west side. He wasn't there, but the bartender told me he was probably at his other location over by the football stadium off Dale Mabry further north, so off I went. I gathered the bartender would call ahead and warn him of my intent. When I arrived, my assumptions were correct. I'd heard about Hernandez from several detectives that knew him from his bolita running days and his lounge operations. They all had nice things to say. If you needed a doctor, he knew the ten best. If you needed a mechanic, one would show up at your door within the hour. Pappy Hernandez liked making people happy it seemed. I imagined there were a few that took advantage of his generosities and put him in danger.

After a bouncer checked me over, he led me towards the back of the building where Hernandez waited in a smoke-hazed office. I held out my hand to this tall man with dark hair similar to Elvis Presley's. He had a dark complexion, wore glasses with thick, black frames, and sported a light yellow guayabera shirt, tan slacks, and brown shoes. He shook my hand firmly.

I attempted a lighthearted icebreaker. "How's your son-in-law?"

Immediately, Hernandez's eyes widened and he smiled. "I've not given away my daughter yet! Besides, the poor boy may not walk for some time, joo know. His legs got burned real bad from the explosion."

"He's lucky to be alive."

"Very. Joo know they found seven more sticks unexploded?"

"It wasn't in the paper."

"Ha-ha!" Hernandez laughed. "They didn't say the car was borrowed, either!"

"Hadn't heard that."

"I told it to this investigator for the police. Didn't they share that with you?"

"Mr. Hernandez, I'm not with the department any longer."

Pappy Hernandez appeared puzzled for only a moment before asking the obvious. "Then why..."

"I'm working with the FBI now. Sure, I still have contacts with the department, but I don't get everything. Who was the detective?"

Hernandez paused momentarily, and so did I when he gave me the name. "I believe his name is Skitter."

So, Robert Skitter was still with the department and even working homicide. The revelation contained more dynamics than I presently had time to digest.

"Skitter, huh."

"You know him?"

I didn't want Hernandez clued too much at the history between Skitter and me. I only desired an honest dialog. If he knew I detested the man, or worse, that he may not have reported every detail Hernandez relayed, it may corrupt my fact-finding ability.

"We worked together." I cut directly to the chase. "I'll be brief, Mr. Hernandez..."

"Please call me Pappy. Everyone calls me Pappy. I hear Mr. Hernandez and I feel like I'm in court."

"Okay, Pappy. All I really need to know is your opinion on who bombed your car."

He gazed at me momentarily, puzzling at my question. "It's very interesting that you should ask me this question."

"Why's that?"

"The detectives were not so interested in my opinion. They only want information about the car, my daughter's boyfriend, and what I was doing."

"That *is* interesting." My body language insinuated my desire for his continuance, which he obliged.

"You wanna know who I think did it?"

"Angel Vargas?"

"Angel? Are you kidding me? He's like a brother to me. I couldn't run my places without him."

"Wait. What?"

"Listen, Bill, it's not Angel. If he wanted some of my bars, all he woulda had to do is ask and I'd set him up."

The new information stuck me on a fact I somehow missed. "No, I mean, does Vargas work for you? I thought those bars were *his*?"

"Which bars?"

"Randy's and Liliput's."

Hernandez laughs hysterically. "What? Naw. Vargas *manages* the bars. He's the best operator in town! I own Randy's, but we named it after his brother as a sort of a gift. Lili's is Sal Tresedici's place. You can look it all up downtown."

"I'll take your word for it."

Of course, we still hadn't shared any prognostications on his bombing.

"If not Vargas, then who?" I asked.

"I don't know, honestly."

"Well, when you said 'interesting' a minute ago, I thought you did."

"I said 'interesting' because I had two guys from outta town in here last night trying to tell me they knew who did it. Said they'd help me with the problem if I wanted."

"Did they ever say who?"

"I ran 'em off before they got a chance. Don't want that kind of trash around here, joo know. I ain't got no respect for hoods, Bill."

"I understand, Pappy."

There was a slight hesitation in Hernandez's answer that gave me reason to pause. Pappy was a likeable guy, much the same way Mack described Emilio Letto. For that matter, Angel Vargas and Giuseppe Cantonello were all *likeable* personalities. Where was it written that mobsters were all gruffly Sicilians with poor English skills and short tempers? I hadn't finished with Hernandez, so I reached into my denim shirt's left pocket and tapped out a Winston. Before I could reach into my pocket again, Pappy had his Zippo's aroma seducing my nostrils. I took a long draw and surveyed his office briefly.

"Did you get a good look at them?"

"They were in here for about thirty minutes before they felt like asking for me personally. Yeah, I got a good look at them. One guy was kinda lanky like one of those pasty European types. Short blond hair, blue eyes. A little taller than joo maybe, but less muscular. The other was a guy about the same height, but heavier. He had longer brown hair, some sideburns, and a funny looking nose. I think he was straight."

"Yeah? Why so?" I asked.

"You run a place like this long enough, joo know. Straight guys can't handle the fairy bars too well. They get the heebie jeebies. I see it all the time."

"What about the other?"

"He acted like any other of my customers. Well, not from Randy's joo know. Plays the role of the man. You watch them; joo catch them looking low. The eyes don't lie."

"Never do!"

"Yeah, *joo* know. Bet joo've seen a few too."

"Not as many as you, my friend." I chuckled. "I asked Vargas this once and he didn't give me a straight answer—what makes a straight man want a homo bar?"

Surprisingly, Hernandez didn't take offense to my question.

"Ay, this is simple. Money. I bet Angel told joo the same, no? You got all these places out there, but nobody wants the queers. Bad for business because the straights make the trouble. Queer money is just as good; better even because they spend a lot of it and don't make no trouble. You ask me, that's an easy business decision."

Pappy was right about one thing; the answer was pretty much the same as Vargas'. Money or not, I didn't understand why someone surrounded themselves with such degradation.   I thought the meeting was particularly fruitful with the exception of his dodging of the main question. The guys that paid him a visit; they knew who bombed the car, and I'd bet they were Santa Claus and Danny Boy.

Around the Ben

[click]
"Pappy, this is Sal. What's this going on?"
"You tell me."
"I don't understand these bombings, you know. Not of you; I can see Carlos maybe. He's got a lot of enemies, you know."
"I don't know what's going on, Sal. I don't want to discuss anything more over the phone. Thank you for calling. See you later."
[click]

Ben stopped the recording and gave me one of his trademark smirks before sitting back down.
"Mystery solved?"
"No. Not really." I replied while closing my lighter's lid.
His smirk instantly disappeared. Ben and I enjoyed our friendly debates over the past few years. I supposed that's what kept us fresh. Up until the time the Bureau locked him away in Orlando, we trashed a lot of dope dealers and their assorted thugs, not to mention the careless bolita bunch. He had no qualms mixing business and pleasure either. While my fiasco with the department was ongoing, neither did I. If it was later in the afternoon, you could bet there was a scotch on the rocks melting around somewhere close to his desk. Maybe it was a natural reaction to the enormous stress — dangling like a cliffside boulder.
I could tell Ben was getting impatient for my answer.
"That call asks more questions than it answers, if you ask me. I don't believe for one second that John doesn't know the identity of the bombers. I also think they may be operating independently,

which would definitely be against the rules. Having spoken personally with Hernandez, they consider him a family friend, but I'm not telling you anything you don't already know, Ben."

"You don't think the call implicates Tresedici for Salazar's drive-by?"

"Jeez, Ben. That seems pretty weak to me, even as a corroborative."

He took a larger than normal slug from his glass and finished it off with a piece of ice to gnaw on.

"I think the grand jury ought to hear it anyway," he said.

"Grand jury?" He completely caught me off guard.

"Yep."

"Ben, we don't have enough for a grand jury yet!"

"Oh, you better believe I have plenty for a grand jury—just not enough on the right people yet. Oh sure, I can drag them in there and have a media circus with nothing more than accusations, but I've got to have the hard evidence first. They know we're close, Bill. Why do you think they're going to all the trouble?"

"You mean Mendez and Lewis."

"Hapless pawns. You know we could've scooped them up several weeks ago if it weren't for taking down the others. Do you know what they've been up to the last month?"

"Not since their Orlando run, no. Lenny has me working Lozello, you know."

"They're taking scores on liquor stores and old ladies."

"Well that fits perfectly with what I was thinking."

"What."

"That they are operating independently. Come on. John has unlimited funding if he needs it. All he has to do is ask, and if the family sanctions it, it's a done deal. Otherwise, they have to scrap for themselves." I said.

"Bill, these losers could just be a couple of addicts. Besides, the amounts their robbing. Small potatoes comparatively…at least to some of my more recent defendants."

"True, but that phone call and their desperateness leads me to believe they need a lot of cash for something else."

The warmth of my drink loosened me somewhat. While pondering the motives of Santa and Danny Boy, my friend's last remark finally slid through the murk. I had been meaning to ask him, finally, about his representational selections, but I never had the gumption—until now.

"Speaking of *your defendants*..."

Ben straightened up in his chair and set the last of his drink down. Maybe I inflected too much sarcasm before he interrupted me, but that interruption was nothing more than the knee-jerk of a young professional.

"You know I cannot discuss them." He said.

"Ben, I didn't want to talk about any of them in particular. We keep up with your cases as they go down. I know of your 'victories' defending some of these kooks. I know you probably look at it the same way Gravina does; strictly a law thing."

Ben reached for my glass and offered a refill. I told him just to make it a half glass before I continued. "But I just don't understand why you're doing it at all. We work very hard to bring them to you and you're working the other direction. Why?"

The big man's jovial nature returned. He liked nothing more than an ignorant conversational opponent. I guess any lawyer does.

"Money!"

What little scotch flew through my nose stung horrifically. "What?" I yelled.

"Just kidding. That's what most people tend to think, so I let them enjoy their own, um, triumph."

"Not the money?"

"Let's not kid ourselves. Their money is good and it's usually cash, but that's not the real reason."

"Okay. Then why?"

"Because I was asked to."

"By whom?" The obvious question begged, even though I didn't quite understand yet.

"I can't give a name, Bill. Let's just say they're a few levels above my pay grade."

"Okay. I'm listening."

"Bill, I imagine when we, meaning you or I, keep our heads down buried in our work, we forget that we're only working on a certain level of the larger arena. Even so, some of the basic premises apply even though the scale or scope may be considerably different. You used to work some low-level dealers, street thugs, or bolita handlers. They come in, get processed, serve a term or go free, and return to society. The difference between before and after is that we tag them like an Ocala Herford. What does the law-abiding part of society get out of that?"

"The tab."

"Exactly. Now, on the state and federal levels, things become slightly more complicated." Ben loosened his tie and I could tell I was in for a ride. "The best way I know how to put it in layman's terms..."

"Hey!"

"Sorry, I didn't mean it as a jab at you. I meant it generally. Basically..."

"Yeah, yeah...go on." I couldn't help making the big guy laugh.

"...you have to think of our government on strictly business terms. They let the high rollers pass until they've built up a nice stash; we make a raid, or in some cases, a larger-scale invasion, and that's the game. Sometimes they want some people going back to the pond. Others—maybe not important enough, tactically."

"Vargas?"

"Let me tell you about that bastard; he may be a prime example of what we're discussing, but I'm here to tell ya, Bill; I'll get forty thousand-worth out of him one way or another."

Admittedly, it was wrong of me to question my friend's integrity. Ben was the lawyer's lawyer and I had to respect that. Some of my scientifically-minded friends believe maturation also occurs through some sort of osmosis. My natural reaction was typically resentment because I knew they were cleverly—or so they thought—patting themselves on the back. But they were right to a degree. My observations placed those types, as brilliant as they are, with characteristics including acute low self-esteem. While it would seem that they should have plenty, their educational drive is usually due in part to sate constant belittling; either from the jealous society or from their own parents. The truly wise call it "encouragement". I found myself drawn to these types because, well, I guess I am a masochist to some degree. In the end, however, it all works out. They have needs to excel and pontificate; I am their dope. What they didn't know is that I was probably getting the better part of the deal.

Pappy

By late September, I had been following Lozello around on nearly a daily basis. My family grew tired of my schedule and I could see the growing disappointment on their faces, but school kept Jeffrey and Junior busy during the day, thankfully. Wendy's job also kept her amused, but when everyone came home, I was never there, nor in the vicinity. It wasn't as if I was unreachable, however; if you knew Lozello's location, I was usually within three hundred yards.

For over a month, he rarely left the department unless he was on his way home. Once there, he didn't move for the evening. That usually occurred around 8:30, so at around thirty minutes after which I arrived home; just in time to see the boys to bed and hear my wife's grumblings. She never understood why I smiled every time she complained. I wanted to tell her about the new house, but I lived for surprises. It never dawned on me that *I* didn't like surprises, but now that I think about it, I shouldn't have been surprised when Pappy Hernandez phoned early one morning in a complete state of panic.

"Joo gotta meet me," he said, gasping for air. "They just tried to keel me again. Go to my bar on the Cass Street in South Tampa. Can joo do it?"

"Get ahold of yourself, Pappy. Yeah, I'll be there in a few minutes." And, like that, I was on my way to another meeting with Hernandez—leaving my wife and kids alone in the middle of the night.

When I arrived at the inaptly-named Coliseum Lodge, a newer white Cadillac sat in front of its doors. One tire had gone flat, there was steam drifting from the rear of the hood next to the windshield, and there were several small holes puncturing the driver's side rear quarter panel. It didn't take a genius to figure out what just happened.

Pappy had taken a seat in the restaurant's furthest back corner booth near a doorway leading towards the rear. I remembered thinking to myself that if I were in his shoes, that was a perfect place to sit. The problem was, the worst possible location for me to sit would be across from him. I therefore grabbed a chair and sat next to him where I could at least see the rest of the place with peripheral vision.

Hernandez was still breathing hard, and sweat covered his clothing. He had mostly calmed down, however. The ashtray in front of him already had three butts crumpled inside and Pappy was about to finish his fourth.

"Goddamnit, Bill!" He said while reaching for the cigarettes in his shirt pocket. His mannerisms were certainly far from the calm and confident businessman he had become. Although he wasn't in a panic, Pappy was clearly in a state of shock.

"Are you going to tell me about it?"

"Yeah, gimme a minute," he said while sparking a silver butane lighter.

"Take your time. I already saw the car."

Pappy finally took his eyes off the table and brought them towards mine. "I saw him, Bill. I saw the man who came after me."

"It was just one?"

"There were two, but I only got a good look at the driver. It was him."

"Who?"

"The same son-of-a-bitch that came into my club after they bombed my car, man!"

"Santa Claus?"

Pappy paused for a moment and looked at me somewhat surprised. "Uh, no; it was his partner — the switch hitter."

"I thought he was a just another homo."

"One of the fellas said he heard him hittin' on woman once, so maybe…"

"Okay, I get it. What about the other one?"

"Did not see him too good, but it wasn't the Santa guy. It was some sickly-looking dude. All I could see was that he was white as a ghost and probably not more than five eight and a hundred-fifty."

"So what happened?"

Pappy took a long draw off his smoke. "Was up at a new place off the 22nd. Rough part of town, you know. Night ended normal. I let my night manager handle the deposit—walked him out to his car, making sure nobody did anything stupid. That is part of our procedures, joo know."

"Okay."

"So I watch him pull out of the lot all safe and I go get in my car. I start it up and get ready to leave; this car sitting in the dark across the street starts up and hits the gas, coming right at me. I see the barrel sticking out the window, so I duck down. All I hear next is this loud bang and my ears start ringing. I look up and the car passed right by and starts to turn around for another pass. I do not remember much about how I got on the road, but I got the sucker in gear and took off down the road for Buffalo. I see them throwing their car around and gas it towards me, so I hit the gas too."

"How fast were you going?" I had to ask.

"Oh, man. I dunno, Bill. Joo think I'm gonna give that any consideration with a gun pointed at me?'

"I suppose not."

"So I get down to Buffalo, make a right and then a left on MacDill, I think. They get up right behind me, aiming that shotgun at my car. I think they fired again, but I did not feel anything hit the car…not like the first time. So, we're flying down MacDill coming down this way. There are not any other cars in sight. Never a cop when joo need one, right?"

"I'm here, aren't I?"

"Joo know what I mean."

"Sorry. Please continue."

"We get past the Interstate underpass and I see two squad cars just sitting there."

"Tampa City?"

"Jeah!"

"And they do nothing even though you're speeding right past them."

"Jeah!"

"You and the other car too." I said.

"Uh-huh!"

"Interesting."

"Interesting? Jeah. Interesting all right. They weren't gonna do anything, I figure, so I reach over and grab my pistol from the glove box. We were in the middle lane, so I move over real quick and hit the brakes, taking a shot as they went by…think I hit right behind the right door. Anyway, they hit their brakes too, so I hit the gas and drive on the other side of the street to pass them on the left."

"Clever."

"I think we flew right over Kennedy—couldn't shake them. Perhaps next I threw a left on, I don't know, maybe Cleveland or Platt…it was not that far but, oh; it don't matter. I think I lost a hubcap or two on that turn. It wasn't fast enough though. They started ramming their car into my rear bumper. Maybe that is why my neck hurts a little. Anyway, I swung a right onto Hyde Park and headed towards Davis Island, thinking that maybe I can lose them in there. I think they took another shot when I made that turn too; still didn't feel it hit the car. I tried to ditch them at the main split down there, but they stayed right on me. I think we were doing seventy when we hit the Thrill Hill." (A very small hump of a bridge connecting the islands)

"Holy…"

"I think I went a good eighty feet, Bill. —Beat me up pretty good and almost missed the curve."

"I can't believe your car still ran. You go more than forty and you're in the air."

"That's where I lost them. I crossed over to the east side and came back out the other way."

"You're very lucky, Pappy."

"I know. But…"

"I guess after two attempts, you're a little sour."

"Jour obvious comments are getting a little worn out, man! That was a brand new Cadillac, joo know?"

I laughed, but I couldn't really tell much about Hernandez's frame of mind, not having been around him. He laughed too, so my guesswork paid off.

"Pappy, I think you should maybe not call anyone about this just yet. I'll get the right people on to you first thing in the morning."

He looked at me with the eyes of revelation. "My phones are tapped, aren't they?"

I could not answer, and when I didn't, his disgust followed.

"Joo bastards already know what is going on, Bill. Why joo dangle me out there like that?"

"No, Pappy. We don't. I cannot discuss anything about that either, but I can tell you this; because of what you're telling me, and because I trust you that it's the truth, we only know who is actually gunnin' for you, not who's hiring them or why."

"No. I don't believe it."

"What?"

"No. No 'what' — who!"

"You know who it is?"

"Jes, but I don' believe it. If it is them then it is only a matter of time. I cannot hide, but I gotta know why."

"Who?"

"Don't sit there and insult me, Bill. Joo know who. I just don't believe it!"

Doubt. It was my best friend in any interrogation. It automatically dawned on me that I had a real chance, just like with The Match, to gain a goldmine for Lenny and Ben. I sat there and let my facial expressions guide his emotions. After a few moments, I offered the deal.

"Look Pappy. I cannot say. You know I cannot. I can offer you protection, however."

"Rat? Never." Hernandez folded his arms.

"Wait. Is this a respect thing? Please, Pappy. Don't play the old balls of steel gag with me. I don't see how you can have any respect for someone trying to kill you."

"Yeah. Joo see? Joo know it is them!"

"Think of your family, Pappy. We can make sure they are safe."

"Safe? No one is safe from them, and I mean no one!"

"Pappy, that's not true. My people have placed people safely all the time."

"Ha! Only the ones they do not care about, jefe."

"Come on, Pappy. You know they aren't going to stop. This is twice now. How much luck do you think you have left?"

Hernandez looked around for a few moments and then got up to get a shot of rum from the bar. After lighting yet another cigarette, he walked back over and sat down in exasperation. His throat was choked. His confidence was completely shattered.

"For over ten years now, I operate these clubs, and this is how they do me. Cojones!"

"Talk to me." I said.

For over an hour, Pappy Hernandez told me the story of his life growing up in West Tampa. He ran bolita for the family back in the late '50s and got arrested early—serving a year in a state prison—which earned his rite of passage. He told me the prosecutor was a real son-of-a-bitch that had it out for those in the gambling trades. He told me they offered him a deal back then and turned it down, saying that his two-year sentence wasn't worth cooperation. Prison was the least safe place and he'd be dead in a week.

Pappy complained about the feds constantly harassing him after he got out of prison. They were constantly picking him up, and always at the most publically-embarrassing places. They arrested him at the horse track in Oldsmar for bringing his own bottle, and again for the same offense at the Jai-Alai cancha in South Tampa. After the terms of his parole were up, he became available for a liquor license. Pappy smiled and told me that's all he ever wanted to do; entertain people. But, he didn't have the money.

Word got around and he told me about his sit-down with Sal Tresedici. He said it was a big affair. Sal wasn't a public man at all, but he liked the formal dinners. Pappy remarked that it was only them two in a back office, making a deal for the cash he needed for his first bar. As long as Sal's machines were the only ones in the place, he would front the fourteen grand. Of course, it wasn't Sal's money directly, but from some of his friends. Honestly, it didn't sound much different than many of the no-compete contracts I've heard of, except for one glaring difference; you break the contract and there is no legal process, just a friendly visit.

"You mean like Carlos Salazar?"

"I do not know about this. Joo know I helped that peg leg bastard get his first bar? It's a shame. He is a good guy, but joo know, he got into the vending business."

Pappy continued with how, in just ten years, he and Sal continued on and how the gay bar industry exploded in the late '60s. We had already covered some of that ground so he skipped most of the small details. What I didn't expect was when he said he only got the first loan from Tresedici. After that, he used legitimate banks, often mortgaging the equipment in the bars. In the end, he told me that he now owned more than a dozen bars and was making money, legitimate money, hand over fist. Even though his friends gave him plenty of opportunities in the rackets, drugs, prostitution, or even back with bolita, he politely and graciously declined. They were happy with his businesses and the money he generated. He told me, when it came right down to it, he just didn't want to go back to prison, disappointing his wife and kids…especially the one he adopted a few years ago.

By the time Pappy finished, it was almost daylight. He began feeling safe enough to leave, so I handed him Lenny's business card.

"I could take you to him right now, Pappy."

"No, no. I must get home before the wife and kids wake up, if they haven't already. It is not fair to make them worry so."

"You sure?"

"Can joo give me a ride? My engine is blown, I think."

"No problem."

He had a swank two-story home on Davis Islands with one of those driveways that circle a small fountain. It wasn't as fancy or large as the mansions off of Bayshore Boulevard, but it was nice. Just before he stepped out of the car, he turned around and firmly shook my hand.

"Joo need anything—anything at all, joo just call me, okay?"

I pointed towards his front shirt pocket. "Pappy, call the number on that card."

"Let me think about it."

When I arrived home, Wendy kept her back turned to me, huddling over a cup of coffee. I had been out all night and she had been crying.

"You bastard!" She said, weeping. "Couldn't you at least call and let me know you're okay?"

Expectations. Even though I told her this would happen from time to time, Wendy had issues lately and expected an update if anything happened that was out of the ordinary. I didn't want to worry her, especially in the middle of the night.

"My mistake."

She threw up her right hand, signaling her unwillingness for hearing excuses. I walked past, grabbed the phone, and called Lenny right in front of her so she could hear every part of my report. That didn't interest Wendy, however. In fact, she got up from the table, walked over to the sink, and dumped her remaining coffee.

It was a long weekend in which nobody hardly said a word to each other. The boys sat quietly, watching their requisite cartoons and Tarzan, while Wendy kept herself busy with cleaning projects. I did outside chores. I thought about what a waste of a perfectly good weekend it was, being that the weather was still warm with huge sunsets, and that the tourists were all gone. Then came Monday.

Still of the Night

Just as Wendy and the boys departed for work and school, the kitchen phone rang off the hook. I didn't let it bother me while hugging the boys goodbye for the day and receiving one of the most emotionless cold-kisses Wendy ever pecked. After the ninth ring, I decided the caller either had a burr up their ass or a dire emergency. It turned out to be Lenny, nearly out of breath with excitement.

"Guess who I just spent an hour on the phone with?"

"Please tell me it was Hernandez," I said.

"You are correct, sir."

"Ha! I thought he'd call."

"Very good work, Bill. Very good work, indeed."

"Well?"

"We're setting it all up through Davidson and the Marshals. He said he wants everyone off his back and his family safe in return."

"In return for what?"

"He's going to testify. Tresedici, Vargas, a few of your ex-coworkers — the lot."

"For the love of…really?"

"No kidding. And, he had a personal message he wanted to deliver to you. He said, 'Please tell Bill Brume I will never forget what he did for me and that he should say hello to his ex-boss this afternoon.' What do you make of it?"

"A long evening, probably. I'd better get ready."

"Ooh, the excitement!"

"Ha! Calm down, Len. It's probably just Lozello playing cards with a few of his associates again. We'll see."

"Good luck with this one. The wife and I are skipping town for two weeks back home, so if you hit the jackpot or something, you call Harry Savage. He'll get word to me."

As soon as I hung up the phone, I composed the equipment manifest in my mind while taking a quick shower. The camera needed a new battery and I thought I should probably pick up some film that worked better under the streetlights. The agents in the lab complained of some blurriness due to the fact I couldn't hold the camera absolutely still. Propping it on the car's door, steering wheel, or dashboard helped, but those half-second exposures needed more stability. I called Lenny back and he put me on to his man in charge of the photographic division at the local field office. He set me up with a new battery for the camera and four rolls of a much faster film, allowing me to take distant shots under streetlights without the graininess and blur. I still had to keep the camera as steady as possible, however.

It took until almost 1 p.m. to finally get everything together, and then I immediately sped off towards the Tropicana in Ybor, hoping to catch up with Lozello at his favorite watering hole. I was either too late or he ate somewhere else.

Just about everyone knew me around the department, including the bail bondsmen across the street. Parking anywhere near the station would be risky, I thought, as I came within a couple of blocks of the Aztec Lounge. I had already hit the brakes and ducked around the next corner when Lozello spilled onto the sidewalk from the lounge's front door. He never looked in my direction before traipsing around to his car door. I hit the end of the block and made a fast u-turn, getting back to the intersection a block down from the Aztec just as Lozello pulled out. Instead of heading down the street towards the station, he made his own u-turn and headed my direction. I remember panicking for only a moment before reaching up to grab the visor; yanking it down before he came close enough to make me. As he passed, I looked the other direction to make absolutely sure he didn't see my face. He continued on for another block without any sudden movement, so I let him go down another two blocks before getting back on his tail.

Lozello headed east across the ghettos and around Ybor channel before turning southward towards the docks. I had to stay back quite a bit further than I normally would have because the traffic mostly consisted of tractor-trailers or box vans. There were very few cars in the mix and I was one of them. After two more turns, he came to a stop at Hooker's Point alongside a large cargo truck that was unloading a docked freighter. The ship was a veritable rust heap almost as long as a football field. There wasn't much cover, so I had to take position around a metal building almost two hundred yards away. Too far!

The 300mm lens Lenny issued me was certainly a champ at long distances, but it would take at least twice that if I were to pull any resolution at two hundred yards. I had to get closer. About ninety yards back there was another large metal building with an alley joining the building I was shadowing. My heart was thumping. Sweat immediately poured into my eye sockets. I remembered thinking I would never get the camera focused with all that sweat in my eyes, but it was all academic if I couldn't get close enough.

Lozello was about to climb out of his car, so I made a mad dash around the other side of the building and quietly walked up the gravel alleyway towards the building's corner. It never dawned on me that there might be a stray worker or two attached to one of these warehouses. What if they discovered me? I couldn't worry about that right now; I could shoot Lozello clearly from my new position, and what I saw next made it paramount.

Lozello met and shook the hand of a short but muscular Latino man dressed in a pair of dirty blue overalls. The scruffy man then reached inside a small canvas gym bag and pulled out a plastic brick of brown powder; a full kilogram of heroin. Before I could take the picture, my heart sank. All this time I knew, in the back of my mind, I knew, but the proof was too elusive. At the same time, I didn't want to believe what my eyes were seeing. It was the closest I ever came to crying, not for Lozello, mind you, but for the good, honest people of Tampa. For a split-second, I almost started to feel sorry about the whole mess. I came within an inkling of turning around and walking back to my car. That almost happened if it wasn't for anger's lightning, jolting me back to reality. Lozello ruined my career; he wanted me dead; he destroyed my life, and attempted to do the same for many of those around me. Now, his abuses were as blatant as ever, and the probability of luck has given me the chance to put much of my chosen city's problems to pasture.

With a deep breath, I picked up the camera, flicked on the meter, and zoomed all the way in, perfectly framing Lozello while he evaluated the brick of heroin. The shutter snapped and I wound off two more before noticing the needle on the far right of the viewfinder. Overexposed! I had forgotten to reset the exposure time for daylight. I almost panicked. Three frames wasted, I thought. Only nine more left on this roll and I won't have time for a change.

My throat was dry as I attempted swallowing my mistake. Faster shutter, higher F-stop. I must have repeated that several times in my mind before my arms, hands, and fingers finally made the correct sequence necessary to complete a simple rotation of a ring on the lens and a knob on the camera body. By the time I brought the viewfinder back up to my left eye, Lozello had already given the heroin back to the little dockworker. Oh, what a missed opportunity! I took three more shots anyway and waited. A minute later, the worker lifted open the truck's rear door and revealed enough heroin to supply the entire Tampa Bay area for at least two months. There was well over a hundred kilos, I calculated, while managing two more shots; both with Lozello and the heroin in-frame. Finally.

I could tell they were both about to leave, so I jogged as fast as I could without somehow gaining their peripheral attention. I waited until Lozello's car and the truck passed my car's position before coming out from behind the buildings and reinitiating my tail.

Lozello escorted the truck back north from the harbor and into the south end of Ybor City, making a left on Kennedy, heading west through downtown. I couldn't believe the brazenness of this operation as they bounced over the bricks downtown and over the river. Even if the dope was the lowest quality "Mexican Mud", they still had around half a million dollars worth in the back of that truck. Incredible.

From Kennedy, they made a left onto MacDill Avenue and headed into the heart of South Tampa. Just past the clubhouse entrance to Palma Ceia Country Club's golf course, Lozello's convoy turned right onto a small side street, before backing into a group of small warehouses. I sped past and found a perfect position half a block down across the street. Nestled under some thick oak trees in the parking lot of a sleepy little bank, I picked up the camera and fiercely rewound the exposures I had taken a few minutes earlier. I threw the exposed cartridge in a canister and reloaded with a fresh roll. I closed the camera's back and checked my exposure settings once more before shooting, and then I glanced up once or twice, making sure I hadn't missed a prime shot. Neither Lozello nor the driver he escorted had emerged yet.

About three minutes went by and I was beginning to wonder what the deal was before another car swung into their parking lot. I remembered thinking that I had never won anything in my life! I always wondered what it was like to hear my name called with the winning raffle ticket, or what it might feel like after pulling the lever on a Las Vegas slot machine and seeing all three tumblers stop on "BAR" or the big "7". I wondered how the President felt at his inauguration. I wondered what went through one's mind when lightning struck them. I remembered what it was like when the nurse placed my son Jeffrey in my arms for the first time. I remembered what it was like giving Wendy her ninth. I felt like I was experiencing all of this at the same time when I saw Angel Vargas step out of his Cadillac, shake Henry Lozello's hand, and hearing my camera's shutter take the perfect of perfects—Lozello, Vargas, and a truckload of heroin—all in the same frame.

In all, I took seven incriminating shots that afternoon. I documented the debarkation points, the delivery system, the shipment amount, the shipment type, and those at the highest trafficking level. I could have waltzed right in there like Harry Callahan and blown their heads clean off. I daydreamt for only a moment before realizing that's just not the way it works. I had no real firepower, just my lemon squeezer and five rounds. I had no communications, so I couldn't just call in the cavalry. Worse, I had no element of surprise. The incendiary pictures and an airtight RICO case would have to do.

I didn't have time to set up another roll of film before Lozello climbed back in his taxpayer-supplied wheels and motored back up the street. Vargas climbed in the passenger's side of the truck alongside its little driver and they did the same. I thought about following them, but I had everything I ever wanted and all that I ever really needed, so I carefully packed the camera outfit as if it were Baby Jesus, and headed for the Tampa field office.

Major Development

Halfway over to the field office a few minutes later, my exuberance melted under a newfound stressor: with Lenny on vacation, how could I trust anyone there with these photos? I didn't really know Agent Savage entirely well, nor any of the lab techs. If my loot ran into anyone sympathetic to the other side, they'd blow the whole operation and worse, I'd probably never get another chance. Damnit! I made a left on Boulevard and headed home.

When I arrived, I really didn't know what to do other than just call Savage and tell him to get word to Lenny that I had what he wanted, but not to push the panic button on his vacation. That was it. I wasn't going to offer any elaboration even if Savage wanted to know, which he didn't. Maybe I should have trusted him and the rest at the field office, but it was just too risky without Lenny in command. For Christ's sake, all I needed was some photos developed! How hard could it be?

That thought dribbled around upstairs the rest of the afternoon. Wendy and the boys were delighted when they came home from work and school. Daddy was home—on a weekday. After that excitement calmed down, I caught Wendy staring at me longer than normal. She had a familiar smirk to her very expressive eyes. I knew that look. But what I didn't know; I was sporting one of my own.

"Okay, what happened?" She said with a sarcastically playful tone.

"That obvious?"

She moaned, "Yes, sir."

I pointed aimlessly in front us, "You see that little gleam down there? That little flicker?"

"What are you talking about?"

"That little glimmer just down there."

"Where?"

"At the end of the tunnel. Do you see it?"

"No." She laughed.

"I do."

She didn't get it, so I pulled her into the bedroom and pointed up into our tiny closet at the camera rig. She knew what it was and where I kept it.

"Really?" She asked.

"Keep a lid on it, will ya? What's in there is probably the most important thing I've ever possessed."

"Then why are you keeping it…"

Wendy is a smart girl. She didn't make it through the question before figuring it out on her own.

"Bill, isn't that a little hot to be keeping in the house. I mean — are we in danger or anything?"

"No! I just need to get some film developed, that's all."

"Why don't you take it downtown and let *them* deal with it?"

"Can't."

"Why? Oh, never mind."

"Just can't."

"And taking it to the pharmacy is out of the question?"

For all of her intelligence, it's thoughtless questions like those that drove me insane sometimes. I didn't have to answer; the sarcastic look on my face provided her answer.

"I have a coworker who says her husband has his own darkroom. What about him?"

"That's a 'hell no!'…might as well just show up at the Tribune with the negatives. That would be something, wouldn't it?"

"Well, how hard could it be, Bill?"

Jeffrey and Junior both wandered into our room, interested in the discussion.

"Dunno, but what I do know is that I feel like some pizza!"

The boy's faces lit up like Christmas trees and the jumping up and down ensued even before any sugar had been consumed. Ah, the energy of youth.

There was no need for a change of clothes or a shower. Everyone was all ready to go, so just like that, we hopped in the old T-bird for some crabmeat pizza and a game of Pong at Maria's if the line wasn't too long. The kids loved that thing.

We had our fill and played a few dollars worth of games before heading home later that evening. Wendy and I relaxed in our bedroom catching an episode of *All in the Family* before she drifted off. We both had a hard time watching that show without making a comment about our neighbor across the street. As soon as the laughs were over, Wendy conked out, so I got up and changed the channel to Monday Night Football. Wendy woke back up immediately and complained that it was too loud. I knew it wasn't the crowd noise that bothered her; it was Howard Cosell's voice. Down goes the volume! Down goes the volume! Down goes the volume!

Even though the game that night was a slow march for the Redskins against a tough St. Louis team, my mind stayed sharply focused on the pictures. I thought about what Wendy had said. How hard could it be?

I got a call back from Harold Savage at 7:30 the next morning. His voice nervously informed me that he couldn't reach Lenny yesterday and his office was still trying to locate him. He said all they could do was leave a message at his hotel, but the reliability of that sort of system was always questionable. For whatever reason, I was still practically on my own. Well, no more aimless wonder, I thought. After hanging up with Savage, I cleaned myself up and took off in the T-bird to the library downtown.

I hadn't spent too much time in one of those places since high school and barely remembered anything about the index card system. After spending a few minutes looking completely lost, a kind librarian strolled over and offered a hand. I supposed I looked rather helpless and some women find that irresistible. Good thing for me, she must have been in her late fifties with hair resembling a Kentucky cockfight loser.

"Ma'am, can you tell me where to find the books on photography?"

She gushed with omnipotence. "Well, are you looking for photographs, or how to take photographs?"

"Err, I'm sorry. Developing photographs, actually."

"That would be in the Photographic Techniques section, love. Look in the 770s." She smiled egregiously and pointed towards the area I needed to go.

I thanked her and quietly booked over to that section. 770.28. There were two books available on darkroom materials and techniques that fit the bill and both published within the previous two years. I brought the books over to a reading table and began thumbing through, making a mental list of the basic procedures and equipment necessary. One of the books displayed a very basic lab design for amateurs or students and I decided right there I could possibly pull this off depending on the cost of the equipment. The chemicals couldn't be too much; I didn't need a sink...maybe just some roller painting trays would do. How much could a red light bulb cost? I could use the bathroom tub as a tank, I thought. A plan was coming together.

The most intimidating piece would be the enlarger. If I was going to get from the negative to a print, I had to use an enlarger. I flipped through both books and both depicted the same basic process. Playing it safe, I decided to check out both and drive up to a large camera shop located on the north side of town. I took a deep breath and walked back over to the more-than-friendly librarian, realizing when I placed the books on her counter that I did not, in fact, possess a library card. Talk about making you look stupid! Even my kids had library cards. Wendy had a library card. Just about everyone had a library card—except me. That shortcoming cost any "chance" I had with the librarian, who now had her nose more obviously skyward than Jimmy Durante checking out the moon.

The process of filling out the form and waiting for her to type out my card only took a few painful minutes before she returned.

"Is this your first?" She asked with a wide grin.

I bit a lip and smiled back. She had her moment, but I reveled in the fact that *I* wouldn't be the one walking out of here and attacked by a local gnatcatcher looking for a place to nest. With both books in hand, I marched downstairs and hopped in the car.

By mid-morning, I walked through the doors of a large camera shop just a few miles north off of Busch Boulevard. The air was thick with a smell of chemicals and fresh electronics. I loved that smell. It was almost as good as the oil and leather from a gun shop. It screamed "gear", and I had slowly become a gear head. Tools were important!

Towards the back corner sat what appeared to be two enlargers. One was huge and looked capable of making small posters. The other looked like something more feasible, so I checked on the price. $459. I couldn't afford that.

"Is there something I can help you with?" Said a voice over my right shoulder.

I turned around and a man, about my height with black curly hair and a thick mustache, greeted me. He shook my hand and introduced himself as Maxwell Reidman.

"Yes. I am interested in setting up a temporary darkroom. Kinda want to get my feet wet. I can't afford *this* though," I said.

"That is our least expensive *new* model, but you said temporary?"

"Yeah."

"What are you trying to do?"

"I just want to develop a couple of rolls to see if I like it or not."

"I see."

He looked at me peculiarly. I couldn't be too divulging, of course.

"Do I know you?" He asked.

Uh-oh. I started thinking this could get me in trouble if this guy ended up being someone friendly with the other side. My paranoia was getting the better of me, I thought, so I gave him the standard.

"Have I ever arrested you?"

Maxwell laughed. "Not likely! I know who you are now, I think. Is your name Brume?"

Normally surprises didn't bother me, but now wasn't quite the time. "That's right."

"You probably wouldn't remember me, but I left the department around six years ago and worked for the local FBI field office for two more years before opening this shop. I worked a few of your cases."

I couldn't hide my reaction. I thought I was in a seriously compromising situation. If Maxwell...

"Are you still with the Bureau?"

Well, he knows I'm not with the department any longer, but I suppose that's common knowledge. Whether he believes in the nonsense about my case is another matter. The fact he knows I'm with the Bureau is somewhat troublesome, however.

"I can't..." Again, before I could finish my sentence, Maxwell already made the conclusion.

"I know. Guys talk, you know. I still have friends there and they send business my way. Look, you don't need to say anything, friend. I've been keeping up with some of my folks back at the department and know that place has gone to hell in a hand basket."

"You're not retirement age, Maxwell. Is that why you left?"

"Partially. Mostly because my wife and kids were tired of daddy being on-call; partly because of the departmental politics, but you already knew about that. It was mostly just one idiot's overbearing lunacy, but isn't that always the case?"

"No kidding! And the Bureau?"

"Worse. I endured it for two years. Gone every week for God knows what. Wife about killed me with her guilt trips. Only so many ball games and plays you can miss, right? My father passed on and left me enough to stay home and try a business, so I figured, why not?"

"It's a nice place."

"Thank you."

"So, you need some development gear."

"Right, but…"

"Well, if you were only developing the negatives, it's just a matter of some developer, a small tank, a measuring beaker, and an egg timer. Well, and the red light of course. All of that can be had for under $30."

"What about prints. I really need to do prints. At least 8x10. Black and white would be good enough."

"Is that the film you used?"

"What?"

"Black and white. Did you use black and white film?"

"No, color."

"Then you'll need to do the color negative process. There are a few more steps involved but the cost is only eight dollars more."

"The prints?" I guess he forgot.

"Ah, yes. The paper isn't that expensive, nor are the tanks. For that matter, you could probably use a couple of paint trays and your bathtub.

"I had the same idea!"

"The expensive part is the enlarger."

"That's what I thought."

Maxwell rolled his eyes around for a moment before admitting he had two used Beselers available on consignment from a local high school.

"They're a little worn, but will still do the job. The school wants to clear $50 apiece on those, and I normally ask double as a fee. I'll let one go without my commission for a good cause." He winked.

"Seriously? Just $50? Believe me, the cause couldn't be better."

"Grab one by the base and bring it up front. I'll start gathering the other things you'll need and meet you by the counter. Wait. Do you know what you're doing?"

"I picked up a couple of books at the library."

I told him which books they were and he acknowledged those as the best resources, while adding a few practical tips of his own.

"Listen, Bill. Those books will instruct you that your darkroom has to be fairly clean, but I'm here to tell ya—get it as dust free as you can. In this business, one speck in the wrong place can lose you big, understand?"

"Got it."

He rambled off a few more tips as I wrote the check for the gear. After tax, the total came to just over $90. Perfect. It wasn't more than our finances could handle and, after Lenny sees the prints, I was sure he would compensate the full amount. It was all a risk, but I didn't see any other viable alternatives.

Maxwell and I traded a few war stories from our days with the department and I felt like I had a new ally should I ever find myself dancing within his technical domain again. He wished me luck as we shook hands, reminded me of his most important tip—keeping the darkroom dust-free—before personally helping me load the gear in the car. We had to take the T-bird's top down to get the enlarger in the back seat after determining it wouldn't fit in the trunk without leaving the lid open. Some patrolmen already knew my car as it was, but I didn't want to roll down the road looking like a parade float.

"Hey, none of this stuff is flammable is it?" I asked just before firing off a Winston on my way out of the parking lot."

Maxwell yelled back, "Safe as water—but don't go drinking any! And don't smoke in your lab!"

I waved in thanks and motored home, never spotting the first patrol car all the way. The only bother now would be—and it never fails—Ida Heinemann. She was hovering around the front of her driveway with a garden rake and a raised brow at the strange contraption riding in the back of my car. Naturally, she strolled over to have a "friendly look".

"What ya gaut thair, Bill? Something expeerahmentle?"

"Hi Mrs. Heinemann. No. It's for developing photographs."

"Oah yeah? I just yoos the Eckads down the conner a Buffalo. They have it beck to ya in a coupla days."

"Oh, I know Mrs. Heinemann.   This is for special photographs."

"You ar-rent statin' a business or nothing, young man. I don't need no strange cahs runnin' thoo heer evry five minutes!"

"No, Mrs. Heinemann.   I wouldn't do that to the neighborhood. It's a project for work; nothing you need worry about at all."

"Woory? Ha! Ya almost gawt yourself killed with those black people a few yees ago. Don't tell me!"

With that, she trudged back across the street to finish raking her "noives".

I brought the darkroom gear inside and placed it in a rear corner of the master bedroom where the boys wouldn't be horsing around later. It was already too late in the afternoon to get this project started. Wendy and the boys would be home soon and the lab, a.k.a. the bathroom, would be in use. I would have to wait until tomorrow. Now was a good time for reading through the books, which, after a lengthy explanation to my wife, I was able to accomplish without much interruption.

7:15 a.m. Finally. The family zoomed out of the house while I began setting up the lab. The sink's counter was rather small, but had enough room for four paint trays and the negatives "tank", which was really a small container about the size of a small coffee can. I decided I should probably develop the roll taken at the docks first. If I screwed that one up, it was the least incriminating. I replaced the light bulb in the ceiling fixture with the red one, and taped several sheets of newspaper over the bathroom's small window. There was still some light coming through, so I taped a black T-shirt over the paper. That did the trick. The room was ready to go.

Patiently, I followed the instruction steps detailed in the books and, after around twenty minutes, had the first roll drying on the shower curtain rod. I could see that there were pictures on those negatives, so I breathed a huge sigh of relief and got to work on the second roll. Twenty more minutes and both rolls were successfully drying. I had a two-hour wait now, so I took a break and brushed up on the next steps.

The print process was entirely more complicated. I had to get the focus and exposure times just right, which meant more testing.

I looked at my watch and it was getting near 11 a.m., which meant I didn't have a whole lot of time before Wendy and the kids came back home. I didn't know what I was thinking. Those prints may be hanging to dry for several hours…maybe all night. Doing the math, I figured it would probably be best if I simply narrow down the negatives to just two or three of the most damaging shots. The rest would have to wait until Lenny came back from vacation.

I can't fully describe my exhilaration when the prints slowly came to life in the developing tray, but there they were in all their glory. My teeth ground with resolve. I had them!

Around two hours later, my 8x10s were clipped and hanging off the shower rod, dripping into the bathtub under a dim red light, that I could now turn off. I grabbed a can of beer out of the refrigerator and tore off the tab. It was a refreshing end to a long, hot process. I wasn't halfway through my beverage before I heard Wendy's car pull up in the driveway. Both of her doors opened and the cacophony began; boys running with abandon through the front door to give me a hug and plop in front of the television, and Wendy slowly drifted in, tired from her day's work.

She gave me a long kiss, wiping her lips from the beer she just tasted, perhaps wanting one for herself. She put her purse down and lit up a cigarette as I gave her the bad news that her customary after-work shower would have to wait. The explanation was short enough, but she still hated my guts. There was only one bathroom and its sanctimony was unquestionable.

Wendy carried on for two minutes before I walked her back and showed her the hanging prints. Her eyes went wide with excitement, then contemplation, then fear.

"Bill, I don't want those here at all!" She cried.

"They have to dry, honey, and when Lenny comes back, I'll dump everything in his lap. Other than testifying, my job is over. It's all downhill from here!"

She looked at me, took a long drag off her cigarette, and calmed down.

"Are they just drying? Is that all?"

"As far as I know, yes."

"Can't you use my hair dryer?"

My wife. I love her…and hate her. "I didn't think about that."

"Just don't get it too close, Bill. Think about it like your own hair. You'll have them dry in a few minutes."

She was right except the prints immediately curled. They looked great, but they rolled into tubes, so I flattened both and placed them in between a stack of our Time Life books. I still felt like I somehow displaced Wendy and the boys, however. I offered to take them out to eat, but my wife was just home from being out and wanted her shower. One thing at a time.

Per usual, she changed her mind during a lengthy soak, deciding she'd like a cocktail, and not at any ordinary bar either. She wanted one from the Kapok Tree Inn over in Clearwater — probably the fanciest restaurant in the entire state.

We had eaten there several times in the past, especially before the boys were born. The food wasn't all that special in my opinion, but the atmosphere usually set the rest of our famously rambunctious evenings afoot. Even on a Tuesday in the middle of October, the place was crowded. None of the air-conditioned dining rooms were available and the wait was at least twenty minutes according to the host. Given the option, and the fact that the weather wasn't completely intolerable outside, we decided to take an immediate offering by one of the gardens where the peacocks would come and eat out of our hands. The boys found that incredibly amusing until Junior's little mean streak appeared. Instead of just calmly letting the birds eat from his hand or tossing a few morsels on the ground, he jumped up and ran after one, chasing it all the way down the massive atrium before one of the waiters intervened. The birds never came back after that little episode, and I couldn't blame them. The incident didn't ruin the rest of the evening, however. We gave the boys an experience they'll remember forever and, as for Wendy and me, well, Kapok worked its magic once again.

Somewhat groggy from the night before, I stumbled around, put some shorts on, and wandered into the living room where the stack of books were flattening my photos. Careful not to slide them as the topmost books were removed, the prints stayed nice and flat between the protective paper I placed on either side. Once again, I examined the prints. Only one had slightly imperfect focus. The other two were razor sharp in every detail. A moment later, the phone rang.

"Agent Savage informs me you have some news. I assume since you are barging in on my vacation that it concerns something fantastic?"

I detailed my surveillance to Lenny, who took a long breath afterward. It was reminiscent of my own after leaving that bank's parking lot afterward, knowing that what was about to happen would be equivalent of the Cuban Missile Crisis as far as Tampa was concerned. I imagined, or rather daydreamed, that the Media Circus Maximus about to ensue would be much farther reaching.

Lenny laughed, "Jesus, Bill..." And his laughter seemed uncontrollable for more than a minute before he realized that he didn't actually have any pictures or negatives, nor did anyone else at the local field office. I thought he felt hurt by the fact that I didn't trust *everyone* at his department, but understood that, in a case like ours, I had to trust *everyone* at his department. One little hint and who knows what disastrous retaliation could happen.

"Bill, I want you to listen to me very closely on this. What you have — I gather you're very aware of its volatility and the dangers of your carrying it around should someone find out. It needs to be in federal hands immediately. Make copies, do whatever you have to do, but I want you to bring those to Ben Davidson immediately."

"I can't do that Lenny."

There was a brief pause. "Well Jesus, Bill, you're going to have to trust *somebody*!"

"Sorry, Len....can't"

"Bill, you've been an excellent agent. I don't want to get in a tangle with you over this, but you're kind of placing me in a strange predicament here. I'll cut my vacation short. The wife won't like it, but she'll have to get over it or stay with her mother the few days extra and fly down herself. In the meantime, I'm calling Davidson right now and telling him he needs to set up a grand jury in the fastest time possible."

"How long is that?"

"I don't know."

"Well, you call him and then call me right back."

He didn't say another word, he just hung up. Not ten minutes later my phone rang. Lenny didn't bother with any small talk; he just got straight to the point.

"Bill, he said it would take two weeks at the minimum. He also said if you had anything that important you should take it to him immediately...as in right now."

"I'll wait."

No pause this time. "Come on, Bill! This is too important."

"I know, Len, that's why I'm going to hold out until you and I can walk in there personally without any chance of a heads up for the other side. If he can get a grand jury in two weeks, that'll be when this hits the fan."

"Well Bill, it's not like I'm ordering you to take it over there; I very well could, but I just want to say for the record that what you're doing; I don't agree with it whatsoever."

"Does that mean you're not going to pay me back for the photo equipment?"

He hung up.

The argument drained me somewhat, and I felt like I needed to show this to someone I could trust not to say a single word. Right about now, that came down to just about two or three people: Mack, maybe Ray, and my wife, but she's already seen everything, so that meant Mack. When I called him about it, I didn't mention anything or hint in any way, I just told him to meet me at the old huntin' camp and that was all. Within twenty minutes we were both out there, watching the sun blaze over the connecting bridge at the causeway. It was incredibly beautiful that evening. I always thought the sunsets looked extraordinary during that time of year and this one was extraordinarily extraordinary.

Mack and I caught up with some personal news about each other before I lifted my briefcase from the rear floorboard of my car. I opened it, retrieved a letter-sized manila envelope, and removed two of the best prints for Mack's perusal. I didn't think I would ever see an expression quite like the one he gave at that moment. He was pretty white already. In fact, we joked about his chicken legs just about every time he put on a pair of shorts. He didn't wear shorts that often afterwards.

"You have to take this to Ben right now."

"Yeah, that's what Len said. Not gonna happen until the grand jury in two weeks."

"Two weeks? Are you crazy? You're being foolish with that kind of fire, Bill!" And, just like that, Mack was giving me the same lecture as the one Lenny gave me just a couple of hours earlier.

Just like Lenny, I couldn't quite convince Mack either. I thought maybe I should just make copies and send them on to Ben like they want, but my nagging intuition kept pounding, *don't!*

don't! What was I to do but wait? Nobody knew what I had, and even if they did, there wasn't much they could do about it.

"Well, if you're dead set on hanging on to those yourself, I'd stay around your house loaded for bear until the cavalry takes over."

"That's pretty much my plan."

Mack kept staring at the photos and carried a super-wide grin. "Man, I hope I'm there to see the look on his face when they plop this thing up on the overhead projector. I bet he has a heart attack right there!"

"Nah. I don't want him doing any of us any favors. I want to see him locked up in a federal pen."

"It's going to happen, Bill. Tampa is about to see a day like no other."

Mack handed the photos back. I replaced them in the envelope and we started to discuss our game plan for the jury. He mentioned that his files were chock full of systemic offenses worthy of jail time for a good portion of the department, and that he had grown very tired of working in the radio room, even though it was producing a gold mine of raw intelligence on a daily basis. More than anything, we were both ready for this never-ending hurricane to pass.

Two-Week Notice

My housing contractor gave me a call early Thursday morning. It was the 16th and I was getting anxious concerning the ticking bomb locked away in my briefcase, which was leaning against the wall next to my side of the bed. I couldn't help but stare at it during the entire call. I was still staring at the case even when he told me there was a major delay on the home's completion date, but we would be able to move in the week before Christmas. All I did was briefly voice my concern that it definitely needed to be an on-time gift before hanging up, still gazing at the case as if it had "Pandora" stenciled in the middle of it. He gave me his word.

I didn't do much else that day besides doing some of the more menial chores the boys weren't quite old enough or adept enough to do on their own. By the afternoon, I sat down with a Louis L'Amour book Mack had lent me. I wasn't much for westerns, preferring the gritty urban thrillers if I were to pick up anything to read at all, which wasn't too often, admittedly, but there was something about the way L'Amour wrote that had me turning pages. I thought it was an excellent waste of time before Ben called me from his Orlando office.

"I've got two pieces of information you'll be interested in, Bill. Lenny said he's still too put out with you to call himself — so you know."

"And you?"

"I suppose I should be, but it's not like I have much control over that, now do I?"

"Nope."

"Ah well. Actually, now that I think about it, there are three things I need to tell you. First, our friends, you know — the ones that gave you a ride through my neighborhood?"

"Yeah."

"They've been identified by Leonard's men after two more robberies in Tampa. One of the larger superettes down there had a new closed-circuit TV system that taped the whole thing."

"I thought they only had those in banks."

"Well they had one, and it worked like a charm. He said that one of the robbers was a known associate of Vargas' named Peter Lewis."

"I've heard of him; the escape artist fairy they call 'Danny Boy'"

"That's the one."

"Who's the other? Was it Mendez?"

"No. He's been identified as a degenerate by the name of Herbert Talmond Graham."

"Never heard of him."

"You probably wouldn't. He recently escaped from the Glades County lockup down below Okeechobee and has a thirty-five year long rap sheet dating back to reform school at the age of fourteen. He went straight for eleven years after he knocked up and married some teenager. Even became a Baptist minister for two years from what they're telling me."

"A minister?"

"Until they kicked him out for embezzlement and a sexual assault charge."

"I suppose that's why he was in jail?"

"Yes. Repeat offender. Multiple escapes, including this one, of course."

"With Lewis that makes a nice couple, don't you think?"

Ben paused. I took it as the humorous/sarcastic pause and not the out-of-bounds pause.

"Moving on. Our resident pyromaniac had a recent breakthrough session up in Marianna, which, consequently, is where our latest celebrity spent his first three years in obviously-didn't-reform school."

"The Match? What's he up to now?" I asked.

"He fully confessed to most of the arsons and — I love this — implicated Vargas and Tresedici."

"Think the jury will allow his testimony? I mean, the guy's certified, isn't he?"

"Coped a plea for reduced sentence; a chance at parole in forty. You ask me, he'll never make it anyway. But, to answer your question, yes, they'll take it. Oh, and you're gonna like this—jury's set for next Monday, the 27th. By the way, our friend Mack is now on the list of affiants, along with Detective Coleman and Major Fernandez."

Of course, I loved the fact that he was able to have the jury expedite the time frame. Ben went on, describing his vision of how the case presentation would go, including the production of evidence. Both of us laughed and carried on about the potential looks on their faces—Lozello, Tresedici, Vargas; the lot—when Hernandez took the stand, and especially when my photographs hit the big overhead screen. We were pretty high on ourselves. The reality was, I had eleven days to sweat out before the biggest day of my life. That meant sticking around the house more than usual; eating at home, watching shows with the family, getting chores done, and simply staying invisible to the outside world. I've never been so bored, but I knew it would all be over soon.

When Mack phoned to vent his feelings about what Lozello just pulled, he reminded me of the seriousness and desper-ateness of the situation. Mack said he had just left his sister-in-law's house in West Tampa and noticed a car tailing him for several blocks. He said he made the requisite turns and drove all over Drew Park by the airport before stopping in a highly visible location, just on the side of an Eckerd's drugstore.

"And there was the son-of-a-bitch himself," Mack said. "He just sat in his car with the engine running right behind me, so I got out and walked back there. I started to cuss him out and all he did was look straight at my family saying, 'I know what you did, Poole. I know what you did and you just better watch yourself.' Can you believe it? So I tell him, 'No, sir. It's you who better watch yourself and you better get your eyes on me and off my family.'"

"Jesus Christ, Mack. Lozello did that?"

"You bet your ass he did. It took every bit of resistance to not shoot him right there, let alone tell him about next Monday."

"I couldn't have done it. Not knowing what I know."

"Well, the wife and kids were there. What was I gonna do, Bill, traumatize them for life?"

"I suppose not. Honestly, I don't know how I would've reacted if Wendy and the boys were there. I don't even want to think about it!"

I had spent quite a bit of time with Wendy and the boys lately. On the Wednesday before the jury, she came home from work and made a supper that would go down as one of my all time favorites. It was tough enough getting any decent southern cooking in Tampa and there were a few places, but none had everything I liked from back home. Fried okra, collard greens, hominy, and I had long ago forgotten the taste of buttery zipper cream peas. Sure, the local Cuban food was out of this world, and I wouldn't trade anything for a good deviled crab, except maybe my aunt's biscuits 'n gravy, but Wendy's cooking? Take me home!

Her specialty was a slow roast beef; the kind you put in before leaving for work and turning off when you get home. I couldn't tell her it was a fire hazard; it was too good. She made it with all the trimmings: carrots, potatoes, onions. She also made white rice, some fresh biscuits (I didn't quite mind that they came from a can), and a salad. For dessert, she made a pecan pie using a homemade crust from that paper-thin Greek pastry dough.

I ate until I just couldn't eat any longer. The meal was absolute perfection; the four cans of Budweiser afterward were just as perfect, and that first Winston—even better. I was already looking forward to the leftovers, but the slight hangover I woke up with the next morning negated the memory. I had all of my work around the house done for the weekend, so it was going to be just another lazy morning in front of the television watching Robert Stack and crew.

Then came a knock at the front door…

* * *

Luckily, Wendy got a ride home from her supervisor instead of finding out the hard way. She was too broken up to be behind the wheel. Her boss didn't tell her what happened; he just drove her back home. When she saw our street full of law cars and an ambulance, she knew. Steve already had his lighter out to meet the Pall Mall she toiled to dig out of her purse without breaking. She promised me she wouldn't cry. We talked about this. It killed me again to see her break that promise, but I broke my promise too. I understood. I didn't understand how I broke that promise. I didn't understand why her boss drove her home instead of to the hospital, because I should have been on my way there a long time ago. There were a multitude of things I didn't understand until just now.

Part II

It Was Dynamite

We called Salvatore Tresedici "John" because he hated the roots of his last name, yet, out of respect for his elders who weathered immigration through Ellis Island, or, as they called it, "L'Isola delle Lacrime" (The Island of Tears), he was bound to wear that albatross necklace until death. John hated the name because it gave us ammunition. He was a proud guido, but not quite smart enough and not quite popular enough to ever become the family's Number One in Florida. Giuseppe would never tell him that because of loyalty and hope. Those in the family had to hope that maybe, one day, they might become the Boss. John openly talked about what he would do when he became the Boss, and Giuseppe knew about this disrespectful behavior, but there was nothing he could do in reality. Any retaliation against him would likely violate his omertà, and likely anger those up north.

By the middle of the '70s, Giuseppe's powers, although still infinite, were limited to what he could see, and blindness came with age. Giuseppe was getting too old for bothering with the hardcore family duties, just as long as those up in New York were happy with the way things were running. While he was creating his vast empire down in Cuba, John ran the Florida rackets with an iron fist.

After the war, vending machines of all varieties had really taken off. They were everywhere, gobbling up loose change—when loose change was actually valuable—from just about everybody. The families were on top of the world with gambling, drugs, girls; you name it. Fidel Castro had something to say about that.

Giuseppe suddenly found himself locked away in a Havana prison cell awaiting execution. If it weren't for the shrewdness, resourcefulness, and unquestionable loyalty of his legal counsel and friend, Paul Gravina, he would have met his fate long ago. Unfortunately, he lost everything and came back to his less glamorous Florida empire, disenchanted and bitter. By the late '60s, Giuseppe was content letting John continue running operations while he relaxed at his new retreat in Costa Rica; a place many fled when the heat became a little too warm back in the states. Unfortunately for Giuseppe, the distance kept him from seeing the great mistake his Number Two was about to commit.

You see, John grew tired waiting for glory and power. Like Giuseppe, he was getting older too, although not quite as old; he still had a dozen or so years left to reach the pinnacle. Somehow, a smooth-talking, ambitious Cuban-Italian named Angel Vargas convinced John that his omertà didn't include compromised officers of the law. Vargas also convinced him that the families were at war with the government for their very own existence—that whenever a racket became profitable enough, Big Money had Uncle Sam's sucklings massage the codebook either for their own protection, or for revenue. It all depended upon the latest greedy mafioso.

Vargas convinced another loose end as well. His name was Gregory Azzari and he was a short, fifties-something Italian that sported a peppered pencil mustache, still wore a fedora, and kept his pants belted around his stomach. Not in a thousand years would anyone ever consider that homely wreck a menace to society. He barely looked capable of lifting an espresso, let alone a machete, but he was Giuseppe's number four enforcer, and rumor had it that he had efficiently dealt with over a half dozen favors. Azzari was also getting on in the years, but he knew he never had a chance at the top position. He was just smart enough to know he wasn't smart enough nor important enough, so the only way he could break the family ceiling was to hitch on to another horse.

On a Wednesday back in late April, Vargas had Tresedici and Azzari meet with the current contractor for a large number of

Florida's west coast problems—Guillermo "Santa Claus" Mendez. None of the three knew Mendez very well, as it typically went with contractors of his nature. Less involvement meant deniability, should a legal disaster ever arise. The only thing they really knew about Mendez was that he was definitely no mulatto-looking Cuban. He was whiter than the rest of them and had those searchlight blue eyes, but his nose would make Medusa convulse enough to intentionally look her own way. For extra insurance, Tresedici brought along none other than Martin "The Match" Sanchez, who had knowledge of the one they called Santa Claus, but for some reason, Sanchez stayed mostly to himself during the meeting.

"Okay Mendez, before we say a goddman thing, I gotta know why they call you fuckin' 'Santa Claus'." Tresedici asked in his usual low-browed attempt at a belittlement.

Mendez cracked a half-smile before confidently responding, "'Cause I..."

"You don't know?" Interrupted Azzari in his crazed high-pitch cackle.

"Let him finish," said Vargas.

"No, wait. Sal? You don't know?" Azzari cracked again.

"No, I don't fuckin' know. I'm too busy to know what every spic chopper from down south did. You gonna let him tell me, or are you telling me?"

Mendez let the slur roll right off his forehead, like a drop of sweat from George Foreman's glove. Tresedici looked back and forth at both Azzari and Mendez before throwing his hands up at Vargas.

"Go ahead. Tell 'em." Mendez said to Azzari, who was obviously about to explode if he wasn't the Omnipotent Storyteller.

"Okay...so Guillermo here is on his third job a few years back, okay, and he's about to finish off this real big Irishman...said he was a Golden Glover back in '56. One thing led to another, he shot his pistola a few times, the Irishman shot a couple of times, whatever. So Guillermo finally gets him through his right kneecap just as the Irishman's revolver goes all the way around. And there they are, both out of bullets, and the guy's on the ground screamin' about his knee. Well, oh, and I forgot to tell you this was in the guy's garage."

"Get on with it." Tresedici said impatiently.

"All right, all right. So Guillermo here grabs, shall we say, a garden tool off the wall and walks over to the fella, and he says, while in terrible pain, but had on the brass pair 'cause he knows he's done, 'And jest whart are ya gonna do with that one, tough guy.' And, get this, Guillermo here says back to him, 'Hoe, Hoe, Hoe, motherfucker!', and hacks the guy to pieces before bagging him up for a seagull picnic."

Mendez smiled in pride, but there was dead silence after Azzari's punch line delivery.

"I don't get it," said Tresedici, looking at Vargas to see if he understood, which he didn't, evidently, by his shrugging shoulders.

"Hey Match; you get it, dontcha?" Azzari asked, but Sanchez just sat there and mumbled, as if he were ill. "He chopped him into six pieces with a garden hoe!" Azzari laughed. "Six pieces. Can you believe it?"

Vargas and Tresedici sat for a moment with shrugged shoulders until Vargas finally started grinning. "Oh, I get it. You get it, Sal? Garden *hoe*?"

"Yeah, I got it. I just didn't think it was all that funny. Tell me, *Santa Claus*, what kind of sick asshole gets his rocks off cuttin' a man up like that? Huh? Six pieces? Tell me; why six?"

Just like that, Mendez's smile turned to a scowl, but he kept his composure. His eyes exuded their maniacal behavioral condition. "He had it comin'."

"Yeah? Why?" Tresedici demanded.

"I was told he was stealing from his wife. Not just the chattel, mind you, real estate too. Sold some off without her knowing about it. She didn't suspect a thing until she woke up one morning—so they tell me—wildly scratching her jungle cave. You know, the fellas up north don't like it much when you mess with one of 'em's daughters."

Tresedici leaned back in his seat and started rubbing his chin. Mendez looked at him squarely and said, "I didn't decapitate him if that is what you were thinking."

That's all it took to get Tresedici loosened up. "Jesus, Mendez. I was beginning to think you were some kind of sick bastard you read about in the dime novels—goin' around getting' his jollies mutilatin' people and such."

"It's a living."

"Well if he had it coming, I suppose…"

"Speaking of having it coming, isn't that why we're here?" Vargas asked, anxious to get back to his girls.

"You called this, Angel. Tell us what's on your mind," said Tresedici, who just noticed Sanchez holding his stomach and limping towards the restroom. "Hey Match; where the fuck you goin'?"

Sanchez didn't say a word, he just pointed towards his stomach and covered his mouth, pretending as if he was about to vomit. If any of the others suspected he was wearing a wire, he was dead right there and he knew it. If they found out later he was wearing a wire, they'd still liquidate him. He knew this because he performed a few himself. The microphone and its transmitter, after getting smashed under the heel of his boot, quickly found their way into the City of Tampa sewer system, leaving the agents across the street tapping their earphones. They would have barged into the meeting if it weren't for Sanchez's last words whispered into the mic before the boot came. "Sorry. Can't." After viewing the last piece of plastic and metal swirl down the drain, he washed his hands and returned to the bar. Vargas was in the middle of answering Tresedici's question.

"A few people, but I don't know if I'm being too ambitious."

"No." Mendez interrupted. "Ambition depends on the target itself, not the quantity. How many jobs is only a matter of time and compensation."

"What is he getting these days?" Vargas asked.

"Guillermo?" Prompted Tresedici.

"Single job? Depending on merit…you know; worthy cause. Target difficulty, prestige factors."

Vargas nodded to Mendez's stipulations, indicating he agreed.

Mendez continued while chewing on a toothpick; a habit that often gave him away at the poker tables. "I get anywhere between fifteen and twenty five. Like I said, it depends. Whom do you have in mind?"

Vargas, Tresedici, and Azzari looked around at each other before Vargas spoke up. "What if I said I wanted five?"

"Five what?" Mendez asked, confusedly.

"Five marks." Vargas replied.

"Like I said, it depends on the who." He stalled and saw a glimmer of impatient frustration mask Tresedici's complexion. "But I'm sure we can work a package deal. You just have to tell me who first.   And no need for names, just give me the professional description."

"What, like their job or something?" Azzari asked.

"That's part of it. I want to know what they do, if their politically connected, and make sure you don't want to do anything stupid."

"Stupid like what?" Vargas laughed.

"Stupid like wanting me to take out someone more important than I'll live to talk about—that's what."

"Okay, he understands." Tresedici yelped. "Just give him the descriptions, Angel. Nothing more yet."

"All right." Angel prepared by wiping his brow.

"The first is a man in his early forties who runs a business in town."

"What kind of business?" Mendez interrupted, sternly.

"None of yours." Tresedici quipped.

Mendez laughed and started to leave the table, but Azzari put his hand on Mendez's shoulder, having him sit back down. "He's just messin' with, ya. Relax."

"Look, I need to know if the guy's important." Mendez said.

"If I say he's not, he's not, understand? He's just a nobody that's disrespecting an arrangement we have. You can only tell people so often, you know."

"Right. So, he's just an average Joe nobody. All right. No problem. Who's next?"

"Next guy is somewhat important, Guillermo. He's, uh, with the government," said Vargas.

"You guys know I don't do cops, right? The boys up north, Giuseppe included, they won't have it."

"He's not a cop. He's an attorney."

"An attorney?" Mendez wondered.   "That could be a problem. You got any more about this guy."

"Nope. It is just a simple business decision, the way I see it." Vargas coldly stated. "He did some work for me, I paid him. He was hired to do some more work and failed completely, but wants a lot of money, regardless."

"So don't pay him," said Mendez.

"Well, you know that could be a problem eventually. I told him he'd never see a dime, and during our little feud, he oversaw several cases that damaged our operations significantly. In other words, he has become, how would you say, an overbearing liability."

"I woulda just said 'prick', but have it your way." Tresedici added to the amusement of the others.

"He is going to be expensive," said Mendez.

"How expensive?" Vargas asked.

"We'll see. Depends on the others. Who's the third?"

"A cop." Vargas smiled.

Mendez's frown returned as he lit a fresh smoke. Three times, he drew the flame into the fresh tip as it ignited. He exhaled a larger than normal cloud, "I told you, I don't do cops."

"He's technically no cop anymore." Azzari stipulated. "A-and besides, he's a bad cop too!"

"Bad cop?" Mendez asked.

Tresedici cut to the chase. "Some of my associates had him on the take. At the same time he put a real hurtin' on our other enterprises, you see. We lost a lot, and I mean a lot of money because of this guy." He leaned back again in his seat and picked up his glass, taking his scotch below the rocks. "And, a friend thinks he took a score on one of his...err...employees."

Vargas added, "I ran into Big Sam Turner a few weeks ago and asked him if he knew anything about the guy. Turner said the word on the street is he's dirty...tells his kids that too; he says, 'He's a real son-of-a-bitch that don't respect nobody's business...likes to beat up the dealers for information and so forth.'"

"Did he mention his brother-in-law?" Tresedici asked.

"Who's brother-in-law?" Vargas asked.

"Big Sam's."

"Sam's? No. Who's that? Someone important or something?" Vargas asked.

"His brother-in-law is a detective downtown ...another pain in the ass, but he don't disrespect like Wild Bill; he's a pro."

"Him?" Azzari said, hovering a pencil over his notepad, much to Tresedici's dislike.

"No. Our friend downtown has him taken care of for now. And get rid of that fuckin' paper Greggie before you get us all pinched!" Tresedici then returned to Vargas, waiting for his response.

"Uh...no. Sam didn't mention him," said Vargas.

"I don't suppose he would. Crazy, ain't it? Sam and his family? I bet the wives spend every extra minute they have in front of the candles at the Sacred Heart." Tresedici laughed. "Anyway, Brume's a bad cop and that's that.

"No shit." Mendez said, astonished. "I'll do him for half price!"

The others laughed uncontrollably for over a minute. The business was all of the utmost seriousness varieties, however, humor usually provided a stress cushion.

When they finally settled down, Mendez moved the meeting along. "All right, and the other two?"

There was a brief pause while the other three looked at each other. Vargas finally spoke up before the silence became noticeably uncomfortable.

"Why don't we see how the first three go before worrying about the other two." Tresedici said decisively while finishing his drink.

Mendez examined the expressions of Vargas and Azzari, whom were awaiting his answer, which he gave after another long draw on his cigarette. "One-twenty."

Tresedici put his glass down and shook his head. "Not on your life."

Mendez looked at the other two again and put his hands flat on the table folded over each other. "It's a fair price, not knowing the other two."

"Maybe," said Vargas, adjusting his sunglasses. "But how many times do you get five together, huh? Could be a nice payday for you, my friend. And, you must consider there are others like you out there more than willing to take the job for less."

"Who?"

"Come on, Angel, tell him." Ordered Tresedici, who never enjoyed haggling in any of his business dealings. He knew everyone else's business quite well, and if they were asking a reasonable market price for whatever it was they were peddling, he never negotiated further. If you were attempting to do business with him and asked for anything out-of-bounds, unless there were no competitors, you never heard from Tresedici again. You had one shot at his business and one shot only.

"We are authorized for a maximum of $105,000 for the five marks, and that's all we are prepared to pay."

The odd figure intrigued Mendez and he almost asked about the amount if it weren't for Tresedici's cold, emotionless gaze stabbing him repeatedly. He knew there would be no negotiation on the price if he wanted the job. He also knew that offer exceeded his normal fee, which he only retained less than four or five times a year.

"That's fine, but I want twenty grand after the first. No less," he said. "And you know my per diem. That's on your dime while I'm on the job. Also, I don't supply the hardware. Whatever the method you request, that's on your dime too. Transportation— yours. Everything. Same as last time."

Tresedici didn't balk or even blink an eye. "Okay. I don't really care how you do the job; just don't be sloppy about it."

"Okay, so tell me about the first guy."

"Sal tells me you prefer shotguns," said Vargas.

"Untraceable." Mendez replied.

"Anything in particular?"

"12-guage unrifled, automatic, six-shot, one box of double-ought buckshot, and one box of slugs."

"Sounds exactly like the last time, if you ask me." Azzari commented.

Mendez replied smugly, "It is."

"You didn't meet Greggie last time Guillermo." Tresedici said. "He's kind of our 'hardware guy'. Got the last one for us. You need anything, he'll get it for you. He's your man for the duration, got it?"

"Okay. What about the other two?" Mendez asked.

"Other two what?" Tresedici said.

"The other two marks. Any special requests for them?"

"One at a time. Okay?"

There were no toasts afterwards. No handshakes either. Tresedici took one last sip off his scotch and headed for the back office. Vargas straightened his collar and reminded everyone Miss Wednesday was waiting for him by the pool at Randy's, so he got up, walked over to Sanchez, and tapped him on the shoulder. Sanchez didn't say a word on his way outside, he just walked out and got in the car with Vargas, and then spent the next several hours dropped off at a hotel with two prostitutes until his handlers busted down the door.

That left Azzari and lastly, Mendez, who was ready to get to work so he could collect the best payday he'd ever seen.

It took a full week before Azzari summoned Mendez to his house where a fresh Remington Model 1100 semi-automatic shotgun and the two boxes of shells awaited. He arrived late in the morning via cab, wearing the same denim garb he wore just about everywhere. There were two cars in Azzari's driveway and one out front in the street. That car was a White 1972 Chevy Impala that had been stolen, rebadged in Louisiana, and then shipped through the network down to a purposely ambiguous owner pool meant to disguise family property—especially the disposable kind. Mendez figured the car was for him before he ever arrived at Azzari's front door and rang the doorbell. What he forgot to mention to Azzari, was one rather glaring piece of minutia that, perhaps, people in their situation should consider before showing up at someone's front door.

"Who the fuck's this guy, Mendez?" Azzari groaned, not at all happy with this type of surprise.

He thought to himself that he didn't become an old man in this sort of game by taking too many chances, even though he idiotically kept records of everything.

"This is a good friend of mine, Pete Lewis. He's my driver. Why?" Mendez didn't much like the tone of Azzari's voice, but he was ready for any interrogation.

"I just don't like surprises, that's all. If you woulda told me he was coming…"

"Take it easy, old man," assured Mendez.

Azzari scratched his chin and turned towards Lewis. "Driver, huh. Looks kinda funny to me. You sure he's okay?"

"Absolutely. D'you get the things I asked for?"

Azzari peered behind the two men and out into the street, looking around to make sure no one tailed them before he invited them inside.

"Yeah. Follow me."

Azzari took them into his living room where the shotgun and ammunition awaited. He picked up the shotgun, inspected it, cocked the trigger, and dry-fired it once, thus proving the firearm was functional and unloaded before handing it to Mendez.

"Semi-automat…"

"I know what it is, old man." Mendez took the firearm from Azzari's hands, opened, and inspected the chamber to make sure it kept maintained. The chamber closed with a quick snap, and then he grabbed the box of deer slugs, tearing its top open.

In many cases, including my own, a homeowner may become somewhat nervous when a stranger, highly regarded or not, began loading a weapon in your home. That didn't bother Azzari, however. His eyes widened with anticipation.

Mendez opened the other box of shells, and began loading the shotgun; alternating between slugs and double-ought buckshot. The tube magazine underneath the barrel would only hold five rounds, but Mendez slid back the lever, loading the firing chamber so he could nudge a sixth round.

The loaded chamber changed Azzari's expression somewhat. He was generally trustful of respected friends but when a weapon became instantly lethal, his anxieties got the better of him. That is, until Mendez snapped the safety button just behind the trigger, aimed at Azzari's couch and pulled on the trigger several times to make sure it was secure. Immediate relief came to Azzari's face, causing him to pull a handkerchief from his pant's back pocket. He put the handkerchief back in his pocket and reached into his front pocket, retrieving some car keys, which he started to hand to Mendez before turning to Lewis.

"Are those for the Impala out front?" Lewis asked.

Azzari nodded and handed him a slip of paper. "The car's clean. You finish the job, you take it to this address, okay? And you, Santa Claus; you find a spot for that gun like the one you found last time."

That weapon was rusting in the bay somewhere under the Gandy Bridge alongside a few dozen others, or so many of us at the department fathomed long ago.

"Anything else?" Azzari asked.

"That oughta do, old man," said Mendez, knowing it made Azzari wince every time he said "old man".

Azzari took a roll of one hundred dollar bills and silently counted out ten. "Here, take this."

Mendez took the bills and counted them again. "Ten."

"That's right. That's for your expenses. We didn't agree to pay for anyone you employ, of course; that's up to you, but what I gave you oughta be plenty."

"It is. Hey, we're looking for a good place to stay. The last place had carpet that stunk like sweaty feet. Got any recommendations?"

"The Samoan, but don't make a scene there, you know."

"No, I mean about a good club."

"Do I look like fuckin' Elvis Presley to you?"

Mendez stared at him for a few moments and joked with Lewis, "Nope. More like an Italian Errol Flynn on a bad day."

The description was so ruthlessly demeaning, Azzari could only laugh, as did Lewis. As it went with most of these guys, sarcasm was the preferred humor.

Mendez asked again. "So you know any place at all? What about that place down the street where Vargas went?"

Azzari started laughing. "Vargas? Oh…oh, you don't wanna go in there."

"Why not?"

"Trust me; you want to get a date for the night, you go up Dale Mabry. There's a coupla friendly places there."

"All right." Mendez muttered, realizing Azzari was an old loner, which meant he was probably relying on information bragged about by his friends.

Azzari opened a small address book he kept in the pocket of his jacket, and clicked a pen.

"What's that for?" Mendez asked.

"I'm writing you down as staying at the Samoan. You call me first thing when you get a room number, understand?"

Lewis jumped in front. "I would rather you not write…"

"It's the only way I can remember who's where and what, you know," said Azzari.

"People get in trouble over that sort of thing, Greggie. Can I call you Greggie?"

"Everyone else does, and you'll just have to live with it. Call me first thing."

Mendez and Lewis started to turn away and head outside. "In the morning — unless you want a call at four, that is."

"Yeah, good luck with the ladies."

Mendez didn't bother telling him about Lewis. It wasn't important and he didn't want any potential negativity scuttling his payday. All Mendez and Lewis saw were high-rollin' good times. Instead of checking into a room directly after leaving Azzari's, they packed the shotgun into the car's trunk and headed over to Dale Mabry for an indulgent evening complete with narcotic-induced hangovers that lasted until almost noon the next day; nearly giving Azzari a heart attack, thinking they ran off with a car, a shotgun, and one thousand dollars.

When they finally called, Azzari gave Carlos Salazar's name and an address on the west side of the airport in a newer waterfront subdivision. Mendez wasn't the sharpest of assassins, and actually, his associate was wiser than he led on. They both hopped in the car and took the ten-minute ride out to that part of town, slowly cruising through the family-laden streets.

"This is pretty busy for a school day, Guillermo."

"Yeah; can't say I'm onboard with this, man. The house is on a corner lot, but it's on a street with a cul-de-sac. We'll have to sit down at the other end and hit him on the way out. Got it?"

"Yeah, but when?"

"I say we pick him up after he comes home for lunch, or maybe later in the afternoon. Seven or Eight, just after dark. You can see through his windows better and nobody will see us."

As planned, Mendez and Lewis drove around, surveying the neighborhood for the most expeditious exit route, as well as the routines of one Carlos Louis Salazar; a disabled Korean veteran in his late 40s. As inept as assassins as they actually were, they were luckily able to track him down and be in position for a hit the next evening, but not at Salazar's house. They caught him right in front of his office's main window that overlooked the parking lot and loading dock. It was a rather large window that allowed Salazar a commanding view, since his prosthetic leg gave him too much trouble to be walking around constantly. He would have never guessed that the view came at a premium where security was concerned. Salazar was a sitting duck, floating just in front of that window, nervously limping back and forth while on the phone.

"This will be like shooting a fucking grouper in a twenty gallon aquarium. Hold the car right here," ordered Mendez, as Lewis pulled the large white sedan right in front of the window at the far end of the parking lot, perhaps less than 50 yards away.

In haste, Mendez rolled down his window and jammed the shotgun through its opening, not being too careful with his aim. The first round was a deer slug and, although it is one of the largest caliber rounds freely available, Mendez still managed missing Salazar completely. Instead, the round shattered the main pane of glass and sent the panicky man behind it straight to his office's knee-deep, aqua-colored shag carpet.

"Ay Dios mio!" He yelled.

"You better take him out, man!" Lewis yelled. "Didn't you see him on the phone? He could be calling anybody right now."

"He's too busy screaming like a little girl!" Mendez laughed in a craze from behind the sights of the Remington. "Besides, I can't see him."

"Jesus Chris, man! The building's sheet metal for crying out loud. He's hiding below the window, can't you see? Take a freakin' shot down there and I bet he starts runnin'; then kill him."

Mendez kept the shotgun firmly pressed into his right shoulder and kept his gaze down the length of the barrel, only breaking his concentration long enough to roll his eyes at Lewis. He took careful aim about a foot and a half just above where he guessed the floor level was and pulled the trigger. He missed Salazar, but scared him into getting up momentarily, just as Lewis predicted. While the buckshot round had no trouble penetrating the sheet metal outer wall, the plaster wall on the inside took most of the energy out of the volley. To be successful, he'd have to hit him with the slug, and that was the next round. Fortunately for Salazar, he had placed his robust cherry office desk between him and the outside wall, protecting most of his body while he reached for the phone so he could dial the police, which he successfully did while his office received the balance of Mendez's magazine.

"He's calling the cops, man!" Lewis yelled.

Mendez fiddled with the idea of reloading, this time with nothing but slugs, but shotgun blasts in the middle of town, in the middle of a busy weekday, were apt to garner too much attention to stick around more than the two or three minutes they had. The longer they stayed, the greater chance someone would get their tag number not that it would matter), or get a detailed description, or worse, in direct contact with a patrolman that coincidentally parked nearby and had his window down in mid-80s heat. That was it; the hit was over.

When Salazar survived unscathed, he took extra precautions and received assurances from the police department. Disappointed but not disillusioned, Mendez and Lewis paced the sidelines waiting for another chance at Tresedici's competitor. After three weeks and burning through their advance, they decided to move ahead with their second score and come back to Salazar at such a time when he calmed down enough to let his guard down.

Tracking down Benjamin Davidson was no easy business, and he was never findable in an accessible location at or near his office downtown. He came later in the morning when the city was bustling, and left early before everyone else departed for the day. They had a hard time trying to locate where he lived, since they never had much of a chance for a tail. Ben's fee would have to be earned, and not easily.

Tresedici, Vargas, and Azzari were becoming impatient for results, but refused to cough up any more allotments for living expenses, nor offer a chance at their third score. They decided, and rightfully so, that if Mendez and Lewis could not handle two simple contracts, there was no reason to continue subsidizing non-results. They offered another equitable solution instead: taking a score on an unfriendly competitor. In this case, the act would be a simple robbery of a busy gas station on the east side of town.

Azzari knew the details on the place: who owned it, the number of employees, and most importantly, what time of day usually had the most cash in their drawers. That happened to be after lunch for that particular store. Lewis had no problem waiting around its corner, standing on the brake pedal waiting for Mendez to calmly get in, holding a paper sack full of small denominations. They both had envisioned that scenario for two days while casing the joint, and their vision became reality when Mendez did indeed climb into the Impala's front passenger seat with a large paper sack completely stuffed with cash. After their tribute was paid, they cleared over $2,200 from the job. The amount was enough to keep them inebriated and complacent until the second week of June.

Salazar was still completely spooked and timid wherever he went. The Tampa Police Department, however, no longer warranted the extra patrols around his properties.

"Hey old timer, I'm gonna need some plastic. You get my drift?" Mendez said, automatically annoying Azzari.

"Do you know what you are doing with that stuff?"

"Absolutely. Must've rigged several dozen in 'Nam."

"How much do you need?"

"Oh, I guess two blocks oughta do."

"Two blocks. What is that?"

"What, weight?"

"Yeah, don't it go by the pound?"

"Oh, I dunno. It's a little over a pound, so two or two and a half pounds will do."

"That's not all is it?"

"No. I'll need about eight feet of det. cord, a cap and some duct tape. You writing this down?"

"Got it right up here." Azzari points to his head, dismissing Mendez's concern.

"Well don't forget any of that."

"I got it, I got it! …Was in a war too, ya know."

"What—as a desk pogue?"

"Don't push it, spic. Anything else?"

"Ooh—lively today, aren't we? Nope. That oughta do it." Mendez confidently assured him."

"All right. I'll have everything arranged with my contact which will take a coupla days, you know."

"What do we do until then?" Lewis asked.

Azzari whipped out his roll and flicked out fifteen fresh Franklins. "Five is for the merchandise you're gonna buy through my contact. Shouldn't take more than that—not even close—so keep the change. The rest is comin' off the top of your take."

Azzari held out the cash to Mendez, who hesitated before he begrudgingly swiped it from the old man's grasp.

Three days later, Azzari mustered his contact to meet Mendez and Lewis at Lilliput's just after the lunch regulars oozed back to work. Azzari's contact was a man in his late 30s with an average height, average build, and one incredibly obvious and distinguishable, but certainly not distinguished feature; a curly, thick, and dyed black mustache. Along with his overgrown black sideburns and a light blue leisure suit that appeared painfully too tight, Santa Claus' eyes rolled back to his partner at the sight of him. Of course, Azzari had been used to this man as a stable contact over the years, and had completely forgotten how ridiculous his associate looked—especially beside an old-school Italian hood and his dated fedora. Equally amusing was the obvious demeanor of Lewis that afternoon.

"Greggie tells me you're good with a car?" Azzari's contact asks.

"That's what they say, among other things," replied Lewis, batting his eyes back at him.

"What the…hey, Greggie, is this guy some sorta homo?"

Lewis sighed deeply—like steam venting from a nineteenth century locomotive—and folded his arms because he was used to this type of response. He had grown quite accustomed to rejection, which became more irrelevant on each attempted pass.

"So what if he is? He's my driver and that's that," barked Mendez.

"Are you?" The insistent contact asked.

"Greggie, introduce us to your friend here so I know which tombstone I'm gonna pay my respects at in a few weeks."

"Hey, hey! I don't need none of that, you understand?" Azzari yelled.

His control over the situation was tepid at best, and everyone knew it but him. "This is a good friend of mine named Jerry…Jerry Molinar."

Molinar stuck his hand in front of Mendez as a show of bravado, which the Spanish usually regarded with respect, not contempt. Mendez didn't care either way, but shook his hand tentatively because this was his supplier and, without him, there was no contract and therefore no payday. What Molinar did not do is offer his hand to Lewis, which was a clear sign of his homophobia, and not so much of another kind of distasteful emotion—hate. Instead he just nodded his acknowledgement and got down to business.

"Greggie's taking the Impala back. It's too hot, just so you know. Thing is, we won't have a replacement until next week."

"Well, how the fu…" Lewis started mouthing off.

"Patience, friend. Listen up; I've got another car arranged for Saturday morning at ten. Greggie and I are gonna swing by and pick you up at a quarter 'til that morning. Got it?"

Both Mendez and Lewis didn't like it much that they were going to be without transportation for the next two days, but they had enough cash to afford cab fare. There wasn't much else to do but hit the bars and lose a few bucks to the local pool sharks, who were more than happy to oblige.

When Saturday morning rolled around, Mendez and Lewis had their fill of the nightlife, at least until their task was complete. By 9:30, they were checking the room's alarm clock constantly, watching metallic number plates flip over in anticipation. Precisely at 9:45, Molinar knocked and led them out to Azzari's pale yellow Cadillac and its ice-cold air conditioning; an observation Peter Lewis instantly noticed.

"Jesus freakin' Christ, it's a meat locker in here!" He said.

"Good thing for you, it's only a three minute ride," quipped Molinar. "You don't want to make any money later, you just let me know."

"Don't worry about it," said Mendez, not caring much for his partner's constant complaining either. "Where we headed?"

"A coupla blocks away offa Himes. We gotta friend with a real nice car," said Molinar.

Like he said, they were only in the road for three minutes before Azzari pulled his Cadillac into a dense residential area in West Tampa. The car came to rest in front of a home where a few cars had parked, but it was quite obvious which one they would be borrowing that day. Almost dwarfing the house, a glistening, black, brand new Lincoln Continental coupe sat waiting.

The front door of the house opened and a huge man wearing no less than a three-piece suit stepped outside.

"Who is that?" Lewis asked.

"I've heard of him, but just once in passing at a club," said Mendez.

"Let's go fellas; Big Sam don't like to wait," ordered Molinar, who thanked Azzari before getting out of the car and walking up the short driveway with the group.

Before he shook any hands, Big Sam Turner asked, "Okay, who's driving?"

Both Molinar and Mendez looked at Lewis before Lewis knew he was supposed to answer. After all, he was the driver Mendez brought along and he was supposedly good with a car. If you were the driver, there should never be any question.

"Me, I guess," answered Lewis.

"You guess? What the…are you the driver or not?"

Obviously, the meek Peter Lewis felt completely intimidated by the figure towering before him in a fancy suit with an unbuttoned collar. Lewis realized that Big Sam had evidently been out all night and had just arrived back home tired, sweaty, and ready for bed, which meant his temper had a short fuse.

"Y-yeah, I'm the driver. Jeez."

"Look fella, I'm about to give you the keys to my Lincoln, so don't get smart with me."

Lewis was right, Big Sam didn't much like having to wait more than an hour longer than his regular bedtime.

"Take care of my car now. It drinks the gas, but it'll get you there and back fast. Real fast. Rides like a magic carpet."

"The Lincoln? Jesus Christ, It's a fucking ocean liner, man," complained Lewis, but Big Sam rolled right over him.

"That's right, but it's fast, got a huge trunk, and has a good air conditioner. Just bring it back by three the way you got it, hear? My wife loves that car."

"Three? Where are we headed?" Mendez asked Molinar, who was amused at Lewis' struggling under Big Sam's weight.

"Straight east on 60 almost to the coast...place called Yeehaw Junction. It's just an old hotel and bar out by the turnpike. Should take us about two hours to get there, maybe less."

"Where? I ain't nevah heard of it. Yeehaw fuckin' Junction? Who the hell came up with that?" Yeehaw? Some hillbillies come up with that? Jesus H." Lewis squawked.

Big Sam started laughing, as did the rest of the men before Mendez took care of his partner. "You rather have an AA meeting?" (meaning Alligator Alley, but many folks confused that stretch of highway with the Tamiami Trail)

"Tamiami? Hell no! I was hoping for something a little more exciting than a service station out past some old waterin' hole for rednecks," Lewis complained.

"Did I mention the car was fast?" Big Sam laughed as he handed the keys to him.

The three climbed in the massive automobile and booked it down Highway 60 towards Vero Beach. Lewis noticed too many patrolmen to let the car go until they were on the other side of Lake Wales, which was a veritable no man's land. Flying the Lincoln at over ninety, they made it to the small intersection called Yeehaw Junction in just under two hours. Sam was right; the car was fast, but he was also right in that it was a major gas hog—not that anything going almost forty miles per hour faster than the top speed limit wouldn't be. But they had arrived at approximately at the time they promised, and their contact, a seedy individual by the name of Willie "Nano" Brunoli, Jr., had been soaking his teeth at the only cold tap for thirty miles around.

Brunoli was a scraggly white man in his early 40s who could have trimmed his beard several weeks ago, but didn't have the sense even though it was the middle of summer and he was living in the tropics. No one had the decency, let alone the courage, to tell the poor bastard he had bits of peanut shells scattered all over that beard, so they simply looked the other way. This had the effect of annoying the man because he, like most of us, preferred people speaking face to face as an indicator of sincerity, or perhaps a gauge for honesty. Nonetheless, the group was not there to socialize; they were there for their explosives and nothing else.

After downing the last of his draft, and forcibly belching because he downed it too quickly, Brunoli and a man waiting in a dark corner of the bar that the group never noticed until after he appeared, began walking outside to their car, which was located on the back side of the building where the rare patrolman wouldn't take suspicion if he coincidentally happened by.

"Come on; let's go get your merchandise," he said to Jerry Molinar.

Lewis took out a cigarette and started to light it before the tall stranger grabbed his hand and silently reminded him what type of cargo they were picking up.

"Go get the car, Pete." Mendez ordered, annoyed by his partner's lack of attention.

Brunoli felt intimidated somewhat by Mendez's tone, but was curious about people that few knew about, let alone made acquaintance without becoming dead shortly thereafter.

"Are you the one they call Santa Claus?" He asked.

Brunoli already knew the answer; he just wanted to ease his own tensions with light conversation. Mendez didn't answer; he preferred someone else tout his reputation.

"Yes, he is." Molinar obliged.

Around the backside of the building rested an older Cadillac Deville with a pool of condensation underneath that had not yet evaporated, indicating that the car had not been resting very long. It rested just long enough for Brunoli to run into the bar and quaff two pints of beer before handling what was certain to become a tricky situation. When he unlocked the truck, lifted a blanket, and brought out a small case, Mendez's mind had already become skeptical. His disappointment became most apparent when Brunoli unlocked and opened the case, however.

"What the fuck is this?" Mendez turned sideways in a defensive posture so he could also address the muscle that was there for Brunoli.

"Well, what the hell does it look like?" Brunoli said.

"Hey, Hey! Relax fellas." Molinar didn't want any unwarranted entanglements, however, in this business, you're expected to deliver what you promise — nothing else. He continued, "Guillermo, go call our friend and see what's going on, will ya?"

Mendez threw his arms up in disgust. All his preparation and planning, the loaned car, Azzari's money — everything — had been wasted he thought, but he kept his cool.

"I'll be right back. Don't you two go anywhere," he pointed.

Mendez walked around to the front side of the hotel where the only payphone existed for thirty miles. He had no trouble coming up with the seventy-five cents for the long distance call back to Tampa, and Azzari fortunately picked up his call by the second ring. Azzari wasn't the smartest or most prominent man in the family, but he was wise enough to know that when you don't give someone exactly what they ask for, you'd better expect a call. He did, and had been waiting by his phone for the last hour in case there was a problem, which he already knew Mendez had.

"That wasn't the merchandise we discussed, Greggie."

"You listen to me and you listen good. This ain't no general store, you got that? We had a last minute complication with the previous request. Pay the man, bring back the goods, and I'll tell you what you need to know, okay?"

"Your money," said Mendez, just before hanging up and walking back to a few nervous individuals.

He gave them the $400 they expected plus another $100 to cover their bar tab and pay for the two girls upstairs he knew were probably waiting for their afternoon appointments. Mendez didn't have to cough up any more than the deal usually needed, but he made memorable contacts over the years by rewarding friends this way.

Lewis and Molinar loaded the case into the back of the Lincoln and waited for Mendez to climb into the back seat — his preferred position.

"So what was the big deal back there?" Lewis asked.

"We didn't get what we asked for. Not exactly, anyway," answered Molinar.

"Greggie better know what he's doing." Mendez added.

"I don't get it," complained Lewis, who hated not being in the loop. "What's in the case?"

[sic] and Tired

Mendez didn't much like the fact that Azzari kept him in the dark on the explosives, but after all, there was no use in working himself up about it since he didn't have a single dime invested. In fact, Azzari had completely subsidized Mendez and Lewis for over two months with money that they hadn't really earned yet, with one exception being the robbery committed a month prior. Now, it seemed, Azzari brought his assassin and his glorified reputation under his own tutelage and demeanor. Mendez became nothing more than a simple enforcer, hand-fed only enough for no warranted complaints until he was able to get back to business. That time had arrived.

"I still don't like the fact that you went ahead with this deal, old man," said Mendez, still getting his jabs in when he thought appropriate.

"Do you wanna learn how to work this stuff or not?" Azzari griped, whose temper had grown short. "Pay attention here or you're gonna blow us all up."

A few minutes prior, Mendez and Lewis returned from returning Big Sam's car. He was asleep, so they just left the keys in the mailbox by the front door as he instructed. Azzari had a cab waiting for them out on the street, so they were back at his place in only moments.

The dynamite's metal container managed to stay just cool enough not to sweat after its ride in the Lincoln's trunk, which could have created a very serious condition if it weren't for the fact that modern construction explosives contain different stabilizers than those thirty years ago, preventing such hazardous conditions. Modern dynamite could take a fair amount of ambient heat, so long as it wasn't excessive. Certainly the trunk of a black car in central Florida heat would usually qualify as "excessive" if it weren't for the fact that Peter Lewis kept the car's interior cold enough to warrant jackets, and that cool air likely leaked towards the rear. Even if he didn't run the air conditioner, the car never saw less than ninety miles per hour unless they were cruising through the small towns. Those retardations only lasted for a few minutes.

Azzari opened the small case revealing eight sticks of dynamite packed beneath some electrical wire and two blasting caps. He removed everything on top of the sticks and slowly removed six, placing them side by side on a small plywood square.

"Get that roll of duct tape on the wall over there and tape these down to the plate while I get this wire sorted out," he said.

Azzari unrolled about eight feet of some 18-guage insulated wire and made a cut. He then shaved off about an inch of insulation from both ends and then twisted the bare end of his cable with the bare end of the wire leading from the blasting cap. "That's it." He said proudly.

"That's what?" Lewis asked with arms folded with a hand scratching his chin.

"That's it! It's finished."

"What are we gonna do with that?" Lewis asked, as if he didn't know.

"You're gonna make $19,000 with it, that's what."

"Pipe down, Pete. I think I know what he wants to do." Mendez interrupted. "Ignition coil?"

"Oldest, most reliable gag in the world," said Azzari.

"Six is enough?" Lewis asked.

"Two is enough under most conditions. Six? Let me tell you something; there won't be anything left when this goes up. Guillermo, you keep the detonator and the wire away from anything metal until the time comes, understand? You can trip the newer caps with a stinkin' radio battery, let alone a static jolt. Just be careful about it, eh?"

"One detonator will set off all six? Why not use both and be safe?" Mendez asked. "You know, just in case."

"It'll go off, no problem. When the time comes, just shove the cap into one of the middle sticks. Kaboom! Just don't be anywhere around."

It had been nearly two months since their botched assassination attempt on Carlos Salazar. He never quite recovered emotionally and stuck close to home after dark unless he had an employee or two handy for a late delivery. At home, however, he was still openly vulnerable.

The City of Tampa Police Department had ceased extra patrols around his house after a few weeks and generally wrote the first attempt as a one-time occurrence. Still, some patrolmen passed by Salazar's warehouse from time to time just to make sure there weren't any stray automobiles hanging around. On an even rarer occasion—happened only once, actually—a patrolman stopped by the warehouse and checked on Salazar personally, giving him the impression policemen watched him regularly when, in reality, they didn't.

Late on the next Monday night, or rather Tuesday morning since it was after two, Lewis dropped Mendez off in perfect darkness a little over a block from Salazar's corner. From there, Mendez carried the bomb and ignition wiring in a black pillowcase roughly two hundred yards to Salazar's corner, dodging the streetlights in case some insomniac just happened to be looking outside. A streetlight illuminated Salazar's yard brightly on its corner, but that left the opposite side completely dark. Before he rounded the corner, Mendez started thinking to himself that the passenger side of Salazar's Buick would be out of the light, not the driver's side that he had intended to rig. It would mean exposure to that light while rigging the device, since the Buick was too low to the ground for him to crawl under and work, let alone hide. He didn't care. It was past 2 a.m. and he was going to risk it. If Salazar woke up and started moving around, Mendez would just take him out with his pistol through the window. None of that happened, however. As soon as Mendez rounded the block, he breathed a sigh of relief. Salazar had backed his car into the driveway, placing the driver's side in the dark.

The first thing Mendez did was crawl as far under the front left corner of the car as his body's thickness would allow, and then reach up into the engine compartment, feeling around for the sparkplug wires. He had to be careful not to yank the wire from the coil; otherwise, the bomb would never go off. Instead, he had to unhook one of the sparkplugs themselves. He found the #1 cylinder wire and yanked it right off the plug, letting it dangle on the ground. He then reached around for his pocketknife and sliced off the jacketed end of the plug wire, exposing the bare copper. All he had to do next was twist together the lead from the engine to the blasting cap lead, shove the cap into one of the middle sticks of the bomb, and then wedge the bomb over one of the exhaust pipes under the driver's seat. Mendez had no problems performing all of those tasks until it came time to wedge the bomb under the floorboard.

After struggling with the car's low stance, and the fact he couldn't exactly see what he was doing, Mendez finally got the bomb to stay wedged over the pipe with the bomb's board-side facing the concrete driveway, almost exactly the way Azzari described. I say "almost" because there was only one minor flaw to Mendez's bomb planting execution: the dynamite wasn't exactly facing directly at the driver's seat. His shimmying and shoving eventually left the bomb rather cockeyed. Mendez thought it wouldn't matter. According to Azzari, if two sticks of dynamite would normally be enough to blast the car sky high, six should be more than enough to smithereen just about anything, let alone Salazar's posterior.

Mendez joyfully escaped back through the shadows to where Lewis patiently waited, softly listening to a radio station that, much to his liking, was in the midst of an extended set playing David Bowie's "Diamond Dogs" album in its entirety as a sort of protest for their disdain of his newer record.

As soon as he closed the car door, Lewis placed the transmission in gear, idled their way around the block and back towards the front entrance of the subdivision—just as quietly as they came. Both immediately reached for their shirt pockets and withdrew their smokes.

"I smell nineteen grand, what about you?" Lewis asked.

"That bomb better go off, Pete. We probably won't get another chance if it don't, you know."

"It'll go off, man; have faith! As soon as he turns the key he'll be on his way to that Skylab thing."

Both cruised back to their hotel, which was a different spot in Clearwater Beach that Azzari had previously set up, so they were located well away from the aftermath. Mendez and Lewis wouldn't know the full outcome until the noon local news later that day. Azzari, however, had been trying to reach their hotel room since 10:30 a.m., but was unsuccessful because Mendez and Lewis had stayed up for three more hours trying to defeat their anxieties. After a fifth of Beefeaters and half gallon of orange juice, they finally conked out around five in the morning. Their vodka comas were way too powerful for the semi-muted telephone to overcome. Somehow though, they made it back up in time for the noon news that had one of Tampa's first remote cameras on the scene, showing the blackened hulk that Salazar managed to escape with his life, but with third degree burns on his only remaining leg—the other one blown apart just as the original in Korea over thirty years before.

Naturally, Mendez and Lewis were shocked and angry with the news that they failed for the second and probably last time with Salazar. Picking up the phone's handset was a painful task Mendez had to do, but calling Azzari was the next logical step. Obviously, something didn't work correctly. Either the dynamite was defective or Azzari's wiring instructions weren't up to snuff. Lewis offered his opinions and came to the same conclusion as Mendez; the explosives were not only the type they wanted, they must have been bad.

Of course, Gregory Azzari was having none of it. As far as he was concerned, his instructions were rock-solid and his supplier was not someone that entertained notions of messing around with Giuseppe Cantonello's people, even if he was out of the country. He decided patience was the best policy for now, given the circumstances and that they wouldn't know what happened until a mutual friend at the police department was able to relay an official cause.

No explanation reached Mendez until a month later when forensic investigators determined that the only reason Salazar survived was because the bomb was likely on the ground at the moment it exploded, and only one or perhaps two sticks actually detonated fully while the others simply fell apart and burned in a less percussive fireball. Salazar never lost consciousness and rolled out of the car into a blanket his wife thoughtfully grabbed from their living room couch.

There were just too many unbelievable circumstances for an angry Mendez to believe, even though the report suggested the bomb simply fell apart on the ground before detonation. Azzari knew Mendez screwed this one up and there was nobody else to blame. The only thing that kept Mendez around was the fact that he had a successful resume and, after all, he didn't get the materials he originally requested. In other words, Azzari felt that he shared some of the responsibility for the failure, but he wasn't going to admit so much to Mendez. Lewis sat expressionless, hatching an idea that he would keep to himself until the time was right.

The (un)Official

Seemingly, Angel Vargas' enterprises and duties transpired all over town and possibly all over the state. On occasion, however, global matters summoned his attentions. In the beginning of July 1975, his problem involved a complication with a public official—one of the highest-ranking law enforcement officers in Oklahoma City—a Town Marshal named Phillip Jackson.

Vargas' narcotics trafficking enterprises were virtually at a standstill in the Midwest due to Mr. Jackson's efforts during the previous two years, and it had gotten to the point where the local family members were all screaming for a solution. To make matters worse, Jackson's task force shot and killed the brother of a close narcotics trafficking family member of Vargas' in Pennsylvania a few weeks prior. This created somewhat of a conundrum for the Pennsylvania connection in that people in Vargas' particular business couldn't run around with weak appearances—not without punishment, anyway. Acts of revenge were normal in that industry, but those practicing omertà strictly prohibited retaliatory actions against legitimate law enforcement officers performing their mandated duties. Nonetheless, there was an unsanctioned contract placed on Phillip Jackson in the amount of $25,000.

Of course, Tresedici's ethics wouldn't allow the killing of a law enforcement officer, which meant his underlings would have to find another solution. While it wasn't acceptable for any family member to carry out such a contract let alone sanction one, Vargas felt he had discovered an elegant solution. And, as long as he could deny involvement if the operation belly flopped, nobody would be the wiser.

Andrew "Drew" Geraldson floated in and out of the FBI's "grey zone" ever since he became Florida State's Beverage Controller. He was quite the excessive type; in his early 50s, around 6'3", weighed upwards of 300 pounds, trimmed white hair and beard, usually wore a tweed sport coat, and always wore his favorite alligator cowboy boots.

Before his days as a questionable beverage controller, he spent twenty years in the Ocala Police Department. At the time of his involvement, state and federal law agencies considered him friendly even tapping his testimony as an informant on several occasions. (But we know about informants!) Even though Geraldson enjoyed his police pension, after his state office run, he continued as a private investigator. At least, that's what his official job description stated. In reality, he was purportedly Vargas' regional boss in the narcotics trade and did little investigating, other than diligence on the people with which he or others in the narcotics trade did business. Indeed, Drew Geraldson seemed like a power to be reckoned with. Many in Tallahassee's local government were likely in his back pocket, as well were many of the local newspaper and television reporters that weren't immune to such a charismatic and talented con artist.

It may have been unclear who was who's boss, but Vargas brought Geraldson in on the contract killing that he planned with Mendez, whom he managed to snake away for a week without Peter "Danny Boy" Lewis' knowledge. For all Geraldson knew, he wouldn't be personally executing the contract; he was only there for diligence and surveillance, knowing that he was a highly recognizable person that, after years of business trips to Oklahoma City and personally meeting with him on several occasions, Jackson would know. Using himself instead of Mendez, he thought, would surely compromise the element of surprise. The cash offered, however, distorted Geraldson's self-vision as effectively as a funhouse mirror.

What none of the group knew was that Marshal Jackson had already been tipped off to his contract by a mutual friend in Pennsylvania, and he had armed himself to the teeth with a various assortment of small arms should anyone come calling.

Vargas was perhaps more intelligent than many of his counterparts anticipated. This fact became most apparent by including Geraldson in the first place. If they were successful, they earned a large amount of cash and a great friend in

Pennsylvania—someone they could always count on if they ever needed a favor, and Vargas always needed favors. If Geraldson botched the assault and was recognized or captured, Vargas would certainly inherit the entirety of his narcotics operations in the Florida panhandle.

Vargas certainly grew more aggressive and cunning, but his weakness—trusting that no one would dare rat him out if they were ever caught—could come back to haunt him. After all, he made Geraldson acutely aware of Mendez's reputation, and although ironically, it was Geraldson who, in a few years perhaps, would actually resemble Santa Claus. Geraldson internally theorized that Mendez was along as a triggerman because nobody near the top of the ladder was stupid enough to risk prison, well, for something as serious as murder anyway. The death penalty, or more directly, the electric chair, still served its purpose as more of a deterrent than a form of justice. Unfortunately, risk incentive also had its price, and that price, at least on this occasion, was $25,000.

Just before Independence Day, Geraldson parked his Apollo Yellow 1974 Cadillac El Dorado convertible about 150 yards down the street from Sheriff Jackson's property. Geraldson had settled in with a pair of binoculars and a shotgun for less than ten minutes before Jackson came from around his house and into the street, toting his standard-issued service revolver, which he wasted no time bringing the sights directly at Geraldson. Two or three seconds went by, so Geraldson panicked and hit the gas, prompting the cool-as-ice marshal to take two steps off the pavement and sling two rounds through Geraldson's windshield from about 40 yards away; a difficult feat for any professional at that distance. Geraldson's reaction seemed antithetical to most, who usually keep running, but Geraldson kept his shotgun inaccurately aimed at Jackson while coming to a complete stop just beside him.

Jackson's curiosity kept him from squeezing off the round that most definitely would have come awfully close to a decapitation. Instead, he kept his sights on Geraldson's skull while he fumbled with his shotgun. The jig was up and Geraldson knew it, but how was he ever going to get out of this one? There were at least two curious neighbors gawking at both of them by that time, and probably a few more—some of whom had already called backup for the marshal. Carefully, Geraldson lowered his weapon and conceded to the old-timer, figuring that he had not actually broken any laws.

As far as Geraldson was concerned, there were no laws against loitering on a public right-of-way, no laws against accelerating from his parking spot, and no laws prohibiting the use, or threat of use, of a firearm in self-defense. In fact, he likely had the marshal at a disadvantage since no one else saw the shotgun sticking out of the window before Jackson let the windshield have it. There was also no method of demonstrating whether the marshal was a poor shot who was shooting with intent to kill, or—what the truth of the matter was—that he had multiple trophies on his fireplace mantle from his competitive shooting days at the department and was therefore an expert marksman. If Jackson wanted him dead, and he could easily claim a case of self-defense in that Geraldson had a weapon in his hand, Jackson could have easily killed him, and that would be that. Except, Jackson had been around long enough to know that a hitman was his best lead if he wanted to take down all those behind a conspiracy. He had the drop on Geraldson and knew it, now all he had to do was take his prisoner to jail and start interrogating.

Jackson had huge tactical problems, however: The side effect of being a popular elected public figure is that you are, in fact, accessible and accountable at all times to the public. Translation: reporters constantly at your doorstep. Now imagine how a large city's local press reacted when some radio plug caught the emergency traffic dispatched after the first phone call from Jackson's neighbors. Within minutes, the ever-vigilant press core sprung into action, often beating certain government respondents to the scene. In Jackson's case, three patrolmen who felt their political chances could increase dramatically should they arrive at the scene first, arrived within moments after the call went over the airwaves. From then on, Jackson didn't have the luxury of helping expedite his investigation personally; he delegated the entire operation to those that would normally take care of such matters as these when they aren't happening to high-visibility elected officials. It was an error Jackson wished he could overcome because, at heart, he liked the chase. Unfortunately, so did the reporters who occupied his every waking hour over the next two weeks.

Spanning Jackson's lengthy law enforcement career, the newspaper reporters had become quite enamored with his "down home" midwestern straightforwardness and colorful expressions. Most of them were interested in the exact moments between Jackson's recognition that he was in danger, and the moment when Geraldson finally dropped his weapon. When the reporters asked how Jackson realized he was being stalked, his reply was, "The only folks drivin' big automobiles like that are the greasy big city mob types or ranchers, but I didn't see longhorns mounted on the front like you see some do on TV. No, this big feller was as conspicuous as hippopotamus in a bathtub."

What infuriated Jackson in the meantime was the almost instantaneous coalition of high-profile legal practitioners descending like turkey buzzards on a fresh armadillo carcass. Like the reporters, they smelled opportunity for notoriety and were frothing at the mouth since, it appeared, Geraldson's quick thinking may have won him a technicality from full prosecution as a murder conspirator. The judge concurred and granted Geraldson's eventual release under bail until his exact charge could be determined.

The judge, much to Jackson's complaints, ultimately reduced that charge to Felony Gun Pointing; a rather obscure and archaic piece of double-standard legislature carried over from the previous century. As a matter of convenience, such as times like these, the law prosecutes to its fullest extent. The spirit of this law involved intent and offense/defense. Most judges felt it safe to assume that citizens aiming a loaded weapon at other citizens are, in fact, committing assault akin terrorism. The double standard occurs when law enforcement officers draw their weapons and aim them towards someone as a preventative defense. Therein the matter becomes a dilemma of intent. An officer may take aim and fire upon you if he feels threatened, and the law affords any normal citizen the same conditional power, provided their local laws allow for self-defense. Someone pointing a weapon in an *offensive* manner, however, is where the law's spirit resides. The law gave Geraldson's attorneys more than necessary to overcome the firearms pointing charge, allowing for his speedy return to Tallahassee. When no witnesses were immediately available, the ambiguity of self-defense dismissed Jackson's angle for incarceration during the conspiracy investigation.

But Jackson was distraught over the matter after nearly being run down by a man he previously considered a trusted friend in law enforcement. Betrayal, even in its smallest scope, tears at a man. He vowed to continue his investigation into Geraldson's ties with the underworld, but the old man was already ten years past normal retirement age and his body couldn't handle the stress. Only four months after the attempt on his life, Oklahoma City's Town Marshal passed away after suffering a massive stroke. The departments that he oversaw, in conjunction with the FBI, continued investigating Geraldson, Vargas, and their Pennsylvania connections.

Two for the Show

Salvatore Tresedici was inconsolable by the reckless incompetence exhibited by those in his employment, but he was stuck with them in any regard. By mid-July, two attempts on Carlos Salazar had been unsuccessful, causing the amputee to become even more reclusive and evasive. Even though the organization had some of the most powerful individuals in offices of the local government, their reach only extended so far. They could not be so obvious as to compromise their own positions. The feds were nabbing his underlings by increased pressures on informants and less interference by uncooperative, sympathetic cops. The war over Tampa's control raged on.

The focal point at the federal level had been, and still continued to be, Ben Davidson, whom the mobsters had also been unsuccessful in dispatching. For months, they've concentrated on getting rid of the opposition to their operations, while not spending enough attention and focus on their operations in the first place. After Vargas' and Mendez's third botched mission, faith in their ability to execute those matters came into question.

Tresedici stood aside and let Vargas continue his narcotics dealing, knowing he was becoming more of an impotent patriarch on a daily basis. For all of Vargas' misdealing, he was, after all, very effective in the management of their legitimate establishments and other fronts for the latest and best moneymaker, cocaine; particularly, the purest varieties imported through their connections in Colombia and Central America. Guillermo Mendez, however, had been a semi-pro hitman his entire career and was making adjustments as a mule for Vargas, since his allowances and other ill-gotten income had vanished.

Dry spells in the murder-for-hire industry were not unusual, however. When everyone behaved, as watered-down as the definition of "behaved" can be, assassins were often-times useful in surveillance and other intelligence gathering, as well as raw muscle (if they had the intimidating physique) or as a discreet courier. With these types of individuals, encouragement in any direction was easy as long as you had the cash. And the deal, if properly implemented, carried an acceptable amount of risk.

"You and Greggie just want me and my partner to run this down to Nano in Miami; that's it?" Mendez said, gazing at the small, clear, plastic bag that held another small bag wrapped in cellophane and taped across its middle.

"Joo be careful with that, my friend," said Vargas.

"Yeah, man. I know what it is, but what am I supposed to get for it?"

"You may think you know what it is, but you may not."

"It's coke; what of it?" Mendez asked.

"Not just any, mind you. It's eighty-eight percent uncut Colombian."

"Oh yeah? Good stuff, huh? Okay, so it's special. Two, three grand? What's in it for me and my partner?"

Mendez took the best guess he could, considering his light involvement with the drug as a user and the few — very few, sales he had made in the past. Most of those, however, were at the retail level and not wholesale or post-wholesale. As well, his former dealings revolved around cut cocaine taken down as far as the 12% purity level.

"Well, let me see," said Vargas, sitting at his office desk behind a worn-out Hermes adding machine. This wasn't his regular office at Randy's, though. That facility was far too visible and far too predisposed for interruptions from people that need no knowledge of Vargas' other businesses — especially his women that allowed themselves the nickname de jour.

"That's six ounces; about 170 grams pure. You don't need to know exactly what I'm buying it for, but let's just say I'm letting you have it all for $4,000. That's fair enough, no?" Vargas said.

"Seems high to me, but beggars...you know," said Mendez.

"Exactly, but I should tell you for uncut quality such as this, the price is more than fair on the third level."

"Yeah, Angel, but what's Nano agreed to pay?"

"A good question, my friend, but there it has more incentive for you as well."

Vargas laughed and sat back in his seat. He valued the surprise and smile most entertainers enjoy.

"What if I was to say to you that this friend in Miami was willing to pay $1,800 per ounce? That should keep you and Danny Boy in tonics until you get another job."

Mendez continued his stare at the small bag of cocaine. "Hey man, the 'Danny Boy' gag—probably shouldn't say that in front of Pete. It drives him insane."

Vargas never blinked before getting his answer from Mendez.

"And yeah; that's a fair enough deal. He gets his six zees; I bring you four grand and keep the change, which should be close to around seven grand. Suits me." Mendez said, stuffing the package in his denim jacket pocket, which made Vargas simultaneously wonder how anyone could wear such clothing in the middle of summer. But that was the fashion of the day, and the air conditioners kept him in ice.

Of course, Mendez had already cooked up his plan to cut the coke with an extra ounce of baking powder, giving him an extra 170 grams of a slightly less pure variety—something he and Lewis could have some fun with if they wanted.

In a newly issued 1972 Ford LTD which was nearly as monstrous as Big Sam's Lincoln, Lewis drove his partner the entire five and a half hours straight to the destination listed on a small scrap of paper Gregory Azzari had slipped in Mendez's pocket the morning they left; Willie Brunoli's home, located just outside Coral Gables.

His place was a spectacularly bland home off 69th Avenue on the west side; something so easy to find, it only took Lewis two turns to get there from the Turnpike in the middle of a summer downpour. By the time they had arrived, Mendez had carefully poured the eyesight equivalent of baking powder into the small pack of cocaine. To ensure an even cut, he vigorously shook the mixture for around ten minutes and then poured an ounce (roughly the same amount that would comfortably fit into the palm of an average hand without spilling) into a temporary small baggie before closing up the original bag. Mendez then made two half-ounce bags from the bag he cut before.

"There. Still have the six zees for Nano, and a half for some extra if we wanna."

"What about the other half?" A skeptical Lewis asked.

"What other half?" Mendez smiled.

"Don't fuck with me, Santa." Lewis joked. "What are you doing with the other half z? Come on!"

"I know a little club off the beach. Probably be a good stop for both of us later tonight. Good place — you'll like it."

Before reaching Brunoli's front door, Mendez surveyed the area, checking for nosey neighbors while he adjusted the .357 wedged in his blue jeans behind his back. The doorbell gave an odd ring; more like chimes from a melody he knew he had heard before but couldn't quite recognize because the mechanism was a little out of sync and the notes seemed slightly off key.

"Ha ha!" Lewis laughed.

"What *is* that?" Mendez said.

 "Beethoven's Fifth. Don't you get it?"

"Yeah; Victory…so?"

"No, well, I mean, yeah, it is, but I mean from that flick with McDowell…um…or was that the Ninth?"

"Hey! What are you two meatheads doin' out here? Get your asses inside." Brunoli laughed as he threw the door open, surprising the men.

All three walked inside and took a seat at the kitchen table, which had half of it occupied with unwashed dinner plates and flatware, some of which looked like it had been there for more than a couple of days.

"Come on in here; tell me what you have for me," said Brunoli as they took a seat. "Six uncut right? Let's see it."

As Brunoli said it, both his and Mendez's eyes met in a severe test of honesty. Brunoli was no idiot. He was a connoisseur as much as they were, only they never noticed the small barrel of a .22 rifle bearing down on their foreheads from a dark room down the main hallway. The mysterious man they noticed prior at Yeehaw Junction was completely forgotten about in their moment of greed.

Mendez withdrew the larger pack of cocaine from his jacket pocket, again drawing a strange facial expression from someone bewildered by anyone wearing such a garment in Miami at any time of year, let alone summer. Brunoli quickly dropped the funny look as soon as the bag hit the table in front of him. He didn't say anything; he simply reached down into the chair beside him, picked up a one foot square mirrored glass tile, and dumped a portion of the bag on its surface that couldn't have weighed more than a half gram. He then licked his right index finger, pressed it into the powder, and then brought it back up for a taste. He did so while looking directly into Mendez's eyes, apparently looking for any sign of deviance. Mendez was a cool player though. He knew 88% would be nearly undetectable with baking powder, which gave no real indication on its own. If he cut it with just about anything else, especially sugar, the man down the hallway would have summarily executed them right there in the dining room. Luckily for Mendez and Lewis, Brunoli's tongue was no more sensitive than a child's after eating a Pixy Stix. In fact, it was probably already numb from a line he did thirty minutes before their arrival.

"Oh yeah! Good shit." Brunoli smacked. "You had any?"

Lewis immediately jumped in. "No! Is it that good?"

"Here.   Finish the rest," said Brunoli, handing Lewis a shortened drinking straw.

Lewis wasted no time sticking his nose in their business, snorting the remains of the loose half and reacting wildly to its potency. Obviously, he wasn't prepared for, nor experienced with, cocaine that potent. What he just consumed, if cut in a typical fashion (which Brunoli would likely do just after they left), was the equivalent of four full lines—a shattering head butt from The Bull. Olé!

"Holy Shi—"

"Relax my man. It will calm down in a few minutes," said Brunoli.

Lewis was having a hard time with burning sensation deep within his nose. "Jesus!"

"So, six at eighteen. That's ten-eight, and I'm a gonna throw in an extra couple hundred for you two to have a good time tonight—my treat."

For the moment, Mendez forgot he was a cold-blooded executioner and felt that he found a much easier and lucrative career in trafficking. The job was easy, the risk was relatively low, the pay was incredible, and the work could potentially be more frequent. Alas, he concluded that the work was easy with one major exception; the supplier. That was Angel Vargas and he would probably prefer his spike stay on one side of the fence. The thought fluttered when Brunoli handed him a nice stack of hundreds.

"I have another half if you want it," said Mendez.

Slowly, Brunoli's eyes rolled upwards, meeting Mendez's with the look of remorse should he have to take his life for suspected embezzlement. As far as he knew, he was receiving six ounces of uncut pure Colombian. The distrusting ways of these businessmen dictated skepticism, but greed usually won out in the end. Brunoli was not immune to the powers of that particular sin. Instead of interrogation and a formal test of his main shipment, his mind moved ahead with the deal.

"I don't have cash, but..." He said.

"Then we're done. I can sell it at the beach over a coupla days." Mendez got up.

"Hey. Hey! You better not sell nuttin' at the beach or at least not get seen by nobody sellin' it out there. You wanna get smoked?"

"By who?" Lewis jumped in.

"By the people that control the area, you high motherfucker. Geez; give a guy a taste and he thinks he owns the town. Ha!"

"Okay. Jesus, Nano, it's just a question." Lewis said.

Brunoli spun and pointed his finger at Lewis in a crazed anger. "What'd you call me?"

Still reeling from his coke, Lewis shrugged the question off. "What. I said, 'by who?'"

"No, after that." Brunoli growled, still pointing.

"What? I said, Jesus." Lewis said, confused.

"Jesus what?" Brunoli demanded.

Lewis sighed, trying to remember exactly what he said. Cautiously he repeated, "Jesus Nano, it's just a question?"

Brunoli jumped up and grabbed Lewis by the base of his skull, slamming him up against the back wall. "Don't you ever call me that name. Don't you ever fucking call me that name. You understand, you little faggot? Never!"

He released a stunned Lewis, realizing his intimidations were ineffective. Actually, Lewis rather liked being strong-armed by the man, and along with his leveling cocaine rush, became rather turned on by the experience.

"Do you want the half or not?" Mendez asked.

Brunoli panted and sat back down, dismayed by Lewis' lack of respect. "I don't have enough extra cash on me for that."

"Well, I guess we'll be on our way then." Mendez said as he got up and turned towards the door.

"Wait. What about something else?" Said Brunoli, wondering if he could barter.

"Something else? You got $900 worth of something else that I actually want?" Mendez laughed.

"Well, let's see, tough guy. You attempting any more mayhem back north?" Brunoli laughed right back, displaying his knowledge of Mendez's bad luck in the assassination racket.

"Maybe."

"Explosives?"

"Didn't work the last time, so probably not."

"It didn't work because you didn't do it right and you know it."

Of course, Mendez wasn't exactly amused with Brunoli's tact in the matter, but he was undoubtedly correct.

"So. What of it? I wanted plastic. That's what I'm used to, so that's what I'm gonna use if I blow anything else."

"Plastic? I can't get plastic. Nobody can get plastic right now because it's in short supply, and well, too much trouble to get through the usual sources. Tell you what I do have, though. I've got thirty sticks of the same stuff you blew a few weeks ago right out in the garage. It's worth $1,250 to anybody else. Thirty sticks. That should be enough for five or six jobs, or maybe three if you want their pieces in orbit."

During his pitch, Brunoli knew he had Mendez interested. He could do a lot of damage with thirty sticks of dynamite and having that much around never hurt. Someone just about always needed blowing up, he thought, so he didn't bother with more discussion, he just reached into his jacket's pocket and flipped a small baggie on the table.

Brunoli got up and slapped him on the back, knowing that for $900 worth of explosives sitting around in his garage, he just nailed another eight or nine grand of coke.

"Oh this is like Celia and Johnny," he said, "¡Azúcar!"

Brunoli led them both to his air-conditioned garage where he kept the suitcase of dynamite under a blanket.

"I don't have no wire, man, but I'll give you six detonators with it. That's all I have. That good?"

"Perfect," said Mendez after loading the box into the back seat of the LTD and taking the car keys from Lewis, who was obviously three hours from being able to drive.

Once outside, neither he nor Lewis noticed the front bedroom's window curtain swinging ever so slightly behind the glass. They never noticed Brunoli's companion at any time, since it was usually better if you didn't.

Two blocks away, Lewis asked, "All right, Santa fucking Claus, I thought his name was Nano. What the…"

"It is; he just hates it when anyone tries to call him that."

"Why? What does it mean?" Lewis asked.

"Use your imagination."

The celebration started with a stop by a South Beach liquor store just off Alton Road, where they picked up two cartons of smokes, a fifth of Tanqueray, tonic water, limes, and a 12-pack of Löwenbräu. Lewis had been chattering non-stop since he and Mendez scooted from West Miami, and Mendez figured he'd better level him out within a few hours if they were going to have any fun at the club.

"I got a key to my uncle's apartment just off the beach. We'll drop this stuff off and relax for a bit, got it? Stay the night there later." Mendez said, interrupting Lewis' mindless chatter about some piece of meat he'd like to get ahold of later, which was making Mendez nauseous.

"What? Where is that place? It's not too far from the club scene is it? What about your uncle? Isn't he there? Where is he? Is he cool? Huh? Talk to me!"

"You need to just chill for a few, ace. My uncle is at his summer pad up in Manhattan. It's not a problem and the choice clubs don't start hoppin' around here until after eleven anyway. I'm gonna take a nap."

Of course, Lewis had a hard time falling asleep, so he took a walk down to Lincoln Road and did some shopping. He was flush with cash and thought his wardrobe wasn't nearly fashionable enough if he wanted to get lucky later. Almost four hours after he stepped out, he returned carrying two large bags filled with three complete new outfits. None of the ruffling bags woke Mendez, who was out like a light. Lewis sat down in the living room and started planning his outfit for later that evening. He poured a gin and tonic, and before the next hour had passed, crashed completely under the vigilant rumble of the window's air conditioner.

What eventually awakened Lewis was a passing car's horn blasting just underneath the apartment as the beach's nightly

Latin soiree began heating up. The noise wouldn't have normally penetrated the building's thick façade if it weren't for Mendez leaving the sliding glass doors wide open. He enjoyed sitting on the balcony, ogling pedestrians while the air conditioning seeped around his feet—checking the ungodly swelter to a minimal perspiration, if anything.

The headlights and taillights blurred below, creating slowly pumped arterial canyons through which Mendez contemplated. By the time Lewis dried off his shower and exacted what he thought was the evening's perfect wardrobe choice, Mendez was sliding the glass doors shut and placing an empty cocktail glass in the sink. He turned the water off, reached into his jacket's pocket, and threw the last half gram of coke on the dining room table.

"One time." He said to Lewis, who was practically frothing upon the bag's sight. "But don't go crazy, you know."

"Don't worry man; stuff's like a freight train. Half a line for me. You?"

"That's fine."

Lewis never noticed the blood trickling down his upper lip until Mendez arose from the table himself, pointing towards his own nose, which was something Lewis really didn't want to look at intensely. Ten minutes it took for both of them to simmer enough before trekking downstairs without appearing completely obvious to anyone else. They almost seemed normal by the time they walked one block over to Alton Road to summon a cab, but that was almost a problem within itself since just about everyone else that was moving around at that hour, and in that part of the jungle were even more hipsters outlandishly dressed and doped to the nines. Where they were going, fashion took a back seat. Your appearance didn't matter as long as you had cash and *other* accoutrements.

Mendez tipped the cabbie an extra ten for pulling into a dark alley fully one block from their secretive destination, which was invisible to prying eyes, being located behind a rather dull appearing laundromat. The outside metal door didn't look like much either if it weren't for the small cloth awning overhead and a rather large, black, middle-aged heavyweight, (as if bouncers are ever anything but large) who was dressed in black pants, black dress shirt and tie, and who never let the semi-smirk disappear from his face during their door-front interrogative. Mendez slipped him a Grant, folded once, accepted a pat-down, and strolled to the next door, waiting to get buzzed in. Lewis followed Mendez's lead, but didn't have anything less than a Franklin, which he palmed to the hulking bouncer, expecting change before he received his pat down. He just stood there high on his idiocy, staring up into the eyes of El Tormento Negro, as his employers nicknamed him years ago.

"Well, come on, don't just stand there." Lewis insisted.

The bouncer said nothing and looked at Mendez down the hall in such a way that Mendez knew that Lewis was jeopardizing their evening if he didn't simply turn around and accept the fact that he wasn't going to get any change from his hundred, and take the pat-down, or else they were both going to see the alleyway from a rat's perspective within five seconds—and without their buck-fifty. Mendez quickly jogged back to Lewis, whispered what was about to happen in his ear, and then smiled at the bouncer, acknowledging the resolution. Lewis finally turned around and put his hands up in the customary position for frisking, but the bouncer didn't simply pat him down. After he finished with Lewis' lower left ankle he reached around and bear-hugged him from behind, grabbing his chest and his package firmly, but not in such a way that was painful. Lewis, still floating in powdered euphoria, was scared out of his mind when the bouncer pulled him in real tight and whispered in his ear.

"Ain't no bank teller, man. But if you need sometin' later, you just look for me or Jimmy, dig?" And, he let Lewis go right afterward.

"Whoa!" Said Lewis, who actually regained his sense of humor upon release—pointing back towards the bouncer. "Now *that* was worth the price of admission!"

Lewis limped alongside Mendez back towards the entrance as the bouncer hit a switch, causing the door's lock to momentarily open. They pushed their way inside and past another large man, who, Lewis guessed, was likely Jimmy. Lewis couldn't help but notice his rather strange smirk as well, but reckoned he should probably steer clear of any more witticisms, which Mendez appreciated. Besides, as soon as their eyes adjusted to the glare from the many high-powered disco lights swarming around the room, they realized they were existing on another plane.

Cigarette and incense smoke choked the main ballroom with haze and didn't do a very good job at all masking Mary Jane and her best friends. The air conditioners kept the place tolerable, but not enough to keep the humidity down, adding to an already greasy feel.   There was another penetrating odor too—unmistakably latex, which an explanation became quickly apparent when Mendez's and Lewis' eyes were able to focus between the blasts of strobe lights.

Some were dancing, albeit in the most provocative manner. Others were either watching or participating in one form or another, in either or both the acts of illicit drug use or sex. Suffice to say, the club was an ongoing orgy. Topless women explored each other in intentional full view of anxious spectators, while muscular men paraded in thongs selling cocktails. There was a topless girl selling cigarettes, as well as connections for those in want, but Mendez gravitated towards the bizarre ongoings at the far side of the ballroom.

There were two large alcoves in the Mediterranean-themed interior that had large, white curtains covering the entrances. One room had a powerfully bright light silhouetting the heterosexual acts performed inside and their spectators, who paid twenty bucks for the ringside seat. The other alcove had the same setup with a major difference; those performers were homosexual— sometimes women, sometimes men.   This club carried no preference rules except for one; desire.

Mendez and Lewis smiled at each other and wandered in, not seeing each other for a few hours until both of their prostitutes brought them together for some blow in an upstairs studio. That's where Lewis revealed his plan.

At a moment when the hired help took a breather, Lewis, in an almost incoherent state said, "Hey, Santa. You know that first one we missed? What if..."

Mendez's evening was almost over because it was nearly 3 a.m. and most of the cash he budgeted, probably two grand, was all gone. He had his final cocktail over an hour ago and the sound of Lewis' voice normally raked his coals anyway—except this time.

"What if what?" Mendez said. "Hurry up; I wanna get outta here in a few, man."

"No, listen. That guy we hit. What if I said I wanna have a little talk? ...tell him who did it."

Mendez's sense of humor was about as bland as a British pizzeria in any regard, so naturally the large razor he kept in a secret sleeve near his collarbone—a place never checked during pat-downs—made its grand appearance adjacent Lewis' jugular.

"What'd you say?" Mendez whispered.

Lewis would have normally panicked by now if it weren't for his clown-like reactions when death knocked, or rather pounded furiously, at his door. As soon as he calmed down enough to clear the mucous clogging his nasal passageway, Lewis explained, "No! I didn't say I would tell him *we* did it."

"Then who?"

"What about that guy, Hernandez? Doesn't he own half the bars around there?"

"Yeah...and?"

"So we tell the stump, what's his? ...Salazar, right? We tell him Hernandez hired someone we know and then he'll want him out of the way too. Easy money!"

Mendez withdrew his blade and let go of Lewis' brand new shirt and its oversized collar. He sat back down and tried, as much as his concentration would allow, contemplating such a double-cross. He knew Hernandez was friendly with Tresedici, but it was a working relationship, not quite the hands-off variety if he were a family member. After a moment, Mendez didn't say much of anything; he simply smiled, put a glass tube up his nose, and cleaned part of hand mirror he prepped moments earlier. Lewis had no idea if he had summoned the wrong side of Santa until Mendez sat back and handed him the mirror with a smile.

Echoing the lyrics blaring from a loudspeaker below, Mendez instructed, "Do a little dance..."

Sinkholes

Pundits define serendipity as somehow having good luck finding desirable things by accident. In my experience, good police work often operated with a degree of serendipity from time to time, however, there were times when you found things you didn't want, also by accident. Some would call that a misfortunate occurrence. There is always a moment when the epiphany occurs, individuals instinctively pause and decide whether continuing their foray into the unknown is worthwhile, or perhaps they should turn back for the sake of peace and progression. Race winners need only face the track, for all purposes considered.

Misfortune handed Gregory Azzari such a conundrum when gossip reached his ear in regard to Brunoli's "happiness with his six and a half ounces". Six *and a half?* Azzari thought. Consequently, his mind raced for over an hour contemplating whether he should phone Vargas or just keep it to himself. Azzari didn't care much for confrontations and he certainly despised it when forced into the role of the bad news messenger. As far as he was concerned, everyone was happy and there wasn't any good reason why he should be the one to go around messing up everyone's good time, so he didn't.

Nobody said anything after Mendez and Lewis rolled back into town, ready to begin their side business. Azzari and Tresedici were to meet with them to discuss their lack of progress with the List of Five, and talk about more runs to Miami. With Mendez's exception, they were flush with cash, so that meant spreading it around at the friend's establishments. In this case, they met at one of Tampa's first strip clubs; a small place off West Hillsborough Avenue called The Twilight.

Tresedici was a married man, so appearances dictated he and Azzari take position on the backside of the bar, where there was a booth with a commanding view of the entire facility. No sense in advertising, they thought.

Mendez and Lewis strolled in like a couple of whales about to blow their holes on the main floor of Caesar's Palace. The only problem was, neither one had the looks most of the women on the floor that night would break any concentration over, let alone interrupt their current marks' business. All they were interested in were the bulges in their front pockets and not any others.

Lewis was not entertained at all, as a matter of fact. For him, it was the equivalent of using a porcupine to masturbate, except he had to pay for it too. His attitude the entire evening had Mendez apologizing more than he'd like, which called his management capability into question with Tresedici. He had become quite annoyed with Lewis as well, but bit his lip for the sake of peace.

The main problem was that everyone was trying too hard. Mendez was trying to impress Azzari, so he'd get more side jobs. Azzari was kissing up to Tresedici, because that's what people with his rank tended to do as long as they thought breathing was a nice part of life. Mendez kept trying to impress both to the point of embarrassment. Lewis didn't care about anything but himself at the moment, considering his nature was under assault. Even worse, he had the propensity to drink until nothing but insults driveled from his tongue's tip. That was what Danny Boy craved more than anything when it came right down to it — danger.

A rather juicy brunette finished her dance on the other side of the bar and moseyed up to the men's table, completely unaware she was interrupting a meeting her boss would rather she never saw. Mendez, eager to make a compliment, encouraged her with his eyes. Playing around, he decided to have some fun with Lewis.

"Hey Pete, whadayou think 'o that huh?" Mendez said while waiving his arm down the length of the girl's body, as if she were some kind of game show prize.

"Hey man, that's not my kind of action. And if it were, I'd need a fuckin' machete to get through there. "Hey cave girl? Ever hear of a fuckin' razor?"

The girl brought up her arm getting ready to slap Lewis cold until Mendez's lightning reactions grabbed her arm before the downstroke.

After a moment, Mendez let it go. "Don't worry about him, honey. He's uh, not your type anyway." She smiled back at Mendez and stepped over to the bar for a chiller.

Mendez turned back towards Lewis in a show of bravado for all at the table to hear, and spoke just loud enough for the girl as well. "Pete, you ever talk that way to one of these girls again, and I'll take you out myself."

If it weren't from the ice-cold stares received from Azzari and Tresedici, Lewis would have never taken him seriously. In fact, he probably would have egged on more violence up until the point of actual bodily harm because that was Lewis. Tresedici was a patient man and had grown accustomed to Vargas' management, or rather, Vargas' handling of his affairs to the point of speaking on his behalf even when he was in attendance. Tresedici became rather annoyed when no one took any initiative while they were obviously there to discuss business, so he came straight to the point.

"Look, Guillermo, we gotta get moving on our main venture here, understand? Greggie has some news for ya, so I wanna let him tell you all about it."

Mendez wasn't pleased with the tone in which Tresedici spoke, and his body language echoed the same, causing a momentary pause before Azzari elaborated.

"Me and Jerry have been talking things over concerning our difficulties, and came up with a solution for you, if you should want to give it a shot, that is."

"What?" Mendez said, coldly.

Azzari paused once again, recognizing but not exactly catering to Mendez's rudeness. "We've acquired a new van that I think will be perfect for what you need."

"A what?" Mendez laughed. "A van? We don't need a van, man."

He lit up a cigarette and exhaled the first puff into the ceiling, which no doubt contributed to its pale yellow dinginess.

"It's not no ordinary van. We put two extra, err, windows in it." Azzari said, noticing he now had Mendez somewhat curious. Or, at least, that was the indication he received from Mendez's raised brow, which fortunately distracted from his nose.

"What kind of windows?"

"The small kind with no glass." Azzari said, with his characteristically maniacal grin that stretched his thin mustache wide enough to almost disappear.

Azzari's description of the van fascinated Mendez; so much in fact, he broke concentration from one of the girls he had been so obviously and rudely staring at the entire time both Azzari and Tresedici spoke. "Where is it?" He asked.

"It's at Jerry's house. I'm gonna take you two over there tomorrow morning." Azzari replied, sipping at his tonic.

Mendez briefly glanced across the table and locked eyes with his partner—both quite aware of what the other was thinking at that very moment. Sure, the van would help sneak up on one of the marks, but right now, they had a good opportunity to make a double off of one of them before they turned the gun around. Lewis and Mendez completely understood the entire scenario just off that very brief stare.

Mendez turned back towards his employers, rattled the ice in his glass, and said, "All right," before craning his neck to see if the girl on which he had focused his obvious desires was still in a close enough vicinity to summon. She was, and he did—wrapping his left arm around her buttocks as he arose from the table—excusing himself for the rest of the afternoon.

Without further invitation, Lewis dispatched the rest of his actionable offenses and got up to have the bartender call a taxi. Azzari didn't bother chasing him down to give a ride, since he would rather not be seen with his type in public. All Azzari said to Lewis was, "around ten," and that was the end of their meeting.

What Lewis never saw as he hit the door, were the two girls that came and took his and Mendez's place at the table. Tresedici was a shrewd businessman who didn't waste too much time on small talk. Unlike Azzari, who preferred more discreetness by wandering off into a backroom with his date, Tresedici took his pleasures right there under the table with no one the wiser—not even the bartender, who knew he was better off not knowing anything, so staying on the opposite side of the bar's island was in his better interest.

A few minutes after ten the next morning, a cab pulled away from Azzari's driveway, depositing two men that had two completely different stress levels. Lewis' prior evening entailed more frustration, since he rolled into one of the trendier gay bars in town, but wasn't quite attractive or trendy enough for its clientele, which resigned him to an unexpectedly short and fruitless evening. His was now a case of too much restlessness and anxiousness in waiting.

Mendez, on the other hand, had spent the last twelve hours keeping up with a girl fifteen years his minor. After boorishly enduring spot comments including terms such as, "all night", "and again and again", and "like rabbits" from him, Lewis had no problem speaking his mind.

"Look Santa, nobody gives a shit about your expedition down the Nile, so give it a rest, huh! Besides, she's either blind or has some sort of crazy nose fetish, or something."

Mendez, probably due to the fact that he couldn't possibly muster any more testosterone-induced bravado in the first place, took Lewis' jabs in the jocular sense. After all, if he thought for one moment Lewis wasn't just plain grumpy from jealousy, he'd probably drop him off the Skyway Bridge late that night. Besides, Lewis was prone to foolhardy and masochistic undertakings at regular intervals, so his audacity had become rather unremarkable if not completely ignored.

They took off in Azzari's Cadillac for the short ride to Jerry Molinar's, and Lewis refrained from making another snide comment regarding Azzari's tendency for keeping the car's inside temperature perfect enough for storing wine. It was only a few minute's ride to Molinar's house, so Lewis made do by lighting a cigarette and keeping its stoked tip at a tolerable distance underneath his left hand's palm. He forgot all about Azzari's rolling cellar when they turned the corner on Molinar's street.

If it weren't for some of the other car's loud colors echoing from other driveways down the street, the orange and black Dodge sport van would have been more appropriate as a cartoon model. Even so, it never dawned on these folks how easily identifiable that van really was. Instead, the extra "windows" on each side of the van captivated their imag-inations.

Of course, Lewis had his mind on other things since his tensions were building and Mendez's were quite obviously relieved from the night before. A van, he thought, had plenty of extra room in the back. He didn't have much time to dream about any extraneous liaisons or other uses the van may incur, other than its intended purpose, before Jerry Molinar caught Lewis' attention with his clever blue and white leisure suit.

Molinar practically danced down the three steps of his bungalow's front porch, dangling the keys for what Lewis would jokingly christen as "The Pumpkin". He didn't hand the keys to Lewis, however, even though he knew Lewis was the driver; he handed them to Mendez, who gave a slight expression of annoyance and immediately relayed them to his partner. That didn't matter one bit to Molinar because, as far as he was concerned, he avoided contact with Lewis. It was as if he innately knew Lewis secretly desired him and his body automatically dictated repulsion before his brain could say otherwise. Lewis never said he was a homosexual to Molinar; instead, he decided it was better to have fun with Molinar's homophobia by pretending he *wasn't* gay — even going so far as hitting on women (in the most awkward and obvious fashion, mind you!) when he knew Molinar was paying attention. Molinar eventually ignored him because he knew otherwise, but thought Lewis' kind were typically as harmless as dragonflies.

"Come on; let's go inside for a minute. Too hot out here to be standin' around. Anyone want somethin' to drink?" Molinar asked as he traipsed back up his porch's stairs.

The men walked down a short hallway to Molinar's kitchen, where Jenny, his younger wife, had been waiting with several sweating glasses of iced cranberry juice on a tray. She was a frizzy doe-eyed brunette that would have been very attractive a dozen or so years ago if it weren't for too many cartons of Virginia Slims that roughed her voice, and too many bourbon and colas that left more wrinkles than her tight curves could overcome. That didn't stop Lewis from attempting a new reputation as a philanderer, which quickly met with fierce opposition from Molinar's wife when she slammed the drinks on the kitchen table.

"Lewis. That's your name right…Lewis? You know you're not interested in me; you're interested in Jerry!"

Of course, Lewis just stood there with his mouth wide open while the other three men howled. Lewis took his humiliation in stride, though, letting Jenny Molinar have her moment in the sun while the others laughed it up. They drank their juice and carried on until she left the room for them to discuss the best strategies for making use of their new van. Mendez and Lewis, however, just wanted to get in the van and head over to Salazar's shop where they knew they'd have a captive audience, but Molinar's phone rang with coded instructions.

Molinar spoke cryptically for only a few moments and then hung up.

"That was Sal. He says to drive over to his bar off Kennedy. Has a job he needs you two for; right now, he said. Oh, and he said park around back."

"What the fuck does *he* want?" Lewis said.

"Don't ask me, man. I'm just passing it on," said Molinar, waiving his hands in front of his body.

As instructed, Mendez and Lewis drove straight over to Lilliput's, parked the van around back, and walked in through that entrance where Salvatore Tresedici waited with a small roll of hundreds and a business card with an address and driving instructions on the backside.

"Here, Guillermo, take this. In a few minutes, Angel's gonna be driving up with a car that I want you two to use on a run by this address on the other side of Orlando. I don't want you to stop there for any reason whatsoever; I just want you to drive by it. There's a twelve-gauge pump shotgun in the back floorboard, but you ain't gonna need it, because this ain't a real job. It has to look like a job though."

"Why, what's the deal, man?" Mendez asked.

"You just gotta drive by that address, that's it."

"I know, but why that address? Whose is it?"

"You remember the list we made? That's the second one's house."

"Vargas' lawyer? He doesn't live there, he..." Mendez said before Tresedici interrupted him.

"FBI safe house."

"Holy Jesus," said Lewis, who threw up his arms.

Tresedici shrugged and said, "Don't worry about it. They can't touch you unless you stop, so don't stop, understand?"

Next, he walked closer to the building's tinted front windows and pointed across the street. Mendez and Lewis were too timid to follow at first, deeming Tresedici out of his mind, but they finally stepped over to the windows.

"Don't worry about it; they can't see you; it's one-way glass. Look, you see those two numbskulls across the street at the beauty parlor...in the brown wrapper? They're waiting for our friend, Angel, but he needs them off his back for the afternoon so's he can take a shipment from the docks. You gotta make sure that car follows you though, so you make double sure of that. Got it? There's Angel now."

Both Mendez and Lewis nodded before drifting back towards the bar for a soda. Tresedici had one last instruction just as Vargas walked through the front door.

"If that car doesn't follow you, just go pick me up a carton of Chesterfield Kings and come right back."

That didn't happen, however, Vargas handed them the keys and they led Agent Savage and me on a wild goose chase all over Winter Park before they came back to the bar a few hours later, laughing like hyenas.

"I assume they followed you all the way after they pulled out." Tresedici said.

"You shoulda seen the look on their faces when we didn't pull into the driveway, man. The place was crawling with feds. Lewis almost shit his pants!" Mendez laughed.

"I did not!" Lewis yelled in an unplanned falsetto, causing him to sit back down slowly in embarrassment while Mendez, Vargas, and Tresedici all rolled.

They shared a round of drinks together before going their different ways. Vargas took his keys back and drove straight down the boulevard to Randy's and Miss Day-of-the-Week. Mendez winked and nodded for Lewis to follow him out the back door where they climbed into The Pumpkin, trying to see if they could still catch Salazar at his office.

They pulled into the parking lot and indeed saw the man hobbling back and forth torturing his phone's extended cord into an unmanageable knot. Naturally, Salazar couldn't help but notice the bright orange mass that now blocked out a large chunk of his office's window, nor the two men that saddled right in front of it.

"Joo let me call you back in a few minutes, okay? I have some customers that just pulled in," was overheard by Salazar's secretary as Mendez and Lewis stepped out of the van. She didn't have any view of the outside world, but after several years working for Salazar, she became aware of his mannerisms, particularly when he indicated there was someone on their way inside. He nearly reacted the same way each time that happened, but after his second-attempted murder, his actions became rather exaggerated.

Mendez and Lewis were somewhat puzzled by the fractional smile the secretary gave just after they opened the front door. What they were not, nor ever would be, aware of, was that secretary's secretive ongoing battle with her own intuitions. The smirk was nothing more than a small acknowledgement of the fact she had won—for the moment, anyway. Nonetheless, Mendez took it as a possible warning of some sorts and went so far as to kick the back of Lewis' heel while they both waited for a greeting.

"Good Morning, gentlemen. How can I help you today?" She said, still smiling, but her teeth were a small distraction to Mendez, since they were three different shades of yellow to grey. This was something that, for a brief moment, confounded him because he figured that any man of taste and business sense would place someone more attractive as the person giving first impressions. Not that the secretary wasn't attractive, for the most part she was until she—as so many people do with poor dialects—opened her mouth. But Mendez's aside broke quickly, and he introduced himself and Lewis, asking for a meeting with Salazar.

Of course, it was an out-of-the-ordinary request since most professionals usually made appointments. Regardless, she deduced by their casual dress that they were definitely not there for anything professional, but likely some club managers looking for vending. She looked them up and down before writing their names on a small card and wiggled her skirt through Salazar's door. One moment later, she stood back at the office's entrance and invited them both inside.

Salazar stood up from behind his desk, carefully inspecting both men with his eyes to make sure they were not armed. It bothered him greatly that Mendez wore a denim jacket in the middle of summer and that concealing a weapon would be quite easy. He focused so much on Mendez's attire that he never noticed his guests' eyes were also busy making a visual inspection of his repairs to their work from over a month ago. Salazar labored in walking around his desk for the handshake, and he didn't make too big of a production about it because he didn't want to appear as any sort of weakling. Lewis consciously kept his eyes even with Salazar's during his handshake, but Mendez couldn't help looking down at the prosthetic before ending his. Salazar wasn't troubled as much as he normally would have been because he was more curious with his visitors and what possible business they could want. What Carlos Salazar didn't know, and never knew until much later, was that both Mendez and Lewis gave false names at their introductions.

"Please, have a seat. What can I do for joo today?"

"Mr. Salazar, we've come here not so you can help us," said Mendez, "but for what we can do for you."

Salazar rubbed his chin and looked at them both. "Well, I am afraid that I am at a bit of a loss. What do you mean?"

Mendez glanced at Lewis and smiled. Lewis leaned forward and looked Salazar right in the eyes.

"Suppose I tell you we know who's been trying to get rid of you."

Lewis lived for the epiphanic moment when someone suddenly realized danger had come knocking on an open door. Both he and Mendez couldn't help but smile, ever so subtly however, when Salazar slung himself back in his seat in an immediate sweat.

"B-but h-how could joo know this?" He said, with his breathing becoming so rapid, he was in danger of hyperventilation. "Joo must call the police…call the police right now!"

Salazar reached for the phone and started to pick up the handset when Mendez suddenly sat all the way forward on his chair and slapped his palm down heavily across Salazar's.

"There will be no need for the police, Mr. Salazar. We aren't here for any heat, okay?"

Salazar was trembling ferociously with his hand underneath Mendez's, wondering if they were there for his life. Mendez patiently waited for Salazar to remove his hand from the telephone, and he nervously complied just after Mendez removed his own.

"Now, Mr. Salazar," Mendez said slowly, "do you want to know who the person is or not?"

Salazar's rattle never quite settled and his curiosity was slow to return. "W-what do joo want from me?"

"It's what you'll want from us." Lewis said.

"I don't u-understand." Salazar said, reaching for his handkerchief, which made Mendez reach into his jacket simultaneously.

Salazar slowly finished withdrawing the cloth and wiped his gushing forehead and back of his neck. Mendez withdrew his hand, thankful because he actually had nothing more than a pocket comb and cigarettes in that pocket—nothing more.

"May I smoke?" Mendez asked.

"Y-yes, of course."

Mendez reached back into his jacket, took the pack out, shook it once, and withdrew a cigarette with his lips. He returned the pack, flicked his lighter, and floated a huge ball of smoke upward.

"Suppose we tell you who did the number on your leg, would you want to do something about it?…other than call the police, that is."

Salazar moved his head back and forth between Lewis and Mendez almost as fast as a net-side Wimbledon spectator during finals. "Joo mean the first time or the last time?"

"What?" Said Lewis, surprised by Salazar's response.

"Well, because the first time was back in de war, joo know. Korea. Not much joo or anyone can do about that!"

Mendez laughed, "Wait, your leg was blown off twice?"

"Jes." Salazar nodded.

"Oh, that *is* ironic," said Lewis. "No old man, the last time."

"Well, j-jes. Jes! Of course, so I would," said Salazar. "Joo know who deed this to me, I want hees head…no, I want him to suffer the same…maybe more."

Mendez and Lewis finally heard what they wanted to hear all along, so they wasted no time getting to the crucial question.

"And how much would that be worth to you, Mr. Salazar." Mendez said, leaning forward again.

Salazar pointed his finger at them both and said, "Joo mean…" His finger came back up to his chin while contemplating the scenario. "…Joo would do this? Que cojones!"

"That's right. We would…and just the way you want, too," said Lewis, sensing a deal in the making.

"Jes, maybe so, but how do I know eet is who joo say eet is, no? How do I know?"

Mendez sat back in his chair and folded his hands. "Mr. Salazar, as soon as I tell you the name, you will know we are telling you the truth."

It was a risky guess, but Mendez remembered some of the stories passed around at Lilliput's by none other than Salvatore Tresedici himself.

"But we need an agreement up front before we tell you who it is…or else we walk right out that door and you will never know.

Well, except maybe until they try it again." Mendez leaned forward in his chair once again and pointed his finger back at Salazar. "And viejo, they *will* try again."

Salazar once again swapped scrutinizations with Mendez and Lewis before continuing. "What ees it joo want to make this happen. I am not a rich man, joo know, but I will pay."

Lewis wasted no time throwing out his starting figure. "We normally get $20,000 plus or minus depending, but for you, we'll take fifteen."

Salazar's eyes bulged at the expense, which was far higher than he had imagined. Even though his imagination of such a scenario only stretched back for several minutes, this was not a carefully considered plan. What he *did* know was bargaining reason. As fast as any worthy businessman could diagnose, Salazar presumed that the men before him were nothing more than opportunists, and by the look of their clothes, and the average vehicle they drove, they weren't exactly the most professional nor discreet contractors.

"Thees ees much more than I can pay, I'm afraid."

"Well what did you have in mind?" Lewis returned hurriedly, which Mendez didn't approve of, but had little choice but to allow unless they would appear incohesive and unrehearsed in Salazar's mind.

"I did not have anything in mind, señor; I only know what I can pay and what I cannot. The price joo ask is more than double what I can pay."

"What? $7,500? That's all? It's outrageous!"

Salazar sat back and knew he would have to come up with more, but if he did, he wasn't going to get just a killing. Something else had to be done.

Lewis started to carry on about how he and Mendez felt insulted by such a low offer, even though Salazar had technically made no offer—only what he could afford—but Mendez threw a blocking arm in front of Lewis before he made the first audile syllable.

"We'll take it, but you also pay expenses."

"And how much are jour expenses?"

"Five hundred. It's not much, and you can afford that, so don't try to jew your way out of it," said Mendez.

Salazar contemplated the deal for more than a moment and decided it was time he found out just who was trying to kill him. "Agreed."

Lewis sat back, but wasn't content in letting Mendez give anything up without something on the table. "We'll need twenty percent up front." He said.

Mendez didn't blink at Lewis suggesting, knowing it was the prudent course of action. He just sat back and refolded his hand in his lap, expecting Salazar to capitulate before making any petty excuses. After all, right behind Salazar's chair was a large coin hopper and wrappers for bills in every denomination. They didn't have to see the large steel safe under Salazar's desk to know they were in a cash room. Salazar reached down and across his right knee, twisting the knob that unlocked his safe, and began withdrawing several stacks of bills. $1,500 was on the table within a minute and both Salazar and Mendez looked at each other expectantly.

"Plus expenses," said Lewis.

Salazar sighed and reached back down into the safe, yanking out a stack of tens and throwing it on top of the other cash. "There eet ees, two thousand. Now, I want to know. Tell me."

Mendez reached across the desk and collected his payment slowly, unnerving Salazar who would speak no more until he got what he paid for. When Mendez finished placing the cash in his pockets he leaned back in his chair, took a quick look at his partner and then back at Salazar.

"So tell me, Carlos (he now felt comfortable calling him by his first name), what did you do to piss off Augusto Her-nandez?"

Salazar's head twitched to one side, trying to recall the name because he hadn't heard it that way in a very, very long time.

"Augusto? You mean Pappy?" He asked in complete disbelief.

Mendez tried to pretend he didn't know Pappy Hernandez, even though he previously had a working relationship with him. "If that's what they're calling the guy that owns several of the homo bars around town, yeah."

Salazar focused on Mendez too much to notice Lewis' reaction to the derogatory. He simply couldn't believe what he was hearing.

"Pappy? I don't understand. I mean, thees is not impossible, joo know. I thought we were friends, but joo know, he hasn't said too much to me after I quit the bar business and went into the machines. Joo know, he set me up with my very first place. I remember heem telling me not to do vending, but I didn't think...Jesus, that bastard!"

Salazar's disbelief soon became an anger exemplified by many Latino men, renowned for tempestuous tirades, especially after the discovery of a betrayal. It's almost as if he caught his wife in bed with another man while he was holding a pistol; the reaction became automatic.

Reaching back down into his safe, Salazar withdrew another $500 and threw it on the desk in front of Mendez. "I want joo to do something else for me and that ees a down payment."

"What?" Mendez asked. He wasn't reaching for the cash, but rather treating it as tainted goods for the moment.

"I want joo to burn that fucking circus side show hees got over on Lafa..err...Kennedy. I want joo to burn it down to the fucking ground!" Salazar yelled while slamming his fist on the desk.

The secretary heard her boss' tone through the door, however, her personal policy for occupational longevity involved non-interference and ignorance. The entire time the meeting had gone on in the room behind her, she filed her nails and listened to the talk radio station Salazar allowed during office hours when there were no visitors. She would never know her boss had just sanctioned the murder of a man she secretly had a crush on, even though he was happily married. She wasn't thinking about him at the time, however, she was daydreaming of an escape to Las Vegas with the money she had slowly embezzled over the past four years. Salazar wouldn't find out about that either, so long as she didn't get too greedy, which, after $12,000, she thought it was a safe amount, and plenty for two weeks of high rolling at the Sands. She was right in the middle of laughing it up with Elvis and Sinatra on each arm when Salazar flung the office door open, ushering Mendez and Lewis back out to the lobby and sending them on their way. That was how most of her dreams ended around that office — always at the whim of another. She never lost that little smile, though. It was a mystery Salazar, nor any other man in her life, would ever unravel because she never made it back to Tampa that fall. Instead, she discovered just how wild the west still was.

As audacious as The Pumpkin appeared when cruising around town, its color was meaningless in the middle of the night.

Mendez and Lewis used this to their advantage, inconspicuously driving into the heart of Davis Islands and running the same routine on Pappy Hernandez that they pulled on Salazar not two months earlier. The glaring difference this time was that Mendez wasn't taking any chances with the dynamite. This time, he wrapped ten full sticks in a bundle and used two detonators. The bombing took place only three days after Salazar's contract, and if Mendez took more time in his surveillance, he would have known that Pappy's future son-in-law regularly borrowed his Cadillac for errands in the morning while Pappy was still asleep. Once again, Mendez and Lewis' unprecedented string of bad luck continued when only one detonator — the one on an outside stick Mendez wired as a backup — fired off with only three other sticks, blasting the others away from the car and poor Christopher Garcia through the windshield.

"What the hell, man?" Lewis said when the police report finally hit the radio waves.

Making matters worse was their amateurish attempt at burning down Randy's by lobbing a Molotov cocktail on the roof. While it did catch on fire, the club only suffered damage to one section of the roof that was easily repairable. Pappy Hernandez instructed Vargas to replace the whole thing since the roof's particular color tiles were no longer available. Mendez couldn't muster the bravery to do the professional thing and called Salazar with an apology and a renewed vow; he did nothing and decided that if he gets another chance, he'll take it and come calling later. A contract is a contract, he thought.

Mendez's growing frustration wasn't what he was worried about so much as his reputation as an esteemed executioner, however. What he didn't realize was that he placed Tresedici in a most precarious situation. Mendez and Lewis never gave a second thought that if word ever got to Pappy Hernandez that one of Tresedici's men tried to liquidate him, there would be hell to pay all the way up to New York. Neither Tresedici nor Azzari had any proof that Mendez and Lewis carried out Pappy's bombing, but if they did, a preemptive move by the bungling duo against Tresedici wasn't off the table. That is, if they could actually pull it off, which Tresedici had serious doubts after they missed Ben Davidson and twice Carlos Salazar. Tresedici loved Pappy Hernandez as much as the next guy and he did business with him all over town. In the end, however, Pappy wasn't Italian and therefore not protected. If the price of his own neck meant letting Pappy's execution go ahead, that's the way it would have to be. That was the end of the debate for Azzari and Tresedici; neither had the need nor the gumption in digging further.

But Tresedici was no fool and that's how he became Florida's Number Two in the first place—covering his ass. Pappy Hernandez was no fool either. As soon as his family had recovered from the emergency a few days later, more than one of his bartenders overheard drunken theories about who would attempt such a thing. There were several such plots going in different directions but three of the stories seemed somewhat plausible. The common name in all three of them was none other than "Santa Claus", and Pappy overheard Tresedici mention that name a couple of years ago—making him wonder if he should continue spelunking in the darkest, deepest canyon. His phone rang.

"Pappy, this is Sal. What's this going on?"
"You tell me."

Tangled Angles

"Hey man, look, it's like this; Sal took us off the deal."

"What?" Lewis yelled on the other end of the line.

"We're fired, man. That's it," said Mendez.

"Jesus Christ, I don't fuckin' believe it." Lewis mumbled. "After all we did for that son-of-a-bitch, he cans us? Mother Fu —
"

"Listen man, settle down. It'll be all right. We've got enough dough to hold us around until the next job anyway."

Lewis' temper forbade him relaxation in the matter entirely, and having Guillermo Mendez tell him to settle down had quite the opposite effect.

"No, you settle down, goddamnit! If it wasn't for your stupid mistakes, we wouldn't..."

"Mine? Okay, if that's the way you want to play this, man; fair enough. I've got my merchandise, you know, and when they want me to go back to work, that's fine. I don't need a partner, you know."

Lewis didn't let the severance make him any angrier than he had already become, and instead hung up and prepped a larger-than-normal line of coke. He didn't care about the blood trickling down his upper lip afterward, but his facility for coming up with ideas — mostly devious ideas — never vacated that sick little mind of his.

Mendez tried to track him down, but lost contact and never heard from Lewis again; at least, not directly. Without any provocation, Lewis had gone on a binge that lasted for over two weeks and sprawled everywhere from Tampa to Miami. After leaving Tampa, he lost track of how many men in which he came in contact, but he had a knack for keeping his expenses low during those dates because, after his institutional education, he usually took the role as the submissive, meaning he never spent a dime as long as he wasn't alone.

Lewis finally ended back in Tampa, sober and nearly out of cash from his escapade, which nobody knew had more than a singular purpose. The second person that became aware of his intentions was Angel Vargas, and he listened to Lewis' idea late one night at Randy's. Vargas never knew Lewis and Mendez were the ones that threw the Molotov on his roof, costing him over eight thousand dollars. As far as Lewis was concerned, that was between him and his client—privileged information.

Early September in Tampa was still a hot part of the year, but the daily thunderstorms had begun to recede. The night Lewis came calling on Vargas was not unlike any other; hot and humid, which meant a full house, queen's high and for all to see by the pool. Lewis was a homosexual, but not the flaming sort that maliciously intimidates—as if no one could possibly misinterpret their mannerisms in the first place. Lewis found Randy's almost as repulsive as the straight men, with the exception of Vargas, who only saw them as animated dollar signs with strobe lights and disco balls.

"Man, I'm serious. You don't have to spill a word of this to Sal, okay? You don't tell him about nobody. After the job is done, you just say you took care of it and you can make up any name you want; he doesn't have to know."

"You take a big risk making an offer such as this, my friend. It is a very dangerous thing to work around our people, you know?" Vargas said.

"What? Your people? You ain't Italian, man. They don't give a shit about you unless you're bringing them their—what the fuck do you people call that? Oh yeah—tribute." Lewis replied.

"Nonetheless, joo know what it will mean. But I think it is an interesting proposition after all." Said Vargas, taking a sip from his tequila sunrise and licking his lips from its sourness. "I tell you what I do. Let me get a friend of ours on board with this. You know him...Gregory Azzari."

"The old man?"

"Yes, him."

"Why him?" Lewis asked in such an uncomplimentary manner that Vargas rolled his eyes before responding.

"I could say, simply 'because I said so' but we are not school children here. The reason is very simple: he is our bone fetcher—

the best person for getting things that won't come back to haunt you, you know, and burying it later. You need something, he'll get it, and he doesn't ask for much in return."

"The guy's a nut job! Every time we get in the car with the dude, he's got the thing as cold as an icebox. And, he talks to himself too. You should hear him sometime. Freakin' nuts!"

Lewis waved his right finger around his right temple waiting for Vargas reaction, but Vargas wasn't so weak-minded as to fall into Lewis' sadist trap. Half the people Vargas dealt with on a nightly basis were practically certifiable as well as practiced sadists, so Lewis' gambit had no effect other than causing Vargas to order another sunrise.

"We'll see. I don't even know if he will go for it, anyway. I have a feeling he will, but maybe, well, you may be rid of him anyway."

Lewis didn't discuss the matter any further that night, opting to take Vargas' advice and head over to another club that he would find more likable. Vargas settled back in his chair next to Miss Monday, who had herself just returned from a rampaging gigglefest at the other end of the pool with several of the raging regulars.

"Give me a few moments, darling; I must make a phone call."

Vargas snapped his fingers, ordering a telephone brought over from the bar on a long extension cord he had installed just so he wouldn't have to get up, and, well, made him look like a cool number. When the bartender arrived with the phone, he started dialing while directing the bartender.

"And bring Miss Monday whatever she wants."

Gregory Azzari let his phone harmonize as well as it could with the dozen or so ticking clocks scattered about his residence. He had some on the walls, some on tables, and others in unexpected places such as the bathroom and hallway. They ticked relentlessly as his playing cards fell in the marathon solitaire sessions he used for passing time because his wife had divorced him several years ago. He secretly blamed the astral counterpart that occupied the other ninety percent of his body for his wife's hatred, and felt smoking would eventually purge those demons. Nobody ever saw Azzari without a cigarette in his hand unless he was in the process of lighting another, and it was the first order of gossip amongst his prostitutes. On the fourth ring, he finally awoke from his meditative game and picked up the phone.

"Yeah?"

"Greggie, it's Angel."

"Well hey there Mr. Vargas. How's the...what day is this? Monday?"

"Quite well, thank you—and even better later." Vargas laughed. "Listen, I want you to come by as soon as you can. I have some business you may be interested in."

"Sure thing, Angel. Which place?"

"Randy's"

There was a brief moment before Azzari spoke, which Vargas recognized as his apprehension with Randy's. Azzari was a free man, but he was the straight and traditional type, which meant Randy's wasn't preferred. He could not say so much, however.

"Joo don't have to come in; I can meet you by the side pool entrance. Just knock on the gate; I'm less than a few feet away. Okay?"

"Yeah, that's fine. See you in a few minutes."

Azzari looked down at his cards and realized his last flip gave no chance for a solution, so he gathered them together and placed them neatly by an ashtray that was about the size of one of his Cadillac's hubcaps. It had been only four days since he last emptied that ashtray, but it was completely full of the squashed filters and filth that three and a half packs a day could accumulate.

He arrived at Vargas' gate not ten minutes after he departed, knocking at it and getting more of an eyeful than he wanted. Vargas excused himself with Monday and sauntered over to Azzari. They discussed Lewis' idea at length and Azzari thought at first that it was a bad idea risking the ire of Tresedici, let alone Cantonello, if they should ever discover the truth. Vargas' salesmanship won him over after he described how they could obtain their goals secretively and without any culpability should things go wrong. They also had Mendez still in their back pocket, so creating one extra job afterward, as long as Mendez was actually capable, wouldn't be a problem.

They agreed to meet again in a few days to start getting logistics together for Lewis, and parted for the evening. Vargas, happy at the prospect of finally moving forward with his businesses, sat down and toasted Miss Monday, who didn't have a clue what they were celebrating, as if it mattered. Monday, when it came right down to it, only cared about Monday; the rest of the week was free.

Lewis had been on another weeklong binge by the time Vargas phoned him with the good news. It took another two full days of sobering up for the trip he planned, but during that time, Lewis had several psychotic episodes from cocaine and heroin withdrawals. Most of those episodes were painful and contained, but sometimes they were terribly severe. He eventually dealt with those the same way he had learned how to deal with any antagonizing situation over the years; sadism. Except this time, he was his own torturer. Towards the last day Lewis' self containment failed, and the outside world, in this case Salvatore Tresedici, suffered the side effects of his malicious self-torment.

"Hello?" Tresedici answered his telephone late one night, to the castigation of his wife.

The caller didn't immediately respond and instead made Tresedici listen to loud breathing. Sensing he was about to hang up, Lewis finally spoke.

"Well, well, you stinking little alky, you got all of us in a lot of hot water over these bombings, you know. But that's all right; you're going to get yours."

"Who the hell is this?" Tresedici yelled, shocking his wife.

"We've been watching you the whole time, you little wop. We've been watching you so long your little white dog in the back yard loves us more than he loves you! That's rather sad, isn't it?"

"Listen here you fuck, I'll meet you anytime, anywhere. You name the place and I'll be there. Name it! I'll cut your goddamned neck!"

"Sal!" His wife screamed, frightened by her husband's tone.

He covered the mouthpiece and yelled back at her. "Shut the hell up, Martha."

By the time he brought the handset back up to his ear, Lewis had hung up. Tresedici's wife fussed for another three minutes, causing him to fire more words back at her than he's spoken in prior three months combined. Unfortunately, they were mostly profane. She started to roll over and shut herself from the world by using a pillow, when the phone suddenly rang again.

Sal picked it up and just listened. Again, there was heavy breathing for a few moments, so Tresedici started swearing into the mouthpiece once again. After he exhausted himself, the only response was a slight giggle and the "We're still watching" Lewis repeated before hanging up. Mrs. Tresedici wasn't quite sure how the phone could survive such a slamming afterward and also wasn't sure it would ever work again, but after her husband pummeled the handset into the phone's base and it started ringing for the third time, she went into hysterics.

"Don't answer the damn thing, Sal! It's just him again!"

Of course, all Tresedici wanted was for the person on the other end of the line to get his earful of Italian rage, but Lewis played it just as cool as the second time; letting him blast until he had to take a breath.

"You just wait until I find out who you are and come knocking you piece of shit; you're finished! You got that? Done!

"We're still watching."

[click]

Never Glades

Trouble mostly followed Herbert Talmond Graham since adolescency. Every time he turned around, it seemed, calamity was there to shake his hand and send him back home to the institutions.

When he was just a fourteen-year-old boy, Graham spent three years in a Marianna reform school for stabbing an upperclassman in the belly with a cafeteria fork. After his school years, the authorities arrested and incarcerated him several times for offenses ranging from grand theft auto, to armed robbery, to grand larceny, and finally kidnapping. Each time, he quickly figured out the operational patterns of the correctional institutions and escaped into the countryside.

By the time he reached his late twenties, Graham decided he'd had enough of "the life" and tried to go straight, or that's what his immediate family thought. Graham had settled in Sarasota, took a wife, and, after nine years, became an ordained Baptist minister. He did fine for almost two years until the gossip concerning police calls to his house for domestic violence circulated throughout the congregation. They launched an internal audit after his wife filed for divorce and found that he had embezzled over $24,000. They weren't able to lock him up for that, however; Graham fled to the Miami area and started taking contracts.

His last job as a mafia assassin was why they had him incarcerated; charged with first-degree murder for the killing of a heroin trafficker who made two mistakes with the local mob. First, he made the mistake of cutting the dope more than fifteen percent from pure, which was easily detectible to any trained tongue. He never considered the consequences because that fifteen percent wasn't for money; it was for his own addictions. The last mistake Graham made was when they caught him on the company yacht with his pants down behind his boss' girlfriend. He smiled. She smiled. The first mate didn't.

The problem with Graham was that he simply took too much pleasure in his work to pay close attention to the details, which was usually the reason he made mistakes. In this case, he was too busy tasting the blood of his mark—after chopping him up with a table saw and sealing the body parts in a 55-gallon drum—to remember punching a few holes in it so the gases from decomposition could escape. A few days after Graham dumped that drum and two others into Dumfoundling Bay, the Coast Guard made a most gruesome discovery.

Graham was closing in on the age of fifty and hadn't learned much of anything in his entire life with the exceptions of killing and escaping. One would think that the prison system would recognize Graham as an artist after his seventh escape, but no, that wasn't the case. Each time he managed overcoming a simple flaw in the institutions operations, allowing for an easy getaway.

The first recurring flaw in the prison system was the lack of intrastate reporting, which should have certainly meant locking Graham tightly away in a maximum-security situation. That wasn't the case, however; Graham always weaseled his way into a *minimum*-security pen. Even so, most escapes were still difficult, but Graham usually found a way to get around the final challenges.

Twice before, he claimed an illness he didn't have, and both times he walked right out of the infirmary in a doctor's coat to an unsecured parking lot adjacent its wing. Even after committing his most heinous offense, Glades Correctional Institute hadn't received any prior history before someone had sent Graham a coded note from one of his old cellmates stating that he would have transportation waiting just outside the northwest perimeter. Graham never considered escaping from Glades because he was secretly self-destructive and, for one honest moment in his life, preferred his torture to come to an end. An irresistible opportunity once again whisked him away for another round of deviance, however.

Using his trusty finger, Graham pointed his own way to the infirmary by sticking it down his throat and displaying the cafeteria's menu all over the front floor of his cell. This naturally had the side effect of disgusting the adjacent prisoners into screaming for a cleanup. Graham never had to tell anyone he was sick, the prisoners did all the talking for him. All he had to do was lie face down on the floor and endure a few moments of his own ejection.

Later that night in the infirmary, he waited for the right moment—in this case, a male nurse shutting the department down for the evening using a light switch located at the opposite end of the barrack. Graham decked the nurse with a loose tube of steel railing he slowly unscrewed during the afternoon. Although he made enough noise to awaken the dead—and most certainly the near-dead, which were two other patients in the infirmary that evening—waking them would have been a monumental feat considering the fact they were both stabbed in a fight earlier that afternoon and pumped full of morphine. Graham wasted no time exchanging clothes with the nurse and tripped the emergency exit—only to discover he had entered a small exercise courtyard that had a twelve-foot, barbwire-topped fence.   Graham contemplated the obstacle for only a moment, knowing that a guard would probably be on his way from the opposite side of the complex, which meant he only had about three or four minutes head start if he quickly overcame the fence.

As fast as he could, he surveyed the entire room before his eyes arrived at his feet, which were standing on a small rug that he thought was just right for tossing on top of the barbwire. Even at the age of forty-eight, Graham was in good enough condition to scale the fence and plow right through the straight wires at the very top. He descended down the other side and waited for his eyes to adjust to the darkness for a moment before dashing willy-nilly into a chigger-infested sawgrass thicket that probably had a gator or fifty waiting for a gourmet meal. His eyes soon adjusted and caught Peter Lewis' cigarette's red hot cherry pulsating about eighty yards further up the swampy southeastern banks of Lake Okeechobee.

"Over here ya fuckin' slow poke!" Lewis waved, trying to keep his balance in the small canoe he had acquired two nights before.

"Danny? That yew, boy?"

"Don't you call…oh never mind. Get your hillbilly ass in here, we gotta go!"

Graham climbed into the front of the canoe, grabbed a paddle, and helped turn the craft around, rowing into and onto the football field-wide sawgrass barrier protecting the lake's southeastern shoreline.

"Doesn't this thang have a gotdamn motor?" Graham asked in a heavy drawl.

"Yeah, but we can't start it until we're in open water. Besides, it's not exactly quiet. Did you get away clean?"

"Nu-uh…not exactly," said Graham in a low volume.

"What do you mean, not exactly?" Lewis yelled.

"Shhhh! You wanna get caught, man? Damn!"

"What do you mean?" Lewis whispered.

"I mean I didn't…well…we only got about two minutes or so before them sirens start a'going off."

Just at that moment a loud wailing reminiscent of MacDill's air raid drills skewered the humid night air.

"Or maybe not two minutes."

"Row your ass off you…never mind, just row!"

The sirens faded as the two slowly made more distance between them and the prison, whose planners never conceived, let alone planned, contingencies for an escape into the glades. Long ago, they decided that any fool that attempted escape in that direction just did the taxpayers a huge favor. They probably could have heard Lewis firing up that little three horsepower Johnson if it weren't for the blasting sirens, but they designed the complex without that consideration, and the sirens actually provided cover for the launch. Lewis and Graham arrived on the southwest side of the lake just east of Clewiston, where Lewis had parked a car. They sank the canoe and jumped in the car, bound for Tampa on US Highway 27, which was a lonely stretch of road running right through the middle of the state. At around 3 a.m. the next morning, Lewis and Graham rolled into a small motel just on the west side of Plant City — a small strawberry farmer's town just east of Tampa.

That particular motel only had twenty-eight rooms, half of which transients or sublettors rented by the hour. Lewis kept his old cellmate and lover there for over a week until the heat from Graham's escape died down to a point where he felt comfortable enough to mingle in town.

A Small Matter

Vargas and Azzari met Herb Graham for the first time during a luncheon at a Cuban sandwich shop just on the east side of Ybor City. To everyone except Azzari, Graham's personality soon displayed more than just a peculiar twitchiness likely associated with his paranoid schizophrenia, bisexuality, and his dreadfully loquacious drawl; it became apparent to Vargas that Graham's terminal behavior made him a perfect candidate as a disposable point man. When Vargas offered the job, Lewis actually embraced the notion of Graham's instant promotion. After all, Lewis was a better driver and, well, figured it was the safest position to play should anything ever go wrong. There were also the legal ramifications in consideration with his decision. Lewis would never take a Murder One rap.

"Pete, I want Mr. Graham to take the lead on this one." Vargas said.

"That's fine by me, angel cakes, I'm just the driver, you know."

Even though Vargas dealt with the sleaziest of homosexuals on a daily basis, he usually did so with mutual respect that dictated his inviolableness as a straight man. Lewis' brash greasiness gave him the crawls.

"That's...never mind." Vargas sighed.

Azzari had just replaced his handkerchief after filling it full of a summertime cold he picked up the week before.

"Reverend Graham?" Azzari sniffed. "Is that what you want us to call you?"

"Jesus, man, I don't much care whut ya call me as long as yew gotta nice paycheck for me later. You can call me Graham, Reverend Graham, The Reverend, Herb Graham, Herb..."

"Okay, we get it." Vargas said.

"Yew get whut?" Graham joshed.

"Your name; we get it."

"Okay because if yew whant ta call me sumpin' else, I don…"

"Okay…" Vargas threw his hand up and turned aside in frustration. "The Reverend. That okay?"

"Yessir, because…"

Again, Vargas threw the hand and then gave time for Graham to stop trying to speak. "Greggie here has a car for you and Peter."

"What about the Pumpkin?" Lewis asked.

"Forget about the van. Sal's using it. Tell them about the car, Greggie."

"I do have the car, but we have to pick it up from Jerry Molinar's place. You remember him, right Petey?"

"Of course."

"He's gotta make a run to our friend down in Miami first." Azzari continued.

"Nano?" Lewis asked.

"Yes him. Why? You want to go?"

"Whut the hell is a nano?" Graham asked, much to everyone's annoyance.

"Yeah," said Lewis without elaboration.

"All right, then. I'll set it up."

Vargas said on his way out of the bar, "Petey, get your *Reverend* a tan for Christ's sake. He's whiter than a ghost!"

Indeed, Graham's stint in prison and hiding out during the day had taken their toll on his complexion.

Of course, Azzari *didn't* set anything up with Jerry Molinar earlier that week, and when he drove up with his Cadillac full of people, Molinar became a little fidgety, especially when he saw Lewis get out of the back seat.

"What the hell is he doing here?"

"Hey, honey!" Lewis yelled across the lawn affectionately, playing with Molinar's insecurities. "How's the missus?"

"All right Greggie, that's enough. Why the…you shut the fuck up, homo! Why did you bring them here?"

Lewis laughed because that's the kind of person he was, but Graham didn't much care for Molinar's affront. He made sure Molinar got a good look at his Colt 1911A1 tucked most inconspicuously into the front beltline of his trousers. Molinar abruptly halted any more resistance, allowing Azzari an explanation.

"Thought you might like some company on your ride down, Jerry. Maybe they can drum up some extra business for you, you know, since you all had such a fabulous time the last go'round."

"I don't need no passengers Greggie," said Molinar, still fixated on Graham's reaper.

"Well suppose I says their goin' anyway?"

Molinar shrugged his shoulders and drooped, realizing his place. "Well, damnit Greggie, you know I have to let him ride if you won't have it any other way."

Azzari winked and tilted his head, letting Molinar know that he wouldn't have it any other way.

"Tell me one thing though, Greg; is he queer too?"

Graham drew the Colt and said, "That thar does it," but Azzari was still quick enough, even in his late fifties, to throw his thumb in front of the pistol's hammer before Graham squeezed Molinar off.

"Come on, Rev, Jerry's just kidding!" Lewis laughed.

Molinar may have thought he was kidding, but he was probably speaking the truth in some form. Graham, the pale and not-so-super welterweight, was showing his quick temper, but he too had a sense of humor if only someone made sure he used it.

"I got something for yew, buddy; right here." He jammed the pistol back down in his pants.

"See you 'round, Greggie," said Molinar as he opened the driver's door of a green Plymouth Satellite coupe with a black vinyl roof.

"Uh-uh!" Lewis said, stopping him before he sat down. "You know who's the driver."

"Shawtgun!" Graham yelled as he ran around to the other side and opened that door.

Azzari laughed, climbed back inside his over-sized banana popsicle, and drove back home to his hands.

"Come on, man; climb in the back." Lewis said, holding his seat forward. "You know you like seeing me from behind, anyway."

"Oh goddamit!" Molinar said, complaining the entire time as he wrestled himself into the tight rear quarters of the coupe. "But don't go over sixty. I don't want no trouble."

"Jesus, it'll take over six hours at that rate!" Lewis said.

"I don't care, man. I just came back from there a couple of weeks ago and the fuzz was choppin' em left and right...for a hundred dollars a pop too."

"It's a revenue scam is what it is, big guy. These cars; they don't get no better mileage at fifty-five than they do at seventy-five, you know. These big blocks are still practically idling at that speed."

"Yeah, I know, man, but I don't want no trouble."

"Don't worry about it, okay? We don't want any either. Reverend over there's kind of...hot right now."

"Whaddya mean, hot? Molinar asked, somewhat surprised.

"We uh...lifted him from the Glades a little over a week ago."

"Oh shit, he's on the run? Jesus H., man! What was he in there for?"

"Calm down, Jerry. It's okay."

"No, Lewis, it's not okay. What the fuck was he in there for? And it better not be nothing messed up, like raping a little leaguer."

"He did a job for someone and it turned back up."

"What kinda of job?"

"Just a little house cleaning, that's all. Body turned back up...cops did some magic and he got a midnight knock on the door. That's it."

"Oh! That's different, then. What did that coyote in the cartoon used to say? 'Occupational hazard'?" Molinar laughed. "What are you—some kind of tough guy, ace? Why are you mumbling?"

Lewis glanced over at Graham just before he entered the on-ramp for Interstate 75. Graham continued mumbling angrily and unintelligibly for a few moments more until he finally broke his blank stare and turned around facing Molinar with the pistol in his hand.

"Whut's a matter with yew shithaids? Yew think yew gotta be some kinda ox to bring a fella down? She-et. Them girly gooks was blowin' em up left in right in the Vietnam, weren't they? I mean..."

"You sure you was a preacher, Herb?" Lewis laughed.

"Whut do yew mean?"

"I mean you don't sound much like a preacher. Were you?"

"He was a preacher?" Molinar laughed, pointing his finger and moving the pistols barrel away from his direction.

"Baptist minister," said Graham.

"Really? Jesus Christ, they'll take anybody."

"That ain't funny." Graham said, slowly and unconsciously aiming the pistol towards the back seat again, causing Molinar's hand to instinctively brush it away slowly.

Not quite six hours and a tank of gasoline later, Lewis brought the Plymouth to a stop in front of Willie Brunoli's house in West Miami, but its front door was wide open. Lewis let the car idle for a few more moments while the men decided what to do.

"There are two cars in the driveway. He's gotta be home, man," said Molinar.

"Then why did he leave the door open?" Lewis said. "Reverend?"

"Don't rightly know. He coulda just left it that way, or he's just sittin' there, or maybe the A/C went out, or maybe his wife done went and burnt sumpin', or..."

Lewis turned the car's ignition off and opened his door, but there was still no movement near the doorway. He held his seat forward and let Molinar grunt his way around before finally untangling himself from the seatbelt and squeezing through the car's doorway onto the street.

"Fuck me!" Molinar griped, reaching for his aching back.

"No thanks," said Graham emotionlessly, knowing Lewis would find the punch line delectable, which he did.

"What do you want to do, Jerry?" Lewis asked as he kept his eyes on the front door.

"What he came here to do. You think I suffered six hours in the back seat just to come here and turn around? Hell no! Come on, let's go."

The three men walked slowly up the driveway and into the front porch, surveying the entrance. There were no sounds that they could hear, nor any signs indicating that anyone was home. The living room was just inside that front door and it didn't take but a few moments before all three of them simultaneously focused on the large stacks of hundred dollar bills just sitting there unprotected on the coffee table. Molinar was the first to enter, tiptoeing towards the table while the other two looked on. Molinar then motioned for Lewis and Graham to join him inside so they could see the other discovered loot.

"Holy crap, man! There's got to be a couple hundred thousand sitting there. And what's this?" Lewis picked up two small cellophane bags containing white powder.

"Looks like two zees at least," said Molinar.

"That's what I think."

Lewis began to open one of the bags so he can test the purity using a snort from his pinky nail. He did, and was just about to make a comment; something to the effect of "Ahh—it's just half and half", when a figure from about halfway down the connecting hallway appeared in a bathrobe holding a 12-gauge pump shotgun pointed straight at them. Graham didn't bother waiting for any question and answer session, he simply reacted, yanking the Colt from his belt line and blasting two rounds towards the dark silhouette.

"No!" Molinar yelled, reaching for Graham's arm, but his reaction was far too late.

The first round scorched past Brunoli and knocked a large chunk of plasterboard from the wall on the right side of the man. The second shot, however, flew right under his chin, blowing out two vertebrae and severing the spinal column, causing instant collapse.

Molinar and Lewis stood back covering their ears and shuddering from the loudness of the percussion, but as soon as the initial smoke drifted upward and away, urgency became paramount. Lewis just stood there while Molinar finally reacted, grabbing the pistol away from Graham, who also stood there, studying his victim while maintaining a strange grin.

"Who was that?" Lewis asked, pointing to the corpse.

Molinar scrambled over to the hallway and got a good look at the person he didn't recognize because of a newly-grown handlebar mustache.

"Holy shit. It's Brunoli!"

"That was Nano? No fucking way."

"I'm not kidding you! Come take a look."

"Nano didn't have a…aw shit, it *is* him."

"Uh-uh…" Molinar started to panic.

Lewis looked around the room and also began panicking. Graham, however, kept reliving the moment with his fingers—pointing at the place where Brunoli stood, pretending his hand was the pistol.

"Herb, you crazy shit; give us a hand here!" Lewis said.

Molinar's eyes darted around the room before coming up with the plan of action. Uh-Herb. Yeah...go back the car up to the door here. We're gonna take everything and get rid of Nano on the way home."

"Whar?" Graham said.

Lewis slapped him on the backside of his head. "Where do you think?"

"Well, if I was to…"

"Herb, shut up and go get the fucking car!" Molinar said.

"I'll be right back." Lewis ran into the kitchen and started opening drawers until he found some paper grocery bags. He took one out, ran with it back into the living room, and began stuffing the cash and cocaine inside.

Graham backed the Plymouth up to the front entrance of the house, and unlocked the trunk before jogging back in the house. At this point, no neighbors gave any indication of curiosity, even after the pistol's blasts boomed through the entire block.

"Gimme a hand with this," said Molinar, holding Brunoli by both ankles while waiting for Graham to pick him up at the other end—the bloody end.

Lewis had already thrown the stacks of hundreds and the cocaine in the grocery sack, folded it closed, and waited for the other two to get Brunoli outside and into the trunk.

"Hey, Pete…" Molinar said, turning his head around to give Lewis instructions. "Go get that shotgun back in the hallway; throw it in the back seat, will ya?"

By the time Lewis returned with the shotgun, Graham and Molinar had thrown Brunoli's body into the back of the car and closed the trunk. Molinar jumped into the back seat without complaint and Graham just shut his door after reaching over and re-starting the car. Lewis climbed in and gave the bag to Graham, put the car in gear and calmly departed the neigh-borhood as if nothing ever happened.

"Please tell me you have enough to get to Naples?" Molinar pined from the back seat, concerned with stopping for gas with a cadaver in the trunk.

"Plenty," said Lewis.

"Hey *Reverend*, when you guys toss our cargo, lose the Colt too. That gun's no good now, you know."

Lewis pulled over at the first rest stop after crossing into Alligator Alley because the daylight hadn't quite slipped beyond the horizon. They needed absolute darkness and a fair gap with any traffic to their rear if they were going to successfully jettison Brunoli's body without any witnesses. They were fortunate that evening in that there was almost no traffic the entire trip across the swamp. When Lewis saw no headlights to the rear of a twenty mile straightaway, he slammed on the brakes and jumped out with Graham, tossing Brunoli, the pistol, and the trunk's carpet he bled on, into an adjacent canal about twenty feet from the highway's shoulder. After the initial splashes, they heard nothing for at least ten steps, and then some light splashing occurred, followed by the more violent type; tossing, rolling, turning, and tearing poor, unsuspecting Nano to bits smaller than his nickname. It was at that point both Lewis and Graham looked at each other and ran back to the car, realizing they had previously walked right into an alligator nest. I could only imagine it akin to some World War II soldier walking through a meadow, coming to the backside of a posted sign, and then walking around to the other side just so he could read the words, "Danger! Mine Field." There is no justice in nature, only luck. Brunoli could have been a doctor, a president, a Girl Scout, or a thieving, cannibalistic child rapist. The alligators wouldn't know the difference.

"Come on you two! Let's get the hell out of here!" Molinar yelled, noticing there were a set of headlights from a car that must have been traveling at well over the speed limit. He thought it must have been a patrolman until a convertible Chevelle SS rocked by with its radio blaring. Jerry Molinar's nerves were showing, and Graham became rather annoyed.

"Hay Jerr, hadn't yew ever been on a job before? Pigs'll take you in five seconds runnin' around like a scared sissy."

"Well, damnit, no; I haven't been a part of a killing before, you homo. What did you have to go off and pop him, anyway?"

"Well, let's see... Y'all obviously didn't know who he wuz, and even if yew did, he wuz still a gotdamn moran—leaving his front door wide open like that. And whut the hell wuz he doin' pointin' that damn scattergun at yew anyway? Don't he know yew? Say?"

"Well yeah, he knows me, but he...or maybe he was having some sort of freak-out or something. Who the hell knows, he's dead now anyway. Ah shit, if someone finds out about it, they're gonna know it was... Aw man!

Molinar's panic was mostly unfounded, as is most panic. True, he was involved in a killing, but he wasn't the triggerman, nor did he intend the murder of his associate. In fact, Brunoli's killing could be argued as purely accidental or possibly in self-defense, although the other circumstances would certainly complicate that argument—especially without any untainted witnesses to corroborate the story. Molinar only had to worry about Brunoli's death if word ever made it to Gregory Azzari or Sal Tresedici, since they originally found him in the first place and had worked with him several years ago. They've been out of personal contact since Jerry Molinar took over that post, and Molinar was the only person who would alert his bosses if there was a problem with a source. There was only one other person who could blow the lid off their mistake.

Frankie Cooper, who owned a well drilling business in Homestead, sold the last two shipments of dynamite to Brunoli and was at the time under investigation by the Bureau of Alcohol, Tobacco, and Firearms (ATF) when an unscheduled inventory uncovered over forty missing sticks.

When Molinar stepped through his home's front entrance late that night, Jenny was sitting at their kitchen dinette table, trembling over a cup of coffee and a half-smoked cigarette. Lewis and Graham kept the car and its headlights grew dimmer through the home's front widows as they backed away—heading home with their share of the loot. When the motor's rumble dissipated down the street, Jenny found the courage to speak.

"Jerry? Can you tell me what just happened earlier?"

She had been married long enough to know her husband was lying when he shrugged and said, "Nothing."

Jenny sniffled, wiped her cheeks from the tears that welled, and exhaled another cloud of smoke.

"Nothing? She said. "Do you call the phone ringing three times from some guy down below Miami wanting to know where his friend was, nothing? He says he thinks you had something to do with his..."

The phone rang at that very moment, which, even under those circumstances was highly unusual for that time of the evening. Molinar stared at the phone with look of dread, wondering what could happen if he answered. By the third ring, he also wondered what would happen if he didn't answer. Obviously, this person knew about him somehow, but he knew nothing about this person. If he didn't engage in conversation, he threw away any chance of further knowledge; so, he picked up the receiver.

"Kinda late whoever this is," said Molinar, trying to ease any onset friction.

"Is this Jerry Molinar?"

"Yeah."

"Listen man, this is a friend of Nano's. My name is Frankie Cooper."

"Never heard of you. How'd you get this number?"

"Don't worry about that."

Molinar muted the phones mouthpiece and leaned over to his wife. "He says don't worry about it. Can you believe this guy?"

"I wanna know how you got the number." Molinar demanded.

"I found it a few hours ago in a notebook on Nano's coffee table. Understand now?"

Of course, Molinar's cockiness completely fell away and utter apprehension replaced it. Yet, he still had to know more about this person. A name wasn't good enough.

"What is my name doing in a fucking notebook?"

"Look man, Nano wrote everything down. You understand, man? Everything. Do you know where he is? I need to speak to him real bad, man."

Molinar paused for a moment. "No. Not a clue."

"Shit. Well, look man, I need to know something, okay?"

"All right."

"Man, I don't want no trouble with nobody. I just do some well digging down here, you know. Nano is a friend and all, and I sold him some stuff a couple of times because I needed the money."

"I don't know nothing about no stuff."

"Man, he's got you written down in this book two times for the stuff I sold him." Cooper paused for a moment to catch his breath. "Like I said, I don't want no trouble…"

"Then don't ask for any." Molinar said coldly, finally figuring out that Cooper really suspected nothing of Brunoli's death and had evidently overlooked the mess in the hallway.

"Shit. Man, all I want to do is get that stuff back before I get in trouble with the feds."

"What about the feds?"

"If I don't get it back, there's gonna be hell to pay, man!"

"Then you shouldn't have sold it to him."

"I just thought he was gonna use it for some fun, you know? Fourth of July and shit, out in the woods?"

"Like I said, I don't know nothing about that."

"But the notebook says…"

"Hey look. You do what you gotta do. I'm hanging up." Molinar slammed the phone's handset down on the cradle, upsetting Jenny.

"Aw knock it off, pussycat; look what I brung ya." Molinar opened the paper sack he sat on the table, reached inside, and then threw a little bag of white powder on the table.

She broke from her sniffles and looked up into his eyes. "Oh, honey!"

She never noticed the rest of the paper sack's contents until late the next morning when she stumbled back into the kitchen for her coffee. It was unlike her husband to irresponsibly leave something so obviously important in a highly exposed place, but after his nose followed hers in an all-night conga line, the bag, for the most part, might as well been invisible. Once the percolator's dance lost her attention and the refrigerator door no longer needed to support her, she slowly turned around towards the table and coveted the brown sack upon it. She approached the table slowly, looking around for her husband who hated her nosiness sometimes. And with the hangover he was about to endure, she knew there was a certain amount of risk involved if she should need to satisfy her curiosity.

Jenny started unfolding the top of the grocery sack, but when it made crackling noises, she nervously flinched away and thought she'd better make absolutely sure her husband was still unconscious. She stood back up and walked down their short hallway wondering if the coffee had awakened him as it usually did, but when she closed within a few feet of their bedroom door, Jerry's chainsaw was in the middle of another cord. No further bedroom inspection was necessary, so she snuck back into the kitchen and slowly opened the bag. She didn't quite comprehend what she was looking at, so she reached inside and brought out one of the stacks of freshly minted hundred dollar bills and gazed cross-eyed into it for several moments.

"Put it back," said her husband, in a low, scratchy morning voice that his unshaven stubble and stained white undershirt made somehow gruffer than normal.

Jenny couldn't replace it immediately because the bundle was currently on the floor. She dropped it during her automatic scream.

"Jerry!"

"Pick it up and put it back."

She scrambled down to the floor and reached under the table where the $5,000 bundle fell. She returned it to the bag, but not before taking a spot accounting of the other bundles, which were eight in total. "But..." She paused, calculating the total in a spasmodic fit. "There's forty thousand dollars in there! Wher..."

"Forty-five, and don't you worry your little head where it came from, got it? We can't use it for a long time, so just close the bag and forget about it. I'm gonna get a cup of that coffee. Smells good."

Molinar watched her fold the bag as he turned around and stepped into the kitchen.

"But..."

"I said don't worry about it, woman!"

"You're not going to tell me what happened?" She sobbed.

Jerry and Jenny Molinar had been married for almost fourteen years, and it was a good marriage between two people that, although both were highly promiscuous with certain friends and openly so, had slowly grown more fidelic. Molinar had always kept an open dialog with Jenny, never keeping secrets, which was why their open marriage had worked for so long. She became greatly upset anytime he attempted to do so, which was rare, but he always capitulated in the end.

"Look, we just had a little...um...problem down there and it's all over now."

"Problem? What kind of a problem?"

"Nothin'. It's over, and maybe next year we can go out to California like we wanted."

Jenny just shook her head and enjoyed his hug from behind as he kissed her on the side of her neck. She sometimes had a reputation for curiosity, but lived by the old axiom: "if you won't like the answer, don't ask the question".

Thrill Hill

Lewis and Graham spent two days laying low at another seedy hotel, this time located in the Westshore district. They were just about to pay for a half-case of beer and two cartons of cigarettes when the convenience store's clerk did a double-take looking at the hundred they floated. She was a middle-aged gal that had seen all types come and go, and never had a problem with anyone until they tried to violate a store policy. This one — written in large, black capital letters with a magic marker on a small piece of poster paper, and unevenly taped on the wall behind her — stated, "NO BILLS OVER $20 ACCEPTED". She made sure Lewis was looking at her when she turned her head and glanced at the rule, but she took and examined the bill, regardless.

"Hey David, come over here for a second." She said, summoning the store's manager from a side office.

David was a lean man in his early forties, who wore thick round glasses and a well-maintained goatee. He appeared from his foxhole within a moment of the clerk's request and straightened his frames just before inquiring what her issue entailed.

"Have a look at this bill, would ya?" She said.

He saw what was in her hand, turned towards Lewis, and apologized. "I'm sorry sir; our store's policies prohibit anything larger than a twenty."

David's eyes blinked rapidly because he had taken several one hundred dollar bills in his career without incident, yet he had to keep appearances with the help.

"No, silly. Take a look at the bill," said his clerk.

"I saw it. It's a hundred. We don't take hundreds."

The policy astonished Lewis since he and Graham were trying to spend over $40 after filling the tank on their car. He was on the verge of a protest, citing that he had already pumped the gas, and that he had no other money to pay—which always worked in these situations—but the clerk shoved the bill in front of her manager's face again and insisted he inspect it. He sighed, readjusted his bifocals, and was immediately dumbstruck.

"Huh." He scrutinized every part of the bill on both sides, looked astonishingly at his clerk, who relished in her affirmation, and then peered over the top of his rims, saying, "Sir, this is a phony and we cannot accept it. Do you have anything else?"

Lewis' brow furled and he was just about to say something when Graham lurched forward and snatched the bill from David's hand. "Lemme see that," he said, examining the bill for himself.

"How do yew know?" Graham asked.

David spoke up. "You see the blurred ink on the front? The printing is messy, but the easiest way to tell is the missing fibers."

"Whut fibers, man. What are yew talkin' 'bout?" Graham said.

"The paper. There are little blue and red threads in the paper that money's printed on." David explained.

Lewis didn't want to cause a scene, so he reached into his pocket and withdrew the last three twenties he had. Before he handed them to the clerk, David fidgeted momentarily while he contemplated asking his next question. He was a backroom type that preferred avoiding confrontation however, some sense of duty mixed with curiosity overcame his inhibition.

"Sir, if you don't mind, where did you get that bill?"

Lewis turned towards Graham, who was still holding the counterfeit in all manners towards the light, trying to see if it actually was as David described. Lewis then turned back around, feeling safer knowing that his sideman had retained the bill, and if the manger had intended calling the police or something else dangerous, he could leave abruptly.

"Why it just came from my bank this morning." Lewis said.

"Which bank?" David laughed.

"The one downtown...uh...Barnett."

David looked at Lewis over his rims again in disbelief, but didn't want any further complexities in his store. After all, the transaction delay had already accrued four more customers queued behind Lewis and Graham. He simply turned around after Lewis handed his clerk the real money and inaudibly mumbled, "My ass!"

Lewis and Graham gathered their supplies and walked swiftly out of the store. Their pace wasn't quickened by embarrassment or the risk of detection, or other complexities from their illegal labors, it was from anger in the realization that they were not only out of over $90,000 in spoils from Brunoli's misfortune, they were now flat broke.

"What the hell are we gonna do, man?" Graham asked.

Lewis opened his car door and moved his seat forward so he could place the beer and cigarettes in the back. That's when he noticed the barrel of the twelve-gauge pump shotgun Molinar left behind in the rear floorboard.

"We're gonna go make some money, that's what we're gonna go do." He sat their supplies in the back seat, and when Graham climbed in his side and closed the door, Lewis reached over the seat and into the floorboard for the weapon.

"Holy Son of God!" Graham said. "Blessed are the peacemakers. Whar we headed?"

"Back to the room, Reverend. I'm gonna throw the beer on ice and make a phone call. You know that job I told you about with the bar guy that looked like Elvis?"

"The one yew all missed?"

"No the second one."

"Yew missed two? Whut the hell are..."

Lewis twitched, "Yeah, two...never...look, anyway; there's an open job right now that the others don't need to know about; you follow me?"

"Din' yew dew that wun with that other fella? Don't he know about it?"

"Yeah, but he's out of the picture."

"All right. Whut's it pay, buddy?"

"We gotta do two things actually. Burn the place down and take care of the owner."

"Whut's first?"

"Don't matter, man. At least, I don't think it does."

Lewis and Graham drove back to their motel and relaxed with a few beers before Lewis worked up the courage to call Carlos Salazar. Historically, Lewis was just the driver and sidekick, never the point man or negotiator, but this was the exception.

They were broke and it was going to take some immediate action to get them back on their financial feet. Salazar would elaborate over the phone, but Lewis did a fair job of codifying the conversation using words like "job" and "client". He was wrong about one thing however. When Salazar inquired as to which job Lewis intended executing first, he did so with the foreknowledge of the logical choice. Unfortunately, when Lewis answered "redecorate", Salazar was lighting fast with his rebuttal.

"I don't mean to tell joo your business, but joo should know that doing one before the other would make it much harder for joo."

"What do you mean?" Lewis asked.

"I mean, the…client will be much harder to reach if you scare him off, joo know?"

"I see. It's your call, jefe."

Salazar laughed, "That's right! Good luck to you," and started to hang up.

"Wait!" Lewis yelled. "I need to know where to find him today."

"Today?"

"Yes—Today."

"I don't know that, but if joo see a brand new, white car—joo know, like the one they had before—then they will be there."

"Got it; thanks." Lewis then hung up the motel's parking lot payphone and turned around towards Graham, smiling.

Lewis and Graham threw themselves back in bed for a few hours, smoking the place to a dense fog and imbibing most of the twelve-pack they had purchased earlier, save a few for the victory dance should they be successful. When darkness finally oozed its way over the western horizon, and the streetlights summoned their flying sideshows, Lewis emerged from the bathroom wearing a fresh shirt he was tucking into the beltline.

"I'm ready." He told Graham, who had already been sitting at the edge of the bed, polishing off a cigarette and combing the grease through his scalp.

They rode over to Dale Mabry Highway first, riding by the football stadium and Al Lopez field looking for Pappy's club, and, only another half-mile further down on the left, there it was, but no new white Cadillac. Undeterred, Lewis turned the car around and headed all the way back south to Randy's, which was almost five miles away. Another fifteen minutes were wasted and Graham became impatient.

"Well shit Pete, how many bars does the man have?"

"I'm told more than eight, but I only know of five."

"Man, we're gonna run outta gas before we find him, yew watch. Probly already gone home too, what yew wanna bet? Say?"

Lewis ignored him because he wasn't necessarily attracted to Graham with the occasional exception of their low-conscious romps. Otherwise, the man's voice made him thankful there were no cliffs conveniently hanging around to tempt him into justice. Graham had it coming for everything he had done, and Lewis sensed the inevitability, but it wasn't Graham's time yet. He intended riding his plug for as long as Graham was useful.

"Say?" Graham insisted.

"No! I don't know! Will you just shut up a moment and let me think?"

It didn't bother Graham so much when Lewis' short temper verged on verbal abusiveness, but when he picked up the shotgun from the back seat and started cycling the chamber, Lewis began to wonder if he was too terse. After all, he thought, Graham plugged Nano at the drop of a hat. If he found out exactly who the mark was and who was paying for him, he might go off and do something stupid.

"What do you think you're doing?" Lewis nervously asked. "That isn't a toy, you know."

"Whut?   I'm just makin' sure this thang has got some farpower. Ain't none of us bothered lookin'. If the cockamamie thing ain't got nothin' but bird shot or rock salt, we might as well try to do it with a pellet gun."

"That's good thinking, Reverend. So what's in there?"

"Number Nine buck. I guess 'ole Brunoli wasn't messin' around."

Lewis pulled out of a parking lot just a few hundred yards down from Randy's and headed towards downtown. Graham placed the shotgun pointing downward into the floorboard and popped his head outside the door's window so he could take in the view of the 36-story Lykes Building.

"Whar we headin'?"

"North side of Ybor. That's one of the last places I can remember."

"All right." Graham said, noticing that Tampa's downtown at that time of night was almost completely devoid of traffic—not that Lewis minded, since he hated nothing more than boiling at a traffic light.

They cruised up 22nd Street about a mile until just after it intersected with Buffalo Avenue, where a small bar was located across the corner from a cemetery.

"You see it?"

"Yew bet your gourd, I do!"

Lewis surveyed the area, but there weren't any other places to park within viewing distance of the parking lot. He and Graham took up a position under the shade of some live oaks at the far end of the lot where an old vegetable market had vacated that part of the plaza long ago. Since it was nighttime, the trees wouldn't have normally provided any effective cover; however, the streetlight located at the front corner of their side of the lot cast a perfect shadow over their car. Even though their car was quite visible, they were not.

The wait was longer than either one of them had endured before. While most anyone could stand five hours riding in an air-conditioned car, lounging on vinyl upholstery with 85-degree swelter, high humidity, and a jungle full of mosquitoes, was almost intolerable after the first thirty minutes. The only help keeping the bugs away was their chain smoking, and even they couldn't keep up that pace after a few hours. Tired, hungry, and nearly unconscious, Lewis and Graham watched people come and go until around two in the morning. There were only two cars left in the lot and they were absolutely positive one of those, a brand new white Cadillac Coupe de Ville convertible, was Pappy Hernandez's. The other was just a Ford Pinto and they assumed that belonged to the help.

Patiently they waited until, finally, a younger man appeared who was holding a deposit bag under his arm. He maintained the front door open with his foot as he searched through his chain ring full of keys.

"There he is," said Lewis, after a much taller man strolled through the front entrance.

"You're right, Pete. He does look a little like Elvis, 'cept for them big as hell glasses he's got on."

"Shhh. Get that shotgun ready."

Graham slowly picked up the gun with his right hand and ever so carefully released its safety by pressing the small button behind the trigger's guard.

"Look; the other one's getting in his car to leave. How do you want to do this, man?" Lewis whispered.

"Let him get on his way, okay. As soon as he's gone, and your man's by himself, you just get on this sucker and get me close enough, okay?"

Not more than a moment after Pappy Hernandez's night manager safely departed with the deposit, Hernandez walked around to his car, unlocked it, and stepped in.

"Do it!" Graham yelled.

Lewis hit the ignition and the Plymouth roared to life, grabbing Hernandez's attention. Lewis mashed the gas, squalling both tires as Graham awkwardly maneuvered the shotgun's lengthy barrel through his door's window and in the direction of its huge white target. The car built speed rapidly across the lot and Graham began having trouble holding his sights steady due to the car's bouncing. They passed within ten yards of Hernandez; close enough for Lewis to see the panic in Hernandez's eyes just before Graham let him have it. But that moment became very unclear when Graham excitedly yanked on the trigger because the shotgun's blast in a confined space severely amplified its percussion. The ringing in Lewis' ears was so intense, it affected his sense of balance. Raw adrenalin overcame his problem by the time they reached the other end of the parking lot.

"Gotdamnit!" Graham yelled.

Lewis knew Graham missed without having to ask, because the last thing he remembered when passing Hernandez's car was the fact that he ducked. That didn't matter, however. Graham never came close to the Cadillac's front compartment, let alone a bull's-eye on their mark. Lewis threw the steering wheel around and spun the car until it once again faced Hernandez's Cadillac — as if going for a second joust — but Pappy didn't panic so much he couldn't function. With no time wasted, he threw the key into the ignition and the Cadillac roared alive like it never had in its short life. Hernandez threw it in gear and bolted out of the parking lot and then south down 22nd Street before Lewis and Graham could get their car turned around in time.

"Come on, Pete, we're gonna loose him!" Yelled Graham, but Lewis was already on the gas in pursuit.

At the first corner, Hernandez squalled his car's tires, slinging the massive hunk of American excess around to the right, making a beeline westward on Buffalo Avenue. Lewis' expert driving skills barely chirped the Plymouth's tires when making the same turn, and it wasn't a half of a mile before they were on Hernandez's tail. Graham pumped the shotgun's action, throwing out the smoking spent cartridge into the floorboard, and then he leaned outside his window trying to get a shot through the Hernandez's back glass. Faster they went, reaching twice the speed allowed for the road, but neither one was remotely concerned with a speeding ticket.

Just before Graham felt confident enough to throw more lead, Hernandez cut to the left down MacDill Avenue heading south and accelerating the entire way. Graham was forced to wait again, but Lewis kept up on the turn, also laying on the pedal for everything the Plymouth was worth. At over 80 MPH, Graham could barely make out his target, but took the shot anyway, completely missing the car.

"Come on, gotdamnit! Kick this thing in the ass and git me alongside him, man!" Graham yelled.

But Hernandez was all over the road trying to prevent exactly that. He knew if he took his foot off the gas and gave them room on his left, it would be the end of him. For all the cubic inches under the hood of Pappy's car, its gross tonnage kept it from escaping the relatively lighter, more nimble Plymouth. When both cars screamed past the two Tampa City patrol cars parked just off to the right under the overpass for I-275, for different reasons, both Hernandez and his pursuers couldn't believe that those officers didn't bother joining the chase. After all, they had just blown by them at over 95 MPH, and on a fairly narrow street. Hernandez almost started crying about it ever since he left his club's parking lot, praying that he would attract a patrolman. At their speed and with guns blazing how could they not? And here they were, virtually walking up to those patrolmen, removing their side arms, and shooting them in their feet, only to see that they might as well have been mannequins.

Lewis and Graham were both astounded as well, but relieved that the police didn't bother. In fact, they both joked afterward, theorizing that God had favored them that night and Hernandez must have it coming. It never dawned on those geniuses that if God really was on their side, Graham wouldn't have missed on the first shot.

What neither one of them knew was that there were no officers sitting in those cars. To be exact, those were no *live* officers; they actually *were* mannequins intentionally placed there as a behavioral observation experiment. Normally, there would have been patrolmen surveilling those patrol cars too, but coincidentally, those men had slipped away for a coffee break when Hernandez, Lewis, and Graham blew past. Their high velocities rocked the patrol cars so violently, both dummies slumped over, which puzzled the real officers upon their return.

"Damnit!" Lewis cried in frustration, trying to somehow maneuver the car so Graham could take a shot. Hernandez had slammed on his brakes and dropped behind Graham too fast for him to take any shots. Graham got an even bigger surprise when Hernandez held a pistol out the window and blasted a hole just to the rear of his door.

"Son-of-a…" Graham yelled, pumping another round into the shotgun's chamber and leaning outside of his window facing backwards.

Lewis hit his brakes too, so Hernandez couldn't escape down a side road without being chased. At the same time he did so, Hernandez laid on his new Cadillac's accelerator all the way into the carpet as far it would go, and then slung another squealing, hard left onto Platt Street, streaking eastward towards Hyde Park, near downtown.

Even though Hernandez's actions seemed erratic and unplanned, Lewis and Graham had no idea he was leading them into a trap when he lost the last two surviving hubcaps on a scorching right turn southward onto Hyde Park Avenue—the main access road to Davis Islands, which was Hernandez's home turf. Only half a minute later, they were burning down the east side of the islands, barreling towards a short, but steep bridge connecting the two islands. Hernandez didn't have too much of a plan other than flying over that bridge in an attempt to disable the car tearing up his rear. He was a Cadillac loyalist and felt they must have built it more solidly than the piece of junk following him.

Graham just managed another shot, but missed Hernandez once again. He climbed back inside the car and pumped the shotgun one more time, keeping his finger on the trigger. He had his head down at the moment Hernandez flew over Thrill Hill, so he had no idea to brace himself before impact. When Lewis realized they had made a terrible mistake, it was at the exact time the impact rammed his head into the steering wheel, and Graham's reaction pulled the shotgun's trigger, blasting a two-inch hole into and shattering the windshield. When they landed, the car stalled and coasted into some hedges a full two blocks down the street. Both Lewis and Graham never knew how, exactly, they arrived in the bushes, nor how long they had been there. All they knew was that they had stopped, their car was dead, and there was no white Cadillac in sight.

"Aw shiat, man. I think I busted a…no, I guess it's all right." Graham mumbled, holding his right kneecap in agony.

Lewis didn't say anything when he awoke; he just looked around for a moment and hit the car's ignition, praying it would start. After turning over a few times longer than normal, the Plymouth finally started, but it had a loud knock in the engine and the fan belt was slipping.

Hernandez was long gone and they knew it, but they had bigger problems now. They would be lucky if their car made it out off the islands, but if it didn't, Lewis wondered where they could hide the car at this time of night.

The Scores

Azzari shook his head in anger when hard knocks arrived at his door in the middle of that morning, but it wasn't the first time that happened. Ever since he earned his reputation as the go-to guy, if someone needed anything around the Bay area, he got the call. He usually dealt only with enforcers in the organization unless it involved a deal in which he was making a cut; the other people—dope dealers, bolita writers, bagmen—used other channels. Typically, customers returned Azzari's cordiality in kind. People were courteous, showed respect, and only visited during normal hours, etc. Occasionally, though, something would go wrong, someone would panic, and for one reason or another, somehow thought Azzari would take care of that problem too. Such was an occurrence late one evening when The Match showed up at Azzari's front door after a botched arson.

In the early 1960s, Martin Sanchez had already amassed quite a resume of burnings to his name. He torched entire apartment buildings, incinerated bungalows, cooked grocery stores, and cremated several of the non-compliant types along the way. What Sanchez had become after several of those contracts, was a bored and sadistic practical joker with little regard for property and human life, except perhaps his own. Those facts became evident after The Match showed up at Azzari's house just before dawn with his clothes torn and tattered with soot, his long hair singed on one side, and wheezing heavily from smoke inhalation. Azzari looked around making sure he wasn't under surveillance and then let Sanchez inside to clean up.

While Azzari disappeared to retrieve a fresh set of towels, filthy Sanchez decided to take a seat on the white linen sofa Azzari's sister had hand-picked earlier that month, but he didn't do so before setting all of Azzari's clocks to chime about the same time Azzari returned from his closet.

"Get out!"

That was the expression Azzari yelled after dropping the towels on the floor and reaching for a .38 special he kept in his trouser's right-front pocket. Azzari aimed just to Sanchez's left and blew two rounds right through that new couch, letting him know he was just as crazy if provoked. But The Match cared not and strolled back out of the front door in hysterics.

Those two stitched holes were the only blemishes on that couch, and they aggravated Azzari relentlessly because he knew he could never part with it without enduring years of sibling guilt. When Lewis and Graham's Plymouth showed up in his driveway, looking like it had just gone through a gun battle in a tornado, he guessed that it had done exactly that...and now it was his problem.

"What do you want?" Azzari snarled, still half asleep and reliving his self-inflicted hell from over a decade ago.

"Nothing!" Reacted Lewis, sensing Azzari's rising temperature. "Well, we...uh..."

"...Need me to take care of that boiled-over heap in my front yard; is that right?"

Lewis stalled for a moment before answering, but he knew he should just tell it like it is. "Yeah."

"What happened?"

"Just a bad run, man. Passed right by him, he ducked at the right moment—you know."

"Hmm. That right?" Azzari scratched his forehead. "So you missed him..." Azzari leaned to the side of Lewis and looked at the Plymouth again. "...while shooting through the windshield?"

"No...I-I mean...yes...I mean, it wasn't like that man!"

"Keep it down, I don't want to wake Nora across the street...real bitch. Now what happened? And tell it to me slow."

"Man, I'm telling you, it's nothing."

"Lewis, you tell me that crooked heap with the busted up windshield is nothing again, and I'm gonna get on the phone; understand?"

"All right, man. We were on a run, missed the first time, got into a long chase and, almost when we had him over on Davis Islands...

"Davis Islands? What the fuck you doing over there?"

Lewis almost forgot Azzari wasn't in on the Hernandez job, and almost said his name. "That's where he ran, man. Look; he went over there and about the time Herb lit him up, we hit this humongous pothole."

"Pothole? Are you high? There aren't any potholes over there; it's the richest place in town besides Bayshore."

"Pothole, bump, whatever. We hit something and Herb got bounced around with his finger on the trigger."

Azzari squinted tightly behind his glasses, completely distrustful of Lewis' story given the evidence, but he was stuck with the car, regardless. He could have, and probably should have kicked them to the corner, but he would have never made any friends if he always played such a hard ass. He was never as tough and unrelenting as his boss, which was why everyone came to him with their problems instead of Tresedici, but that was the real reason his associates gave him less respect than due.

"Park it around back by the shed and get everything out of it. I'll make some coffee while we wait this out until around 7:30 or so when everybody's too busy to look."

"Why don't yew call us a cab?" Graham said.

"I call you a cab and there will only be three of you people out there: the cab, you, and the police. You go out in the morning and everyone thinks we're just going to work like everybody else."

"Fine by me, old timer."

All three sat around talking shop for a few hours, playing no-stakes poker and emptying two pots of coffee trying to overcome each other's boredom. When it seemed the clock couldn't drag on any slower than a nineteenth century correspondence chess match, Azzari finally stood up, swallowed the last sip of orange juice in his glass, grabbed the telephone on his kitchen wall, and dialed for a cab. He then dialed his friend who owned a local service station and gave him the directions to his house.

After he hung up, he turned to Lewis and said, "Gimme a hand with your car outside. I have to get the windshield off before they come and get it, or else everyone starts asking questions."

Lewis followed him outside and together they kicked the glass panel out with their feet. It took both of them to carry the folded and fragile panel behind Azzari's garden shed and dump it out of sight. Moments later, a brown Cigar City Cab came to a stop in front of his house and tooted its horn, causing Azzari to droop his head in disbelief after noticing a window blind rise from a bedroom across the street. After Lewis and Graham departed, Azzari shuffled back inside to his frosty living room and awaited the wrecker.

Around an hour after he made the call, his friend from the service station pulled into the driveway and towards the rear of the house where the Plymouth sat.

"What the hell happened to that?" The overweight driver said.

"Some friends ran into a hole or something."

"Christ, Greggie; it looks like they fell off a parking garage! And where's the windshield?"

"Popped out. They left it on the side of the road. How long's it gonna take?"

"Hmmm…I'll have to order the windshield, of course. Two broken shocks up front, if that's all. (He opened the hood) Got a busted motor mount too. Damn…and a cracked exhaust manifold gasket." He turned back towards Azzari and gave him a strange look. "I'm not askin'."

"How long, Ricky. I ain't got all morning."

The mechanic rubbed his chin for a moment and closed the hood. "Depending on the windshield, which is probably sitting at the state warehouse in Orlando…I dunno. Three days, maybe four. That okay?"

"Yeah. Take it."

Azzari strolled back inside, threw his feet up on the couch, napped for a few hours, and was awakened by a phone call from a strung out heroin runner, looking to make a score on some old lady he had been casing for over a month, but didn't have the wits or the guts to hit her on his own. Azzari met him in the stock room of a friendly convenience store nearby and, when the addict said the mark was easily worth eight or nine grand, it intrigued Azzari enough to walk outside to the payphone and buzz Lewis' hotel room.

"Somebody must be looking out for you guys."

A groggy Lewis replied, "And why is that, old man?"

"I don't know why I put up with you; I really don't."

Graham fully interpreted his friend's facetiousness when Lewis rolled over towards him in bed and sarcastically gave the international sign language phrase for "yack, yack, yack!"

Azzari continued, "I've got a friend that has a job worth around eight or nine. Simple in and out, and you and your friend are cut at seven points. You want it or do I need to call somebody else."

Lewis sat straight up and quieted Graham, who was poking him in the side. "Yeah, yeah. When? Set it up as soon as possible, all right?"

"Sure," said Azzari. "But it's gonna be at least three days because of the car thing, you know."

"That's how long it's going to take?"

"What's the matter?"

"We're…uh…kinda tight right now, you know?"

"Don't worry about it. Meet me at Angel's parking lot around ten. You know; the place off Hillsborough that has the hairy broads."

"I hate that place!"

"I know." Azzari laughed.

Ten o'clock came sooner than anticipated due to their sleep deprivation, but Lewis and Graham reluctantly trudged over to Twilights with the punctuality of a typical Cuban housewife; always fifteen minutes late and never an apology. While that would normally rile anyone trying to carry on business, especially business as serious as theirs, they were, after all, at a strip club and the only people in a hurry were the lap dancers. None of the scenery mattered to Lewis and Graham, having quashed any chance of a stray heterosexual inkling hours earlier. What made matters worse for them was the fact that their tardiness met with the best response one could manufacture — greater tardiness.

Gregory Azzari didn't arrive for another twenty minutes, which had Graham wondering how long his last four dollars would hold out.

"Hey old man, you gonna keep us in this zoo all night or are we gonna make some dough?" Lewis yelled across the bar to Azzari, who somewhat ignored him in favor of the young blond trying to purloin the bankroll so obviously bulging from his trousers. He walked over to their booth and sat down after a few more minutes.

"You know how it is." He said, looking back towards his evening's entertainment.

"So whut is it, old timer? Whut's the deal." Graham said.

Azzari reached into his sport coat and withdrew small scrap of paper that had an address scribbled on it. He placed it on the table in front of Lewis and said, "It's perfect. My guy says this is some old, and I mean older than me, lady..."

"Whut? Aw come on, man. At some point ya gotta draw the line, ya know?" Graham sat back and folded his arms.

"Shh!" Lewis shunted Graham before he started one of his endless rambles. "So what about her? He asked Azzari. "She rich or something?"

Azzari sighed and continued. "My guy's been hanging outside her window in the late afternoons. Says he's seen her constantly go in between her mattress, pull out stacks of cash, and then puts them back. Says there's probably over eight or nine grand in there. That too small beans for you *Reverend,* or should I dish it out to Santa or Jerry?"

Lewis jumped before Graham could spend their last two dollars. "No, no, no! We could use an easy one, you know."

He reached for the scrap of paper, took a long look at the handwriting, and remembered the address near the Hillsborough River in Seminole Heights. He then rolled the scrap into a small ball, torched it with his cigarette lighter and threw it into an ashtray as it smoldered into ashes. Azzari had one of his hands under the table and started bumping Lewis on the knee.

"Take this. I want it back after you're done, understand?"

Lewis reached down and grabbed the two crisp hundred dollar bills from Azzari's hand. Even if they weren't successful, it was enough to get by for a couple of weeks if he and Graham couldn't scare up any more work. Neither one of them had reason to lack confidence, however. It was just a little old lady with some money under her mattress.

Lewis wasn't so confident as to lower his guard even slightly because he regularly paid attention whenever there was a national news story regarding some crotchety blue hair blowing the gourd off some unlucky intruder. The regular people always rooted for the underdog no matter what the situation. An old man bare-knuckled some out-of-line punk? Perfect. Someone robbed a bank that charged excessive fees? Just deserves.

I suppose folks could make a case for poor, unsuspecting Esmeralda Greene who had her door kicked down and a shotgun shoved in her face three nights later. Some would have gone so far as to say that crazy old broad should have kept her money in a bank, while others would say she should have remarried or settled into some nursing home over a decade ago. Esmeralda wouldn't get a featured national news article like some of her lucky peers because she fell into the statistic that, akin car wrecks, happened with such a regular frequency, the public grew tired of those redundant stories long ago.

After he woke her, wearing nothing but her silks and robbed of her dignity, Graham kept the barrel of his freshly reloaded shotgun aimed directly at her chest. Esmeralda didn't beg and she didn't cry; she was a mean old bird who just stood there, giving them an evil scowl while Lewis fumbled around in between the mattress and box springs until he struck gold.

As it turned out, Azzari's contact had exaggerated slightly, because there wasn't eight or nine thousand dollars under the mattress. After Lewis became frustrated and destroyed the entire mattress, believing that Ms. Greene must have separated the funds, there simply weren't any more; there was only $4,200. Lewis held up the bundles so Graham could see they were successful, at which point Graham lowered the shotgun, ripped the cables leading to her phones, and apologized on his way outside.

"Don't apologize to me, you bastard. Rot in hell!"

Lewis pocketed the funds and interrogated her in case there were more funds she had hidden, threatening her life if he caught her lying. She pointed at one of her dresser's drawers, and when Lewis opened it, he found several pieces of jewelry neatly kept in their original boxes. Family rings, strings of pearls, gold necklaces. There was an extra two thousand worth and, when Lewis began to leave through her bedroom doorway, that was the moment Esmeralda could no longer hold back, sobbing for several weeks afterward, mourning all of her lost history.

Graham had already walked down the block to where they parked the restored Plymouth and jumped into the driver's seat waiting for Lewis to come along with their loot. Lewis finally showed up a few seconds behind, demanding Graham's seat.

"Uh-uh! You know I'm the driver, man. Scoot over."

Graham sighed and moved over, not pleased with the way Lewis handled the robbery. He knew it could have gone a lot worse, but it wasn't the kind of action he had envisioned while rowing across Lake Okeechobee.

"Man, that's just nawt my thing; you know it? I mean; I've taken from them types before, yew know, but not like that; not directly like that."

"No difference in what you did a minute ago and what you did back in Sarasota, Rev. You're still going to hell!" Lewis laughed. "Take a look at this."

Lewis handed Graham a small box full of the jewelry and his disappointment soon faded. Sure, they made off with only half of the cash promised, but they padded the loss with the jewelry — something Lewis quickly decided should go to Azzari and his contact for getting the deal wrong.

Of course, Azzari wasn't at all pleased with the proposition Lewis offered when it came time for the split a few days later. He warned both Lewis and Graham that if he caught them skimming the cash, that would be the last job they ever worked; not just for him — for anybody.

Lewis' lack of expertise in fine jewels actually paid off, however, when Azzari took the time to look inside the box and feast his eyes on the objects that made poor Esmeralda cry for so long. There was no way for Azzari to know the full history behind the large and unusual string of black pearls glistening under several tangled gold necklaces and a half dozen silver rings. It didn't matter that Esmeralda's deceased husband and a bunch of his World War II buddies dove for them while stationed on Bora Bora during Operation Bobcat. There was no way to know that, but even if he did, there was no way he was going to give that $8,000 necklace back, nor tell Graham and Lewis the true value of it. Azzari simply took the necklace out of the box, stuffed it into his coat's breast pocket, and gave the rest of the jewelry to his contact a day later.

"I got another job for you two."

"Better nawt be no old ladies or nothing, 'cause if that's the deal, I'm gonna have to pass. I didn't like that last job one bit, I gotta say, so..."

"I know you're hating the two grand in your pocket for a few minutes work, too."

"That ain't the point, old timer, it's just whar..."

"Well don't worry about it because that's not the next job. Jerry's got a line on a grocery store over on the east side and says they do their cash deposits every day at the same time. He said about a half hour before the manager leaves with the escort, there's probably ten or twelve grand in the bag. It's just sittin' there behind a counter, he says."

"Grocery store? In the daytime? Oh, I dunno about that, old man. Seems to me the risk is too high…and after the split, what's in it for us?"

"Jerry said he'd do it for two points." Azzari thought about it for a moment and decided what he'd make off his pearls would be more than adequate to make up for a freebie. "And I'll take nothing this time. You boys did good on the bag in Seminole, so maybe you're better suited for this kind of work, you know?"

"Nothing?" Lewis asked.

"That's right. I want you guys on your feet for a while, okay? So don't go around blowin' it all up your noses."

Graham didn't quite know what to make of Azzari's sly accusation of their drug use, but he became a little paranoid, wondering how the old man knew so much about their private life, as if simple observation couldn't answer most questions one would have about somebody.

"How nice of you!" Lewis quipped.

"Look, uh, fellas…this job, you know, isn't like the last one. You're gonna have to do some ground work this time." Azzari said in a lower tone and volume. "This is during the daytime, you know, with people all around. I don't want you two doing nothing stupid like you did in Miami."

Lewis' attention to Azzari had been intermittent at best, only catching what was important and completely disregarding the small talk. On the other hand, Graham had been paying strict attention to everything Azzari had to say; so much so, the slider Azzari hurled almost slid beneath his swing. Graham's temper was automatic.

"Whut the fuck you talking about Miami, old man?" Graham stood up and started pointing angrily.

"Sit down." Azzari said with his teeth clenched, trying as calmly as he could to maintain control over the situation he just created. "Jerry told me all about it, so relax. I know it wasn't your fault, and if you woulda asked me beforehand, I'd say the dumb son-of-a-bitch was askin' for it."

"Damn right he wuz. I don't know whut all Pete told yew about me, but he shoulda said I don't take too well when someone takes aim in my direction. Yew do that and, well, yew heard whut he got." Graham sat back down.

"What else did Jerry say, pops?" Lewis asked.

"Nothin else. Just said you took the dope and let Brunoli return to nature was all. Did I miss anything?"

"Oh, no, no. That was it. Kinda messed up the trip but…"

"All right then, that's the last of it. Nobody else gotta know. Not Angel; not Sal; not anybody—especially Giuseppe, 'cause if he finds out about it, that means the folks up north will know too, and that won't be good."

"Suits me." Lewis said.

"Yeah, I kinda thought the same from the git-go, old timer. The less the better."

"Well I'm glad you two feel that way 'cause after you get through with this little job with Jerry, you gotta make another run down to Miami to take care of a loose end you left."

"What? What do you mean?" Lewis cracked.

"Jerry told me about some guy that called his house trying to find Brunoli because he was in hot water with the ATF over the merchandise he sold you those two times. Started making threats."

Graham laughed. "Whut's the dumbass gonna do; go to the police?"

"Yeah, so what, let him cry, Greggie. He can't do anything to us."

"Hey—wake up. He had Jerry's number and if he gets nailed and starts talkin to the feds, they're gonna start lookin' his direction. And that ain't exactly wonderful."

Lewis hadn't been thrilled with the rollercoaster ride Azzari's had him on all evening and started letting his anxieties take control, but Graham kept him in check with his assuredness.

"Seems like a good idear to me, gramps."

"Knock it off. Besides, you're not that far behind me."

"I hear that a lot." Graham smirked, looking towards Lewis.

Azzari nearly puked at the thought and stood up looking around for his favorite gal, thinking he needed her around to keep him from absolute nausea, but he made matters worse when two packaged condoms fell out of his trousers and into plain view in front of the table. The result of which sent Lewis' high-pitched cackle straight to the ceiling, and was so loud, even Graham stuck fingers in his ears.

"Two?" Lewis laughed. "That's rather optimistic, isn't it, pops?"

The girl for whom the prophylactics were meant, rolled her eyes and tried to defend her paycheck as best as she could by reaching down and picking them up quickly.

"You sure these are gonna work this time? You broke the last three in a row, you know." She winked and then hauled him into a private lounge.

Grocery Getters

Wearing the most nondescript clothing his closet offered that Saturday afternoon, Jerry Molinar buttoned his plain blue denim shirt up to a point just in the middle of his chest. After teasing the bed out of his almost afro-like curls—a task his wife enjoyed spying on him like a giddy peeping tom outside the window of a slumber party—Molinar finished with a few light pumps from his wife's hairspray bottle, kissed her, and grabbed several items from the kitchen table on his way to the garage.

Lewis, who was equally dressed down with plain brown slacks and a grey shirt, sat and mostly watched Graham's razor finesse a half gram of once-cut cocaine on the kitchenette table. Graham wasn't quite done separating his first line before both he and Lewis heard Molinar's signature "X knock" on their room's door. Molinar learned the knock after hearing a war story from a buddy of his that spent time in a prisoner camp. The tap code was simple; five quick knocks followed by three more. Graham asked about the knock once before and Molinar told him about the simple five by five lettering grid, and that the letter X was used for breaking up sentences. Molinar joked later that he liked the knock's significance because he wanted to break up the room whenever he arrived. Graham never gave him anything more than the knock's recognition.

"It's Jerry." Graham said.

"Perfect timing as always, the mooch." Lewis replied before floating over and opening the door.

Molinar came inside and took a few moments for his eyes to adjust to the room's dark brown interior.

"Are we ready?"

Just after asking, he caught the lines Graham had been grooming. "Oh, man, are we ready!"

Graham didn't have a straw handy, so he rolled up a crisp five-dollar bill and handed it to Molinar while Lewis watched.

"What are we talkin' about here?" Molinar asked, wondering if he should take no more than one line.

"Once." Lewis replied.

"Nice." Molinar thankfully replied before turning back around and vacuuming one of four lines Graham had prepared.

As he stood up, he felt Lewis' hand pat his behind, which would have normally made him feel uncomfortable had it not been for the extreme rush he was undergoing. Lewis took his turn, carefully cleaning almost every grain from a line before standing up, almost certain his nose would start bleeding within moments, as his was prone to do. Graham and Molinar couldn't help but snicker at Lewis' suffering, which ended when Graham furthered the insult by snorting both the remaining lines.

"Jesus Christ, Reverend! You gonna be able to hold it together in a minute or what? What'd you have to do two lines for?" Molinar scowled and then emptied a brown sack's contents on the table. Three surgical masks, three pairs of sunglasses, and three pairs of latex surgical gloves. "Take one each. We're gonna put this stuff on before we go in the store."

Graham hadn't overcome his enormous coke rush and struggled to keep the contents of his nasal cavity where it belonged. Even so, you could tell he was trying to laugh along with Lewis, who was also struggling with his nose after it began dripping.

"What; are we going in as doctors or something, Jerry?" Lewis whined in a pinched nasally tone.

"Yeah, that's right; doctors. This is a daytime thing, you know. I don't want anybody seeing our faces, okay? I also don't want us calling each other by name. If we gotta talk to each other it's Doctor this or Doctor that, understand?"

Graham started to come down from his initial rush and nodded affirmatively, while Lewis held a napkin tightly against his nose as he bent down to gather his allotment.

"Oh, I'm going to have fun with this," said Lewis. "Doctor Jekyll."

Molinar turned towards Lewis and smirked. "You should call Herb that since he's the ax man around here."

Graham tried pretending he was angry for a moment, reaching into his pants' pocket and retrieving a small automatic pistol. He placed it on the table as a show of force, but Molinar looked upon it with a furled brow after noticing that Graham had forgotten to load the magazine. Even if he left one in the pistol's chamber, the safety was still engaged, prompting Molinar to call for an inspection.

"What are you gonna do, Rev, hit me over the head with it? Molinar laughed. "Come on, take the clip out and let's get everything on the table. I don't wanna go in there with you two…uh…half-cocked."

Lewis laughed and then covered his nose again before staining the floor. "Man, don't do that to me, Jer!"

"All right, all right. Come on, you guys." Molinar said.

Lewis stepped over towards the front window and retrieved a shotgun hidden behind one of the curtains while Graham dug into his trousers for the ammunition magazine. Both put their weapons on the table and then waited for Molinar to do the same.

"Come on Jerry; what did you bring?" Lewis urged.

"Don't you worry about it," said Molinar.

"Hey! We had to. So do you. If you get nailed, I wanna know what you got, okay?"

Molinar grimaced, reached behind his back beltline, and whipped out a nickel-plated Smith & Wesson .357 magnum revolver with a four-inch barrel.

"Ooh, sizzling!" Lewis gleamed.

"Loud gun." Graham said.

"Yup. You want to get someone's attention, it's kinda like that shotgun right there; you just squeeze one shell off and everyone's hittin' the floor," said Molinar.

Molinar looked around the motel room for anything his partners may have forgotten before deciding that he should have probably stayed home since he wasn't making that much money. This was more of a favor to Azzari than anything because Azzari had a knack for dishing him a nice score anytime money became too tight for his wife to bear. "Come on. Let's do this before I change my mind."

"Change your mind?" Lewis asked.

"Yeah. Didn't really need this, you know…after Miami."

Lewis looked at Graham, who shrugged before lighting a cigarette.

"Wait." Lewis said. "You don't know?"

"Know what?" Molinar replied.

"Oh shit, Herb—he doesn't know!" Lewis laughed, almost bursting his nosebleed's fragile recession.

"What's so fuckin' funny?" Molinar demanded.

Graham exhaled with a slight cough from holding back more laughter. "That wuz scat bacon, man."

"What? What the fuck does he mean, Lewis?"

"He means it was phony."

"What?" Molinar asked incredulously.

"Jesus, Jerry—the money!" Lewis shouted.

"The money from Miami?"

"Yes!"

"Man, you deaf or sumthin'?" Graham said.

"Shut the hell up, man." Molinar became understandably angry at the news. "You better not be jiving me on this, Pete."

"Well , Jerry we thought you knew! Heck, if that money was good, Herb and I would be on our way to Vegas for a few days. Is that why you're taking so little on this job?"

"Yeah, Jer. We wuz wonderin'."

Molinar nodded and rolled his eyes. "Yup."

Lewis and Graham looked at each other before Lewis spoke up. "Tell you what. If it ends up being a good payday—say, above twelve large, you can keep your cut and the change. Well, that is, up to a point. It gets to fifteen and we'll have to talk about it. That kosher?"

Molinar's face lifted with the generous offer. "Yeah. Yeah, of course. Thanks."

Lewis winked at Graham before adding, "But there's one more thing we would like in return."

Molinar turned back around with a regretful express-ion. "What?"

Lewis tried keeping his composure as best as he could. "We get a night with you."

Molinar rolled his eyes, replaced the .357 revolver behind his back, and bolted outside—but not before yelling, "Fuck you two," over his shoulder.

Both Graham and Lewis heard him mumble something about keeping their (expletive) money on their way out to the car and that's when they decided they would tease Molinar relentlessly all the way to the job.

"Come on, Jerry, just one night." Lewis begged.

Graham made kissing noises and laughed endlessly at Molinar's homophobia. Of course, neither he nor Lewis intended spending any time with Molinar even if he capitulated for some strange reason, but Molinar never quite knew when someone was just jerking his chain. He didn't know about Graham, but he was certain Lewis would swarm over him if he gave the slightest indication.

"Goddamnit, no! And, if I hear another word about it, I gonna..."

"Okay then, how about an hour?" Graham laughed.

Molinar reached around for his pistol, but Graham had already raised the barrel of his shotgun to just over the top of the seatback where Molinar could see he was already beaten.

"Whoa, big feller. No need getting' outta line or nothin'. We're just messin' with ya, that's all."

Molinar left his pistol crammed into his rear beltline, sat back, and grumbled at his situation.

"I'm not!" Lewis laughed. "What about ten minutes, Jerry. Just ten minutes!"

"All right, that's does it!" Molinar yelled, but again both Lewis and Graham just laughed—even when Molinar pointed his pistol at both of their heads. He wasn't planning on committing a double homicide, however. Their egos were at war—not each other—but that fifteen minute ride became one of the longest ever taken by Molinar as he helplessly rode in the back seat. The ride's length seemed exactly the opposite for Lewis and Graham, whose humor helped relieve their hypertension.

"We're here." Lewis said, after he calmed down from laughing so hard his nose started bleeding again.

When the car came to a stop at the far end of Bread and Bear's parking lot on the east side of town, Molinar reached into his paper sack and pulled out their costumes.

"Doctors," he said cordially.

All three men removed their sunglasses and tied their surgical masks over their faces. Next, they struggled getting their surgical gloves on tight enough so as not to interfere with firearms operation. Molinar was feeling some anxiety since his fingers were slightly larger than average, making the task more difficult than he imagined.

"Ready?" He asked before giving the order.

Lewis and Graham turned around to nod, but when they did, Molinar noticed something wrong with Lewis' mask.

"Pete—your mask." Molinar pointed towards the middle of his own.

"What about it? I put it on right."

"You're still bleeding, man."

Lewis looked at Graham for confirmation and indeed, his nose had bled right through the surgical mask, leaving a large red stain on its front. He stripped it off and looked at the stain in disgust, knowing that he wasn't going in on the robbery unmasked.

"Don't worry about it, man." Graham said. "I wuz kinda wantin' yew to stay back and keep the car runnin'. This place ain't that big. Me and Jerry can handle it. Don'cha think, Jer?"

Molinar didn't agree verbally, but rather tapped on the back of Graham's seat, motioning him to climb out of the car so he could too.

"Pull the car around to the side of the building, Pete. If we ain't out in five, get your ass outta here," said Molinar just before he and Graham walked briskly across the lot and into the store's front entrance.

Not too many people gave Molinar a second look as he entered the store with a surgical mask, rubber gloves, sunglasses, and a revolver, because Graham's shotgun completely distracted them. The Bread and Bear wasn't as large as one of the super-sized grocery store chains, but it was definitely not a superette either. It was just large enough and just busy enough to keep five register lines busy with three or four customers waiting in each. It also had a supervisory open "office" that was actually three tall counters forming a square against the middle of the front wall. As soon as Graham strolled inside with the shotgun, some of the younger women in the lines began screaming in panic.

"Everybody hit the floor!" Molinar yelled.

The older ones became angry and turned back around, ignoring the situation as if it would somehow go away. Of course, the screaming garnered the attention of those few occupying the front office, causing their heads to pop up from behind the counter like prairie dogs from a hole. Two women stood up back there and immediately cowered behind a tall, thin, balding gentleman who wore a long-sleeved shirt, a tie, and sunglasses. Given that this man had never gained much respect or admiration, with the exception of when payday came around, he suddenly felt like a real he-man for the first time in his middle-aged life. He did not, however, feel powerful enough to confront his store's intruders, opting for the warmth of the secretaries at his back.

Only half of the people in the checkout lines actually laid on the floor. The others didn't feel threatened enough by the men in doctor's masks, so they just stood there and pretended to mind their own business. Molinar again shouted for everyone to get on the floor and even drew his revolver to strengthen his resolve. He pointed that pistol around, but never directly at any of those standing. Nonetheless, just about everyone hit the polished concrete floor with the exception of one belligerent cashier.

He was a younger black man that was tall, muscular, and had been in and out of jail on minor offenses after losing his Florida football scholarship to a shattered ankle at his high school's homecoming. A local Episcopal pastor finally con-vinced him that his life wasn't over and that God had other wonderful plans ahead, so he stayed out of trouble and worked his way into the cashier's position after a coworker accidentally discovered his freakishly fast talent with the register. But the brave cashier still had his faults when it came to common sense. Instead of making an impression as a resilient hero, just about everyone, including the baldy behind the front counter, begged his compliance so they could get on with the inevitable. When he didn't, and Molinar stalled because he wasn't a killer, nor strong enough to muscle the cashier. Graham lost his patience. With a swift pace, he angrily walked down the store's main aisle, stopped in front of the entrance to that cashier's line, and, while standing over two crying women, took aim from the hip with his shotgun and fired.

But Graham never corrected his poor aiming skills, however, and yanked on the trigger so severely, he completely missed the cashier and exploded one of the large plate glass windows at the front of the store. The cashier, realizing his mortality, finally panicked and hit the ground in a state of hyperventilation. Graham, somewhat embarrassed, didn't see the need to kill the man after he capitulated, and opted to play it cool — as if he meant to merely scare everyone into compliance in the first place. With none the wiser, his little acting job worked. In fact, it worked so well, if someone drove by the store, they'd think it closed if it weren't for the lights and the open sign. The only two people standing now were Graham and Molinar, who were in complete control of the situation. And now that they were, Molinar settled down enough to remember the entire reason they were there to begin with; the loot.

"Um…Dr. Jeckyll, keep our..er..patients down while I see the manager, will ya?"

"Sure thing Dr. Cream."

Molinar did a double-take on the name Graham gave him, not sure where it came from or what it meant. His curiosity only lasted a moment as he stepped over a few people on his way to the front office. Once there, he found two women huddled around the bald man in the dress shirt. Molinar assumed correctly that the most well-dressed employee must be the manager, so he waved the revolver at the man's face, motioning him to get up. The manager held up his hands and slowly rose to his feet.

"I know you've got some deposit bags down by your feet, so why don't you be a good boy and hand those to me." Molinar said.

Trying to appear suave for his secretaries, the manager played dumb. "What bags? I have no idea what you're talking about."

Molinar wasn't about to take any nonsense from the manager, so he coolly kept his pistol aimed at him while flipping open the counter's entry and walked inside. Just to the side of the manager's feet, under the counter exactly where Azzari's contact said they would find them, were three large deposit bags with locked zippers. The manager twitched nervously upon the discovery of his lie, and sheepishly stepped aside.

"Oh no; you're gonna get those for me." Molinar said.

While the manager stalled, hoping that the police would somehow magically arrive much like the cavalries of old western movies, the same cashier that gave them trouble earlier had been eyeing the handle of a small aluminum baseball bat he had snuck in months earlier and kept behind a trashcan under his register. Graham had not been paying too much attention to the ongoings in the office and had been looking at five cash registers that were wide open for the taking. When he finally decided that those were worth going after, he turned around and caught the cashier reaching for the bat. Graham immediately slammed the butt of the shotgun on the cashier's hand, breaking it in several places and causing two short screams from a couple of customers nearby. Graham next shoved the barrel of his shotgun into the cashier's temple, pinning the man's head to the floor. He put so much pressure on the barrel that it left a circular cut in the cashier's flesh, as well as depositing gunpowder from the previously expended shell. The cashier's focus abruptly switched from his shattered hand to the blood gushing from his temple. Both were equally painful and disorienting to the point the cashier finally made no movements other than constant shaking in agony.

Graham picked up the baseball bat and flung it through the gaping hole in the front of the building where there used to be a window. After he was satisfied there wouldn't be any more bravery, he found a plastic trash bag at one of the registers and began systematically cleaning the cash from each one. In the meantime, Molinar was beginning to lose patience with the manager who had yet to deliver the deposit bags. Frustrated, he cocked his revolver and stuck it in the man's face; something he had never done in his life and thought at the time that it must have been the cocaine. One of the manager's secretaries suddenly split away from him and reached for the bags.

"For God sakes, Tim! Stop playing around and give him what he wants." She said.

The manager pushed her aside just before she picked one of the bags up and said, "No. I'll do it."

He would have to lecture her later about his grand plan and how she completely ruined it, but for now, he was giving Molinar what he wanted. Molinar opened a small duffel bag, had the manager place the three deposit bags inside, and made his way out of the office. Graham had completed his pilfering of the registers and slowly exited backwards, keeping his shotgun aimlessly pointed at everyone in the checkout area. Without further action, both walked briskly outside and around the corner to where Lewis had patiently been waiting for just over four minutes with the engine running. He reached over and opened the passenger door, allowing Graham to throw his bag on the front seat while he reached down, unlatching the front seat so Molinar could stuff himself and the duffle bag in the back seat. As soon as he did, Graham propped the shotgun against the front seat and floorboard, climbed in, and slammed the door. Lewis hit the gas and the Plymouth roared out of the store's parking lot, leaving behind a mess of emotional distress and suffering.

"Not too fast." Molinar said, noticing Lewis would probably get nailed for a speeding ticket before anyone knew what they had just done.

"Where are we going?" Lewis said.

"Back to my place. We can hide the car in the garage for a few days until this dies down."

"I don't think nobody saw us leave," said Graham.

"I don't care if they did or didn't; we're not taking any chances with that. If I was doing this proper, we'd be on our way to the salvage lot, understand? And Reverend, you can take the mask off now."

"Whutever you say, doc."

"Yeah, and what did you call me back there, anyway?"

"Dr. Cream."

"Who's that?"

"Jack the Ripper."

"Jack the...wait a minute. I thought they never figured that one out? And how the fuck would you know anyway?"

"Whut? You think because I'm frum down here, we don't read none? Plenty of time for that in the can, feller."

"Yeah, well, you coulda fooled me, but I thought..."

"Naw, man. They don't know who it was. Many of 'em's got opinions on whew did it, and I think it wuz that Dr. Cream feller 'cause he's the only one I read about that wasn't neither gay or Jewish."

"Rev, if you've read so many books how come you talk like...oh, never mind."

"Let's talk business for a second, can we?" Lewis interrupted. "I see that you two picked up more than we thought?"

"I hit them registers. Probably got over a grand just off them." Graham said.

"Yeah, that was a good idea, man." Molinar added while stoking a fresh cigarette.

"Whut about them bags?" Graham said.

"Don't know, but I can say this—there were three; not two, and they were all stuffed."

"Can we take a look?" Lewis asked.

"I ain't touching nothin' until we get to my garage," snapped Molinar.

When they arrived at Molinar's house, Graham jumped out so he could unlock the front door and open the garage. Once he did,

Lewis backed into the space just in case he had to make a fast exit. All three unloaded the car and brought everything into Molinar's kitchen.

The first thing Molinar did was find an empty coffee can, place it on top of the stove's burner, and turn on the exhaust fan. Next, he took the surgical masks and gloves from the pile on the table, threw them in the can and set them ablaze. He didn't anticipate the amount of smoke he created, which immediately choked the room in a black haze, even with the exhaust fan on high. Molinar quickly jacked two windows open to get rid of the fumes, which had summoned his wife from the bedroom down the hall.

"What the hell, Jerry? What's this burning in the can?"

"Nothing. Just…we don't need it anymore."

"Can we get the show on the road here?" Lewis complained, sitting in front of the large duffel bag in anticipation.

Graham and Molinar sat down at the table while Molinar's wife stood over him, coughing occasionally from the toxic smoke still lingering in the room. Graham took out the cash from his haul and immediately began counting. Molinar reached over the black duffel bag, unzipped it, and took out the three bank deposit bags.

"How are you gonna get into those, Jer?" Jenny asked.

"What do ya mean? They're made of cloth. Go get me a pair of scissors, will ya?"

Molinar tried cutting the heavy nylon cloth with the scissors for a few minutes before determining they wouldn't do the job. Graham had just about finished with his second count and interrupted himself to reach into one of his pockets, pull out a larger-than-normal pocketknife, unfold it, and hand it to Molinar. The sharp blade made easy work of the fabric, creating gaping holes in each of the three bags large enough for him to reach inside and remove the banded bills. One of the bags, however, contained mostly checks. Molinar and Lewis gathered all of the checks and then handed them to Jenny Molinar.

"Stick those in the coffee can; they're useless," said her husband. "Never got to play Robin Hood before."

"What do you mean?" Lewis asked.

"Those checks — free groceries for the ones that wrote 'em."

"Ah!" Lewis agreed.

Jenny interrupted, "Some will go back and pay once they find out."

"Not all of them," said Lewis.

"Hardly any of them," said Molinar. "You write a check and it doesn't go through; what do you do? You tell me you're gonna call them so you can pay them? Uh-uh. Not me. If they messed up my check, that's their problem."

"Eleven hundred and one." Graham spouted, but he barely caught the attention of the other three in the room, as they were fixated on the first bundle of bills Molinar extracted from the second bag; a band of fifty hundreds.

"Oh, I like the way this is starting!" Lewis said.

But that was the only bonanza of the evening. The rest of the bundles were twenties and some singles. The other denominations were kept for making change or transferred in when the store ran out, which happened on a daily basis. After they counted everything twice, Lewis and Molinar added their sums.

"Eleven thousand, nine hundred and fourteen. Plus your eleven hundred and one gives us…um…thirteen thousand and fifteen." Molinar said.

"I say split that there fifteen three ways right now so we don't have to think about it," said Graham.

Lewis didn't hesitate before grabbing ten singles from a stack and splitting it with his partner. "All right, where does that leave us?"

"He said two points, right?" Graham asked.

"Yeah, that's right." Molinar answered.

"And we said he could keep anything above twelve?"

"Uh-huh." Molinar said.

"Wait a minute." Lewis interrupted. "Was that two points coming from the twelve or from the thirteen?"

"What's the difference? Two hundred?" Molinar asked.

"Hey, but that's…" Jenny uttered before her husband silenced her.

"Do it from the twelve, Pete. Heck, I was only expecting maybe two grand from this at best."

"Thirty-four hundred." Graham said.

"Okay, so why are they giving you the extra thousand?" Jenny asked, puzzled by the bonus.

"Because," said her husband.

"Because why?"

"He said you would spend the night with us." Lewis laughed.

"Oh, ha ha!" Molinar's wife said sarcastically. "We know better."

"That shit ain't funny," said Jerry. He didn't say so in anger, however.

"No, really, why the extra grand?" She asked.

Nobody said anything because they didn't want to give her the bad news. Her husband knew she never reacted well to letdowns, and with the haul they just made, it wasn't welcome. But Graham didn't care about anyone's feelings when he saved Molinar's grief.

"Because the money yew thought yew had ain't no good." He laughed.

"What? Jerry, what does he mean?"

"He says the money we brought back from the last time is fake; counterfeit."

She didn't say anything immediately and reacted as if she had just passed gas and didn't want anyone else to know. "Oh."

"Don't worry about it, honey bunch. Easy come, easy go, easy come. Right fellas?" Molinar laughed and hugged his wife around her bottom.

She just smiled sheepishly and carried on as if nothing were wrong. Lewis and Graham both laughed as they counted their shares and bundled them up.

"C'mon, let's celebrate. What do we got, honey?"

"Umm." She paused.

Graham reached into his trousers and threw a small plastic bag on the table. "Hell, I'll spot the first gram."

"Righteous!" Molinar said. "That's your new nickname—Gram."

There was a hell of a coke binge that night at the Molinar residence, as the four consumed almost two grams, and, in addition, a half a case of beer and the last of Jenny Molinar's Seagram's.

Just after 3 a.m., which was around the middle of Jerry Molinar's coke hum and well after his wife had passed out, he faintly remembered that he still had to get rid of the counterfeit money. So, he stumbled into the bathroom where they kept it and the other "flushables" should the authorities demand an inspection, and took a last look at the money. It was still in the bag where he left it, but before closing the bag, he caught the fact that one of the bands of hundreds seemed loose. He took it out and the bills practically fell out of the band, so he became paranoid; throwing the bag to the floor and counting the loose bills. As he had feared, it was a thousand dollars short.

Jerry Molinar looked around the room and became highly incensed, so he returned to the bedroom and rummaged through his wife's purse, finding only one of $100 bills. He knew she had to have spent the other $900 somewhere and slumped next to the bed in hysteric paranoia, but Lewis, in a drunken tumble, fell next to Molinar and insisted he take a sip of his whiskey. Naturally, Lewis didn't tell him he laced the drink with a hit of LSD because he and Graham had a running bet that they could get Molinar to kiss one of them before the night was over. Neither Graham nor Lewis reckoned Molinar would immediately pass out and stay that way for over twelve hours. They didn't wait around that long, however; grabbing a cab several hours later while the Molinars were sawing logs.

Jerry Molinar didn't remember anything after the robbery by the next evening, when he finally managed his first coherent thoughts. He didn't remember the drink, nor much else that occurred after they switched from beer to the Seagram's, but his splitting hangover made remembering anything impossible with the exception of the $3,400 he left on the kitchen table. After a brief revisitation from his nemesis, paranoia, he discovered his stake right on the kitchen table where he left it. The only thing missing were his partners, whom he would not bother contacting for a few days.

Mrs. Molinar, on the other hand, had been quietly resting on the couch in front of the television, pounding cup after cup of black coffee after she discovered her rummaged purse and its contents scattered on top of her dresser. She stayed silent and generally under the radar in hopes that her husband would forget about the missing money; the last hundred of which she shredded and flushed down the toilet while he slept. She also cleaned up the bottles and trash from the previous night, spraying Lysol everywhere, hoping that it too would erase any chance of triggering his memory. But she had nothing to worry about with her husband; the acid reduced Molinar's mind to that of an infant's that night, and she kept him busy with other ideas for the next two days.

Snapped

"What's that, hoss?" Henry Lozello said as he peered through his rather large bifocals at a grainy photograph. Salvatore Tresedici called him over in a panic late on a Monday afternoon in the third week of October and sat him down at the counting table in his vending warehouse.

"That's you getting your picture taken, you dumb shit!" Tresedici yelled. "Just what the hell were you doing down at the docks anyway?"

Lozello slowly peeled away his silver-rimmed frames and stared blankly into Tresedici's incensed glower. While gaining rank and position, Lozello never quite gained the popularity or commensurate respect, and that grated on him his entire life. He also never endeavored in reasoning his own ascension, other than plain entitlement. Sure, Lozello came through the ranks, but it was always at the easiest expense and usually through the surreptitious plotting with other immaterial officers. He never did the difficult police work; he just let everyone else do it for him while he collected the accolades. Anytime someone discovered his worthlessness and actually confronted him about it, Lozello would just sit there and stare blankly at his accuser—just as he stared at Tresedici—knowing the highest familial authority would eventually rescue and restore his ascribed power.

But Giuseppe Cantonello was back in Costa Rica after testifying before a US Senate's Church Committee's investigation into abuses the Central Intelligence Agency purportedly made in attempting to assassinate Fidel Castro. He left the day-to-day operations in the hands of Tresedici, who, because of the bungling of his inept and overly greedy associates, had foreseen the end of their empire.

"Joo gotta be crazy, man. I ain't had my picture taken by nobody, and you disrespect me with your..."

"Shut up, Henry, or so help me—look—" Tresedici relaxed for one moment. "I had a guy sent to keep tabs on Angel's delivery down at the docks the other day because we heard the feds were sniffing around."

Lozello squinted and placed his bifocals back on, reexamining the photograph. Tresedici, wiped the sweat from his brow and continued.

"You know this guy?"

Lozello looked closer. "Coño! Yeah, I do, but he's not got anything or else I woulda known about it. You can't get a picture developed without me knowing about it."

"So what! I found out he bought a bunch of stuff from a shop on the north side of town. You know which one?"

Lozello slumped in his chair, remembering the one technical officer he badgered relentlessly until he finally quit the department—Max Reidman. He took a deep breath and titled his head towards Tresedici. "Yeah, I do."

Lozello angrily clenched the photo, crumpling it into a wrinkled ball. "You know, if he's got a picture of me down at those docks with Angel that's gonna be bad for a lot of people—not just me. But I haven't heard nothing about no picture, so I gotta figure he's sittin on it until this goddamn grand jury they've called in a couple of weeks."

"So you think he's just laying low with that over at his house? C'mon, Henry. Nobody's that stupid. Why doesn't he take it to his friends at the FBI, huh? How do you know they don't already have your mug plastered all over some wall downtown?"

"Joo gotta trust me on this, Sal. If something this hot went through my friends downtown, I would have known about it in less than a minute."

"Your friends downtown." Tresedici repeated sarcastically. "You mean the idiots that let what's-his-face post those pictures on his goddamn refrigerator?"

"Coño! Joo think I got to where I am because I don't know nothing about police work?"

"Huh!" Tresedici laughed. "I know exactly how you got to where you are now, and you're conveniently forgetting about that."

Lozello's cold stare returned, having secretly resented any condescending tone regarding his path to the Chief's office. His mind never accepted anything that disagreed with the entitlement he believed he had earned simply by stamping a time card for almost thirty years. It simply blocked all the easy assignments his sympathetic superiors had given over those years.

Lozello folded his arms. "I'm not gonna listen to this bologna of yours."

"Oh yes you are! You thought we were joking about taking this one out and now look."

"You gonna do it now?"

"Have to. If there's any chance he's squatting on the picture as you say, yeah, I suppose there's no avoiding it."

"Then you understand I don't know nothing about it."

Lozello stood up, put on a pair of large, square sunglasses and timidly departed, walking with a slight limp as if he had been injured somehow, but it was more likely that his leg had fallen asleep. After he left, Tresedici picked up the phone and dialed the back office number for Randy's, looking for Angel Vargas.

Silenced

The phone rang several times until a huffing bartender finally picked up and took a message that Tresedici was looking for his boss. That was one of Vargas' lightning-rod traits for criticisms of his generation; somewhere down the line, modern culture preached narcissism and vanity to the point that merely getting up to answer the telephone portended a subservient demeanor. Worse, Vargas never showed interest in ringing phones at all, pretending to be far too busy for menial tasks. He wanted his voyeurs to observe him as a sought-after rare gemstone at all times.

The bartender scribbled "Sal" on a paper slip and trudged around the pool delivering the phone to Vargas' table. Vargas and Miss Monday, who was a voluptuous freckle-faced brunette, had enjoyed the last swim of the season in Randy's pool and were still soaking wet.   The bartender helped Vargas with his abundantly fluffed terry cloth robe, mocking James Brown, who was currently funking up the patio's feed from the jukebox indoors. After the applause from his smarmy patrons still wading in the pool, Vargas settled into his teak lounge chair, took a sip from his lime-twisted tonic, and dialed Tresedici.

"What took you so long?"

"I was in the pool. How are you?"

"You're gonna' catch something from that pool you won't be able to get rid of, Angel."

"Not to worry, my friend. I keep enough chlorine in that thing to kill cancer! What can I do for you today?"

"You can come over to the shop as soon as you're able. We have a problem."

Vargas didn't respond, he simply hung up and stared at the lights shimmering in the aqua ripples just past his feet. He wasn't going to jump up immediately as his bartenders do when he summoned them; Vargas kept his pretentions to the hilt—slowly sipping his tonic into the ice and ogling his patrons through the haze of his newly-lit Marlboro. He didn't dare depart until he was finished with it, either.

"How's the thing going in Oklahoma?" Tresedici asked.

"It's not a problem. He'll get off eventually because he technically did nothing wrong." Vargas replied.

"As long as he doesn't mention any of you."

"Aye, c'mon Sal; he knows better."

"You never know about some people, Angel."

Vargas paused and wasn't at all pleased with the needling from his boss, especially given the money they all made recently from one of the largest heroin shipments ever to reach the city.

"Well, what is it that you need, jefe."

"One of our friends downtown has some trouble."

"Bad?"

"Let me put it to you this way: if *he's* in trouble, then *we* are in trouble." Tresedici grabbed a shop rag and wiped his sweating brow. "You remember the third guy on the list?"

"Yes. Too bad, really. I liked him before he went bad, you know. I still don't believe it, but what you gonna do? So, what about him?"

"He was taking pictures of the docks a couple of weeks ago, understand?"

"Of us?"

"Don't know, but that doesn't matter. We need him done on the double."

"Anything special?"

"Yeah, has to get him at home. Those pictures might be there, so make sure they get them, or make sure he doesn't have them, so we'll know what the deal is. And use someone else besides that friend of yours, Guillermo what's-his-name."

"Santa Claus."

"Yeah, him. Forget about him; get someone else."

"All right. He won't like it, but I'll get Greggie on this first thing in the morning." Vargas said on his way towards the exit.

"No; tonight. Tell Miss Monday you'll see her next week."

"I'll send her your regards." Vargas said sarcastically.

Vargas stopped by Randy's and slammed another cocktail with Miss Monday, apologizing that he had yet another errand before they could consummate the evening. The "gals" on stage seemed as though they were keeping her busy in any regard, trading fashion and post-operative advice for those still undergoing the transition from man to some form of individualized transsexual. Vargas bid her adieu and slipped over to Gregory Azzari's house where he greeted him with an ashtray aroma, a sweaty glass of iced tea, and the cacophony of ticking clocks, the only break from which came from a young calico kitten that pounced into Vargas' lap the moment he sat down on the couch.

"Well, hello there little one," said Vargas as he reached over and stroked the purring animal's back. "Oh, I see you are still in one piece, my young friend."

"Unlike some of your customers, eh?" Azzari quipped.

"Hey Greggie, you better get this one fixed before he destroys your house, man." Vargas let go of the kitten long enough to light a smoke, figuring his would cover up the older stench coating everything in the room including the kitten, which sneezed incessantly.

"I'll get it done when he starts the trouble; not before. I don't wanna think about cutting anyone's cojones, you know."

Azzari returned to the living room with his own fresh iced tea and sat down in a chair opposite Vargas. He never visited him unless he was there for business; never socially, and never under any other circumstances. If Vargas came over, it was only because he needed something.

"So what is it you need Angel. You never come here unless you need me for some reason, you know."

"This is the way of things, Greggie, and besides, the less you are around me, the better off you are." Vargas was usually comfortable around the family members, but he could tell just by looking around the room that Azzari was fast becoming a reclusive curmudgeon. "You know that job we've been working on with Santa?"

Azzari laughed because of Vargas' looseness with the term "working on", since they've gone after three contracts, some more than once, and failed miserably. "Yeah, I know the ones."

"Well, they want a rush job on the third because he's causing some trouble with our friend downtown."

"What kind of trouble?"

"Serious trouble. The kind that would make a lot of trouble for us."

"I see, and when does this need to happen?"

"As soon as possible, otherwise…"

"Otherwise, we would be having this meeting so late and Miss Monday would be wrapped around you like a boa snake."

Vargas grinned. "Exactly."

"So what's the drill on this one," asked Azzari as he opened his small leather notebook.

"They just said quick and mentioned some photographs that might be at his house, so they have to do it there and get those."

"Pictures? Of what?"

"Of the docks. He said there might be some pictures of us at the docks, so if there are any, get those.

"So it has to be there. At the house, I mean."

"Yeah."

"That makes it a lot more difficult, you know."

"Look, Greggie, I don't really care how difficult it is for you or anyone you get to do this. I just know it's important to our friends, well, and for us, that we get it done and get it done as soon as possible."

"So why ain't you getting' your guy on this?" Azzari asked with a smart tone that aggravated Vargas' concentration. "Never mind. I'll get on it first thing in the morning, don't you worry."

"Oh, no!" Vargas yelled. "They said as soon as possible, and if I gotta break a date, you gotta lose some of your, ugh, beauty rest."

"Now?" Azzari complained.

"Yes, now."

Vargas finished the last sip of his iced tea and placed it next to his old, black, rotary telephone he's had since the Korean War. He picked up the phone's handset and, even though it was getting toward the end of the generally-accepted etiquette window for placing calls, and even though there were two dozen clocks scattered about the living room, he checked his wristwatch before dialing Jerry Molinar's number. After the fifth ring, and just before Azzari put the handset back down, an exasperated Molinar finally picked up.

"Hey, uh, Jerry, this is Greg." Azzari fumbled for words having apparently disrupted or awakened Molinar from something he really didn't want to know about.

"Jesus, Greggie; what you calling this time of night for?"

"Yeah, sorry about that, Jerry; I gotta talk to you about some more work…uh…" Azzari capped the mouthpiece and looked over towards Vargas, who was motioning with his finger pointing down, meaning tonight. "…uh…tonight, man. "

"Tonight? It can't wait until the morning?"

"Sorry, Jerry — gotta be tonight."

Vargas again motioned towards Azzari, who relayed his message to Molinar, "And Angels comin' with me."

"Aw shit. Must be something important. I'll get the kitchen fixed up."

With that, Molinar and Azzari hung up and met slightly more than fifteen minutes after doing so.

Azzari and Vargas arrived in separate Cadillacs out in front of Jerry Molinar's house, which normally would have drawn some attention if it weren't for the Giants and Bills game on television that night, flooding the neighborhood streets with synchronous flickering, and crowd noise emanating from each household. Both men walked up to the front entrance and Azzari knocked on the door. Molinar opened it and stepped back allowing the other two to step inside. Vargas shook his head on the way in because Molinar chose to clean the kitchen over cleaning himself, which was evident by his unshaven face and the bathrobe he wore that was a size too small.

"So what is it?" Molinar asked after taking a seat with the others.

Azzari looked at Vargas first and spoke up. "I got another job for you."

"Already? Man, I don't know. I mean, don't you think I'm hot enough already?"

"Yeah, we heard about the store. Congratulations. Did you come out all right on that?"

Molinar sheepishly fidgeted for a moment. "Well, yeah, sure did. Better than expected, in fact."

"Oh yeah? How much?" Vargas asked.

"Well, uh, Angel, the guys were pretty generous and all…gave me more than I asked for because of the trouble you know."

"Trouble, huh? I saw that. So, what happened?"

"One of their people got a little too heroic for one of the guys, that's all. Got a little pissed off at him so he took a shot. Good thing he missed too, because I don't want that kind of trouble. In fact, if this is anything like that again, I don't want no part of it," said Molinar as he tapped the table top with his index finger.

"No, this is different, but it does involve direct involvement," said Azzari.

"Direct involvement? What do you mean?"

"He means you walk into a guy's house, you take him out, you look for something while you're there; if it's there, you take it; if not, you just leave."

Molinar sat back and laughed. "You think I'm a fool or something? That's suicide going into someone's den like that."

He continued laughing, but soon calmed down after his guest found no humor in his answer.

"What about the guys that went on that job with me. Their perfect for some shit job like that?"

"Shit job, Jerry? It's paying fifteen grand!" Azzari countered.

"Fifteen, huh?" Molinar paused. "No…can't…uh-uh. Out of the question. Get those other two. They're crazy enough. It was that one guy, the Reverend, who got trigger-happy to begin with. If you ask me, he ought to be your man on this one too, the asshole."

Vargas and Azzari both sighed and understood that Molinar wasn't going on the job, so they started to leave.

"Hold on a second," said Molinar, holding up a finger. "You're gonna need something for that kind of work, you know.

You can't just walk in there, blast a guy and linger around for the neighbors to get a good look."

Azzari looked at him with a strange grin, knowing Molinar had done *exactly* that in Miami. He couldn't say anything about it because of Vargas, but it was enough to make Molinar pause and remember.

"Umm, wait right there, I'll be right back."

Molinar scooted down the hall while the other two shrugged and waited near the kitchen door. Molinar returned with a small wooden box that had a black metal pipe inside. He showed the pipe to Azzari, who picked it up and examined it thoroughly with his bifocals.

"This what I think it is?" Azzari asked.

"Yup. It goes with the automatic Danny Boy is carrying."

"Who?" Vargas asked.

"Pete…you know. You want it?"

Vargas reached into his pocket, withdrew a small plastic bag containing five grams of uncut cocaine, and handed it to Molinar. "That's sufficient, no?"

Molinar's eyes sparkled at the bag's glitter as he paused momentarily. "Um, yeah. Yeah, that will do quite nicely."

Azzari snatched the small box from Molinar's other hand while Molinar stood mindlessly fixated on the twinkling bag. "We'll see ya around, Jerry."

"Yeah," was all Molinar could muster, not paying any attention to the others.

Vargas looked at Azzari, laughed, and waltzed back out to his car, eager in returning to Miss Monday and her particular delights. Azzari didn't bother speaking with Molinar any more either, shuffling down to his car and quietly easing that elephant off into the night. But Azzari suddenly found his involvement unsettling after witnessing Molinar's weakness firsthand. They were in a business with moral dilemmas, and dealing with one abuse sometimes meant committing others. Azzari didn't drive straight home that evening, opting for a stop at his local package store for a fifth of gin. Upon arriving home, he began his slow downward spiral into the evening, passing out after four hours of solitaire and late-night television reruns.

He woke up late the next morning, still fully clothed and in a pool of sweat, dealing with the beginning of a massive hangover. He had forgotten to load up on water, so he dealt with the problem the same way fireman dealt with forest fires: fighting with fire. Azzari's fire came in the form of the last cup from his gin bottle — hair of the dog — that he swilled through a few cubes cranked from a half-empty aluminum ice tray. Even though he's in a room full of ticking clocks, he still preferred twisting his cuff out of the way in getting at his wristwatch, which told him he had overslept until 10:30, and that was an hour he hadn't slept to in a couple of decades. When Azzari came to this realization in a brief moment of absolute clarity, he slightly panicked and wondered if he had missed any important phone calls. The clocks were ticking louder every second, pounding his conscience relentlessly until a different pounding interrupted his temporary dementia.

"C'mon Jerry; open up!" A voice said from outside his front door.

"Yeah, old man. We's ain't got all day, ya know," added someone.

Azzari straightened himself right away because he recognized that horrendous accent as Herb Graham's. Before he reached the door, he abruptly realized that, although he was supposed to set up a meeting for today, he hadn't called Graham or Lewis yet. His saturated mind fogged over with alternative reasons, but he couldn't think, let alone reason, with Lewis' incessant knock hammering every last brain cell that had previously evaded extermination. They, along with Azzari were corralled at the front door and given no other option but to open it before it was opened for him.

"I'm coming, I'm coming!" Azzari yelled, further aggravating his condition.

He opened the door and let the men inside as they dried themselves off from a morning shower.

"Geez, Greggie; we've been calling all morning. Didn't you hear the phone ringing?" Lewis asked.

"I guess not."

"Your man Vargas called us and said to meet you here. Said he couldn't get in touch with you; that the phone lines must be messed up or something." Lewis added.

"Holy mother. Hay old man, you look like shit!" Graham laughed, noticing the open gin bottle on the table and the blanket on the couch. "Whut you been up to?"

"Nothing. Hang on a minute and let me get a drink of water. Have a seat at the table over there." Azzari pointed.

He grabbed a glass from the counter, sloshed in some straight tap water without any ice, and downed it all at once.

"That bad, huh?" Lewis laughed.

"Never you mind that." Azzari griped. "You boys got a job to do. Did Angel tell you about it?"

"No," said Lewis. "He just said it was important and we had to see you right now."

Azzari turned around to face them, and in his sweaty demeanor, said, "We gotta take that cop out."

"Cop? Whut cop? Nobody never said nothin about killin' no policeman."

Lewis interrupted. "Pipe down, Herb, this was before you got up here, and besides, he ain't no cop. He's some private detective that's on the take; a bad ex-cop."

"That's right." Azzari said.

Graham unfurled his brow and said, "All right then. How's this gonna go?"

"Job's worth fifteen. I figure a three-way split, but I gotta know how you'd do this first." Azzari asked.

"I don't know Greggie. You haven't told me much about this guy yet and you haven't told me if there's a special request." Lewis said.

"Special request? What, you think this is a fuckin' radio station for crying out loud? They just want him gone, that's all."

"All right, all right. No need for hostilities, man! You got an address?"

"His house; that's it."

"All right, so we wait for him down the block, follow him to wherever he's going, wait until he steps out and let him have it." Lewis said.

"What? Like you did with Hernandez? Forget it," said Azzari in disgust. "Man, I miss the old days, you know? You wanted someone gone, you just walk right up and let 'em have it. No dancing around giving them any chances or any of that shit…just face to face and it's over…done. That's what your gonna do this time, understand?"

"Face-to-face?" Lewis asked.

"Yeah, face-to-face."

"I ain't got no problem with that, old timer." Graham intervened.

"Let me get this straight; you want us to walk right up to his front door, wait until he answers, and blast him right there in the middle of the daytime with all of his neighbors watching?" Lewis whined.

"Take a look at that box on the table. You see what's inside there? That goes on that peashooter you got behind you."

Wondering how the old man knew he was carrying a pistol in his rear beltline, Lewis reached around his back and placed the firearm on the table. Graham picked up the silencer and examined it thoroughly.

"How does it, um, work?" He asked.

"You mean, how does it work, or how do you operate it?" Azzari replied, swallowing another gulp of water.

"Both."

"Well first, you gotta unscrew the top of that thing and stuff it with filter fibers. Then you close it back and screw the whole thing onto the barrel of that pistol."

"Filter fibers? What? A coffee filter?" Lewis cackled.

"Air conditioner. Follow me to the shed out back. I've got a couple back there."

Azzari gulped another half glass of water and opened a sliding glass door to his back yard where the shed stood near the back fence. He reached into his pocket for some keys, searched around for a moment, and inserted one into the lock, twisting until it opened. He swung the door open and reached into the front of its left side, withdrawing two flat, air conditioner filters that had brilliant blue fibers matted into a thick sheet. He sat one down and used a pocketknife to shred the other, creating a large handful of loose blue fibers. Graham unscrewed one end of the silencer and handed it to Azzari, who packed the fibers into the cylinder, careful not to obstruct its inner perforated barrel. Graham handed the silencer's end cap to Azzari and he screwed it back on tightly, allowing no chance of accidental failure. That was something he witnessed firsthand in an accident involving another friend almost a decade earlier; someone didn't properly tighten the silencer and it exploded on the first shot, sending the man to the hospital with facial burns and lacerations. Azzari wasn't taking any chances that he'd make the same mistake, or that he may arouse suspicion with a neighbor because, as quiet as they were, "poor-man's silencers" still made a fairly loud noise with a distinct sound—something akin to a pellet rifle or an overflow valve's release on a commercial air compressor. He had Lewis and Graham follow him back indoors, where he took aim at his ex-wife's favorite couch and pumped two rounds right through the middle of it.

Azzari then held the pistol up and said, "How's that working for you?"

Neither Lewis nor Graham said anything; they were just standing there slack-jawed at Azzari's apparent destruction of his own sofa. There were two fresh, smoking bullet holes in the middle of one of the back cushions, and a few of the blue fibers, now blackened with soot, stuck into the same cushion near the holes. Azzari was evidently too hung over to notice, turning around and handing the pistol to Graham.

"Stay right there," said Azzari, disappearing down a hallway.

"The man's clearly off his rocker, Herb."

"Yeah, I know it, but he's got the right idea, man."

Azzari reappeared with an old, brown Florsheim shoebox and tested whether the pistol fit inside. Since Azzari had larger than normal feet for a man of his height, the gun fit nicely inside with the lid closed.

"There you go. Just walk right up, pretending to make a delivery and that's that."

Lewis and Graham left Azzari to deal with his hangover and returned to their motel after deciding it was already too late in the day to for an attempt. Instead they hit the local clubs, drinking, dancing and generally slumming around the west side of town until coming back to their room, half lit from two snorts in a restroom less than an hour earlier.

Lewis, who preferred taking his showers in the morning before venturing out for the day, sat on the bed's corner watching a late-night Creature Feature repeat hosted by Paul Bearer.

Graham emerged from the bathroom several minutes later, wrapped in a towel and beading water in several places he missed drying, which were mainly his back and legs.

"So how are you gonna do it?" Lewis asked.

"Whut do ya mean, man?

"Are you just going to walk up and shoot after he answers the door?"

"Well, yeah." Graham answered blankly. "Whut else is there to do?"

"I don't know," said Lewis, "Maybe say something cool right before you do it. You know, like they do in the movies."

"Man, you hit some acid or somethin' while I wuz in there?"

"No, I'm serious. It would be cool. Just between me and you. You say something really—I don't know—angry, or something, right before you pull the trigger."

"Whut, like 'Take that!' or something?"

"No; cooler than that. Like, 'this is for…' or something like that, you know."

"Aw, man, I don't know about nuthin' like that." Graham said bashfully.

"Aw, c'mon. Can't you think of anything?"

"Nope." Graham said just before removing his towel, causing Lewis to forget everything else until the next morning when he woke up and saw Graham combing his hair in front of the bathroom mirror saying, "I got a message," and using the comb as a pistol, shooting at himself in the mirror. He did so for over five minutes while Lewis watched in fascination, wondering if he really would remember the line when the time came.

"And what's the message?" Lewis asked, startling Graham, who pretended that he wasn't doing anything with the comb, hiding it around his back.

"Uh – nuthin'; just gonna kill 'em, that's all."

"Hurry up and get ready, it's almost eight."

Graham looked puzzled and said, "Well ain't yew gonna clean all that off before we hit it?"

"Nah. I'll take one when we get back, man. Sometimes you wanna stay dirty when the job calls for it."

Graham buttoned up his polo shirt and straightened his collar, disagreeing. "Not me, man. I like the calm, cool thang. And, for me, that goes with the clean."

Lewis picked himself up from the corner of the bed and changed a few channels on the television before turning it off in frustration and lying back down.

"So what's it gonna be?" He asked.

"Whut's that?" Graham replied.

"I mean, what are you going to say to him when you pull the trigger?"

"Uh, man, I haven't got that quite figured yet."

"Well, don't forget. C'mon, we have to go get the car from Jerry. Cab oughta be here in a minute. Here—hit this, I'm through."

Graham walked over, took a rolled dollar bill from Lewis' hand, and snorted the last two lines of cocaine Lewis left on a hand mirror. After recovering, he quickly finished dressing and surveyed the room in case they were missing anything before departing. He took the silencer out of its box, shoved it into the pocket of his trousers, and slid the Mambo .32 automatic pistol into his back beltline before donning a dark blue windbreaker. Lewis had shredded the other air conditioner filter earlier that morning, and stuffed a handful of its fibers into the shoebox given by Azzari before leaving with it.

Both exited their motel room into a crisp October morning, where a bright yellow cab perspired onto the parking lot. Before they were able to climb inside, an elderly lady from the manager's office bolted around the corner and started complaining about their week's rent being two days overdue.

"We're going to the bank right now, lady, calm down!" Lewis said, throwing his cigarette butt to the ground in front of her.

"You better, or I'll have all your belongings in a locker!"

Lewis closed his door and laughed, "Same place she parks her broom, I bet."

Around fifteen minutes later, they arrived at Jerry Molinar's house, knocked on his door, and rolled the green Plymouth out of the garage and quietly out of the neighborhood. Within a few more minutes, they sat idling at the corner down at the end of my block in Seminole Heights contemplating their next moves.

Graham withdrew the pistol from his backside and placed it in his lap while retrieving the silencer from his pocket. Lewis picked the shoebox up and grabbed a handful of the blue air conditioner fibers from inside. He handed those to Graham, who opened one end of the silencer and packed fibers around its inner barrel until he felt it was full enough. Graham screwed the silencer's end cap on tightly and then screwed the assembly onto the barrel of the Mambo. He then cocked the weapon, placed it inside the shoebox with the safety off and closed the lid.

"You ready?" Lewis asked.

"Um, no, not really, man. How about yew go around the block one time before we just pull up there."

"All right."

Lewis idled the Plymouth down the street and by the house where there was only one vehicle parked in the carport—my '66 T-bird. He circled the block and stopped again at the same corner they were previously, letting Graham work up his courage.

"All right, man. I'm going to drop you off at the driveway and go around the block just like we did. So, it'll take that long for me to get back around."

"You ain't staying out front?"

"Nope. The car isn't a delivery van, you know. He should think you're parked down the street or something."

"Aw, man, I dunno 'bout that." Graham quivered.

"You'll be fine," said Lewis, trying to keep Graham focused. "So what are you going to say when you do it?"

"I, uh—what?" Graham stuttered.

"C'mon, man! I can't be there when you say it, so tell me!"

"Man, I don't know, dang it! Yew just drive over there before I change my mind."

Lewis threw his hands back on the Plymouth's steering wheel and placed the shifter in Drive. The car slowly crept forward down the block, slowly gathering speed until Lewis stopped in front of the house. Graham took the shoebox, stepped outside, and closed the door behind him. After he straightened his tie in the door window's reflection, Lewis drove away and around the block. Graham walked up the two steps onto the small front patio, rang the doorbell, and turned around, so as to obscure his reaching into the shoebox. When I answered the door, he thought about his line and the coolest thing he could come up with was, "I've got a message for you, cop," before sending me to the floor.

When it was over, he ran back outside, picked up the shoebox, and dove inside the car that Lewis had just parked out in front of the driveway. He only caught a glimpse at Ida Heinemann screaming, "Oy, a broch!" as he trotted the thirty or so feet to the end of the driveway. When Graham slammed the passenger door shut, Lewis hit the gas and sped off down the block.

"Is it done?"

"Hell yeah, it is!" Graham howled, clutching his right ear.

"What happened to you?"

"Aw, the damned son-of-a-bitch went and hit me upside the head with a flower pot."

"A flower pot?"

"Or a big ass ashtray." Graham said, noticing that Lewis was having a hard time believing the excuse. "A big ashtray, maybe! One them big 'ole glass ones."

"Oh, I get it. So I guess it wasn't that smooth then."

Graham just sat there and bled into his hand. "No, it wasn't. I missed 'em a couple shawts before he fell. That little gun ain't worth shit, man. I had to hit him five times before he saw the floor."

"Right, well, you don't need a hospital or anything do you, because you know we can't…"

"Oh, hell no, man. Just get us where we're going…wherever that is."

"Salvage. I'm gonna call Greggie from there." Lewis paused. "So, did you say it?"

"Whut?"

"The message! Did you say it?" Lewis insisted.

"Oh, yeah. Yeah, I said it," replied Graham softly as he watched people going about their lives within the blur of the passing landscape.

"Ha-ha!" Lewis shouted. "That's my man."

When they arrived at the salvage yard, they left the keys in the floorboard and went inside the front office to call Azzari. While Lewis was on the phone, Graham watched as a crane slammed its electromagnetic lifter on top of the car just next to the Plymouth, smashing its roof down before lifting the car into a crusher.

Azzari arrived minutes later in his "rolling freezer", as Lewis called it, and gave them a ride back to his house.

"Hey Greggie, aren't they going to take care of our car?"

"What?" Azzari turned towards Lewis. "No! What do you think this is, the movies? That car's too hot and besides, it has to be stripped of gas and other stuff before they can stick it into one of them compactors, otherwise they blow up."

"Oh," Lewis said.

"We got a guy that's gonna deposit it in Land 'O Lakes."

"Deposit it?"

"The ponds aren't just for fishing, you know. Anyway, I got a call from a friend who listens to a police scanner. Said it was busier than during the '68 riots, so I'm guessing you fellas had some luck. How'd it go, Rev? That piece work okay for you?" Azzari turned around towards the back seat as he said it and noticed Graham holding his ear. "He okay?"

"Yeah, he's fine." Lewis said.

Azzari reached over into the glove box and removed some napkins he had amassed from every restaurant he had eaten at in the last year, handing them to Graham.

"Here, and don't bleed on the upholstery. It's a Cadillac for crying out loud."

"Stop yackin' old timer. I just bought yew a new'in."

"You gonna tell me how it went?"

"He's done, and that's it."

"That's all you can say? What happened to you?"

"He got hit with an ashtray." Lewis laughed.

"An ashtray?" Azzari smirked.

"Yeah, a godderned ashtray. That piece of shit .32 you lent us ain't worth squat. Had to hit the fella five times just to get him down."

"Is he dead?"

"Well he wasn't breathin' too good when I left."

Both Lewis and Azzari turned backwards towards Graham who sat with his eyes diverted.

"You don't know?" Azzari's tone soured. "You left without making sure he was dead?"

"I don't know!" Graham yelled.

"Aw shit, Reverend, you're gonna get us all in trouble if he makes it to the hospital," said Azzari.

"Oh Jesus, man, I thought you said..." Lewis started to complain, but Graham interrupted.

"I know whut I said, Petey. He ain't gonna make it so relax."

"Relax? Oh Christ!"

Azzari lit up a cigarette and rolled the window down just long enough to flick the last one out. "What about the pictures? Did you get the pictures?"

Lewis and Graham both looked at each other before Lewis asked, "What pictures?"

Part III

Commencement

After the department informed Wendy, her sorrows began with an incurable crying hysteria. The first responders dared not engage her accusations, fully knowing the circumstances and the probabilities just as well as she did—only they stayed within their spineless flocks this time. When she finished with her tirade and re-entered the arms of her supervisor, the crying resumed. She demanded an escort to the hospital where they took me, and only then did it appear as if someone was lifting more than a pinkie to help her. A patrolman saddled up on his Harley and did her bidding, rushing her down through Hyde Park and over the bridge to the north end of Davis Islands. The ambulance had just arrived at Tampa General, but there was no sense of emergency, and the men that witnessed my arrival hung their heads, giving Wendy every indication of what happened. She never lost hope however, and didn't cry until a tall, grey-haired surgeon emerged from the first bay down the emergency rooms' main hallway. He looked her squarely in the eye, and said nothing. She ran towards the doors, but he blocked her, saying it was simply too late; I was already gone.

I wanted clarity, but sometimes that commodity is overbearingly expensive. Tampa became a pressure cooker sitting on a burner that I set much too high, and it cost everything—my hopes, my dreams, my honor, and my family— but this was really just the beginning.

Wendy fell to the ground at the doctor's feet, hugging his legs and crying. He was powerless as he searched the hallway for someone, anyone, that could have helped her. For several moments there was no one until Mack Poole appeared through the same door she flung open just minutes before. Wendy got up and cried for almost two hours in his arms, repeating, "Those bastards killed him, Mack; you know who did it, don't you!" And Mack kept repeating that he wouldn't rest until he caught who did this. That's all she wanted to hear.

Lewis and Graham went with Azzari back to his house, cracked open a fresh fifth of Seagram's and sat down discussing the particulars of the hit. An hour and a half pack of cigarettes almost passed before Salvatore Tresedici rang Azzari's phone. In their easily deciphered code, both Graham and Lewis knew he was calling to confirm the hit. He asked about the photos right away, and Azzari never stuttered in his cover-up, stating twice that there weren't any—right in front of Lewis and Graham so they thought he was doing them a favor, even though it was for himself. Tresedici became rather pissed-off however, and told them that he wasn't going to make any disbursements until he read it in the newspaper. He then instructed Azzari to set his friends up at the beach, which actually meant driving them to an Indian Rocks condo they used regularly for parties—Lozello's. On the way there, Graham lowered his passenger's window and sailed the Mambo pistol, along with the silencer, off the highest part of the Gandy Bridge. Even though the bay was unusually calm and infested with grouper fisherman, none of them saw the gun hit the water.

Tresedici had the most terrible misfortune in playing the role of the shot messenger when delivering the news of the still-missing photographs to Lozello. The chief's temper tantrum was enough to send the head of the floor's secretary all the way around until he slammed the door to his office for privacy. He immediately telephoned Lt. Wexler to take charge of the crime scene and recover the photographs. Wexler stated he couldn't go it alone, so he tapped Det. Skitter to back him up in case some of the local patrolmen decided to become a little too curious.

If I had time to think about it, the all-important photographs would have been hidden in a much better spot than in my gray plastic briefcase under the bed, because Skitter had no trouble finding what he and Wexler came for—removing them from the crime scene under Wexler's sport coat, undetected. They also mucked up other evidence, such as wiping off the shell casings Graham left behind. Lenny's feds were stunned upon the scene when they arrived and commandeered the investigation. The scene was completely useless.

When Lozello's devoted minions arrived and placed the manila envelope on his desk, his brow furled well above the dark circles clouding his eye sockets.

"Got a little careless, did we?" Skitter jabbed, automatically unleashing Lozello's temper because Lozello had no tolerance for smart-alecks, especially since he had no talent in that regard.

"Not another word about this, Skitter or I'll have jour ass walking the Thirteen!"

But Skitter couldn't stop laughing when he said, "And you'll be right there with me if you do!" And that further angered Lozello.

"Get him out of here Ned, before I do somethin' I oughta not."

Lt. Wexler found some humor in Lozello's predicament as well, but kept his expressions to no more than a slight smirk as he escorted Skitter back to the elevator. Lozello sat back down and placed his face in his palms, exhausted from the stress of so much guilt. He was free now, or at least he thought he was. He stared at the envelope for over ten minutes before locking it away in a desk drawer.

By the end of the day, the shooting was all over the local media, which meant that Tresedici's terms were satisfied. He sent Vargas alone to the beach that evening with the cash, and Vargas carried a couple of uncut grams with him as well, ensuring a pleasant reception.

Two days afterward, officials finally allowed Wendy and the boys back into the house, only to find that the technicians had not fully cleansed the crime scene. There were still drops of blood on certain parts of the floor, and some insensitive moron with the paramedics left a body bag wrapper on the kitchen counter near where they found me. Further confirming Wendy's suspicions of a raging snow job, she and Jeffrey found two of the bullets that missed me. One had bounced around and came to rest up under a newspaper on the living room floor, and the other sat embedded on the back wall of the same room. Indeed, hardly any evidence had been documented at the scene, other than those from Wexler's imagination in a later report.

The first thing Wendy did was pick up the phone and call Mack, but Mack cautioned her not to say anything after hearing the telltale clicks indicating a phone tap. He said he could not meet her, fearing for their safety, and instead gave her Lenny's home number. Wendy immediately hung up and called him, keeping her misplaced anger in check during the call. She felt that he could have prevented this somehow, knowing those photographs were much too dangerous to keep, but she was more concerned about progress than hindsight.

Lenny's string of misfortune didn't stop with my death because, when he hung up with Wendy, Pappy Hernandez called to inform him that he was no longer willing to testify under the circumstances. No matter how hard Lenny tried to convince him otherwise, Hernandez didn't want to leave the life and reputation he worked so unrelentingly hard to amass.

"They got to Bill, and he was one of joo! They can get to me too. Besides, the wife likes the weather around here, understand, jefe? She don't want me to testify now. What can I say?"

Hernandez's withdrawal plowed Lenny's confidence almost entirely until he made a conference with Ben Davidson, who said there were plenty other exhibits and evidence that would, at the very least, cause a lot of pain throughout the city. Due to my murder, he postponed the grand jury until the first week of December so they could let the heat die down for Hernandez and The Match. They thought if some more hands were tied, or more preferably shackled, witnesses might find their bravery once again.

Pressure mounted on Lozello from every angle—the newspapers, television, the mayor (but only as a show), state agencies, and federal investigators—to solve my case as rapidly as possible. The ranks within the department grew angrier and more despondent by the hour, even threatening a walkout if I wasn't reinstated with a full pension awarded to Wendy. But Lozello never made mistakes, especially when one had publically broadcast ramifications. He fired me for not taking a polygraph and knew it was against the law to do so, but revisiting something that he considered buried several months earlier would reopen an investigation.

With the exception of his devoted followers and a couple dozen others sworn in with their fingers crossed behind their backs, the department was mostly against Lozello. In a show of solidarity, most of those officers — the ones who could make it — showed up for a makeshift formal ceremony at my burial. After a moving eulogy, marking many of my practical jokes, many of which Ray Coleman didn't want to relive, the captain called for steadfast diligence in justice, and patience with the leaders, "while they weigh the best course of action in bringing about the right solution." I believe he was the only one at the funeral that didn't think he was full of it. People tend to embarrass themselves more often than the other way around, but Wendy quickly forgot about it when he handed a folded flag to Junior. My boy sat there, emotionless in his plaid jacket, not quite sure what anyone was saying, nor why they gave him the flag, other than to hold it.

I used to kid folks at funerals and other functions where people were absent, saying, "You weren't gone until you were missed." I could tell some people in the small crowd missed me while the sun shined and a passing cloud spat upon the wind. Some of the department noticed who else was missing and "Where's Linus?" was heard whispered loudly several times from rear ranks, who frankly didn't care if they were overheard or not. But they didn't whisper about the several detectives who were also missing because those folks were currently collecting their confidential informant dossiers and burning them in a trashcan behind the Aztec Lounge. Mack and a few others toasted me afterward and drove by the gravesite, leaving a few empty cans of my favorite beer sitting atop the headstone in tribute. I suppose that is when everyone realized I was truly gone.

Passing the Buck

"You people want to deny that there's evil for evil; that it takes people like me to get rid of your trash without all the vain exposure you crave from the newspapers and TV. You don't want the Klan or Panthers around because they make you look bad!" Martin Sanchez said under questioning by Lenny's men outside Tallahassee.

The Match connected two people in Boston that may have been involved with the shooting, but it became apparent after their interrogation, that Sanchez had aligned his allegiances with former employers. While those suspects were facing convictions for small roles in the Boston arsons, they had absolutely nothing to do with the Tampa shootings. Sanchez's employers had previously instructed him to direct the attentions of his captors as far away from the scene as possible. His wasn't the only lead that sprang up in the case; it was just part of the dog-and-pony show put on by the local department and its highest official.

Lozello disappeared into the bowels of his office, having instructed his secretary to run interference and deflect calls pertinent to the case unless they were emanating from certain friends. When asked about my reinstatement, he passed responsibility on to the mayor, who passed that on to the city council. The newspapers badgered Lozello relentlessly, to and from his issued car; in the mornings and in the afternoons. Only one reporter ever received more than a shanked grin when Lozello rolled down his window and angrily answered only one of the highly-circulated rumors.

"Everyone on the street says it's a mob hit." The reporter asked.

"Look, I want this bad; just as bad as anyone else. I'm even putting one of his best friends on the case. We just don't have any evidence to say this was done one way or another. The FBI says there's no way it was a professional job, and I think so too. Joo let us work on the investigation, okay?"

While it was true, one of the men from Lenny's office offered his opinion on the hit, the reporter took his full answer out of context. He said, "It didn't look like the work of professionals," but he never said it wasn't a contract killing. When reporters asked about the impending patrolmen and detectives' walkout, Lozello's window knob began turning.

The pressure was far too much on Wendy too. Reporters were constantly stalking her; first, at the hotel, then at a friend's home, and after the crime scene tape had been removed, at our house, which she couldn't stand being inside for more than a few minutes at a time so she could gather personal belongings. She cried while dialing Lenny's number, having exhausted all others that evening, almost two weeks after the shooting. He gave her as good advice as I could have given her in that he said to simply go back home. That meant the small Houston, Texas suburb where she grew up, and that's where she moved with the boys. But moving there only changed the scenery. Tampa would be on her mind forever it seemed, especially after the first call she received was Lenny informing her that the city council had once again voted down my reinstatement (by a one vote margin), testing the willpower of the department who again threatened a walkout. Those officers also had the backing of the local Police Benevolent Association, who, along with a mystery donor, offered $10,000 as a reward for the information leading to the arrest of the perpetrators.

Tampa had become a three-ring circus centered around the investigation, its grand jury, and those seeking attention from it. Not a day after Wendy settled in back home in Texas, one of my informants (a guy who ran an office specializing in supplying waitresses and go-go dancers to several clubs partnered by Vargas and Tresedici, among others, but we all knew he was just a glorified pimp), testified he was shot at six times as soon as he tried to leave his second-floor office off Buffalo Avenue in West Tampa. It turned out that the grand jury and the subpoenas they issued only helped round up informants connected with me, and they leveraged them against providing any clues. That same evening, Lozello's men busted two small-time dealers-turned-informants for trafficking cocaine in unheard-of amounts—

amounts that only some high-level trafficker such as Vargas could supply.

None of it made sense to Lenny or Ben Davidson, who knew Cantonello wouldn't have sanctioned it without some vital piece of information missing. So they made every attempt at personally getting Cantonello's attention, even having his attorney's license suspended for tax evasion. Sure, it got Cantonello's attention, but he shunned everyone except the Colombians and kept quiet in Costa Rica. Paul Gravina was already broken from dealings gone bad, and with the suspension, prosecutors hoped he would offer something in return. Yet Gravina always considered himself the consummate professional and never once considered violating the attorney-client privilege. Because of that, he bankrupted himself entirely, and the only person that could help him was Cantonello.

"Ask me for anything you want. You name it—anything...except money," said Cantonello in a jocular reply when Gravina begged. In a nutshell, his response defined the nature of their relationship.

The men at the department were on the verge of walking, but the city council, five members to be exact, weren't budging. They felt the pension money that Wendy would receive for my 11 years was far too much to pay during a budget crisis, but the prospect of not having a police department at all would soon change their minds. The wait wasn't over, however, and they voted to stab my wife once more and watch her bleed for another two months.

Azzari, meanwhile, slowly began losing the fight with his own conscience. While Tresedici's attendants held a meeting at Lilliput's, Azzari imbibed an unusual amount of rum. It wasn't uncharacteristic of him to drink a lot of anything, but it was highly unusual in that he hardly ever drank more than one rum drink in any given night. Rum's effect on Azzari was not unlike that of sodium pentothal or other truth agent, in that he began blabbing incoherently until one sentence caught Tresedici's attention.

"Just another one fer The Reverend, s-s-so he says," Azzari slurred.

Tresedici interrupted the punch line of a joke he was finishing, emptied the room, and angrily interrogated the entire story from Azzari's compromised locker. Azzari spilled everything from the Miami shooting, to the grocery store caper. Tresedici became enraged with Azzari, but recognized he was far too drunk to reason and would wait to hear everything again when he was sober. Tresedici spent that entire evening in a fit of anger and anxiety, wondering what his mismanagement and trust had gotten him into.

When Azzari gave him the full scoop the next morning, Tresedici reclused at home, wondering what his next move entailed. He called Vargas and met with him early that afternoon, and after Vargas heard the story, he panicked and asked to hide at Cantonello's estate in Costa Rica. Tresedici didn't yet feel that the situation was out of control and told him to hold off. Lewis and Graham, on the other hand, were doing nothing of the kind.

Using most of the money left over after two weeks of partying and other nonstop pleasures, the men scammed their way into another narcotics dealer's nest in Miami, netting nearly $100,000 in counterfeit hundreds and a kilo of cocaine. When they returned, they gave the kilo to Vargas as a show of good faith, which negated the lecturing Vargas had intended to serve. They also gave $60,000 of the fake cash to Molinar to split with Azzari, regardless if they wanted it or not. They gave almost everything away because it was never their intention to bother with merchandise types that were immovable. Instead, they used the deal as a conversation piece, securing the whereabouts of their Miami contacts, whom they robbed at gunpoint the next week. That job netted a half kilo of cut cocaine, around four dozen speed capsules, a rather large coin collection worth $8,000, a large diamond ring, and $2,300 of their original cash stashed along with it.

When they returned from Miami, Vargas met with them directly and let them know how close they were to a miserable death for dishonesty with him and Tresedici. In a subsequent meeting that included Jerry Molinar, Vargas laid out his path to salvation, which meant taking care of their loose end in Miami — the dynamite supplier that was currently in trouble with the ATF. But Molinar, Graham, and Lewis suddenly became superstitious of Miami, having perhaps worn out their welcome with the local soldiers. Instead, they decided to try and hire their own dupe using the counterfeit cash in large supply as the stipend. Over the next two weeks, Lewis and Graham traveled all the way to New Jersey in their search, leaving a trail of those counterfeit bills all along the way. When the Secret Service began investigating, they had unwittingly stumbled upon a tangential case that set the dominoes in motion.

As Jerry Molinar had once feared, but had completely forgotten about after playing Colombian roulette with Lewis and Graham, his wife had been passing hundred dollar bills all over neighboring Pinellas County. He never recalled the slightest inkling of his wife's misdeeds until returning from a liquor store run, unlocking his front door, and seeing her cuffed on the couch with two Secret Servicemen patiently awaiting his return.

"Good afternoon, Jerry."

Molinar's immediate thoughts were on the logistics, as in where they parked, because he didn't see any other cars in front or down the street. By the end of that afternoon, the Molinars had been processed and entered into questioning, but Molinar knew exceedingly well what would happen if he snitched on the rest. Before the interrogators thought to keep them separated, Jerry Molinar had already threatened his wife if she said one word referring to the others. Both remained tightlipped about the cash and how they came to possess it because their lawyer knew the Secret Service had nothing more than a possess-ion/circulation charge—nothing more—as long as they didn't give it away.

As soon as Azzari, Vargas, and Tresedici found out about the arrest and interrogation, they immediately tried to get in touch with Lewis and Graham in order to expedite the job in Miami. They were nowhere to be found, however, having lost themselves in Jersey City, where Graham's accent and demeanor were nothing less than conspicuous.

The Grand Listeners

By the middle of November, Ben Davidson's team held it together long enough to present the state grand jury with witnesses and evidence of the police department's corruption during the murder investigation, but a friendly and ambitious state attorney attempted every delay—from claiming Davidson's team wasn't sharing information, to claiming Lozello hadn't fully discussed the jury with him yet. The jury convened anyway, and Lozello vehemently denied corruption—any corruption—existed in his department. If it weren't for the serious issues on the matter, the prosecutors' smirks after the jury may have adjoined Lozello's statements, but as it was, Davidson's team struggled to produce any hard evidence other than witnesses' testimony.

Davidson's team wasn't without any maneuverability in comingling elements of my discharge as partial reasoning for the corruption charges. While the department released composite drawings of Lewis and Graham as seen by Ida Heinemann to the newspapers, the jury grilled Lozello for mandating polygraphs and firing me for refusing to take one. So naturally, prosecutors made a formal request asking that he take a polygraph himself. Lozello's eyes widened at the thought, and he searched for the best excuse for refusing one.

He said, "It would set a bad precedent for the department," which, again met with muffled giggles and choking noises from the prosecutor's side of the room.

Lozello became incensed with his lack of respect, as did a few of the jury, but they knew what the prosecutors just accomplished, which was not so much a victory for the corruption implications as it was for Wendy.

The jury backed the city council into a corner now. If they voted to install the use of polygrahphs, they risked exposing half of their ranks to endless prosecution. If they voted to ban their use, Lozello's argument for firing me became inert, and would certainly lead to my reinstatement. The city council weighed their decision carefully, but any arguments among them became moot when a clerk walked into their boardroom the next day and delivered notice that a US grand jury was commencing their corruption probe immediately. That same day, the Tampa City Council voted to officially forbid the use of polygraphs on policemen and other city officials. Davidson had his little victory, but the war still raged.

One outspoken councilwoman put out a notice requesting that the governor seek a special prosecutor in the murder case — without the backing or knowledge of the other council members, who were quite upset over her act of insubordination. The governor swiftly replied that he trusted the state attorney's handling of the grand jury, which made total sense given that those two had worked so closely together in the past. Old connections never die. Lozello was playing it safe, however, and wanted a fall guy just in case momentum shifted away. After an emergency private meeting with Wexler, Lozello decided that person was Skitter.

Skitter went out of his mind, but not so much that he would expose himself and the rest of the department by his illegal activities. Instead, Lozello calmed him down enough to trust the advice of their city attorney named Eugene Wiggins, who promised Skitter he could plead the Fifth Amendment without any repercussion. In doing so, however, Lozello told Skitter that he'd have to suspend him for 30 days as a show of good intention. Skitter agreed to the scheme and, when his turn came up in the grand jury, he followed the plan precisely. Lozello followed the plan as well, suspending him while the reporters were in his office, and going so far as to threaten firing Skitter if he didn't cooperate. Linus, it seemed, missed his calling as a character actor for the local theater, but he wasn't the only actor in the department.

During the grand juries, someone shot a city detective by the name of Floyd Moreland while he was walking towards his apartment just on the other side of the Hillsborough River from Seminole Heights. While in the hospital, nursing the wound to his left side, he said he'd probably be dead if it weren't for his hearing some shuffling from behind. He said he turned around and shot at his attacker just as the attacker shot, but he missed. As the time of occurrence was in the middle of the night, there were no witnesses. Nevertheless, prosecutor Jimmy Willard received a package with documents from the FBI showing that the gun that shot Moreland had previously been sent to the FBI's crime lab. They were able to recover the serial number that someone filed off, or so they thought. That number led them to the gun's owner, who testified under oath that Moreland confiscated the gun from him months earlier. The gun never saw the property room according to the report, and Moreland's costly charade only momentarily deflected the grand jury's investigation. By December, more witnesses were emboldened to testify and one of the most damaging of those was Mack Poole's.

Mack laid his accounting carefully, colorfully detail-ing every movement by Lozello, the disbanding of the Criminal Intelligence Unit, his reassignment to the radio room, how informants were being rounded up or gone missing just after my shooting, and his thoughts on the investigation. But the prosecutors saved the pièce de résistance until the last question.

"Did Sergeant Brume (Willard insisted on hammering my police rank, mocking Lozello and the city council) ever show you photographs of Chief Lozello socializing with alleged members of a criminal organization during the commission of an illegal act — namely, supervising a shipment of heroin for a one Angel Vargas?"

Of course, the defense threw every protest possible, and, legally, they were in the right to do so. As much as Mack did for exposing the truth to the grand jury, and logically laying out the scenario in which they could believe, it was all for not. No matter how brilliantly Mack and the others testified, and no matter the bedamning stories of crime and corruption, the bottom line was that none of the witnesses could produce a single shred of hard evidence. The jury struck everything as hearsay and opinion, so Davidson and Willard concentrated once again on Skitter.

Skitter plead the Fifth, and since the city council favored the path of least resistance, they agreed with their attorney's opinion regarding the civil rights of their own employees, maintaining his ability to utilize the Fifth and avoid further prosecution. Pleading the Fifth in the first place brought natural suspicion, however. The jury knew something was amiss, but the prosecutors were simply falling short in proving their case. That frustrated

Davidson enough to bypass protocols and blatantly complain to the newspapers that Tampa had become a crime seat at every level. Lozello, meanwhile, was grandstanding for those reporters on what to do with Skitter. Lozello had a plan for Skitter all along, however, and that was to keep tabs on his latest rival—Mack. Lozello sent Skitter to the radio room, and that was the beginning of the end of Lenny's information pipeline.

Skitter's assignment was temporary, and after two months, he was reassigned to Vice. The detectives in Vice abandoned Skitter's camaraderie almost instantly, and when they had a clear opportunity during a raid almost a year later, they let Skitter get shot in the right thigh, severing his femoral artery. The paramedics arrived quickly enough, but they were the same paramedics that worked my shooting, and Skitter's ride to the hospital proved permanently disabling.

Davidson and Willard weren't finished, though. Lozello made his second appearance in mid-December; this time at the federal grand jury, where they probed him about the fourteen detectives' photographs that ended up on an Ybor City tavern's refrigerator.

He claimed that a longtime traffic judge—an overweight, renowned excessive drinker named John M. Robertson— had requested those and sent them down the chain. The next witness, a major named Hammond, verified he acted on Lozello's direct orders and forwarded the photos to one of his lieutenants, and so on. While Judge Robertson claimed that his office did in fact receive the photographs, which prompted an appearance from his secretary, his explanation for "losing" the photos was that they must have been stolen; from the main floor of the police station, no less. When asked why he needed the photos to begin with, Robertson concocted some story that he needed them so he could identify when undercover detectives were asking to have minor violations dismissed for their informants. That explanation wasn't good enough for the jury. Willard brought Ray Coleman to the stand next, and Lover Boy's secretive investigation of the "stolen" photographs brought up a frequent visitor of Robertson's named Gerome Franks, Sr.

Along with his son, Franks pimped prostitutes all over town, and one of his regular clients, as it turned out, was Judge Robertson. Franks wasn't about to divulge any of that information, only stating that Robertson had inquired about *twelve* photos, which made little sense other than confirming the two were regular visitors.

He added, "We happened to show up that particular day with two fine young girls that were with me to help pluck some chickens at my Plant City farm, you know, for dinner later. Nobody was havin' any sex or any impropriety such as. I needed some family advice and he was on the way. We had a couple of drinks, but that's normal, right? I'd do it again if I had to do it over." The real explanation, however, came to light when the previously missing call girl named Deborah Lyons took the stand.

She spilled everything; from Robertson's almost daily appointments, to picking up the photographs from Robertson's secretary (who knew of the request), to Franks and Son's lucrative side businesses. All of which the reporters got wind of as soon as that day's session ended. Naturally, reporters inundated Robertson's office asking for commentary, to which Robertson replied that he knew of a great new fishing spot in Land 'O Lakes. Robertson knew he was untouchable as long as he and Franks stuck to their stories. On a technicality, they had done nothing illegal, and ethics had no say in the matter.

Towards the end of the holiday season, the 18-member US panel met with various individuals, including eight detectives with the department, which also meant that Mack had another shot at the stand. He, along with the others, were examined to no end concerning recent increases in narcotics trafficking, gambling, and prostitution. Afterwards, the jury foreman, a squat Latino named Rodriguez who was well known for distrusting certain factions of the government, stood up in front of Lozello, Major Hammond, and the county Sheriff, asking them why none of their agencies had presented even one gambling case. All were silent.

"But there's open bolita all over the streets. I've seen it with my own eyes!" Rodriguez said.

"In every community there are known crime figures; here, and in Pinellas. But this is happening elsewhere, not here." Lozello replied.

His statement left the jury scratching their heads, but Rodriguez opened a new line. Lozello acted shocked when Rodriguez asked him about a recent case involving Maj. Hammond stepping in for a friend caught in a Sunday beer-selling raid. Lozello's complexion went faint because he thought none of the detectives knew about Hammond's offense. He should have known better since his building was completely full of trained interrogators, but that was just another chasm in Lozello's logic. He didn't think anyone would ask questions after he quietly shifted Hammond's Tactical Division job as a commander in Vice to the Uniformed Division; without any decrease in rank or pay. His only explanation to the jury was acknowledgement of the incident, and that Hammond was "counseled".

But it wasn't the only surprise the detectives left for Lozello. Rodriguez also asked about another incident involving Hammond where he interceded for his father-in-law after a hit-and-run wreck two years earlier.

"I'll be looking into that." Lozello said coldly.

Finally, Rodriguez and his panel drilled Lozello on the case of a detective whose fingerprint showed up on a bolita slip at a gas station when technicians gathered evidence after a raid. When the panel discovered that the slip was made from a piece of paper taken from Lozello's car—a car that happened to be undergoing service and was brought to that gas station by that detective, who also happened to be Lozello's wife's first cousin—they began losing faith in Lozello's testimony. They lost even more faith when Lozello explained that he believed that one of the gas station employees must have taken the slip from the car. Nonetheless, that detective, a tall, sickly man who wore Coke bottle glasses and had an insanely large, grotesque mole just to the right of his mouth, was allowed to retire just four months earlier with a full pension.

The panel was aghast at the misconduct and ethics sidestepping, but there was nothing illegal enough to warrant a trial. Lozello bragged that eventually the grand jury would find that his department was one of the better outfits in the nation, and that any corruption surely wasn't systemic, but rather isolated incidences of bad behavior and broken rules dealt with individually.

The last few weeks of 1975 were rather ugly. Nobody trusted anyone else, and that was especially apparent between the state and US attorneys. The state attorney finally came out to the news reporters and blatantly accused Willard and Davidson of not sharing their transcripts in a timely matter, which was true, actually, because Davidson proceeded through the proper channels, and that those transcripts had to be released by a US

District Judge, not through their office. The attorney disagreed, opining that they only used that procedure for local trials and not grand juries. If the truth were contained in later actions, it sided with the US grand jury since the state attorney continued to receive transcripts through the District Judge. And the number of transcripts increased congruent with the increase in federal probes of the Tampa Police Department, which found itself increasingly dysfunctional.

Lozello, meanwhile, officially called the murder invest-igation dead—because he wanted it that way—and concentrated on shuffling the department further. The investigation was far from dead, at least from the federal point of view.

The Little Guy

The bicentennial anniversary of our nation began with as much tumultuousness as the previous year finished. The city council found itself painted into a corner and, by the second week of January, finally surrendered to the notion of my reinstatement and would vote again soon. Davidson won that little battle for Wendy and the boys, who would likely see some financial security while growing up in Texas. But the war was far from over; Wendy and Davidson couldn't sleep at night, restlessly wondering when the murderers would come before justice, if at all.

Lewis and Graham were running out of money, luck, and help in Jersey. Most of the players up there, the ones with any sense anyway, were staying as far away from Tampa as possible during the federal murder investigation. Out of alternatives, the fugitives, who were toying around just under the FBI's Ten Most Wanted list, decided to come back to warmer climates.

Upon their return, Lewis called Azzari, who filled him in on the Molinar's disappearance.

"You better not go nowhere around there, fellas. My friends are telling me the g-men got the place watched. Where the hell have you guys been, anyway? We've been trying to contact you for weeks."

"What for?" Lewis asked.

"Tell me where you are and I'll let you know all about it, okay?"

"Okay, pops, if that's the way you want to play it."

"Don't…"

"We're at our usual place; Room 15."

"Don't go nowhere; I'll be right over."

Azzari arrived half an hour later and briefed them on their new contract. He also gave them another shock.

"Vargas and Tresedici know everything now, including the way you killed Brunoli down in Miami. They told me to tell you that if you fucked this one up, you're next."

Lewis laughed hysterically, "Who's he gonna send, *Santa Claus*?"

"Don't joke about this one Pete, I'm tellin' ya. Jerry won't say nothing, but if the feds put that little dynamite guy's telephone calls to him, they might get something out of it, understand?"

"Well that's just the problem, Greggie. We're hot enough as it is, you know? Rather get someone else to do the work for us if we can," said Lewis.

Graham nodded in agreement from the corner of the bed he sat on, smoke wafting upward through his nose while he flipped through all four television stations looking for something other than a soap opera.

Azzari lit another cigarette, and upon exhaling the first drag, said, "I really don't care who pulls the trigger or lights the fuse, Pete. Just get it done."

"Whuts the pay?" Graham asked.

Azzari became enraged. "Pay? Christ, Reverend, there ain't no pay for this because there wouldn't have been any problems to begin with if you hadn't blown away Brunoli!"

Lewis intervened, "All right, all right. Settle down before you have a stroke or something. Herb and I'll take care of it."

With some sense of urgency, thinking their lives depended on it, Lewis and Graham haphazardly departed for Miami that afternoon.

The probes of the Tampa City Police Department, meanwhile, continued with more policemen testifying before the grand jury. The last of which, a mere patrolman named Howard Williams, gave the most intriguing testimony, stating he initiated his own investigation in 1974 after hearing some buzz of Lozello's corruption. Williams elaborated further, detailing a large-scale narcotics, weapons, and prostitution network involving Lozello, Wexler, the deputy chief, various detectives including Skitter, and certain informants. All of whom were in regular communication with various members of known and monitored crime figures, namely Vargas, Tresedici, and Cantonello. He even went so far as to say Lozello had occupied a house given to him by Cantonello, although the legal records couldn't conclusively prove anything. When asked about his information source, Williams said a good portion was from personal observation after receiving tips from one of his informants. He also stated one of Wexler's men, consequently, recently picked up that informant.

When jury foreman Rodriguez brought Lozello back for cross-examination, he asked him directly about the relationships and the house. Lozello offered the classical deviant's response: If you can't prove it, it's not true.

"Where's the facts?   Where's the proof?"   He said. "Everything jour hearing is part of an elaborate scheme to smear the current leadership of the department in some sort of a struggle for the power."

Rodriguez became increasingly frustrated with Lozello's responses and threw up his arms while looking down the length of the panel in disgust. After fulfilling his duties that day, Rodriguez asked to be excused by the district's chief judge citing bias conflicts, and the judge was happy to oblige, impaneling an alternate the next day. Even so, without Rodriguez, the probes began to fizzle during the month of February, but Davidson's quest was far from over, and an unexpected phone call from Lenny lit up his office.

"We got 'em, Ben."

Almost a full month earlier, the ATF finally squeezed a confession out of a small-time contractor from Miami named Frank Cooper, who—because of his atypical Miamian foot-long golden mountain man beard—went by the alias "Frankie the Beard". And the ATF teased Frankie relentlessly because of the fact that he wasn't the original Frankie the Beard; just like so many other copied aliases running around. (There were too many Gents, Lefties and Scarfaces for the Bureau's amusement)

After the successful execution of a subpoena, the ATF reviewed Cooper's phone records and questioned him about one call from Tampa. When they performed a cross-reference with the telephone company, Jerry Molinar's name appeared. That piece of information became a visit from those agents who were surprised by agents of the Secret Service that already had the property staked. It was yet another case of lax communication sharing by federal departments, but when the FBI became involved, the problem was quickly resolved. Lenny had both

Cooper and Molinar in custody and their stories started to unravel.

For the rest of February, the Miami field office installed an agent posing as Cooper hiding in his Homestead mobile home, which was located on a two-acre lot surrounded by palmettos and swamp down at the end limestone-graveled street. A late '60s Ford painter's van served as the three-agent command post that parked at the other end of the street, but maintained a view of Cooper's driveway. From there, they could see anyone who came and went, as well as monitor radio communications from their decoy. Two snipers used experimental Starlight night vision scopes on their rifles and monitored both sides of the trailer from opposite edges of the lot at wood's edge. Their trap was ready.

Around 3:20 a.m. on February 25, Lewis and Graham rolled to a stop halfway down the desolate street and deployed a man named Nacho Ramirez; a dark-complected illegal fresh from Cuba, who unfortunately didn't know enough English to understand what the snipers meant when they yelled, "Drop the weapon!" Instead of complying, he kicked open the trailer's door and ran inside with his revolver drawn, meeting three rounds from the decoy's automatic. Ramirez died instantly.

Simultaneously, two agents from the van had snuck upon Lewis' and Graham's car and cocked their automatic's hammers just outside and behind the open windows of the car's doors.

"Try it." The passenger-side agent said to Graham as Graham reached for his shotgun.

That was the end of the hunt for Lenny, who transferred the two up to Orlando the next afternoon. He brought them there instead of Tampa because he wasn't sure if he still had a mole in town. Information still seemed to trickle its way into the local departments, and they leaked it to the people who needed it the least.

After Lenny called Davidson with the news, he drove to Orlando for the cursory interrogation. He crossed them thoroughly without success, but at the first mention of Old Sparky's "accidents", Lewis broke down.

Crying, he said, "I'll tell you everything. Everything! Anything you want to know, I'll tell it, but you got to make me a deal. They'll come after me, for Christ's sake. I'll need protection!"

"Sorry Danny Boy," said Len, "We'll only promise that you won't see the chair. You killed a cop, and you know they don't like that much on the outside. Prison too for that matter."

Lenny started to walk out of the room, indicating that Lewis was at the end of any potential bargain.

"He wasn't no cop! Or, if he was, he was a bad one!"

Lenny turned back around and got right into Lewis' face. "No, asshole. That's where you're wrong. He was a good cop and he was working for me, and if it was up to me, I'd drop you off naked at the pistol range. But that's not the way it's going to be. Some other folks and myself are going to have a fine time watching you smoke in Tallahassee, and you can bet your ass, that's exactly what's going to happen."

Just before Lenny made it back to the door, Lewis wound up like a young boy who just fell off his tricycle into a fire ant hill.

"I don't want to die!" He cried.

Lenny ignored him once more and opened the door.

"It wasn't just us, it was..." Lewis whimpered.

Lenny turned back around and listened as Lewis laid out the whole scenario — the narcotics, the List of Five — everything.

Thursday, February 26th, 1976 became Leonard Karman's most memorable. In the first light of that morning, agents surrounded Salvatore Tresedici's house, serving an arrest warrant without resistance. Within the same hour, they also surrounded Gregory Azzari's house. Azzari came into custody quietly as well until he saw one of the officers go back inside, braving the raging odor of used cat litter and deluge of ticking clocks to confiscate two notebooks that Azzari stupidly left in plain view on the side table next to his recliner.

"Put those back! Those are mine!" He yelled, gasping for air.

Lenny's investigators had a tough time holding onto Azzari who had begun convulsing wildly. One of the agents radioed for an ambulance while the other performed CPR. Paramedics arrived within fifteen minutes and stabilized Azzari, whose heart simply overloaded. Tampa General medically released him back into federal custody the next afternoon.

Along with the books, the feds confiscated almost $9,000 in counterfeit bills, $5,500 in stolen T-bills, and a full kilogram of uncut cocaine. A week later, Lenny's bunch returned to the house and found two .32 caliber bullets lodged in Azzari's living room wall, right behind the sofa where Lewis told them to look. The bullets would end up matching one of the rounds removed from my chest before the coroner could accidentally lose it. The bullets were some of the strongest verification of conspiracy, but they weren't the most potent.

Of everything confiscated from Azzari's house, the notebooks proved most important later in court after a lengthy battle over an improper seizure charge. Under the "Plain View" rule, the objection was overruled, and the notebooks—containing accountings of almost every caper and transaction in which Azzari was connected—detonated in front of the jury.

In all, fourteen individuals connected with the murder were indicted, placed into custody, and awaited trial. Because of public pressures, the judge naturally expedited the process. Trials such as these had no business waiting where politically connected judges relied on positive press. Vargas and Mendez were still on the lam, and their capture became paramount.

All of the good news sparked a wave of optimism within the city, whose citizens felt like a great evil began exiting their domain. The city council, or rather, the lone holdout needed to swing the vote, finally listened to his constituency in early April and paved the way for my reinstatement with the police department. It was defeat for Lozello's leadership and another victory for Davidson, who had threatened a lawsuit against the city over Lozello's lie detector fiasco. Not everyone in the city was enjoying the news, however.

At the end of April, word leaked from the FBI stating that Lewis entered the Federal Witness Protection Program after accepting a second-degree murder charge in exchange for more information. Shortly afterward, Giuseppe Cantonello, who had recently flown back to Costa Rica after answering questions at an IRS-directed grand jury over his taxes, received a long-distance telephone call from New York.

"You need to take care of some business."

For the Price of Admission

Guillermo "Santa Claus" Mendez was penniless and hope-lessly addicted to cocaine when Tresedici's attorney, Chuck Bartlett, finally caught up with him in a back room at one of Pappy Hernandez's taverns. Mendez, half-slumped in a bar stool, mostly due to depression than substance abuse, listened soberly to Bartlett's plea.

"Guillermo, I have a message from Giuseppe himself. He says you're a good guy and he likes you, but you need to do the right thing and come with me to the police station."

"What?" Mendez almost choked. "Since when did he ever have a conscience?"

"Look man, you're only looking at a minor complication here. They want to question you about Oklahoma — they've got nothing on you there — and they want to hear your story about some dynamite you *didn't* buy at Yeehaw Junction. That's it."

Of course, that wasn't it. The next day Bartlett drove Mendez to the Tampa federal courthouse and flanked him as he climbed its steps into the awaiting arms of awaiting US Marshals who stood alongside Lenny's agents. After booking, they charged him with conspiracy to commit murder, illegal use and trafficking of automatic weapons, silencers, and explosives, attempted murder of Carlos Salazar, contract murder attempt of Pappy Hernandez (which Hernandez didn't find out about until the trial), distribution of cocaine, and the attempted murder of Ben Davidson. When the last of his charges where read, Mendez collapsed to the floor and vomited. Immediately, Bartlett started plea-bargaining for Mendez and some of the others.

Having not pulled the trigger, Tresedici, Mendez, and Azzari all plead innocent to the murder charges at their hearing, opting to accept the drug and other racketeering charges. They didn't know just how much Lewis spilled during his interrogation, but they knew his testimony could result in the most damage.

The next day, technicians played an unannounced tape of Graham's confession. He detailed theories, saying they used him as a front man and almost didn't go through with the shooting if it weren't for the fact he completely "gassed himself" on cocaine that morning, as he put it.

A young court reporter had difficulty understanding his thick drawl, but she recorded, "I almost didn't go through with it, but it was too late when I got to the porch."

Regardless of Graham's remorse, prosecutors charged him with first-degree murder and sought the death penalty. During the legal process, Graham entered into a state of deep depression, rapidly losing weight, and becoming despondent while awaiting his fate in a dank Orlando cell. The presiding judge scheduled his hearing for July 12th on whether to use electrocution, and just ten hours before that hearing, Graham's jailers found him on the floor in front of his bunk with one end of its bed sheet tied to an iron clothes hanger on the wall, and the other end snugly around his neck. The investigation that ensued determined that Graham must have wet the sheet to keep the knot from slipping as he fell towards the floor, and during the night, the sheet stretched enough to allow his body all the way down. That was the official investigation report, anyway.

Ironically, Graham's psychiatrist was scheduled to appear and convince the 12-member sentencing jury that Graham's behavioral pattern over the past year had indicated suicidal intent. Four notes Graham left on a small writing table next to his bed indicated the same. One was a makeshift will, the second was instructions on the disposition of his remains, the third was a rambling farewell to his teen-aged son, and the last was a puzzling manifest of personal effects he wanted the local sheriff to place in certain parts of the prison, which left the sheriff asking questions for weeks. That may have been Graham's final joke on the world; making some politician waste a month of his life for nothing.

Frankie Cooper (formerly "The Beard" because incarceration regulations demanded it shorn) had much better luck, or so he thought. During the first round of trials, the Police Benevolent Association made good on their $10,000 reward and sent the check to a relative while he awaited his fate. The ATF also made good on their promise and had all charges dropped. But Frankie never saw a dime of that reward money because one of the agents that worked his case mugged him just after he cashed his check. Cooper never bothered calling the police and went back to drilling wells because he quickly reasoned he was lucky just to be alive. There were others that had trouble with that concept, however.

La Charada

Cantonello sat comfortably in a goose down-cushioned rattan chair. He gingerly sipped his mojito, filled his table's umbrella with cigar smoke, and rattled some shiners from his Cuban nightclub glory days to Angel Vargas. The thought of never seeing the United States again wrought Vargas with anxiety. Cantonello, in classic passiveness, rolled his cigar around in the ashtray until it revealed its red-hot cherry, and then he broke the news Vargas wanted to hear.

"Our friends have a job for you in New York and there is an absolutely splendid apartment waiting for you in Greenwich. How does that suit you?"

Vargas raised his Aviator glasses above his eyebrows, which was rare for him during the daytime, and said, "Greenwich? For real? Oh man, tell me you're not joking."

"No, no, it's not a joke, Angel. Look, I have your ticket on Pan Am right here. First Class from San Jose to Kennedy. You will arrive late tomorrow afternoon in time to hit the clubs."

When the men stood up to exchange hugs, Vargas noticed Cantonello's embrace was slightly stronger than usual, but he brushed it off as rum-induced euphoria. What Giuseppe Cantonello was really saying when he hugged Vargas so tightly was goodbye. When Vargas arrived the next afternoon at John F. Kennedy Airport, six agents with the FBI and another two from the US Marshals met him at Pan Am's gate.

Lenny wasn't there to witness Vargas' capture firsthand; he received word in Tallahassee during a sentencing hearing for Martin Sanchez, who had just successfully navigated his way back to the asylum after apparent auditory hallucinations had him convinced that the two young black men he laughed at, while on their way to extra crispy status, were now laughing back. It didn't help any that the midnight shift guards kept jokingly referring to him as Smokey the Bear from his days spent there in '63. Within his means, the judge gave him life without parole, sparing him the electric chair if he cooperated. The Match, it seemed, had met his.

By the beginning of August, Tresedici's knot began to unravel. He sat in a lonely cell and said absolutely nothing, with the smallest exception of an occasional "thank you" to his guards when they delivered his aluminum tray at mealtimes. His fate hung with the testimonies of Vargas, whom he thought might betray him after getting the double-cross. He also didn't trust any of Vargas' men, namely the bungling hitmen that botched everything from the beginning—Guillermo Mendez, Peter Lewis, and Herbert Graham. Graham, of course, was no longer a problem, and Lewis could only implicate Azzari, but Azzari was probably the only man Tresedici trusted in the entire outfit. And Azzari proved his worthiness of the most-endeared Italian virtue once again by not implicating either Vargas or Tresedici even though the cause of his heart attacks indicated otherwise. The judge, however, couldn't try Tresedici or Vargas for the actual murder; he could only try them for the conspiracy of it (among the host of other charges including RICO, trafficking, and other various crimes). With Graham dead and Lewis fully cooperating under a guilty plea, Azzari, who plead innocent, would face the jury alone.

Azzari's trial began promptly on a Monday morning in textbook fashion with a seven-woman, five-man, and two alternates jury picked before the end of the day. The proceedings began the next morning with the prosecutor carefully detailing Azzari's jungle—from the elephants, to the tigers, over to the monkeys, and finally, the hyenas—while Azzari sat nervously in a brown suit that seemed one size too small. It took the entire morning to connect all the dots jotted by Azzari and the rest, and many of the jurors kept personal journals just so they could keep track of all his personal connections.

The defense tried every unscrupulous tactic, including once walking in front of a black juror specifically to mention who sparked the '68 riots. The gavel hammered constantly, but in the end, it came down to just a handful of witnesses, and under escort, one of those had just walked his way up to the stand.

Under carefully guided questions from the prosecutor, Peter Lewis ineloquently fingered Azzari, Vargas, and Tresedici as the masterminds behind the List of Five and other various crimes. But Azzari was the only man presently on trial, and the judge told the courtroom so much.

None of the accusations seemed to bother Azzari as he sat blank and emotionless during the entire proceeding. This was in contrast to the only supporter Azzari had in the gallery, which was his sister. As much as she wanted to cry foul on each of Lewis' implications, she feared for her own wellbeing due to the fact that *my* sister, who had flown in from Virginia because she was tired of reading everything secondhand from the newspapers, sat across the center isle from her and made her presence known. My sister carried herself in the most prim and decent fashion any proper lady could, but if you messed with her family, her claws were as terrifying as any paleontologist could dig up. She sat in her pew, weeping when doctor's described how one bullet out of the five shot pierced my heart, killing me within minutes. And while listening, in her mind, she stoned the evil that sat before her, still breathing, still existing. She wasn't the only one.

By the end of week, both the prosecution and the defense were at rest, and according to every prosecutor's wet dream, the jury went into deliberations late that Friday afternoon. After only 90 minutes, they convicted Azzari for first-degree murder and the various other charges. Opting not to come back after the weekend, the sentencing phase ended after only another 20 minutes. The judge, not bound by the jury's recommendation, took it anyway; sentencing Gregory Azzari to death by electrocution.

Some reporters wrote that Azzari never moved a muscle when the judge read his sentence, and some others reported that he slumped over and cried in his attorney's lap. In actuality, Azzari simply pursed his lips and started devising a solution for anti-gravity with divine help promised by his elementary school nuns. Besides a few coherent sentences pieced together during the ensuing years of appeals — which Azzari maintained he didn't do anything wrong, repeating "I didn't pull the trigger!" — he carried on his delusional state, claiming to stay in spiritual conference with historical geniuses and Hollywood celebrities. If anything, he kept his guards completely entertained.

Weeks began rolling by and the avalanche began picking up steam.   In October, because there was no other producible evidence, Davidson facilitated another victory by gaining the owner of Central Stevedore's conviction in an embezzlement sting. Apparently, narcotics trafficking wasn't lucrative enough, so the owner quietly absconded parts of steel shipments from his own wharves, warehouses, and if they sat long enough, his own trucks. Davidson's accountants tallied over $750,000 worth from various companies, but the crime was only worth three years in a minimum-security facility. Davidson took what he could get, and putting Lozello's wife out of a job made it go down a little easier.

By mid-November, it was Lewis' turn to face the music. After fully cooperating, the judge still saw fit to throw him away for 35 years with no parole in a San Diego prison, which was totally unacceptable to Lewis. A year later, he was still trying to get his sentence reduced by spilling the entire mob's gambling rackets, everything from bolita, to football parlays, to Jai Alai, to the horse and greyhound tracks. During an interrogation, he even claimed to know the whereabouts of Emilio Letto.

"Yeah, I know where he is, but you'll never find him. Not him, nor a hundred others. I know a couple of guys they brought from New York just to feed Letto to the alligators... and...and, you know the trucker's union boss? They did the same thing with him the July before last. That's their favorite place, you know—Tamiami Trail, about an hour east of Naples. Been that way ever since they built the thing. Why do you think so many of 'em are sittin' on the side of the busy road down there, eh? They've got them alligators trained!"

"You know a couple of guys..." One of the interrogators drolly replied.

Yet Lewis had no new information regarding Tresedici, Mendez, Vargas, both Molinars, and a few others wrapped into the case who were sitting before an angry Jacksonville judge—who was eager to start his Christmas celebrations. In the middle of December, he threw the book at them with the exception of Jenny Molinar. They gave her five years for passing the counterfeit bills and misdemeanor possession of cocaine. She was released on good behavior after 18 months, divorced Jerry and disappeared somewhere out in Central California. The judge gave Jerry Molinar 30 years for various charges ranging from manslaughter, to aggravated robbery, possession, and on and on.

His first parole hearing ended with rejection and they sent him back for another eight years. He would eventually exit the state's penitentiary system after his third parole hearing, but Jerry had become maladjusted for society and died from major depression within two years.

The judge gave Tresedici the maximum of 40 years with parole available in 13 years. It was the best he could do given the lack of testimony, so prosecutors started chipping away at Vargas' façade. They knew Molinar didn't know much of anything past Azzari, and Tresedici was a family man, which meant he wouldn't say a word because he knew his life depended on it. Vargas knew everything and he was the only one left that knew the entire operation — front to back — that wasn't a made Italian. But getting Vargas to talk would take time.

Lozello had been wreaking havoc on the legitimate leftovers in the department, meanwhile. They harassed Mack, Major Fernandez, Loverboy, and a few dozen other policemen relentlessly in every legal way they knew how. Everything from constantly changing their shifts in and out of midnight, sending them to departments with little criminal oversight, to blatant harassment with surveillance tails and tapped phone lines.

Mack, not sure if he'd survive Lozello's tenure, or his successor's, quietly went back to the University of Tampa, and gained a Master's degree. With Lenny's help and a few other connections, he started teaching part-time at a community college an hour north of town where few cared about the "big city". Tampa wasn't quite through with Mack, however.

During the entire year of 1977, Mack had repeatedly accused Lozello of corruption in the newspapers. He did it so much, the reporters began floating editorials flagrantly disrespecting Lozello's personality, usually poking fun at his infamous lack for words or completely tangential responses when given direct questions. Linus had taken the department from one of the most-respected outfits in the country, with numerous endorsements and affiliations, to a shunned heap of corruption and infamy. By March of the next year, Lozello had enough of Mack's accusations and badgering, so when the opportunity presented itself to get rid of him, Lozello took it.

They decided to take him out in the same manner they attempted with me; some rigmarole internal plan of entrapment. Lozello cooked up his juicy dish when Mack started pressuring

him about throwing away a Driving Under the Influence charge
for a non-immune Colombian consulate member that, in Mack's
and Lenny's circles, was known for running narcotics in
diplomatic pouches, as well as setting up shipments through
Costa Rica. When the story ran in the newspapers, Lozello
accused Mack of the leak and got that power-intoxicated sot,
Wexler, a fast-tracked notary certification. That meant Wexler
could attempt, under the guise of legality, to swear Mack in and
give a statement. Of course, every bit of it was completely illegal,
but that didn't stop Lozello from doing it anyway. He knew he'd
have Mack out of the way during a lengthy legal battle, and the
worst thing that could happen was a slap in the wrist from his
friend in the mayor's office if Mack won. Mack, of course, denied
the charge, so Lozello had him booted for perjury, leaving him to
fight it out with the city over the next several years—just as
Lozello wanted. They tried the same thing on Major Fernandez
too, but it didn't work. Jose walked right in to Lozello's office,
took his "oath", and flatly refuted Mack's supposed leak. They
demoted Jose to captain—the first time that's ever happened in
department history—but Fernandez didn't quit as he very well
could have. He hung around, eventually regaining his rank
before leaving with a tidy retirement.

It didn't bother Mack too much in the scheme of things,
however; he was tired of fighting the mob. Through the same
connections that placed him before, Mack lined up a new career
as a sociology and deviant behavior professor at a private college
in Houston starting that fall. Just before leaving Florida, however,
Mack gathered his internal file on Lozello—the one he wasn't
supposed to have—and left it on his desk with a small
unaddressed "cc" on the bottom left corner, letting Lozello know
it wasn't the only one. Even though the file was supposed to see
Mack's lieutenant first, Skitter confiscated the folder and handed
it directly to Lozello, who promptly torched each page.

While Mack was busy packing his suitcases, Davidson had
Vargas on the ropes after several months' worth of convincing
him that his allegiance carried no value with the Italians, let alone
the police department. At the end of April, Vargas finally agreed
to testify against Tresedici, and even better, bring down
Cantonello's entire criminal empire, including those in the
department.

"I'll fill up Curtis Hixon Hall with the bastards!" Vargas boasted.

Collaterally, however, that meant several people in New York too, but this was all entirely academic.

The mob's intelligence network was unfortunately every bit as effective as the CIA's, and Cantonello received another phone call in Costa Rica before the day was over. Shortly afterward, detention guards found Vargas in his county jail cell, face down and in a pool of blood. Some immediately tried to say it was a drug overdose suicide, but the curious types had a huge problem writing that excuse off without questioning the source of Vargas' narcotics, smuggled while locked away in a max-imum-security cellblock.

The coroner only found trace amount of common sleeping pills in the preliminary autopsy, and disregarded gashes over each of Vargas' eyebrows as incidental. He stated Vargas must have gotten the cuts when he fell off his bunk, and determined the cause of death as a heart attack, likely from early onset heart disease previously undetected. Of course, he completely overlooked any possibility that Vargas had actually been knocked cold with a set of brass knuckles, and before any bruising could take place, his murderer shot 70ml of air into his right-side middle ear with a syringe, causing an undetectable embolism. Both Willard and Davidson had dreamt what songs Vargas might sing, but now began hearing the other's records skipping while their own plastic grooves shattered on the floor.

Cantonello received his phone call late the next afternoon with the news. Upon hanging up, he stoked his Cohiba, drew a long sip from a fresh gin and tonic, and savored the Pacific breezes. Tresedici received the news of Vargas' death from a pernicious guard the next morning, and for a brief moment, wondered if he was next.

The end of the decade saw increased pressures on Tampa's constantly embattled mayor, and most of those were due to the voluminous amounts of negative press the police department had been receiving. Between the card games, the rise in narcotics and other vices, the increasing corruption charges, and general lack of morale, Mayor Richard Pike called Lozello into his office and poured a bourbon for him before asking for his resignation. His 30-year career in law enforcement was at an end, and just after

1979's St. Valentines' Day, Lozello's announcement hit the newspapers with all the ferocity of a classified ad for a used accordion.

Upon hearing the news, Major Wexler ran to Temple Terrace and bragged that he would be the next chief while downing half a fifth of single malt. After which, he weaved his way home, sat on his beloved rock, and prayed to the Almighty. In the fall elections, Tampa decided it was time for a Latin man to take the reins, having suffered enough under Pike. He had his own man in mind for chief and it wasn't Wexler. He would have to wait six more years.

Lozello spent the next two weeks making rounds with his inner circles at the cafes and taverns around town. He schmoozed and shook hands with all of his supporters, few of them as there were, and prepared to turn his office over to the next man. But Lozello had forgotten about the plain manila envelope he tucked into the back of his desk's filing cabinet until his last day when cleaning out the very last of his belongings. The envelope had no identifying marks other than a month and a year—October, 1975. He sat down in his padded high-back and stared at the envelope he dared not open almost four years earlier, but the two scotch and sodas he gargled during lunch helped overcome his fear. He made his decision to finally destroy the contents, but he wanted one peep before doing so; it was his own brand of morbid curiosity. Carefully, he unclasped the envelope's brass fastener and slowly opened the flap. Peering inside, a sudden panic rushed through Lozello's body, which would have caused heart palpitations severe enough to risk cardiac arrest if it weren't for the alcohol, but he kept his body's quivering just under enough control to manage tearing open the envelope and flipping each piece of paper over and over until he slumped back in his seat. The pages were just as blank as his stare.

Just before the Tampa's mayoral election, Tresedici, Molinar, Mendez, and a few others were in the midst of an appeal, complaining their rights had been violated because they were seen at trial wearing chains, and that the sight of those chains presumed the defendant's dangerous nature to the jury. They were marched in the next day without chains, just in time to hear their convictions upheld; with the exception of one. The jury spared Tresedici's murder conspiracy charge and set him free for time served. Everyone else paid the piper.

Peter Danforth Lewis had spent over three years as a model inmate studying his San Diego correctional facility's details while regaining his "Danny Boy" reputation. I still haven't the slightest clue why the federal justice system, in all its wisdom, sent a known escape artist to a minimum-security facility, other than the fact that most, if not all, institutions aren't immune to mistakes. On Halloween night, Lewis spooked his way once again through the infirmary, and fled across the Mexican border into Tijuana. From there, he decided he may be of some use to Giuseppe Cantonello, and decided to hop a flight to Costa Rica via Panama City. It was a poor decision.

The next afternoon, a baggage handler working a Lacsa Airlines gate at Panama's Tocumen International, received emergency treatment after witnessing Lewis' freshly decapitated head bounce down the baggage conveyor and onto the ramp below. When it came to rest, the handler saw that someone had severed Lewis' tongue and stuffed it back into his mouth, which made the handler convulse and scream in complete horror. When Lewis' torso leaked its way down the conveyor, the handler went into convulsions, carelessly running into the path of a departing L-1011 bound for Peru. The port wing's engine would have sucked him into it if not for a fast-thinking tow operator scooping him up at the last moment.

Lewis's execution was simply a favor done for Cantonello by his old CIA connections in Miami, who then enlisted the help of a leader in Panama to help with laundering the voracious amounts of cocaine money flown in daily from the states. Cantonello originally offered $150,000 for the hit because his friends up north weren't too pleased about Lewis' gambling exposé , but they refused his gratitude, saying it was a drop in the bucket compared to the killing they were about to make. And make money they did.

Just as Lewis and Vargas had done so before him, Santa Claus also saw providence from a prison cell. By agreeing to testify against Andrew Geraldson in the murder attempt of that Oklahoma City town marshal, Mendez thought he could have his 60-year sentence commuted. While Geraldson did a fantastic job convincing the newspaper reporters of his innocence, his lawyer failed to convince the six jurors at the trial. They convicted him on conspiracy charges and, just before the holidays, sentenced him to 20 years. The judge gave Mendez pat on the back, but sent him back to prison for the remainder of his sentence.

"Merry Christmas, Santa," said his jailer, whistling "A Holly Jolly Christmas" as he locked Mendez's gate.

For the next four years, Azzari's lawyers attempted every angle in appealing his execution, including insanity due to Azzari's infamously insane ramblings about God and anti-gravity. He was unrepentant and unwavering until the end, never once ratting on his beloved family. The only recognition of which came just before his death when a reporter caught up with Cantonello, who had moved back to Miami the year before. Azzari's lawyer had run out of options and convinced some female reporter to track Cantonello down for help. She only acquired two sentences from the stodgy old-timer:

"Greggie was a good boy. Send him my regards."

Azzari never blinked when a heartless guard teased him with Cantonello's message. He had collapsed within himself entirely, and, when the end came, he wanted no clergy, nor any last meal, but they fed him anyway. He only drank some of his fruit juice and a few sips of coffee while continuing his ramblings on the solution for anti-gravity. Indeed, he intimately understood Newton's law — in the spiritual sense, anyway — on a crisp January morning in 1984, when the State of Florida sent 2,000 volts through his veins.

Afterward, official's cremated Azzari's body and gave it to his sister, who, heeding his instructions, dumped his ashes in Tampa Bay. What she didn't realize is that she dumped those ashes in close proximity to a storm drain where most of the treated sewage went.

Wendy received news of the execution from her sister, who attended it. Her knees buckled just after hanging up the phone. Junior ran over and caught her just before she fell completely to the floor, and she cried into his chest repeating over and over again, "It's over, baby! It's over."

It wasn't over just yet.

Three years later, Giuseppe Cantonello's health had just about given out, and he faced a hospital trip to Texas because there was only one surgeon experienced in the procedure. Cantonello didn't think he would survive. Just before leaving, he flew from Miami to Tampa to reconcile with his old attorney — the one he shunned a few years before — Paul Gravina.

During a strange ride in Gravina's Lincoln that, for almost two hours, sent them in circles up and down Bayshore Boulevard's two-mile length, Cantonello confessed to everything as if Gravina were a Catholic priest. He made wild claims about his bad deals with Jack Mollar, the Trucker's Union boss, and that he wasn't joking when they toasted Kennedy's assassination. He said they should have gone after Bobby instead, but that's how the tumblers stopped. Gravina defended Mollar on numerous occasions, but always assumed they were joking when someone mentioned something that sinister off the cuff. Yet, Cantonello carried on, detailing how he, Mollar, and a Louisiana don (who was still sore over being "kidnapped" by the FBI and taken to Guatemala) set up the hit. He said afterward that Jack Ruby was a regular visitor of his in Havana, and that he hated Kennedy after Cantonello told him of the pictures that he should have taken of the president's infidelity while he vacationed down there. Cantonello rambled on about helping the CIA attempt to assassinate Castro, and that all those rumors were true. And lastly, he talked to Gravina about Tresedici and my contract, and the many regrets he had — staying away too long in Costa Rica and trusting the wrong people. He said he didn't know about any of the problems until matters were completely out of control. "Vargas and Mendez," he said, "…were not my kind of people, and they should have never been allowed to do such stupid things." Gravina just sat and listened, wondering what a book deal might be worth for his story.

Two days after that meeting, Cantonello died from complications during a supposedly routine heart surgery in Houston, of all places.

I can't believe people such as he are all bad. They became suckers into a world that cherished their importance and rewarded them with success for wrongdoing. Mack once said it was nothing more than the dark side of Pavlovian psychology. I agree.

Just one year after his family laid Cantonello to rest in a Tampa cemetery, Florida's cash-strapped government saw an opportunity and threw hypocrisy to the wind — voting for a constitutional amendment creating a state lottery — instantly killing the bolita rackets and invalidating any moral stance against gambling. The entire state witnessed those little white balls transition from an old burlap sack to a fancy clear box fit for live television, and everyone quickly forgot their history.

What very few people knew was that Giuseppe religiously played a token nickel on bolita every week, and he carefully placed his last bet with a writer that kept his gambling secret for over 34 years. When the writer saw Giuseppe's slip—numbers that he never wrote for Cantonello before—he cleared his throat and went about his normal business. Later in the week, he wept incessantly after hearing that Giuseppe's number came up while he was in Houston. He didn't quite know what to do with his customer's won nickel, so he wrapped it carefully in its betting slip, placed it on the musty windowsill behind him, and left it for eternity upon a dream.

Acknowledgements

First and foremost, my loving and supportive family –
Dad, Mom, my wife Maria and Jessica.
You are my favorite editors.

To my enduring godparents, Joe and Gloria.
They are certainly the fittest survivors.

My aunt Annie and cousins Robert and Ron, whose levity kept it real.

The Cloud Family and their ever-vigilant quest
for the peace of justice.

Technical Acknowledgements:
The fine folks at John F. Germany Library – Downtown Tampa
(Thanks for all the microfiche)
Microsoft, Adobe, Dell, Logitech, Google, Dictionary.com,
Public.Resource.Org

The Tampa City Police Department
The Tampa Tribune
The Saint Petersburg Times

To all those that gave their lives in the line of duty
~ whether official or not.

www.ingramcontent.com/pod-product-compliance
Lightning Source LLC
Chambersburg PA
CBHW020742020826
48980CB00021B/829/J